TRITON

TRITON

A JOURNEY OF SEX, BOOZE AND ROCK 'N' ROLL

MORGAN SMITH

The Book Guild Ltd

First published in Great Britain in 2019 by
The Book Guild Ltd
9 Priory Business Park
Wistow Road, Kibworth
Leicestershire, LE8 0RX
Freephone: 0800 999 2982
www.bookguild.co.uk
Email: info@bookguild.co.uk
Twitter: @bookguild

Copyright © 2019 Morgan Smith

The right of Morgan Smith to be identified as the author of this
work has been asserted by her in accordance with the
Copyright, Design and Patents Act 1988.

All rights reserved. No part of this publication may be
reproduced, transmitted, or stored in a retrieval system, in any form or by any means,
without permission in writing from the publisher, nor be otherwise circulated in
any form of binding or cover other than that in which it is published and without
a similar condition being imposed on the subsequent purchaser.

This work is entirely fictitious and bears no resemblance to any persons living or dead.

Typeset in Adobe Caslon Pro

Printed and bound by CPI Group (UK) Ltd, Croydon, CR0 4YY

ISBN 978 1912881 833

British Library Cataloguing in Publication Data.
A catalogue record for this book is available from the British Library.

Dedicated to Ferret, Anastasia and Glynis with thanks for their invaluable technical support and so much more.

Triton:- Greek god: merman: hybrid motorcycle

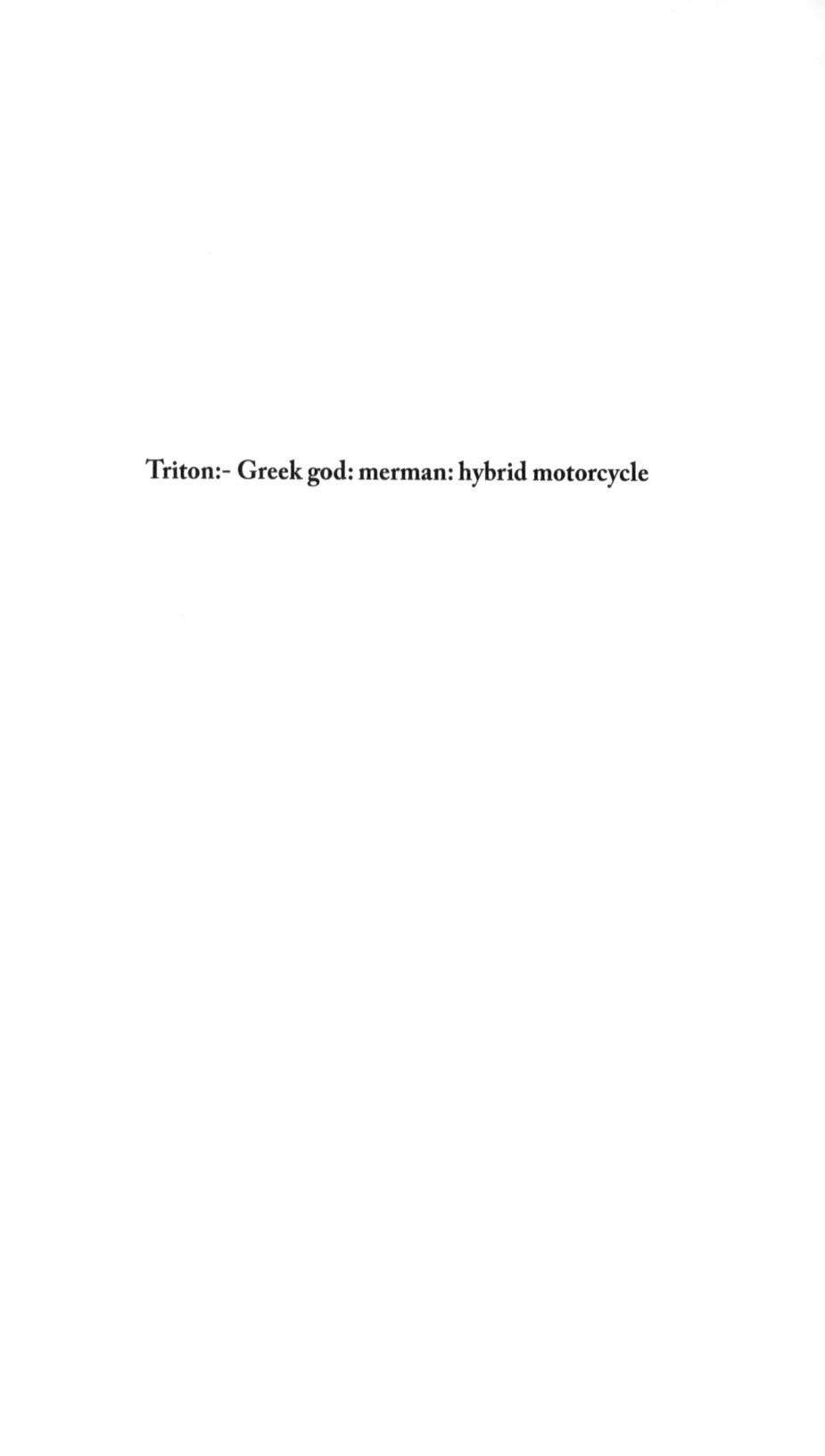

PART ONE
ST ANNE'S

ONE

A heady aroma of coffee, cabbage and tobacco pervaded the café, enhanced by the merest hint of engine oil. The jukebox emitted the exciting new American music which horrified parents, shocked by the on-screen antics of Elvis Presley and Little Richard, were convinced led to bad behaviour and immorality. Teddy boys in drapes and drainpipe trousers and older men with leather jackets had more important matters on their minds, crowded round a table in front of the steamed-up windows, too many for all to be seated, trying to read the *Daily Herald* upside down or over one another's shoulders. Girls huddled round another table, coats piled on an empty chair, full skirts squashed together as they showed off their Saturday morning purchases of spindly plastic bangles, Sunsilk and setting lotion.

The jukebox fell silent. A lanky, dark-haired boy in grease-spattered overalls fed it a sixpence, even his grimy fingernails didn't spoil his good looks. The machinery whirred and clicked and Elvis was altogether shook up.

One of the girls patted her already immaculate hair into place. 'Hi, Johnny.'

The boy winked at her and grinned. 'Anything new?' he asked the men monopolising the newspaper, his West Country twang unmistakable.

'It says the plane tried three times to take off.'

'Dreadful business,' the man behind the counter said; his quiff did little to disguise an incipient bald patch and the apron stretched across his paunch might once have been white. 'United's lost more'n half the team.'

The jukebox whirred again. 'Don't be cruel,' Elvis pleaded.

'How's the bike going?' the proprietor asked Johnny.

'Sweet as a bird.'

'Engine run in yet?'

'Just about.' Johnny gulped the dregs of his tea. 'Gotta get going, I need to be somewhere.'

Johnny dashed up the flight of concrete stairs to his parents' council flat and stripped to the waist, leaving his shirt and overalls on the kitchen floor. He sluiced himself in the sink, found a clean shirt, grabbed his leather jacket and slammed the front door behind him. He paused on the top step to turn up the collar of his jacket, inclined his head to strike a match, drew on the cigarette and leaned against the wall to admire the beautiful rebuilt motorcycle parked at the kerb. He smiled to himself, trotted down the steps, chucked his dog-end in the gutter and eased his fingers into black leather gloves. He caressed the shiny tank and straddled the bike. The engine that had slotted so smoothly into the featherbed frame responded the instant he touched the starter. He eased the throttle open until the noise hit ear-splitting.

Ignoring an angry gesture from across the street he made his getaway, riding the Triton along the front with the wind in his face, savouring the tang of seaweed, stopping only when he ran out of road at the headland. He kept his leather gloves on to enjoy another cigarette before glancing at his watch and speeding back through town to the railway station where he threaded his way between stationary buses to the entrance, on the receiving end of black looks from chatting bus crews and a solitary taxi driver.

It wasn't long before a train chugged in, passengers streamed from the single platform, drivers and conductors boarded their waiting buses. A sailor with his gear slung over his shoulder came into view and Johnny dismounted. The sailor waved his cap revealing hair as fair as Johnny's was dark. He drew level with Johnny and put his kitbag down. They grinned at each other like a pair of Cheshire cats.

'I'm so pleased to see you.' The sailor's refined accent was definitely not local.

'Len, it's great to see you an' all,' said Johnny. 'It seemed like forever.'

'Don't I know it. How's tricks?'

'Finished the bike.' Johnny stepped aside to allow an uninterrupted view of his pride and joy.

Len squatted for a closer look, muscular thighs straining his bell-bottoms.

'Don't pretend you know what you're looking at,' Johnny said.

'I know a good job when I see it; you've done wonders.'

Johnny swung his leg across the saddle. 'Wanna lift?'

Len shouldered his kitbag. 'Can you drop me off at the end of the road?'

At the bottom of the hill out of town they passed an old Vincent. The rider gave a cheerful wave.

'Bollocks!'

'What's wrong?' Len asked when they pulled up on the corner of a tree-lined avenue.

'That was Danny.'

'So?'

'So we might as well have taken out an ad in the paper; now it'll be all over town that you're back.'

'Is that a problem?' Len said.

'I bloody well hope not. I did want you to myself for today at least.'

'Can we meet at the barn? Give me a chance to say hello and change, I can be there in half an hour.'

'Sure thing.'

Johnny rode through winding, hedge-lined lanes and stopped beside a Triumph parked next to a five-barred gate. The rolling fields held grazing sheep and a few distant cattle, the only building in sight a solitary barn. He left his gloves on the saddle and vaulted the gate.

Len emerged from the barn. He too wore a leather jacket and jeans.

Johnny left the barn scowling into the fading light. He zipped up his jacket, brushed straw from his jeans and headed for the gate.

Len ran after him. 'Wait!'

Johnny, with one foot on the gate and the other in mid-air, looked over his shoulder. 'I thought we'd got tonight to ourselves.'

'I'm sorry, I should have mentioned it earlier,' Len said.

'I thought we could nip to the pub for a quick one.'

'It won't be open yet. Besides, you're not old enough.'

'Don't be such a bloody square.' Johnny turned away, swung his leg over the top rail and landed in the lane.

'I need to go home and get ready. I'm really sorry.'

'No you ain't. You already decided who you want to spend your time with.' He rocked the bike off its stand and toed the starter. Triton purred. He took off like a rocket leaving the other boy standing, riding fast through the winding lanes. It was safer after dark; headlights warned of oncoming traffic. He slowed to turn onto a path, crouching to avoid low branches, headlight flickering on the tree trunks. After several hundred yards he emerged onto tarmac. He pulled up in the entrance to a driveway and sat astride the bike with his boots firmly planted in the gravel, engine idling. The beam from his headlight a bright streak along dry brown beech leaves. In the gloom by the hedge his dark hair and clothes were hardly visible. The bike's tank glinted in the light from a street lamp; the rhythmic thud of its heartbeat was the only sound. He cut the engine and lit a cigarette. Triton's cooling metal ticked.

Len pulled into the drive and stopped next to him.

'Fast enough?' Johnny said.

Len shook his head. 'I couldn't keep up.'

Johnny laughed, his condensing breath swirled in the lamplight. A gust of wind snatched it away and the brittle hedge rustled.

'You've done a pretty good job. One would hardly recognise that for the rusty old Norton you bought last year.'

'It's a Triton now, get it right,' Johnny said.

'I don't want a row…'

'Well, don't start one then.'

'It's my first weekend home and she hasn't seen me for months,' Len said.

'Neither have I. Why can't you take her out some other time?'

Len cut his engine and dismounted. 'I'm sorry, but I really can't get out of it now, it'll look suspicious if I change my mind. It's not my fault she found out I'm home.' He laid his hand on Johnny's shoulder. 'Please be reasonable, Johnny. We can meet up tomorrow.'

Johnny touched the throttle. Triton growled angrily.

'For God's sake! You suggested I take her out in the first place.'

'Oh, swan off on your bloody date. See if I care.' Johnny revved his precious new engine and opened the throttle. It was pitch-dark by the time he pulled up outside a farmhouse, light shining from the front-room window illuminating a fence, gate and haystack. He parked a short way from the gate and slunk past outbuildings to a courtyard behind the house. Light shone from the kitchen window. The girl who came to the back door wore jeans and her long, dark hair was drawn back in a ponytail, the scar on her cheek didn't show with the light behind her.

'Danny's out. What do you want?'

'Fancy a ride, Fran?'

'Now?'

'Please yourself.'

'No, I'll come. They're watching telly. I'll say I want an early night.'

She came back pulling a duffel coat over her sweater, following him down the lane. They rode over the bridge, through the village and across the moor. There were several motorbikes and an old banger outside the pub. He had no trouble getting served in the Star, he was nearly as tall as Danny and they asked no questions.

The rain started on the way back, hardly more than a thick mist at first but by the time they reached the farm it was a downpour. The house was in darkness. They ran across the farmyard and she pushed the front door open, putting her finger to his lips, warning him to be quiet.

'I love you,' she whispered and took her brother's crash helmet from the shelf in the passage. 'It'll keep you dry.'

'I'll bring it back tomorrow afternoon. Meet me in the park by the statue.'

'Take care.'

She watched until he was out of sight, heard Triton's engine start up and listened to the sound fade before she closed the door against the driving rain.

TWO

Sunday morning was cold but not freezing, the sun had yet to rise. Gerald Barrington took a sharp left at the entrance to St Anne's Hospital avoiding potholes filled by the previous night's rain. He parked the Bentley outside the casualty department, strode past a mud-spattered ambulance and through the double doors. White walls made the large, brightly lit room gleam even brighter, the strong smell of antiseptic so familiar that Gerald did not notice it. The duty doctor was standing over a motionless form on a trolley, flanked by a nurse and a police constable. The nurse was cutting away clothing with an efficiency born of long practice. Leather and denim were smeared with mud and blood, contaminating the doctor's white coat and the pale grey linoleum.

'Not another one,' said Gerald. 'We've still got the last hooligan cluttering up Men's Surgical.'

'Good morning, sir,' said the doctor. 'Sorry to call you out so early.'

'Have you telephoned the anaesthetist?' Gerald thrust his overcoat at a passing nurse. 'My office!' The girl scurried away.

'On his way, sir. The radiologist has arrived. She should be ready by the time we've got this lot off.'

'What have we this time?'

'Possible head and spinal injuries, multiple fractures including a compound break to this wrist and the hand is a bit of a mess.'

The policeman stepped forward for a closer look, gagged and bolted. Gerald heard the man retching before the doors swung closed.

'Do we know who he is?'

'The police recognised him, they're trying to contact his parents. I think his skid lid saved him but—'

'His what?'

'His safety helmet, sir.'

'Right. Let's get on with it shall we, Doctor?' He peered over the houseman's shoulder. 'Oh no! Oh, bloody no.'

'What's wrong?'

'It's Johnny Hunter.'

'Do you know him?' The doctor looked surprised.

'My son is acquainted with him. I'm going to scrub up, wheel him in as soon as you're ready.'

By the time Gerald had changed back into his suit, Johnny had been taken from the operating theatre to a side ward off Men's Surgical. The surgeon found Johnny's parents waiting for him; Mrs Hunter crying, a headscarf knotted above her brow, Mr Hunter pacing, his unbuttoned raincoat flapping round the knees of his boiler suit.

'We're doing all we can,' the surgeon said, hoping to fend off questions he had no answers to.

Johnny's mother half rose and her coat fell open to reveal a wrap-around overall. 'Can we see him?'

'Just for a moment.' Gerald left them with the ward sister. In the car park he discovered Father O'Brien with his soutane hitched up, standing on one leg like a stork, putting on his bicycle clips.

'Morning,' said Gerald. 'What brings you here?'

'I was called in to the boy on the danger list.'

'Johnny Hunter?'

'That's right,' the priest said.

'I didn't know he was Catholic.'

'Yes, fortunately someone recognised him and they called me in. Surely you don't know him?'

'Lucien does.' Gerald unlocked his car and rummaged in the glove compartment. 'I do wish parents wouldn't insist on seeing their children when it can't help and only causes them more distress.'

'I didn't realise his parents had arrived.' The priest bent down.

'The police notified them. It appears we're not the only ones who work on a Sunday.'

The priest dropped the bicycle clips back in the basket on his handlebars. 'I'd better have a word.'

'Rather you than me,' Gerald said.

'Is there any hope?'

'A slim chance at best. Very slim indeed.' Gerald retrieved his cigarette case. 'Now, if you'll excuse me.' As he locked the car a small piece of card fell to the ground.

'I say!' Father O'Brien called as he strode away, but the surgeon had not heard.

Back in his office Gerald picked up the telephone, hesitated with his finger poised above the dial, then replaced the receiver and lit a cigarette before dialling his home number.

'I need a word with Lucien.' He paused to listen. 'Where did he go? What do you mean, you don't know? Did he say what time he'd be back?' He tapped the handset to end the call then dialled the internal number for Men's Surgical. On hearing that Johnny Hunter's parents had gone off with their priest Gerald made his way to the ward.

'Any change, Sister Denley?'

'Nothing, I'm afraid, Mr Barrington.'

He preceded her to the side ward where a nurse was taking Johnny's blood pressure. The boy lay immobile, the bedclothes supported above his legs, an oxygen mask on his face, dark hair brushed back from his forehead.

'Thank you, Nurse Gomez.'

'Yes, Sister.' The girl left the room.

The sister checked the bottle suspended at the head of the bed. Blood dripped through a tube into Johnny's arm. 'His colour isn't too good, sir.'

'That's hardly surprising. Nobody seems to know how long he lay there. It's a wonder he didn't die from exposure or loss of blood. I've sent to Exeter for more.'

A junior nurse came in. 'Excuse me, Sister. They sent this up from casualty.' She held out a brown paper bag.

'Thank you, Nurse, leave it on the locker. Is that all, Mr Barrington?'

'I might look in on the other youngster while I'm here. I'll be with you shortly.'

Sister Denley followed the nurse out of the room. Gerald studied the chart at the foot of the bed, shook his head and examined the patient's heavily bandaged right hand and arm. He shook his head again, glanced at the paper bag and walked round the bed to take a closer look. It contained a broken comb, a ten-shilling note, coins, keys, a length of string, a box of matches and a packet of Woodbines, crumpled and broken from the impact. A piece of damp card proved upon closer inspection to be a tide table. The final item was a flick-knife.

Gerald joined Sister Denley in the main ward. Halfway down the row of beds a ginger-haired youth slid back against the pillows. At a gesture from Sister a nurse materialised to pull up his pyjama leg and expose a plaster cast.

'Now then, Sidney. How are you getting along with the crutches?'

'All right, sir.'

'He's managing very well, Mr Barrington. He had a practice on the stairs yesterday.'

'Move your toes.'

The boy obediently wiggled his toes.

'Good, good.' Gerald glanced at the numerous drawings and lewd messages scrawled on the youth's plaster cast. Sidney's ears turned a colour that clashed violently with his hair.

'I think we can let you go home.'

'Please sir, how long will it be before I can ride my bike?'

'Foolish boy, you're not seriously planning to ride a motorcycle again? Haven't you learnt anything? Discharge tomorrow, Sister, outpatients appointments for removal of the cast followed by physiotherapy twice weekly.'

THREE

Danny Gomez had no sooner let the cows out of the milking shed and opened the gate than an ambulance came blatting down the road from the village with its bell ringing. The leading cow stood in the lane and bellowed, the rest bolted. With his father's help they quickly rounded up a dozen cows and two more were found half a mile away, trampling a village garden and munching flowers. His father slapped an orange-brown rump and both animals trotted up the road to join the others as if their jaunt was a daily occurrence. By the time they shut the field gate behind the last one, an adventurous brown and white found halfway to the river, his mother had finished bottling the milk.

His father loaded churns and crates in the back of the Land Rover. 'You take these, I'll finish here.'

'Sorry, Dad, it was making such a row and they went every which way.'

Danny drove carefully into town, past the crossroads leading to avenues of large houses, past the park and into terraced streets. He drove through the town square whose central fountain didn't work any more, past the town hall and the bank, to leave the milk churns at the station where a porter saw them safely onto the platform to wait for their train. Returning through the square he stopped at the Bell Inn, a Georgian building whose saloon-bar entrance was opposite the town hall. The public bar and off-sales door was round the corner in a side street. Danny reversed through an archway near the saloon-bar door into a cobbled yard to deliver his crate of rattling bottles to the hotel kitchen. He paused at restaurants and corner shops, dropped the last crates at Bert's café and rushed off without picking up the empties.

Once rid of the milk he put his foot down, cursing the Land Rover's lack of speed up the hill. His father, waiting at the gate, made a circular motion with his arms and Danny did a three-point turn in the road while his mother, his kid brothers and sister trooped across the farmyard. His father had the rear door open almost before he stopped and was unloading crates on the grass verge to make room for the boys in the back. Francesca dived in the front with their mother at her heels.

'I'll sort these out for you.'

'Thanks, Dad.' Danny let in the clutch. 'I haven't had time to change.'

His mother slammed the passenger door. 'Is choice of dirty or late.'

So he drove off in his jeans and jersey leaving his father to deal with stacks of dirty bottles.

He parked beside a bomb-site where desiccated buddleia flower-heads nodded over them as they tumbled out and hurried to St Richard's. The bell fell silent; they were late. They tiptoed in and sat at the back.

After dinner Danny rode his ancient Vincent to the café. He rounded a stationary lorry to ride across the pavement and stop beside a Triumph Thunderbird parked in front of the tall windows. The lorry driver was tucking into his meal while reading a folded newspaper propped against the ketchup bottle.

'Hello, Len.' Danny addressed the T-Bird's owner. 'Is Bert around?'

15

'He was here a moment ago.'

Danny wasn't sure what to make of Len. He'd turned up at the café one day last summer in a tweed jacket, hunched, squinting, on the brand new bike. For some reason Johnny had taken him in hand and the three of them had set off for Exeter one Saturday afternoon to get him kitted out. Len now looked the part in a leather jacket, jeans and proper boots with white sea-boot socks folded over the top. Danny wore wellingtons with the tops turned down to show their white linings. Len had even bought a skid lid. He might look like them now but he still sounded like a BBC announcer. To cap it all, Johnny had gone and introduced Len to his other sister, Maria. Last night wasn't the first time Len had carted her off to listen to some fancy jazz band.

Bert appeared from a door behind the counter. 'Danny boy! Come back for the empties?'

'Sorry about that, I was running a bit late.'

Bert trickled dark brown liquid into a mug and presented it to him with a flourish.

'May I have another coffee, please?' Len said.

'Certainly, squire.' Bert busied himself with the coffee machine behind him and produced a frothy hillock in a glass cup.

'Thank you.' Len picked up the sugar bowl, chunks of tea-stained sugar stuck to the spoon. Len stirred, coffee overflowed into the saucer. 'It's quiet in here today,' he said.

'Not for much longer it ain't,' Bert said.

Danny dropped a coin in the slot, sat down to roll a cigarette and carefully swept stray strands of tobacco into his tin before striking a match. The Everly Brothers lamented harmoniously.

The driver was preparing to leave and Bert emerged from behind his counter to clear the table. He gave the American cloth a cursory wipe, dropped the newspaper on the counter and took the dirty crockery through the door next to the coffee machine. He returned to lower the counter flap. 'How long before you're off to sea again?'

'I've a few more days,' Len said.

'When do you finish your National Service?'

'In August.' Len picked up the *Herald*. 'May I?'

'That's what it's there for, boy.'

Len turned to Danny. 'Unless you want to read it first?'

'No, ta.' Danny didn't need to. Several pages were devoted to the carnage in the snow and he had already seen the pictures of injured passengers in a Munich hospital. The lorry driver's departure let in a blast of cold air and Danny shuddered.

The café began to fill up as the afternoon wore on. Danny had just ordered another tea when his older sister burst in. 'Maria!' He put down his mug. 'What's up? I thought you were at work.'

'I tried phoning home, but when Mama said you'd gone out I thought you might be here. Just a tea, please, Bert.' She curled her fingers round the warm mug.

Len strolled over to offer her a cigarette.

'Oh, thanks.'

Len whipped out his lighter. 'Is everything all right?' he asked.

'Far from it, it's Johnny,' Maria said in a low voice.

'Now what's he done?' Danny said, too loudly he realised when the buzz of conversation ceased and heads turned.

'Over here.' Maria tugged at his sleeve to steer him into the corner by the jukebox. 'They brought him in early this morning.'

'Is he okay?'

'I'm sorry, Dan, he's quite bad. I'm ever so sorry… his parents are in bits.'

Len followed them and stared, uncomprehending, as she whispered. The cigarette burned down to his fingers. 'Shit!'

'Len!'

'Sorry!' He picked up the dog-end and dropped it in the nearest ashtray. 'I'm frightfully sorry.' He ran a hand through his fair hair, making it stand on end.

'You mustn't tell anyone I told you,' she said. 'It's serious misconduct to talk about a patient and I'd be in dreadful trouble if anyone found out. I've got to go.' She dashed out without another word.

Danny rubbed a hole in the condensation and watched her pedal away. Greasy plates were pushed aside, chairs scraped back and everyone began talking at once.

'He'll be all right, mate,' said a teenage boy. 'You know how girls exaggerate.' His girlfriend thumped him with her fist.

'Course 'e will,' someone agreed. 'He'll be chatting up them pretty nurses in no time, trust me. Not yours of course, Len,' he added.

Len went out and kicked his T-Bird into life.

Danny shouted after him from the doorway. 'Where are you going?'

'St Anne's.'

'But they won't let you see him if he's out cold.'

Len roared up the street.

'Where'd he go?' Bert stood behind his counter with a plate of sausage and mash and a puzzled frown. 'And shut that door, you great lummox, you're lettin' all the heat out.'

Danny shut the door and ran to his bike.

Len's bike was in the hospital car park but there was no sign of him. Before Danny had a chance to dismount Len ran down the steps at the main entrance, crossed to his shiny new bike and started it up. He was followed by a man in a suit.

Len turned on the man. 'Why didn't you tell me, Dad?' he shouted.

'I telephoned earlier but you were out.'

'When can I see him?'

'You can't possibly see him.'

Len revved his engine. 'I really need to.'

'Be reasonable, Lucien, his parents are with him. Will you please stop making that dreadful noise?'

A big woman with an elaborate cap anchored on her rigid grey waves marched down the steps and made a beeline for Len. She spoke quietly and Danny only caught a few words but they seemed to be effective because Len cut his engine. The man he had been speaking to left.

Danny dismounted and flipped the stand down. Len made as if to come over but the woman held out her hand. Len gave her his keys.

'Thank you,' she said. 'If you want to do something useful for your friend…'

Danny didn't catch the rest because two more bikes came in and stopped nearby.

The woman came over to them. 'I would prefer it if you switched your engines off before coming in here. This is a hospital, not a playground. My patients need rest, not all this disturbance.'

'Sorry, miss.'

Rumbling heralded the imminent arrival of another bike. Danny dashed through the gateway to wave it down and hopped back as a Norton Dominator came to a halt inches from his toes, its idling engine throbbing menacingly.

The rider was a middle-aged man with more hair in his sideburns than the sparse crescent at the back of his head. 'What?'

'Sorry, Skinner. We've been told to get off here and wheel our bikes in so as not to make too much row.'

'Have we now?' Skinner said. He cut the engine and steered the powerful machine into the car park as if it weighed no more than a child's pushbike. 'I'll man the gate then.' He stationed himself outside the entrance with his arms folded. His denim jacket strained at the seams.

The stout woman had gone and Len was disappearing round the side of the building. Danny ran to catch up with him. 'Where are you off to?'

'I gather Johnny needs another blood transfusion. I'm going to find out if I'm a suitable donor.'

Danny returned to the car park and sat on the stone steps at the main entrance gnawing his thumbnail. More bikes arrived and at Skinner's instruction were wheeled in to form an erratic cluster near Len's Triumph. Their riders stood in small huddles, smoking, saying little. At intervals the groups dispersed and reformed. A couple of older bikers, senior members who'd frequented Bert's place for years, joined Skinner on the pavement.

In the street a bus stopped and disgorged a stream of people; they headed for the steps and Danny moved to let them past. More people arrived on foot, singly or in pairs. A car turned in and parked as far away from the bikes as possible. A smartly dressed couple got out. The line dividing sun from shade crept across the car park.

Maria came down the steps carrying two steaming cups. 'All on your own?'

'Just the job,' said Danny. 'How did you know I was here?'

'I saw your bike from the canteen.' She balanced her cup on the wall alongside the steps and pulled her navy cardigan round her.

'How is he? Is it really as bad as you thought?'

She laid her hand on his arm. 'I'm so sorry, Dan.'

Brother and sister sat together on the steps drinking their tea.

'You're very quiet,' she said.

'I was thinking.'

'Don't get your hopes up too much, most people pass away in the small hours. It's a miracle he survived last night. The ambulance men said he was cold as a corpse when they brought him in.'

'He's a tough nut. Perhaps—'

'Oh, Danny.' She gave his shoulders a quick squeeze. 'I thought Len might be here.'

'He is. When I got here he was sat on his bike arguing with a man in a suit. Then this lady came out and read them the riot act and took away Len's keys. She said she didn't want her patients disturbed by such a racket and we've got to wheel our bikes in and out.'

'What did she look like?'

Danny shrugged. 'A navy dress, no apron but some seriously fancy headgear.'

'Matron! Oh dear. So where's Len now?'

'He's gone to give blood. Did you know his name was Lucien?' Danny asked.

'What?'

'I told you, when I got here this bloke was having a right ding-dong with him; seems it was his father. Len was shouting "Dad" at him and he was calling Len "Lucien". Did you know? And why wouldn't he be suitable?'

'Slow down, Dan. Suitable for what?'

'To give blood. Why mightn't he be suitable?'

'Because it's not all the same. Some people can give blood for anyone, otherwise they need to be the same group as the patient. I'd better go, I was a bit late earlier.' Maria ran up the steps and looked round. 'Tell Len to phone me tonight.'

'Okay, Sis. See you later.'

People began to leave the building; most hurried to the bus stop, the well-heeled couple made for their car. The sun disappeared behind the building. Len reappeared.

'Hey, Lucy!'

A chuckle rippled through the group.

'Lucy Ann!'

The chuckles turned to outright laughter.

Len whirled to face his tormentor, clenched fists raised, not seeming to care that the man was older and heavier and he had little chance of landing a punch.

Skinner came out of nowhere. 'Shut yer mouth,' he said, stepping between them.

The man who had poked fun at Len took a step back and raised his palms. 'No offence, Skinner.'

'Thank you, Mr Skinner,' said Len, 'but I can—'

Skinner, inches shorter than Len, stepped up to him. 'Can you now?' he growled, poking Len in the chest with a podgy finger. 'A posh accent don't cut no ice with me, kid, and it ain't mister, just Skinner. How did it go?'

'How did what go?' Len said.

Danny interrupted. 'Was your blood the right sort?'

'No, unfortunately not, but if anyone wants to donate blood they'll test you round there. It's the second door on the right.'

Men and boys looked at each other, hesitating. Skinner was the first to move, others trickled round the corner after him.

Danny looked around, could anyone else be as nervous as him? Several would-be donors were tested, waited and then were sent away. All too soon it was his turn. He rolled up his shirtsleeve revealing the snake around his arm.

'You don't mind needles, then,' the nurse said.

Danny gulped and looked away. The tattoo had been Johnny's fault; he wanted one and had persuaded Danny to go with him. They'd gone to a pub first and got blind drunk, getting away with it because both were tall for their age.

It was a long time before the nurse came back. Danny got up, ready to leave, but she had come to tell him that his blood was a match. He focused on the watch pinned upside-down to the bib of her apron and held his breath, concentrating on the second hand. For a split second his attention wavered. His eyes strayed to the bottle of blood. His blood.

'Is he all right?'

'Why is it always the strapping great lads who faint?'

'Because they're the weaker sex.'

A different nurse, younger and prettier than the first, gazed at him with a concerned expression in her blue eyes. Danny gave what he hoped was a winning smile. 'I'm fine.'

'Stay where you are.'

'I'm okay, honest,' he insisted.

'You will be when you've had your tea. You have to rest for half an hour afterwards, it's standard procedure. So are the tea and biscuits, so tuck in.'

Danny tucked in. He asked the pretty nurse her name but she wouldn't tell him.

FOUR

Francesca changed into a pair of her kid brother's jeans and cleared off before she got roped in to help with the dishes. She strolled through the park's wrought iron gates along a wide tarmac path and on past shrubberies and empty flowerbeds until she reached a bank of golden crocuses shivering under tall, bare trees opposite a lake. She sat on a bench by the water's edge, close to Triton on his rock with his long, curly hair and his fishes tail rimmed with green algae where wavelets lapped at his grey stone scales. She tore the cellophane off a cigarette packet and optimistic mallards swam over. A gust of wind blew out her match, she shivered and struck another. The disappointed ducks swam away, their spreading wakes lapping at the shallow grass banks and the merman's tail. A church clock struck the quarter. She lit another cigarette and walked to the gateway to meet Johnny. In the west a dark line of cloud promised more rain to come. It had rained last night. She had tiptoed upstairs in the dark hoping nobody had heard the bike but her sister was still awake.

'Where the hell've you been?' Maria came in her room and leant against the door. 'You look like a drowned rat, you won't half catch it if they find out you've been out this late.'

'I've been out with Johnny,' Francesca whispered, rubbing at her hair with a towel. 'Please don't tell.'

'You really shouldn't be running round the countryside at this time of night.'

'We weren't doing anything wrong. Did you have a nice time?'

'We went dancing and afterwards Len took me to the new Italian restaurant.'

'Are you going to marry him?'

'Don't be silly, my lovely, he's not Catholic. And I don't intend to marry anyone yet. Give me your brush, it'll take you half the night to get the knots out.'

'So why do you keep on seeing him? He's no James Dean but you've been going out with him for ages.'

'Looks aren't everything. He's got lovely manners and it's a change to find someone who doesn't trample on your feet – most young men can't even cha-cha. You want to be careful, Johnny Hunter is trouble.'

Excited children ran past laughing and shouting, jolting Francesca to her senses. She wandered along the grassy bank, endangering the crocuses, unable to believe how easily she had been taken in. The girls at school said a boy didn't want to know you once he got what he wanted, stupidly she hadn't believed them. A stiff breeze sprang up and shadows lengthened, but there was still no sign of Johnny. Hot tears trickled down her cheeks. She hoped he would still turn up so that she could walk straight past and ignore him. She would never speak to him again.

She trudged up the hill in the dusk with her head down and her hands in her pockets. At the farm gate she was dazzled by headlights. They went out and her father stepped from the Land Rover's cab.

'Where are you going?' she said.

'To find you. Nobody knew where you were.' He squinted into the gloom as if he had lost something. He reached into the cab to turn off the engine. 'Come in the house.'

The kitchen was too hot, the radio too loud. Her mother stood at the range with her back to them. Her kid brothers sat at the scrubbed pine table toying with their cutlery. She wiped her eyes with the back of her hand.

'Where you been?' Her mother turned round. 'Oh, no.' Her wooden spoon bounced off the coal scuttle and clattered on the brick floor. 'You heard already.'

'Heard what, Mama?'

'Maria telephone earlier. There was accident.'

Watching her mother's face Francesca felt most uncomfortable, as if an insect was crawling up the back of her neck. 'When? Who is it?'

'Johnny Hunter had an accident last night,' her father said.

'I need to see him.' Her hand was on the door handle before her father gently pulled her away.

'You can't, he's in the hospital. They will only let his parents in.'

'But, he'll be all right though, won't he? He had a crash helmet.'

'I don't know.'

'She's got my jeans on, Mama,' Miguel said.

'Never mind that now,' their mother said.

It was a subdued meal. Her youngest brother, Alvaro, who usually chattered non-stop, ate little and spoke less. Francesca pushed food round the plate with her fork. After tea she pleaded a headache and went upstairs to crawl into bed fully dressed. Her brothers came upstairs. When Mama came and opened the door a crack she pretended to be asleep. Mama went to say goodnight to the boys. Maria came up and ran a bath.

When it went quiet Francesca rolled up a blanket, arranged the covers over it and tiptoed onto the landing. Every other tread on the staircase seemed to creak when she stepped on it and her heart thudded deafeningly. The passage smelt of wet coats. A line of light showed under the sitting room door and she dare not pass it to reach the front door. She grabbed her coat and tiptoed past Danny's room to the empty kitchen. She slipped a torch in her pocket and for the second night running quietly let herself out of the back door. The sitting room curtains were open and she would be seen if she crossed the farmyard to borrow Maria's pushbike. Walking into town seemed to take much longer in the dark. It began to drizzle. A car went past, its headlights reflecting on the wet road. An approaching bike sent her cowering by the hedge in fear of being seen but it turned off at the crossroads. It wasn't her brother. The mournful cry of a foghorn led her on through the darkness. She reached houses and pavements and garden walls, and walked on past warm light glowing through red curtains. Light from street lamps transformed the cascading raindrops into sparkling slivers of steel. The rain had almost stopped by the time she walked past the locked park gates and turned a corner. The lights of St Anne's Hospital were straight ahead.

Bert from the café was stationed at the entrance. Bikers were trickling into the car park in ones and twos as the news spread. Most wore leather or denim jackets, a few wore T-shirts and goosepimples to prove how tough they were. Francesca had no idea there would be so many people and she walked in slowly, suddenly shy. She couldn't see her brother until a car turned in through the gates and parked up with its headlights on. Danny's girlfriend got out and people gathered round as she handed out chips wrapped in newspaper.

Danny reached in the boot and tossed a bottle; its deft catcher took his beer over to a tree whose massive trunk had forced the boundary wall out of shape.

Danny spotted her and came over. 'They won't let us in.'

'They had to cut his clothes off,' a voice behind her said.

'Shut up!' Francesca ran blindly, her hands over her ears, tripped on tree roots which had forced their way through the asphalt and sprawled headlong into Len's arms. He held on long enough to stop her falling then let go, embarrassed. He wedged his beer between the roots to offer her a cigarette.

'Thanks,' she said, forgetting that adult eyes were watching. 'Do you know how he is?'

His hand shook as he flicked the lighter for her. 'Critical.'

'What does that mean?' but she had no need to ask; the look on Len's face shattered any lingering hope.

'It means…' He turned away to use the shelter of the tree trunk to light his cigarette. 'It means he's quite badly injured.'

Tears sprang unwanted and she scurried away. She found a dark doorway on the other side of the building, sat on the cold stone step and buried her head in her hands. God had struck Johnny down for their wickedness; what would her punishment be?

Len hurled his empty beer bottle at the tree, it thudded against the trunk and broken glass showered the emergent roots. He took the steps at the hospital entrance two at a time and Danny had to run to catch up. The double doors to a ward stood open. Len walked straight in but stopped by a closed door just inside. While he hesitated it opened and a woman in a navy blue dress and starched white apron came out. She looked at him in surprise.

'Lucien! Your father is with John Hunter's parents. Perhaps you could wait outside.'

'Yes, Sister,' Len said and went to sit on one of the chairs ranged along the wall in the corridor outside the double doors.

Danny hovered nearby. The woman walked past him, stopped and turned. 'It's Daniel Gomez, isn't it?'

Danny took his hands out of his pockets. 'That's right, miss. I'm a friend of Johnny's.'

'Thank you for donating blood this afternoon.'

'Any of us would have. Miss?'

'Yes, Daniel.'

'Is he going to be all right?'

'I can't discuss the patient's condition, you're not a relative.'
'But he's my best friend.'
'I'm sorry, Daniel.'

When the door opened again they were both studying their boots.

Johnny's parents were ushered out. 'We'll contact you immediately if there is any change. If you wish to stay overnight there are some armchairs in the canteen.'

Len jumped to his feet. 'Dad! How is he?'

'Still critical.'

Len, standing in the doorway, took out his cigarettes.

'Not here!' His father pointed into the room. 'Do you want to blow us all to kingdom come?'

'Sorry, I didn't think.' Len put the packet back in his pocket.

'You never do. You can have five minutes, and absolutely no smoking.'

'Thanks, Dad. Don't wait up for me, I might stay at Danny's.' Len disappeared into the dimly lit room. A nurse came out, closing the door behind her. A telephone rang and moments later the nurse was back.

'Matron wants to see you,' she said.

Danny stood up, towering over the woman. 'Who, me?'

'Yes, Miss Turnbull's office is directly below here. You can't miss it, her name is on the door.'

Danny found a door with a brass nameplate and tapped cautiously, hoping it was the right one.

'Come!'

Danny peered round the door. Matron sat at an imposingly large desk.

'Come in, young man. So, you're a friend of Lucien's.'

'He's more Johnny's friend than mine, really.'

'I remembered I still have his keys. Can you look after them for the time being? I don't think he should be driving this evening.'

'Yes, miss, I mean Matron. He isn't going anywhere, I'll see to it. Thank you,' Danny flustered. He thought of something. 'Len's father? Is he, um…'

'Yes, your friend is in good hands. Mr Barrington is one of the finest orthopaedic surgeons in the country. We're very fortunate to have him.'

Danny went back to the front entrance and was waiting at the foot of the steps when Len pushed past, marched over to the tree and bent down. Blood spurted from his wrist.

'Hey!' Danny raced after him. 'Watch it!'

Danny snatched the shard of glass. 'What the bloody hell do you think you're doing?' He steered Len round the corner.

'What's going on?' someone called after them.

'He tripped,' Danny said and shoved Len through the casualty doors before the bloke had a chance to ask any more questions.

'Name?' the doctor said.

'Daniel Gomez,' Len answered without batting an eyelid.

Danny opened his mouth but before he could protest Len jabbed him in the ribs with his elbow, a move that sent blood spattering across the floor. The doctor hurried Len into a cubicle and rattled the curtain across.

Danny sat and waited, elbows on knees, chin resting on interlaced fingers. He straightened up when Bert came in.

'What's occurring?'

'It's just a cut. He tripped and fell on some broken glass,' said Danny. 'It's no big deal, they're sorting it out now.'

Len finally reappeared with his arm in a sling. 'The stitches have to come out next week so I'll do it myself.'

'What gives?' Danny said, walking towards the front of the building where their bikes were.

'Pardon?'

'Why did you tell him my name?'

'Sorry, it was the first thing that came to mind. I can't face a load of questions from my father. He works here.'

'I sort of got that,' Danny said.

'It's okay. That chap didn't recognise me.'

'He looked bloody suspicious if you ask me.'

'Well, nobody's asking you.' Len lagged behind.

'Come on then, if you're coming back with me,' Danny said.

'No, I only said that to shut my father up. I'm staying here.'

'What good will that do?' Danny wheeled his Black Shadow to the gate and looked over his shoulder. 'Come on.'

'Besides my bike is here.'

'Stop arguing and get on.'

Len thrust his arm into his jacket, pulled it across his shoulders, zipped it up over the sling and climbed on behind Danny.

The farmhouse kitchen was hot. Len eased his jacket off and put it on a chair, disengaged the sling and dropped it on the table. 'May I use your bathroom, please, and could you possibly lend me a clean shirt? Then I'll get back.'

Danny, reluctant to let Len loose in a room containing razors, showed him where the outside toilet was and told him to wash in the kitchen sink. He fetched a shirt then ran upstairs to hunt through the bathroom cabinet, taking a small bottle back to the kitchen. Len had taken the safety pin out of the sling and was attempting to fold up the triangle of cotton cloth.

'Here, have one of these,' Danny offered him a tablet.

'They gave me an aspirin or something I think.'

'It's a sleeping pill, you can kip on the sofa in my room.'

'No, I told you, I'm going back to the hospital.'

'Okay then, I'll come with you. We'd better get something to eat first.' He took Len's jacket to the sink. 'I've known him ever since I was five.' Danny used the dishcloth to sponge blood off the leather and wiped it dry with a tea cloth. 'Since my first day at school, our first day at school. What was all that about?'

'It was an accident,' Len said.

'Like hell it was.'

'I slipped.'

Danny didn't answer.

'Please don't say anything. There's no need for anyone to know.'

Half a loaf sat abandoned on the breadboard. Danny buttered the cut end and hacked off a slice. He was sawing at a second slice when his mother came in.

'What you do to my bread?' She took a dish from the oven. 'Francesca gone to bed, poor child worn out.'

'She's…' Danny caught the look of alarm on Len's face just in time. 'I expect she's upset.'

'Of course she is upset.' She ladled out generous platefuls.

Len barely managed a slice of bread and butter. Danny made short work of his own meal and polished off Len's leftovers.

It had stopped raining by the time they got back to the hospital. Danny, torn between looking for his wayward sister and keeping an eye on his unhinged companion, asked his girlfriend to find Francesca and give her a lift home. He found Len leaning on the wall outside the men's ward, the double doors were shut. A lady in navy approached, suggested they go to the canteen and closed the ward doors behind her.

'Why don't we?' Danny said.

'No. His parents will be there and I've no idea what to say to them. I'm going to the pub before they shut. Are you coming?'

Outside Danny made for the group near the tree, his girlfriend's car was missing. 'Anyone seen Penny?'

'She took your kid sister home. She didn't seem too happy about it.'

Danny turned to Len. 'Will you be all right if I stay here for a bit?'

'I can find my own way to the pub,' Len said.

FIVE

Danny woke with a start to find a woman standing over him. The green beads dangling from his fingers clattered to the floor. It took him a moment to figure out where he was. He gathered up his rosary.

'It's four in the morning. Why don't you go home?' she said.

'I can't, Johnny's my best friend.'

She took pity on him. 'Would you like to sit with him for a while?'

'Yes, miss. Thank you.'

'I'm Sister Branch. Please do not touch anything.' She opened the door. 'That is an oxygen cylinder so smoking is absolutely forbidden.'

A dim light glowed above the bed, light from a street lamp shone on the opposite wall. Danny waited for his eyes to adjust after the brightness of the corridor. His leather jacket creaked in the silence, he shrugged it off and hung it on the back of a chair. A mask hid Johnny's face, only his bare shoulders were visible. Bedding was raised above his legs. Curiosity got the better of Danny and he lifted the cover at the foot of the bed.

'*Madre de Dios*,' he whispered.

He crossed himself, went to the window and thrust his hands in his pockets, his fingers found the rosary and the beads clicked automatically. It was drizzling again and he could just make out the knot of bikers huddled under the tree in the corner of the car park. Occasionally a match flared. Eventually a grey day dawned.

The night sister came back, took Johnny's pulse and blood pressure and wrote on a chart at the foot of the bed. 'You'll have to leave now, Daniel.'

Down in the car park he found Len slumped against the tree trunk, a pool of vomit nearby. His leather jacket had kept out the rain but his blonde hair was plastered to his head and his jeans were sodden. Danny gave him an exploratory prod with his boot, an empty bottle rolled from his grasp and he slid sideways.

'Prat!' Danny said.

'Yeah,' agreed a young man. 'He'll have a humdinger of a hangover when he does wake up.'

Danny wheeled his bike into the street. The damp had upset the Vincent and it didn't want to start. Danny swore and gave it a kick. By the time he finally got it going he decided there was no point in going home, his father would have finished morning milking by now. The Black Shadow misfired all the way to the café. Bert stood in the doorway contemplating the empty space which was usually filled with motorbikes. Inside the place was empty, the jukebox silent.

'Any news?' Bert said.

'No, he's still the same.'

'The missus'll serve you,' Bert said and disappeared off down the street.

A plump woman with greasy bottle-blonde hair and scarlet lipstick, universally known as Auntie, came through the door next to the coffee machine.

'Yes?' She fired the word across the counter.

'Tea please, Auntie.'

Auntie lit a cigarette. 'Do they think he'll pull through?'

'It's touch and go.' Danny shovelled sugar into his tea. 'He's always been there, ever since we started school. I ought to 'ave gone home, my dad's gonna kill me.'

Skinner turned up.

'What can I get you?' Auntie said.

Skinner ordered breakfast. Danny shook his head.

'Bloody nightmare,' Skinner said.

'Yeah,' said Danny. 'He's all in plaster, an' all tubes and things.'

Bert returned and dumped a box of vegetables on the counter. 'Take him home will you, mate? He's been up all night.'

The older man mopped up egg yolk with his bread and butter. 'Come on, then. I don't reckon you're safe to ride if you're knackered.'

'I am a bit tired,' Danny admitted.

'Why didn't you take them round the back?' Auntie demanded, picking up the box.

'Forgot my keys,' Bert said.

'Oh heck!' said Danny. 'I don't know what to do about Len.'

Skinner led the way outside. 'Last I saw of him he was spewing his guts up all over St Anne's car park.'

'He's still there, I've got his keys.'

'Best hang on to them.' Skinner's boot hardly touched the starter, the Norton throbbed obediently. 'Get on, I'll give you a lift home.'

Danny was too tired to argue. 'I need to go somewhere first.' He climbed on behind and bawled directions in the big man's ear until they stopped outside St Richard's.

'I won't be long.'

'I'll come with you.'

Danny dipped his fingers in the stoup, crossed himself and went to the Lady Chapel. Skinner followed. Votive candles flickered on a metal stand. A shelf held a stack of candles and a small wooden box with a slot in the top. Danny dropped a penny in the box and held his candle to a flame.

'Can I light one?' Skinner whispered.

'I guess so. Why are you whispering? It ain't a library.'

Skinner lit his candle from Danny's. 'What about his bike?'

'What about it?'

'Has anyone arranged to shift it?'

'I dunno, I hadn't even thought about it.'

'D'you know where it happened?' Skinner asked.

'More or less.'

'Shall we?'

They rode up the hill out of town, past the farm and through the village. A few miles further on they passed a solitary farmhouse and Danny yelled in Skinner's ear. They turned off the main road onto a potholed cart track skirting the moor. The place was cold and grey and windswept.

Skinner rode slowly, pulled over, planted his feet on the ground and cut the engine. Skid marks veered sideways then vanished. Danny dismounted. Near the track a distorted hawthorn crouched with its back to the prevailing wind. The Triton lay on its side as if seeking shelter beneath the leafless tree.

'Look!' Skinner, still astride his bike, pointed to a gouge in its trunk. The Triton had evidently slammed into the thorn tree. It now lay on the stony ground surrounded by a throng of footprints and flattened yellow grass. 'Damn shame, that was a nice machine.'

'Trust him to find the only tree for bloody miles,' Danny said.

'I don't reckon he hit the tree,' said Skinner. 'That mark is way too high. He must have lost it, the bike hit the tree then bounced back and hit him before he could get out the way.'

Danny wandered along with his eyes cast down and squatted beside a large puddle. The dark red mud round its edge was criss-crossed by animal prints and tyre tracks. A tractor and at least two pushbikes had used the lane recently. The motorbike had come in from the moor. Danny scrambled to his feet. 'He'd been riding cross-country.'

Skinner scrutinised the puddle thoughtfully. 'Looks that way. He got in trouble when he came to the road, if you can call it that, and lost it when he hit the pothole.'

Once home Danny went to his room, chucked his jacket on the sofa and flopped exhausted on the bed.

The telephone woke him. He emerged unshaven from his room, rubbing his eyes.

'That was Maria,' his mother said.

'How's Johnny?'

'She don't say. She only say Francesca leave school at dinner time and go to the hospital. Your father bring them home when Maria finish work.'

Danny took a china mug from the dresser and helped himself to stewed tea from the pot skulking on the range under a knitted tea cosy.

His father opened the back door. 'Awake at last! Just in time for milking.'

Danny gulped the last of his tea, put his mug in the sink and leaned on the wall to pull on his wellingtons with one hand, a half-eaten sandwich still in the other.

When they finished Danny drove the cows past the house and opened the gate to the road. A black and white collie bounded up with his tail wagging.

'Hello, boy.' Danny fondled the dog's ears. 'Where've you been?'

When they reached the field the collie made short work of sending the cows through the gate. Carlos went to fetch the girls, leaving Danny to hose out the milking shed. By the time he finished it was raining again, the jeep was back and his father was lifting Maria's bicycle out of the rear door. 'The girls are in the house.'

Danny went in the kitchen. 'How is he?'

'You know I'm not supposed to tell you, even if I could,' Maria said.

'He's still with us, then,' he said.

'Yes, but he's very ill. Sister tried to persuade his parents to go home for a bit, but his mother won't budge.'

'How long will it be before he wakes up?' Francesca asked.

Maria avoided her sister's hopeful gaze. 'He might not.'

Francesca made a small noise, Maria laid a hand on her arm. 'I'm so sorry, my lovely.'

Francesca pulled away, pushing back her chair with such force it toppled over, and stormed out slamming the door so hard it bounced open again.

'Fran!' Maria called after her.

'Leave her, she needs to be on her own. You should have been more, more...' Their mother groped unsuccessfully for the word.

'Tactful? How's that going to help? He's so badly injured, he's not... I mean, even if he does come round he might not be all right. Oh Mama, it's awful when it's someone you know.'

Consuela Gomez picked up the chair. 'But I thought he had the crash helmet.'

'They don't always get away with it, even with a helmet.'

Francesca had exchanged her school uniform for jeans and a cardigan. She stood in the passage red-eyed but composed, putting on her coat. 'He's not going to die. He *is* going to wake up and I'm going to be there when he does,' she declared.

'You can't go out in that,' said Maria. 'It's bucketing down.'

'You come sit down,' their mother said.

Francesca slung her coat over the post at the bottom of the stairs and sat down. Her father came in and hung up his donkey jacket. When he bent to tug off his muddy boots strands of wet hair spilled forward, dark curls streaked with grey.

Maria broke the silence. 'I saw Len this morning.'

'So did I,' said Danny. 'He spent the night in the car park and fell asleep under the tree. He got soaked right through.'

'So that's why he looked like a tramp. He came up to the ward and I had to send him away with a flea in his ear before anyone saw the state of him.'

Len's father, heading home via the tobacconist in the high street, spotted a distinctive bicycle propped at the kerb outside the Bell Inn. He tracked down the priest in the snug bar.

Father O'Brien rose. 'The boy? I'll be with you directly.'

Gerald shook his head. 'He's stable at present. It's incredible the amount of punishment the human body can withstand.'

'Thanks be to God. What can I get you?'

'I'll have a Scotch, please. I gave Lucien a lift into town. He left his motorcycle at the hospital but he wanted to see someone before he collected it so I dropped him off at a seedy looking place. He called it a coffee bar but it looked more like a transport café to me. I simply cannot understand why he wants to mix with these types.'

'And Johnny Hunter?'

'Not good. This is what happens when youths hang around in gangs, showing off with fast girls and faster motorcycles,' said Gerald. 'He has a number of broken bones and he's badly bruised. It looks as though he's been in a fight recently. I do wish Lucien hadn't got mixed up with him. And as if that isn't enough I've got a car park full of juvenile delinquents.'

'What makes you think he's been fighting? Surely his bruises were caused by the accident?'

'A good many contusions are several days old.' Gerald took a sip of whisky. 'I'm pumping him full of penicillin but at best it's a long shot.'

'Penicillin?' Father O'Brien raised an eyebrow. 'For broken bones?'

'Including a messy compound fracture of the right wrist. I'm particularly concerned about that as well as the spinal injury. He's seriously ill and blood poisoning would certainly finish him off.'

'I see. Have them call me at any time.'

'Of course.'

'You dropped this yesterday,' the priest said.

The black and white snapshot of Lucien, incongruous in a tweed jacket astride his brand new Triumph Thunderbird, posing awkwardly between Danny, tall and swarthy in shirtsleeves and jeans, and Johnny, a skinny youth with a black leather jacket and a cocky grin, like a small boy who is up to no good and knows you can't prove it.

'Did I? Lucien had recently bought the confounded thing. I've no idea who the foreign-looking chap is.'

'That's Daniel Gomez.'

Gerald looked blank.

'Nurse Gomez' brother,' Brendan O'Brien explained. 'The family were refugees from the Spanish Civil War. Of course, with Franco in power they couldn't go home and before long they found themselves trapped here in the middle of another war. Mr Gomez is a remarkable man; originally a schoolteacher he found work as a waiter in England, then as a farm labourer, it does seem a dreadful waste of knowledge. After they bombed Guernica he escaped with his pregnant wife on the last boat out.'

'You know a great deal about your parishioners.'

'Not really, the rest of the family are devout but not Carlos.' The priest gave the name an English emphasis, making him sound like a mislaid motor vehicle. 'I happened to discover that he played chess and we have a game from time to time.' Father O'Brien sipped his stout. 'Johnny's face appears remarkably unscathed; surprising considering the extent of his injuries.'

'He'd been wearing a safety helmet. When Lucien came home on Saturday he wasn't wearing his helmet and we had words about it. In fact I insisted he use it tonight if he must ride his motorcycle.'

'Don't be fooled by Johnny's looks. When I came here my predecessor warned me about him; according to him the boy was a lying little hooligan.'

'What did he do, steal the collection?'

'It's not a subject for levity. He told wicked lies, very distressing for everyone, especially his mother. He never attends Mass. Mind you, teenage boys rarely do; they're much too busy up to their elbows in engine oil or taking girls to the cinema. What do you think of his chances?'

'Very slim. His father seems to have some idea that he crashed deliberately to get out of National Service but Lucien is convinced he wouldn't do such a thing. He believes Johnny was most anxious to leave home.'

'I shall pray for him.'

'It'll take more than that.'

'Surely you don't discount the power of prayer.'

'I'll put my faith in penicillin and leave the prayers to you.' Gerald went to the bar. He placed a half of Guinness in front of Father O'Brien. 'Lucien has taken this business rather badly but unfortunately it doesn't seem to have put him off motorcycles. I told Sister Denley to let him sit with the boy provided he makes himself scarce when the parents are about.'

'It's hardly surprising he's upset, it must have brought it all back to him. How old was he when his mother passed away?'

'He was twelve. Still at prep school.'

'You don't regret leaving such a prestigious post?' Father O'Brien asked.

'Never. Far too many memories at the old place, and with the boys at school I was rattling round the house on my own.'

'But your career, surely—'

'Even in this backwater people still have accidents. Fishing and farming seem to be somewhat hazardous occupations and motorcyclists account for a significant number of my patients. I do wish Lucien hadn't bought that confounded machine.'

'Why on earth did you let him?' the priest asked.

'I didn't. He received his mother's legacy when he was eighteen and promptly spent it on unsuitable purchases. Have you seen his clothes?'

'Isn't it rather unusual for one so young to receive a bequest?'

'Daphne persuaded me that if anything happened to us the money would be more use to the boys when they reached eighteen rather than twenty-one. She naturally assumed they would opt for deferment and complete their degrees before National Service.'

Danny planned to walk into town and collect his bike after tea but he fetched up in the village pub. Len tracked him down in the Horse and Hounds staring into an empty glass, oblivious to an animated row over a game of dominoes at an adjacent table.

'Here you are.' Len put his lid on the table.

'Is he…?' Danny was afraid to say what he was thinking.

'No! I've just come from St Anne's. He's still with us.'

Danny breathed a thankful sigh. 'I was thinking about going to the hospital. D'you want a drink?'

'I'll get them.'

'Only a half?' Danny queried when Len put the glasses down.

'I thought I'd take it easy.'

'Yeah, you didn't half hammer it last night.'

'I was looking for you and saw your bike at the café. Bert suggested I might find you here. How did you get home?'

'Skinner gave me a lift.'

'What's his first name?'

'Dunno, he's called Skinner cos he works at the abattoir. Auntie at the caff is his sister, I think she calls him Rick.'

'I gather you've got my keys,' Len said.

'So that's what you came for. You didn't half give me a fright.' Danny stood up carefully, wary of the low beams, and delved in his pocket. 'I'd forgotten about them. How'd you get here?'

'Found the spare key for the bike indoors.'

'What's with the lid?'

'My father insisted. He thinks they're essential but it didn't do Johnny much good did it?'

'I didn't even know he had one,' said Danny. 'His mum was always nagging him about it so I guess he must have given in.'

Len put their empty glasses on the bar. 'Do you want a lift home?'

Len ground to a halt and leant on the handlebars. Light from the hurricane lamp on the cowshed reflected on his lid. 'It's all my fault. We had an argument the other night, if he hadn't gone off in a bad mood he wouldn't have crashed.'

'It ain't your fault so stop upsettin' yourself. How's the wrist?'

'Sore. To be honest it's throbbing in time with my head.'

'You wanna go home and get some sleep.' Danny listened enviously as the T-Bird started with no trouble at all.

SIX

'We'll fetch Johnny's bike after I take the milk,' Carlos announced on Tuesday.

Danny gave a grunt of assent, wiped his hands on his jeans and squelched along the track by the camping field to sit on the steps of a caravan and roll a cigarette. He wasn't looking forward to this expedition.

His father had enlisted help from Hilltop Farm and a flatbed truck was waiting for them at the crash site. Apparently the driver felt the loan of the vehicle was sufficient effort on his part and he watched with his hands in his pockets while father and son heaved the broken bike upright, tugging it from the clinging red mud, and hauled and shoved it up a plank onto the back of the truck.

'A Manx Norton!' said the farmer as he climbed in the cab. 'Good racing bikes, them.'

'Almost,' gasped Danny as he fastened the tailgate. 'It's got a Triumph engine.' He climbed in the jeep beside his father and the little procession set off towards the village. Immediately after the bridge they turned onto a dirt track alongside the stream until they reached an old barn. Danny wheeled the Triton inside to join an elderly Matchless and miscellaneous items of farm machinery. He tried to wipe some of the mud off before reverentially covering the Triton with empty sacks and walking into town to collect his own bike from the café.

Bert and Skinner sat at a table poring over a newspaper. Munich was still front-page news. Auntie was in charge of the counter.

'Sausage and bacon, please,' Danny said.

'Do you want beans or tomatoes with that?' she said.

'Can I have both?'

'Course you can. How's Johnny?'

'He was still the same last night. I haven't heard anything this morning.'

Auntie vanished through the door by the coffee machine and Danny strolled over to the men.

'I'm not surprised the kid came off,' said Skinner. 'He passed me one night on the Exeter road, going like the clappers. I reckon he wanted to see what it would do on the straight. I hear he's not likely to make it and even if he does he'll lose his hand.'

Auntie emerged from the back with a steaming plate. 'That'll do, I've already heard all the grisly details, thank you.' Judging by the expression on her face she wished she had not.

A bike rumbled onto the forecourt. Skinner wiped the window with his sleeve, creating an arc of clear glass in the condensation. 'Here comes the nancy.'

'Just because he's got nice manners?' Bert went behind the counter. 'That is a beautiful machine he's got.'

'Have you heard anything?' Danny asked with his mouth full.

'He's still the same,' Len said. 'I'm glad you're here. Mrs Hunter has given permission for his friends to visit.'

Danny delved in his pocket for tobacco and matches. 'We went to fetch his bike this morning. I shouldn't think his folks will want anything to do with it.'

'It's my fault,' said Len. 'I should never—'

'Don't start all that again,' Danny said.

'It's no good blaming yourself,' Bert put in. 'These things happen. Especially when you kids go tearing round the lanes on such powerful bikes without any experience.'

'Johnny had loads of experience,' said Danny. 'We've been riding since we were thirteen; we'd take it in turns to ride Dad's old Matchless across the fields at weekends.'

Customers were arriving in droves, anxious to place orders and bag seats before the midday rush. Len stood up. 'I'll see you later on.'

Danny followed him out.

Bert lifted the counter flap. 'Bet it won't start,' he said from the doorway.

Skinner gave the window another wipe.

With Bert's eyes boring into the back of his neck Danny brought his boot down on the starter with the force of a jackhammer. Nothing happened.

'What'd I tell you?' Bert said.

'Reckon you be right,' Skinner replied.

Danny tried the starter again, at the third attempt his elderly Black Shadow shook itself into life coughing and spluttering. Their laughter followed him above the noise of the engine as he steered onto the road and took off round the corner in a cloud of smoke. He passed Francesca trudging up the hill.

'Hop on,' he bellowed above the row from the exhaust. 'Did you miss the bus?'

'I'm not going home, I'm going to St Anne's. Do you know how Johnny is?'

'Still the same Len said.'

'How come he gets to see him when we're not allowed in? It's not fair.'

'Johnny's mum said we can go and see him. I'll come and get you at teatime.'

So Francesca sat at Johnny's bedside reading, school tie discarded on the floor. When she left the room she met his mother sobbing in the corridor. She threw her arms round the woman.

'Oh, Mrs Hunter, please don't cry. Supposing he can hear you?'

Winifred Hunter gave her an astonished stare.

Johnny's friends came to stand silently just inside the door; as if death was catching and they were afraid to go too close. An old man came, Jim Trevelyan; weather-beaten, smelling of fish and pipe tobacco. He managed to avoid his daughter Winifred but he couldn't avoid tears for his only grandson.

Johnny defiantly clung to life.

'It's dreadful to see him lying there like that,' Danny said. They had finished tea but nobody seemed inclined to move.

'Johnny always full of the beans,' Ma said.

'Wasn't he just? Do you remember, Fran, when he dropped the stink bombs at youth club?' said Danny. 'They wouldn't let us back in for weeks.'

'I remember this,' said his father. 'You got in trouble. Mr Robinson came round here complaining because he didn't know where Johnny lived. So many times he got you in trouble.'

'He never did anything really bad, he just went a little bit over the top sometimes,' Danny said.

'What about that fight? You can't dismiss GBH as a bit over the top,' Maria said.

'It can't have been that bad,' said Danny. 'He got away with it. Anyway, the other bloke started it.'

'What about that time you two woke us up at the crack of dawn, riding bareback and howling like a pack of wolves?' Miguel piped up.

'That was your fault,' Maria said to Danny. 'You'd convinced him it was a Red Indian ceremony that had to be done at sunrise.'

Miguel let out a scornful snort. 'What, on a carthorse?'

'Not exactly the Wild West was it?' said Danny. 'We used to have such fun.'

'Stop talking about him as if he's already dead.' Francesca stormed out.

For the rest of the evening Danny prowled round the house and yard in the dark, wondering who would help him fix his bike with his father so busy and Johnny out of action. Unable to settle, he rode back to town.

Johnny too was restless, constantly moving his good hand under the covers. Danny pressed the bell, a nurse came to his rescue. 'He's making funny noises and twitching.'

The nurse turfed him out. He waited in the corridor, sitting with his elbows on his knees, his chin cupped in his hands, studying the swirling pattern on the lino.

'Is he all right?' he asked when she reappeared. 'I was afraid he was going to pull the thing out.'

'It's a catheter. He's quiet now. Do you want to go back in?'

Johnny was still fidgeting.

Danny sniggered. 'Oh, you dirty little devil, spark out and still worrying about your dick…' Suddenly aware of someone standing behind him he stuttered to a halt and whirled round. 'I meant—'

'I think I know what you meant, Daniel,' said the night sister. 'It's a good sign, it means he's starting to regain consciousness.'

SEVEN

Johnny jolted awake. Smell of antiseptic. Pins and needles in his arm. He tried to move but something held him down. He forced his eyes open. A woman in a white frock, white ceiling, white walls. He shut his eyes against the glare.

'Did you see? He opened his eyes, he's awake.'

'Mum?' The word came out as a faint groan.

'It may be some time before he's fully conscious, Mrs Hunter, but it is a very good sign. Perhaps you would like to go home for a while, to freshen up and get some rest. It won't help him if you become ill with exhaustion, will it?'

'Perhaps, just for a little while.' The door closed.

Johnny stared at the strange woman. The white dress was dazzling in the bright light. A white seagull perched on her head. While he waited for it to fly away she wiped his arm. A pinprick took away his ability to think.

Fingers stroked his hair. 'Wake up, sleeping beauty.'

He took a deep breath.

A searing tide of pain surged through him. The skin round his mouth itched, he tried to scratch it but there was a mask in the way. He let his hand drop. He mustn't push it away; he didn't want to drown. He forced himself to concentrate. Voices came from a long, long way away. Surfacing from a deep dive. A mermaid came and put her fingers round his wrist, he couldn't understand what she was saying to him. He wanted to see what she looked like but his eyelids were lead heavy.

'Please, Johnny. I'll do anything if only you'll wake up.'

'I think he's coming round,' said the mermaid. 'Johnny, can you hear me?' When she touched him someone began to scream.

'Shh.' A hand on his bare shoulder, the mask lifted from his face. 'It's all right, Johnny. Keep still, calm down.'

'Len? Wha' you doin' in my dream?'

'You're not dreaming, Johnny.'

'Wha' the hell's goin' on?'

'You had an accident, you're in hospital.'

He frowned at this puzzling piece of information. 'Hospil?'

'You fell off your bike, you clot.'

'It don't half hurt.'

'I'm not surprised.'

He kept his eyes firmly shut and pretended to be asleep. If he deserved a thrashing there was no way to avoid it. Last time the bed was wet his father had hit him with a wooden chair. His arm still hurt, it hurt a lot. His back hurt too. The dream was going on too long, he needed to wake up. When a hand touched his other arm he gave a yelp of terror and tried to leap out of bed but he'd kept still for so long that he'd gone numb, try as he might his legs refused to work. Something squeezed his arm; somehow Danny's tattoo had wound itself round him.

'It's all right, Johnny,' said Len. 'She only wants to take your blood pressure. Stop struggling, you must try to calm down.'

'Got t' get up. Need a piss.' The words came out on a rising note of panic.

'You don't need to worry,' said Len. 'That's all taken care of.'

'Do you want to wait until your father gets here?' said the woman.

'Yes please, Sister.'

'Wha's this?' The needle in his arm was held in place with sticking plaster.

'Leave it,' Len said.

Johnny ran his tongue over his lips.

'Do you want some water?'

'Mm. Need t' sit up.'

'No you don't, you can drink from this.' Len held a small white teapot with a long spout.

One of his nightmares was real. When they moved him the pain was atrocious, after that, he couldn't feel what they were doing but he could smell it. The embarrassment was worse than the pain. He endured the process as best he could, staring at the window past the white birds on their heads.

'Johnny? Darling, it's me.' She sounded anxious. When hadn't she sounded anxious?

He rolled his aching head and tried to focus. 'Sorry, Mum,' he mumbled, not altogether sure what he should be sorry about.

'Oh, Johnny.' She stroked his forehead.

'Don't,' he tried to push her hand away.

She recoiled as the tube brushed her arm. 'Johnny dear, you must be careful.'

'Mm.' He was losing the battle to stay awake.

'I'm pleased to catch both of you here.' A loud, authoritative voice disturbed him. 'As you are aware, your son is starting to regain consciousness. I hope to undertake a further operation on his wrist tomorrow and I shall need your signature on the consent form, Mr Hunter.'

'Why didn't you finish it before?' His father's voice came as a surprise.

'It was necessary to wait until the swelling subsided. I see he sustained a previous fracture, how long ago was it?'

'Years ago, when he was six,' his mother said.

'How did it happen?' the loud man asked.

'He slipped on the stairs. The stairs are outside and they're made of concrete.'

'He always was a clumsy child.' His father again.

Johnny clenched his teeth with rage and resentment and grunted.

'I think he's waking up again,' his mother said.

'I must warn you,' said the loud man, 'there are no guarantees. I'll do all I can but he may have very limited use of that hand. I'll leave the consent form with Sister Denley.'

His mother began to cry.

'How do they know he'd broken it before?' said his father. 'Have you gone and said something?'

'No! I suppose they could tell from the X-ray. Do you think it shows the difference between a fall and a hiding?'

'Shut up, woman! How the hell would I know?'

'You always were too hard on him.' She sounded tired. 'He was only little, you never should've been so impatient.'

'A boy needs discipline, Win.'

'Hello, young man.' It was the man who had dared to argue with his father.

He opened his eyes to the blindingly bright, blurred world.

'Can you tell me your name?'

'Johnny.'

'Your full name?'

'Jonathon James Hunter.' He managed with an effort, slurring the words. 'Wha's going on?'

'You're in hospital. How many fingers am I holding up?'

Johnny felt dreadful; his arm hurt, his head ached and there was an agonising pain in his back. He wanted the man to go away and leave him in peace. He tried to focus on the fingers but the light was too bright and it hurt his eyes. 'Three,' he guessed.

'Can you wiggle your toes for me?'

He wondered why the idiot wanted to play stupid games.

'Johnny, wiggle your toes,' the voice insisted.

'Then will you fuck off?'

Someone gasped. The man took no notice. 'Can you feel that?' he said.

'No.' Something was blocking his view and he had no idea what the idiot was doing.

'Now move your fingers for me.'

'For gawd's sake!' Johnny said. The tube in his arm shook when he clenched his fist.

'And the other hand.'

His other hand was lying on a pillow. He tried to move the swollen fingers sticking out of the bandages but they were too stiff.

'Thank you,' said the man. 'Go ahead, Sister.'

The injection brought rapid relief. As he sank gratefully into oblivion a familiar face swam into view. 'Len?'

'I've got to go now, Johnny, but I'll be back first thing tomorrow, I promise.'

He had the feeling he was not alone. He rolled his aching head. A girl was turning the pages of a book carefully as if she didn't want to disturb someone. What was a girl doing in his room? He never brought anyone back to the flat. The light from the window behind him shone on her dark hair. Behind him? The window was in the wrong place! Who was she? Why was the window all wrong? He sighed and pain shot through him.

He closed his eyes and tried to think.

A bell rang. It brought sharp clicking heels.

'He made a noise and he opened his eyes for a moment.'

'Johnny, can you hear me?' a woman said.

'Arm hurts.'

Another dazzling apron. 'You can have a few minutes but don't tire him, he's still very poorly.'

Johnny ground his teeth. 'Not fuckin' poorly.'

Danny hove into view.

'All right, keep your hair on. I came to see if Fran wants a lift home.'

Francesca! Why?

'Stop looming over me, you great lump.'

'Sorry.'

'Bloody clear off,' Johnny ordered.

'But I only just got here.'

'Get out!'

The nurse came in. 'Why did you send your friend away?'

'I don't want him seeing me like this. I don't want anybody seeing me like this.'

'It's a bit late for that, they already have,' she said.

Johnny frowned. 'They? Who's they?'

Strange noises, stranger smells. Discomfort soon turned to pain and he tore at the sheet with his good hand. The nurses came to give him an injection, they rolled him on his side to spread canvas beneath his body, then rolled him back again.

The door opened. 'Can I see him before he goes to theatre?' Len said.

'You won't get much sense out of him, he's already had his pre-med.'

'Len?'

'I thought I'd pop in and see you before the op.'

'Op?' Johnny frowned with the effort to speak.

'They need to set your wrist. How's the pain?'

'Doesn't hurt. They gave me some stuff. Floating. Nice...' His eyes closed in spite of his effort to keep them open.

Len squeezed his good hand. 'You'll be all right.'

'I would be if they didn't keep moving me. Too tired...'

A nurse opened the door. 'He's sedated so don't expect much response.'

Len dropped his hand faster than a red-hot poker. 'Good morning, Mrs Hunter. I'll see you later, Johnny.'

'Len! Fancy you being here. Hello, darling.'

'Mm.' His mouth refused to work. Try as he might he couldn't keep his eyes open. He roused when two men arrived with a trolley and two long wooden poles. The porters pushed the poles through slots in the canvas underneath him. When they lifted him onto the trolley he hardly made a sound. They pushed him along the corridor and through a pair of double doors where a man in a mask wielded yet another syringe.

EIGHT

Francesca took Miguel's jeans with her on Thursday. After school she changed in the hospital toilets, stuffed her gymslip and tie in her satchel, and made her way to the men's ward. The double doors were open, a hum of visitors inside. Johnny's parents were sitting in the corridor, Mrs Hunter in maroon hat and coat, Mr Hunter with his shabby raincoat. To avoid them she dodged through an open door and found herself in a small room with a large sink. Glass bottles and enamel bedpans were ranged on shelves. It was quiet and smelled strongly of disinfectant. A wooden stool lurked in the corner behind the door and she sat down to wait.

Mr Hunter's voice broke the silence. 'We were sat like this at the juvenile court. Near two year ago, now.'

Mrs Hunter offered no response.

'It was his last term at school, assault and affray.'

'But they dropped the wounding charge.' Mrs Hunter's voice rose in Johnny's defence.

'Only because the bloke was too embarrassed to admit a youngster had bested him.'

'He's easily led.' Mrs Hunter tried to excuse Johnny's behaviour.

'Dammit, woman! Can't you see it's him what's doing the leading?'

'How can you go on about that when he's so ill?'

'And did you know about those tattoos?' he went on. 'Whatever possessed him? When did he get them done?'

'It really doesn't matter now, Norman.'

A bell clanged and departing visitors streamed past. Francesca peered out. Johnny's parents were still there.

'I'm going to get a sandwich,' Mr Hunter said.

Francesca withdrew into her hiding place.

More footsteps. The door swung open and Francesca jumped up, but it was only Maria. She took down a bedpan.

'Why are you hiding in the sluice?'

'How's Johnny?'

'They haven't brought him back from the operating theatre yet. Why are you whispering?'

'So's they don't know I'm here.'

It was dusk when the porters whisked a trolley down the brightly lit corridor and into the side room. The porters came out with the unburdened trolley. Mrs Hunter folded and refolded a ruined scrap of cotton which had started life as a hanky.

Mr Hunter came back. Francesca caught a strong whiff of beer as he walked past.

'Have they brought him back yet?'

'Yes.' Mrs Hunter raised her head expectantly as a nurse came along.

'You can sit with him now.'

More footsteps outside. Francesca craned her neck. Len walked straight into the ward and up to the desk.

'Not now, Lucien. Johnny's parents are with him.'

'How is he, Sister?'

'You should ask your father when he's got a moment.'

Len wandered down the corridor with his hands in his pockets. 'He's never got a moment,' he muttered.

'What's that?'

Len jumped. 'Oh! Maria. Nothing, it's not important.'

'Can you keep an eye on Fran for a bit?'

'Yes, I suppose so but—'

'Good, she's in the sluice. Thanks,' Maria added over her shoulder.

'What on earth are you doing in there?' Len stood in the doorway grinning at the sight of her perched on the stool with her school blouse tucked into an old pair of boy's jeans.

'I'm trying to keep out of the way. Any chance of seeing him yet?'

'Not yet, his parents are with him. He'll probably be asleep for quite a while.'

Francesca drooped dejectedly.

'How about a ride to the café?' Len said.

'I want to be here when he wakes up,' Francesca said.

'We need not be long.'

She was surprised when he produced the lid. 'I'm afraid I only have one. Would you like it?'

'I've never worn one,' she said, pulling her hair back and tying it into a ponytail.

Len's headlight reflected in a puddle, he cut the engine and Francesca got off as a group of people left the café laughing and chattering.

'I see Scarface has got another boyfriend already,' one of the girls said.

Francesca scowled at them in the gloom.

Len held the door open and they were greeted by bright lights and a blast of rock 'n' roll. He pulled out a chair for her. 'How very unpleasant.'

'It's best to try and ignore them. If you take any notice they only do it all the more.' She sat down heavily. 'I'm ever so tired.'

Two Teddy boys, elbows on the table, gravity-defying quiffs almost touching, were deep in conversation. One glanced up. 'All right, Len?'

'Yes, thanks.' Len turned his attention back to Francesca. 'You're limping. Have you hurt yourself?'

'My leg aches a bit, that's all.'

'What have you done?'

'Nothing. I broke it ages ago, when I did this.' She touched the scar on her cheek. 'I've been doing a lot of walking lately.'

'Isn't there a bus?'

'If I caught the bus every time I went into town my pocket money wouldn't last five minutes.'

'I'm sorry, I didn't realise. I can take you home if you like, when you're ready.'

'Thanks, I want to see Johnny first, if they'll let me. Danny sometimes gives me a lift back but he's taken Penny to the pictures tonight. It's got worse since I've been seeing Johnny.'

He looked surprised. 'Your leg?'

'No!' She managed a half smile. 'The teasing; I think they're jealous.'

'Are you two going to buy anything or just sit there yakking all night?' Bert called out.

Len ordered coffees. A newspaper lay on the counter and he turned it round to read the headlines. 'It's Valentine's Day tomorrow, I'd quite forgotten.'

Bert brought their coffees over. 'How's Johnny?'

'Holding his own,' Len said.

The Teddy boys sniggered. 'So we heard.'

'Idiot!' Francesca picked up the spoon and played with the froth crowning her coffee. 'He couldn't keep a secret if his life depended on it.'

'Who couldn't?' Len said.

'Danny.'

'Why? What has he said?'

'It doesn't matter.'

'I got ragged at school.'

'Did you? Why?'

'Some chaps thought my Christian name had hilarious possibilities.'

'What did you do?'

'Nothing really. It stopped for a while after...' He twirled his half-empty cup round on the glass saucer. 'After my mother died.'

'Oh Len, I'm sorry. I didn't know.'

'No reason why you should. Do you know what the worst thing was? He didn't bother to come and tell me, he didn't even ask to speak to me. My father...' Len's hand shook and the cup rolled off its saucer dribbling dregs of coffee on the American cloth. Len set the cup upright. 'My father telephoned the school and left a message. Our house matron told me.'

'Oh, Len. But surely—'

'Afterwards he couldn't bear to stay in the house, too many reminders of Mother, I suppose. He stayed at an hotel for a while, then he took the post at St Anne's and we moved down here.'

Francesca couldn't think what to say. The Teddy boys went out discussing their impending National Service and Bert inadvertently came to her rescue.

'That pair are in for a shock when the army treats them to a short back and sides.'

Francesca looked at her watch. 'Do you think we ought to go back?'

Len picked up his crash helmet. 'I've rather enjoyed the navy. I shall miss it.'

'What are you going to do after?'

'I'm going to university in the autumn but I'll get a few weeks off first.'

'University? What will you do there?'

'I'll be reading medicine. I'm expected to follow in my father's footsteps, and my grandfather's.'

When they got back to St Anne's Johnny was alone but still asleep, his long lashes dark against wax-pale cheeks. His arm was now encased in spotless plaster of Paris, discoloured fingers ballooned from the cast. The mermaid on his upper arm was hidden by more bruising and a blood pressure cuff hid the other tattoo. Night sister came in.

'I'll be back shortly,' Len said.

Sister Branch took Johnny's blood pressure, unwound the fabric and raised her eyebrows at Francesca. 'Neptune?'

'It's Triton, because his bike was a Manx Triton.'

'Really. Is there a Manx cat, then?'

Francesca flushed crimson, scurried from the room and nearly collided with Len as he emerged from the gents.

'What you done with your school clothes?' her mother demanded the minute she walked in.

'They're in my satchel. I went to see Johnny.'

'She's pinched my jeans again, Mama,' Mig wailed.

'I only borrowed them and they're too small for you anyway.'

Ma took one look at the crumpled gymslip. 'You better get the iron out.'

'What about my jeans?' Mig said.

'Oh, bother your jeans,' Francesca snapped.

She found Danny in his room doing a fair imitation of Winifred Atwell on the piano.

'How could you? It's one thing to tell us, but to go and blab about the other night all over town.'

'Whoa there. What you on about? I never said a word.'

'You did too. About Johnny. Don't you try and deny it, they were laughing about it in the café.'

'Oh, I thought you meant about Len.'

'Len? What about him?'

'Monday night in the car park, he tried to top himself.'

'He never!'

'He slashed his wrist.'

'I thought that was an accident.'

'Not from what I saw. Ask him if you don't believe me.'

Francesca grabbed Danny's elbow. 'When are you going to learn to keep your big gob shut?'

NINE

The twilight smelled of antiseptic. A young nurse in a pale blue dress dipped a cloth in an enamel bowl, wrung it out and carefully wiped every horizontal surface in the room. Johnny studied the blue and white blur and worked out that nurses wore white aprons not white dresses.

She noticed him watching her. 'Do you need anything?'

'I'd love a cuppa and a smoke.'

Another nurse came in and tried to put a thermometer in his mouth.

He turned his head away. 'What time is it?'

'Just gone seven.'

'Night or morning?'

'Morning, I've just come on duty. Now open your mouth, please.'

'He's been asking for tea and a cigarette,' the girl said.

'If you've finished you can go and get him some tea.'

'Can I have a fag as well?'

'If you're a good boy and open your mouth for me I'll see what I can do.'

They allowed him a cigarette. The girl in the pale blue uniform stood guard while he smoked it. When he finished she stubbed it out in a tin ashtray and left him on his own. The sun rose, daubing a yellow square on the wall. The ward sister came in followed by the pale blue nurse carrying towels and a bowl.

'No! Not again!' Johnny felt on the locker and found the ashtray. There was a clang as it hit the door frame. 'Get out!'

The nurse fled.

Sister Denley was made of sterner stuff and Johnny, far too conscious, gritted his teeth while they turned him on his side.

When he lay emptied, washed and combed, with the sheet folded over the bedspread its regulation number of inches and his right arm resting obediently on its pillow, they finally left him alone. He sneaked a look under the bedding tunnel; white plaster covered his body. He craned his neck. His leg was in plaster too, a yellow tube snaking across the whiteness and out of sight, his toes poking out the end. Voices outside made him drop the sheet.

A larger than usual entourage trailed behind the surgeon. 'Do you mind if some medical students take a look at you?' Mr Barrington asked.

He shook his head, wished he hadn't and hoped this wouldn't take long.

'Wiggle your toes,' Mr Barrington commanded. He raised his eyebrows at someone Johnny couldn't see. 'Well?'

A young man barely older than himself, enveloped in a white coat much too long for him, approached the foot of the bed and took something from his top pocket.

'Can you feel that?'

'No.' Johnny glowered at him. The bedcovers completely obscured his view. They trooped round the side of the bed.

Another student stepped forward at the surgeon's request. 'Can you move your fingers for me?'

'I'm not a bleedin' performing seal,' he complained. Try as he might his fingers wouldn't work; they felt numb, as if he'd slept on his hand.

The door swung open.

'Bloody get out!' Johnny shouted.

'Lucien, you really must stop dropping in at all hours of the day and night,' Sister Denley said.

'Johnny, calm down, it's me,' said Len. 'I can't stay all that long, it's Maria's day off and I promised to take her to the cinema.'

'Why can't I move? When I asked Mum what I've done she told me not to worry.'

'You've broken your leg.'

Johnny dragged the sheet aside, exposing the plaster covering his chest. 'Since when did my legs come up to my armpits?'

'And some ribs,' Len said.

'Look at me!'

Len looked as if he was about to burst into tears.

'I need a fag.'

Len reached across him for the cigarette packet. He lit one and left his lighter on the locker. 'You might as well hang on to that, I've another one at home.'

Johnny took the cigarette and puffed smoke at the ceiling. 'When were they going to tell me?'

'Tell you what?' Len stared at him vacantly.

'Why didn't they just let me die?'

'Johnny, you mustn't talk like that.'

'You lied to me, you bastard,' screamed Johnny. 'I'm not going to get better.'

'I didn't, I'm sorry, I thought—'

'What did you think? That I wouldn't notice?'

'Johnny, I—'

'I've broken my back, haven't I? That's why they've put me in this fuckin' white coffin. They don't do all this for broken ribs.' He put the cigarette in his mouth and dragged the bedcovers aside again.

'Mind out! You'll set the bloody bed alight.' Len took the cigarette away and ground it out in the ashtray.

'Gimme that!'

A nurse came to find out what the shouting was about. 'What's going on?'

'He's in a bit of a state.'

'Fuck off.' Johnny turned his head away. 'Fuck off, both of you.'

Sister Denley came with a syringe in a kidney dish. Johnny stretched out his arm. He was getting the hang of this; it was the way out of the nightmare.

'May I stay for a while?' Len asked.

'He might be a bit groggy,' said Sister Denley. 'I gave him a shot of morphine.'

'They've given me s'more stuff.' Johnny formed the words with difficulty.

'I know,' said Len. 'You'll feel better soon.'

The sister left them.

'I'm fucking scared, Len.'

'You mustn't get so agitated. It's not the end of the world. You might get some movement back eventually.'

'But it is. It's the end of everything, all our dreams.'

'Johnny, please try to relax.'

Minutes passed.

'I don't feel too good,' mumbled Johnny. 'It's ever so cold.'

'Are you still in pain? Shall I ring for a nurse?'

'No, it doesn't hurt now.'

'That's good.'

'Why's it gone so dark?'

Len kept his thumb on the bell until a nurse hurried in and took it away from him. Sister came too, followed by a man in a white coat. They left the door ajar. Out in the corridor an electric floor-polisher droned.

Everything went black.

Len grasped his shoulders. 'Johnny!'

The noise came first. A low rumble. It penetrated the thick sea mist, gradually growing louder. Moments later a pinprick of light pierced the haze, followed by another, then another and another, moving steadily towards him. The lights became brighter, they resolved themselves into headlamps. The bikes seeped through the grey curtain in single file, throbbing past him in the darkness. His pulse raced, he opened the throttle ready to follow and his heart missed a beat. A wave of pain washed through him. From a long way away someone called his name, the sound hung in the air. He turned to see who it was and the light blinded him.

'Johnny!' Len pleaded.

'He can't hear you, lad,' the doctor said.

'I have a pulse, Doctor,' Sister said.

'Mm.' Some fool was shining a light in his eyes. 'Fuck off,' he mumbled.

'Johnny!' Len breathed a sigh of relief.

'For a minute there I thought we'd lost him.' The doctor sounded equally relieved.

Mr Barrington strode in. 'Don't you dare die on me now, boy.'

The school bus let more jabbering kids on at every stop. It was too crowded, too noisy and on impulse Francesca pushed her way through the throng to get off several stops too soon. She walked quickly, wondering what to do when she got to the hospital, but she need not have worried, nobody tried to stop her as she made her way to the men's ward. She hesitated. The double doors were open, Johnny's door was not.

'Are you feeling any better?' Len asked.

'I feel lousy. Stop fiddling with my plaster.'

Len put his pen in his top pocket.

'Hold me.'

'You'll get us into trouble one of these days.' Len glanced through the glass partition in the wall behind him to check the coast was clear.

'I feel like a bloody goldfish stuck here with them all peering at me through that window.'

Len slid his arm round Johnny's neck. 'I'll be back after Whitsun, you'll be so much better by then.'

'How the hell can I be better? I can't even piss for myself.'

Lips brushed his cheek.

'Fool! Someone might see.'

'It's all right, they're halfway down the ward, busy with the drugs trolley,' Len said, unaware that Francesca was walking up to Sister's desk as he spoke. Unaware she was waiting to ask permission to see Johnny. Unaware that she had turned round to be confronted by the goldfish-bowl glass.

He laid his hand on the nape of Len's neck. 'Give me a proper kiss.'

The injection began to take effect. With his cheek resting against the soft cotton of Len's shirt he sank beneath the jangling, anguished surface into quiet, enfolding darkness.

Francesca wandered into the corridor with her head down and nearly bumped into the ward maid coming out of the kitchen.

'Careful! Look where you're going.'

'Sorry.' Francesca stood aside to let her pass. 'Mabel?'

'What is it, dearie?'

'Why do you call him Mr Johnny?'

'I can't call him Mr Hunter, can I? He's only a lad.'

'Why not just Johnny?'

'Oh, no, that wouldn't be right, miss. What with him being such good friends with Mr Barrington's son, an' all.'

Francesca wandered into the street. She didn't understand. She remembered the headlines in the *News of the World*, remembered reading about men being sent to prison, disgraced for doing wicked things. Johnny couldn't be like them, could he? What exactly was gross indecency anyway? More than a kiss surely but even so that wasn't right; men didn't kiss each other.

Last autumn the papers said such things weren't so wicked after all and the law should be changed, but it wasn't. She stumbled on until cold spray from a wave crashing against the harbour wall brought her to her senses. The wind gusted fitfully, rocking sheltering fishing boats. She had no idea how she had got there. She turned her back on the boats to trudge along the tideline in her best school shoes, stopping now and then to pick up pretty pebbles and empty shells. A tremendous sea was running, grey-green breakers rolling dizzyingly towards her, the wind tossing spindrift in the air like smoke. Breaking waves tumbled shoreward to wash up the shallow slope and leave a transient fringe of lacy foam on the yellow sand before the next wave redrew it. A seaweed covered ledge barred her way; she had walked all the way to the promontory. The falling tide had exposed the rock shelf jutting from the base of the dark red cliff. Waves crashed on its seaward rim, tossing plumes of spray high in the air. Buffeted gulls, losing their battle with the gale, were swept sideways to hang above the bay beyond.

She sat in a shelter on the promenade to smoke a cigarette and gaze vacantly at the turmoil on the shore. Daylight faded. Lights flashed along the prom and a rowdy group of boys on pushbikes careered past.

She set off towards the café. The shops were beginning to close but the pubs weren't open yet; it was the time Bert's place was at its busiest. Realising she was in school uniform she retraced her steps to Woolworth's for a fizzy drink and a bar of chocolate. When her English teacher walked into the shop she hid behind the sweet counter.

'Where on earth have you been?' Maria asked when she got home.

'At school.'

'Clearly you haven't because I saw you in town earlier.'

'I've got the curse so I went to Boots for some aspirin,' Francesca said.

'And where have you been ever since? You were nowhere near the shops when I saw you.'

'Sorry.'

'So you should be. It's my last day off before Len goes back and I cancelled a hairdresser's appointment so we could go out today, then he couldn't come. Where would we be if half the population took an afternoon off every month because they had stomach ache?'

TEN

Rock 'n' roll blared from the café's open door, boys gathered outside to discuss the respective merits of their machines and giggling girls vied for their attention. A pretty blonde with pink lipstick, tight jeans and a ponytail abandoned the bench in front of the windows and followed Danny inside.

'Murphy's managed to scratch a team together for next week,' said Bert. 'You'd think, in the circumstances, they'd have let them postpone the match.'

'I'd forgotten about that, I don't even know who they're playing,' Danny said.

'Sheffield Wednesday, don't you read the paper?'

'I haven't had time,' said Danny. 'United haven't got a hope. Wasn't their goalie in the plane crash?'

'He walked away.'

'Lucky blighter.'

Danny chatted up the blonde whilst keeping a sharp lookout for his girlfriend's car. Len's T-Bird nosed onto the pavement and came to a halt next to his Vincent. Danny disentangled himself from the blonde and went to meet him.

'Ain't it great about Johnny?'

'There's nothing great about it,' Len said.

'But he's going to be all right.'

To his astonishment Len grabbed him by the lapels and

pinned him up against the plate glass window. 'You stupid great oaf,' Len yelled in his face.

'But I thought, now he's come round—'

'Don't you realise he'll spend the rest of his life confined to a wheelchair?' Len hissed in his ear.

Danny shoved Len off and got on his bike. He only went round the block. The Black Shadow roared down the road, round the corner and across the pavement. People scattered in all directions. Danny launched himself at Len with fists flying, sending him spinning. Len grabbed the back of the bench to keep his balance and Danny hit him again while his guard was down. They were gathering an audience, motorbikes were wheeled to safety and the few remaining girls scampered inside.

'Fight! Fight!' chanted the bystanders.

A ragged circle formed round the pair. Bert emerged from behind his counter and stood in the doorway to get a better view. Those who hadn't already done so came to shift their bikes out of harm's way.

They swayed in a clinch. 'He's my friend too, you've only known him five minutes,' said Danny. 'And don't you ever call me stupid.'

They pushed apart and started again. Neither would give ground. Blood trickled from a cut on Danny's cheek. He landed a punch on Len's nose, saw blood on Len's shirt cuff. The significance of this hit him. 'Bugger!'

Len hit him, hard.

Danny staggered, regained his balance, raised his fist to block another punch and by a lucky accident caught Len under the chin. This briefly checked the onslaught. Very briefly.

'Hang on!' Danny dodged a swing. 'Whoa there!'

But Len had no intention of stopping. He feinted right and swung a left but Danny was ready for him. Brute force and extra height versus Len's formal boxing lessons made them too well matched.

In the end Bert stepped forward. 'That's enough! Come on, break it up. Come on, you lot,' he shouted, beckoning onlookers. 'Gimme a hand.'

Bert and another burly biker grabbed Len from behind.

'Take it easy, boy,' Bert advised. This remark made Len even angrier and he struggled furiously but the men had a firm hold.

Penny's little Austin was parked at the kerb. Danny hadn't noticed her arrive. She wound the window down.

Danny waved frantically at her. 'Over here.'

'What?' She didn't sound too pleased. Had someone told her about the blonde?

'Give us a lift to the hospital, darling.'

'Are you okay?'

'It's not me, it's Len.'

Penny gave a cursory glance in Len's direction. 'No chance. I'm not having him bleeding all over my car.'

Auntie produced a tea cloth to staunch the blood and Penny grudgingly tipped the passenger seat forward to let Len squeeze onto the back seat holding his wrist up with the allegedly clean cloth firmly wound round it. She dropped them outside St Anne's and drove off, leaving Danny to take Len to the casualty department. He was flustered and almost gave Len's right name. He tried to explain what had happened but got precious little sympathy for his cut cheek and black eye. Len eventually emerged from a cubicle.

'What did they say?' Danny asked.

'They put a couple of extra stitches in.'

Len took a taxi home, leaving their bikes marooned outside the café and dropping Danny off at the crossroads to walk the rest of the way. By the time he got back to collect his bike the café was almost empty.

Auntie sat at a table by the window reading, ash from her cigarette dropped on the magazine. She shook it on the floor and looked up. 'Just look at the state of you. What you need is some raw steak on that eye.' She gathered up her belongings. 'And your jacket's smothered in blood.'

'It's Len's. You should've seen him, standing there bleeding like a stuck pig, and me holding his arm up so it was pouring down me an' all.'

'Is he all right?'

'Yeah. They put some more stitches in and he's right as rain.'

Bert came in and raised the counter flap for Auntie to come through.

'I thought you'd be back,' he said to Danny. 'You seem to be making a habit of abandoning that old heap here.' Bert nodded towards the Vincent.

'She's not a heap.' Danny's voice gained an octave of indignation. 'She's a beauty.'

Bert laughed. 'You spend more time mending it than riding it. Is Len okay?'

'Yeah, till his dad finds out. Then there'll be fireworks.'

'It was hardly your fault,' said Bert. 'We could all see he was spoiling for a fight.'

Danny sighed. 'I don't know what's got into him.'

'Come to think of it, he's been a bit off with everyone lately. You'll have a right shiner there.'

'I know, my mum's going to do her nut.' Danny reached the door. 'What about Len's bike?'

'It'll be fine where it is. I don't mind a nice, shiny new T-Bird out front, that don't lower the tone.'

Danny was nearly home when he passed Maria. He waited for her at the gate.

'What have you done?'

'I had a nosebleed,' he said.

'You've been fighting. Whose girlfriend were you chatting up this time?'

'You've got it all wrong. I didn't do anything, honest.'

She wheeled her bicycle into the harness room. 'Who was it?'

'Len.' A peal of thunder rendered Danny's reply barely audible.

'What! Why?'

'Don't ask me, he started it.'

'Len? A likely story. We'd better get in before it rains. I'll go first or Mama will have a fit when she sees that blood.'

Danny faced an inquest on his black eye before he got the chance for a word alone with Maria.

'Len says that Johnny's not going to get better.'

'Yes he is. Mr Barrington wants to transfer him to another hospital when his condition improves.'

'What sort of hospital?'

'They specialise in spinal injuries.'

'Then it's true that he'll have to spend the rest of his life in a wheelchair.'

'It looks that way. What were you and Len fighting about?'

'I don't know, he just went for me. I thought everything would be okay once Johnny came round.'

ELEVEN

Francesca tiptoed in, unsure at first whether he was asleep or unconscious. The drip was back in. She stared at the cast on his other arm.

'I see you've been busy.' The nurse wasn't much older than her.

'You made me jump,' said Francesca. 'Has anyone else been to see him?'

'Not this morning. His mother was in yesterday.' The girl went out, closing the door behind her.

The plaster on Johnny's right arm was adorned with a wavy line sprouting short stems with flowers and pointed leaves on alternate sides. The leaves resembled bindweed but the flowers looked like hearts with an arc across the V at the top.

He was watching her.

'Johnny, it's me. You weren't asleep, were you?'

He grunted.

She pulled up a chair. 'Why keep your eyes shut, then?'

'Because this fuckin' ceiling's boring.' He rolled his head to look at her. 'You've got a dress on.'

'I'm on my way home from church.'

'How long have I been here?'

'A week.'

'Bloody hell!'

'I prayed for you.'

'Fat lot of good that'll do.'

'Does your hand hurt much?' she asked.

'No, but my back hurts and I've got a bloody awful headache. Why are you gawping at my fingers? Are they—'

'They're a bit puffy. Who's been drawing on your plaster?'

'Len signed it.'

'There's a proper drawing. It's got pointy leaves and the flowers are like little hearts.'

'What flowers?'

'On your plaster.'

'The bloody idiot. Everything would have been all right if I hadn't wound up in here. If anyone asks, say you drew them. Please, Fran, for my sake.'

'They're not that obvious. They hardly show.'

'How the fuck can they not show?'

'Please don't shout or someone will come in.'

'I am not shouting! Tell me exactly what's there,' he continued more quietly.

'It looks like bindweed but the flowers aren't right. I wasn't quite sure what they were at first. And on Friday when I was waiting to ask Sister if I could come in I saw you.' She looked down to undo the button on her left glove. 'I saw you and Len…'

'What do you think you saw?'

'I didn't imagine it.'

'Imagine what? Spit it out.'

'He kissed you,' she said, undoing the other glove.

'Christ all bloody mighty! He told me nobody could see us.'

'What's going on, Johnny?'

'You haven't said anything have you? You mustn't tell.' His voice rose and he grabbed her arm with his free hand. 'You've got no idea how much trouble I'd be in if anyone found out. Promise me, Fran.'

'Please, Johnny, let go. You're hurting me.'

'Promise?'

'I promise, cross my heart and hope to die.'

He let go. 'Don't start crying, for gawd's sake.'

She blinked frantically.

'You mustn't tell anyone what you think you saw. You have no idea how bad it would look if someone misunderstood.'

She took her gloves off, pulling at the tip of each finger separately until it came loose.

'Fran!'

The young nurse interrupted them. 'I'm sorry but you'll have to go now, it's lunchtime.'

Francesca stuffed the gloves in her handbag and left without another word.

The nurse put down the tray and held a spoon to his lips.

He turned his head away. 'What's on my plaster?'

She glanced at his arm. 'Your girlfriend has been doodling on it.'

'What does it say?'

'If you eat this I'll tell you.'

'Nurse!' He wrung two indignant syllables from the word.

'It says get well soon and she's drawn some flowers. Come on now.'

He opened his mouth but gagged on the soup. For the first time that he could remember he wasn't hungry. His mother had done her best through the years of rationing when he was a boy. He would make up the shortfall by scrounging his tea at Danny's and in term time he wolfed down school dinners, even the greasy mutton stew which he detested but ate down to the last grain of pearl barley, leaving his plate bare but for the bones. Now he had no appetite at all.

'Come on, Johnny, just a little. Please, I'll get into trouble if you don't eat anything.'

'Sorry. Can I have a cigarette?'

She looked at him doubtfully.

'I had one this morning; they're in the drawer there.' He jerked his thumb at the locker, then frowned. 'I think it was this morning.'

'If you eat some of this I'll ask Staff Nurse Seddons.'

He could see the little nurse through the glass partition, talking to a thin woman with glasses who looked as though she'd swallowed a wasp. She granted permission to smoke. The nurse came back to light it for him and she hovered over him until he finished.

The scrawny woman came to give him an injection.

'Hello, darling.' His mother bent to kiss him. 'Are you feeling better today? I've brought you some grapes.'

'Thanks.'

'There was a terrible storm last night. We were lucky but half the houses on Ferry Road have got tiles missing.'

'I know, Mum, I heard it.' He explored the locker with his good hand. 'There was a fair bit of lightning an' all.'

'What are you after?'

'Fags, they should be on here somewhere. Can you get me some more?'

'Hello, John.'

His father lurked at the foot of the bed. He hadn't seen him come in. His mother found the cigarettes.

'I can do it.' Johnny snatched the packet and extracted one with his teeth. He offered them to his father, who struck a match and held it at arm's length.

Johnny drew on his cigarette and the match flame shrank.

'Is there anything you need?' his mother asked, clinging to an ashtray like it was a lifebelt.

'Gawd's sake! I just told you, Mum. I need some more fags.'

'There's no need to speak to your mother like that.'

They descended into an uncomfortable silence. He had neither the interest nor the energy to think of anything to talk about;

they never had found much to say to each other. He stubbed the cigarette out, closed his eyes and turned his head away.

'I'm sorry I didn't get in yesterday,' said his father. 'I had to go back to work. Things have been a bit tight, what with your mother being off work an' all.'

Johnny opened his eyes and glared at him. 'Lucky you! I'd rather be flat on my back under a car than flat on my back staring at this bloody ceiling. I don't suppose there's much call for paralysed mechanics, is there?'

His mother searched for her hanky, his father looked away. Johnny wondered if he'd been giving his mother a hard time. The interminable visiting hour finally came to an end.

While Johnny was wishing away visiting hour the Gomez family were battling the elements. Francesca had been relieved to see the jeep still waiting for her outside St Anne's but nothing prepared them for the chaos in store when they reached home. From the farmyard nothing seemed amiss but in the kitchen the coconut matting covering the brick floor was soaking wet. Their mother rolled her sleeves up to pick up the mats. The top section of the stable door was open and they could see the paddock had become a shallow lake, here and there a tuft of grass broke the surface. Their father was stacking sandbags against the door. Francesca ran into Danny's room, the courtyard was awash and water was seeping in under the French doors. He lugged his bed to the far end of the room and started to roll up the carpet.

'Someone gimme a hand in here!'

'I can do that,' said his father. 'Take my waders and go to check the stream. I'll stay and help your mother.'

Miguel and Alvaro ran down the stairs, having shed their Sunday best in favour of jeans and gumboots.

'Here we go again,' said Danny. 'Who's coming with me?'

'I'll be down in a sec,' Francesca said. She changed as fast as she could, leaving her coat and dress in a heap on the bed.

They piled rope and rakes in the back of the jeep. Francesca claimed the passenger seat, Mig and Al scrambled in the back with the tools. Danny drove towards the village, turning off when they reached the track leading to the high barn. Danny slowed to negotiate the rain-filled ruts, the jeep rocked on the rough ground and his kid brothers hung on as best they could. Past the barn only parallel strips of grass breaking the surface of the murky water indicated the edges of the track. Water fountained up on either side as Danny drove towards the willow trees. On their right the pool was brimful and the once shallow stream curving from it was now an overflowing torrent of dirty water carrying rafts of vegetation. The hedge which sheltered the orchard grew on a low bank and held back the rising flood but the roots of the hedge on the east side of the field were completely submerged and water was trickling through the tangle of stems into the paddock.

Heavy, wet leaves brushed the jeep's roof and Danny braked. As he splashed into the muddy water distant thunder rumbled. He shouldered a rake and glanced up. Clouds hung dark over the moor.

'We'd better get a move on, there's more weather on the way.'

Al slid down gingerly and squelched along under the trees. He lost his balance in the ankle-deep water and plunged in his hand to stop himself falling. 'My wellie's got stuck!'

'Don't you go falling in,' said Danny. 'If you can't help go home.'

'For heaven's sake!' Francesca wrenched the boot free.

Little Al pulled his boot back on over his sodden sock. 'What's this?' He opened his fist to show them a blue pebble.

'I dunno and I don't care,' Danny said.

'Don't you take no notice of him, Al.' Francesca held out her hand. She wiped the muddy stone on her jeans, shrugged her shoulders and slipped it in her jeans pocket. They splashed through the water near the bank, feeling their way with the rakes to avoid stepping into the channel where the force of the current might sweep them off their feet. They reached the footbridge, the water which normally ran a couple of feet below the plank now foamed against it, spreading out on either side. A few yards beyond the bridge the channel became rocky, narrow and steep; where water should have been skipping downhill in a series of little waterfalls there was barely a trickle. A large branch had become wedged under the bridge, collecting more debris until it completely blocked the channel.

Mig squatted on the plank, one hand on the length of iron pipe which served as a handrail to steady himself. 'Loads of stuff has got stuck down here.'

'Get over the other side.' Danny glanced at the sky and grasped his end of the broken branch. 'Let's get on with it or it'll be raining again before we're done.'

Francesca and Mig ran across the bridge and got hold of the other end of the branch. It was firmly wedged. They pulled and tugged until Mig fell over backwards, he scrambled to his feet, his backside caked in sticky red mud.

'This is no use,' said Danny. 'Mig, get back over here and fetch the jeep; Al, get the rope.'

Al hitched one end of the rope to the tow bar and dragged it through the water uncoiling it as he went until he got near enough to toss the end to Danny, who lowered himself into water which reached his knees to tie it to the branch.

Mig gently pressed the jeep's accelerator to take up the slack. The engine raced as he eased forward. The rope rose dripping from the filthy water and grew taut under the strain, the branch came away with a jerk and water began to trickle through the gap. Danny and Francesca used rakes to drag out the rest of the blockage. By the time the water gushed downhill big drops of rain were plopping on the surface. Francesca ran upstream to check whether anything else was likely to clog the channel.

Danny opened the driver's door. 'Out you come.'

'Can't I drive home?' Mig said.

'Don't be daft, you're not old enough to go on the road. Where's Fran got to?'

'I'm freezing,' Al said, his teeth chattering.

'Fran!' Danny yelled. 'Buck up.'

Little Al was shivering violently by the time they got home so Danny sent him and Miguel to take first turn in the bath. He chucked the soggy rope out and sat on the floor of the jeep intending to pull off his waders. He stood up quicker than he had sat down. 'Mig's bloody gumboots!' He tipped dirty water out of them.

Francesca tugged at the tangled rope. 'Shall I leave it in the yard?'

'Hang it on the fence and let the rain wash some of the muck off.' He went to help her, with cold bare feet and wet grass soaking the turn-ups of his jeans.

'What are you laughing at?' she said.

'You've got mud on your face where you pushed your hair out the way.'

When Danny finally got his turn in the bathroom there was precious little hot water left. He doused himself with lukewarm water, put on clean clothes and joined his parents in the sitting room, pulling a wooden chair up to the fire and shovelling some more coal on. He wasn't taking much notice while they discussed the summer lettings until his mother mentioned the wheelchair.

'What's that?'

'Someone telephone about the holiday flat, their boy use a wheelchair. I think is possible make a room for him if dining table go in the kitchen and you take a bed downstairs.'

Danny considered the problem. 'I don't see why not.' The holiday flat occupied the far end of the house, the part where old Mr Durrant, their landlord, used to live. 'Easy enough to bring a single bed down the stairs, ain't it, Dad?'

TWELVE

Light from a street lamp shone on the wall. His mother had come in the afternoon but there had been no sign of anyone since. He spent all evening straining his ears for approaching footsteps. None came. Was this only putting off the trouble which was bound to descend sooner or later? He thought he could trust Francesca but supposing she let something slip by accident. There had been no sign of Danny either. What if she'd said something to him, or Maria? But Maria hadn't behaved any differently today, had she?

'Wotcha mate! Y'alright?' Danny's utterance was more greeting than query.

'Look at me!' Johnny glared at him. 'Do I look all right, you idiot?'

'Sorry!' Danny pulled up a chair. 'I looked in the other night but you were out for the count and they wouldn't let me in.'

'Did you?'

'Yeah. I couldn't hang about because I'd promised to take Penny to the Valentine's dance.'

'Go and ask Maria if I can have another pillow.'

'Not allowed and Maria's gone now. I think Len's taking her out, he's still in the doghouse for standing her up on Friday.'

A thought surfaced in Johnny's befuddled brain. 'What's happened to my bike?'

'It's in our barn.'

'I've really done it this time, haven't I?'

'Sure have, kid,' Danny agreed.

'What've you done to your eye?'

Danny thrust his skinned knuckles deep in his pockets. 'Oh, nothing.' His glance darted round the room like a cornered animal seeking an escape route. 'The stream burst its banks yesterday, made a helluva mess. I must have caught it on something when we were unblocking it.'

'I remember once when I came round yours after school. We had to climb over a pile of sandbags to get in and your mum and dad were scraping mud off the kitchen floor with shovels.'

'It wasn't quite that bad this time but it took ages to get all the crap out of the stream. Your bruises are starting to fade. D'you remember when we got our tattoos done?'

'Yeah, you got totally plastered. I'm totally plastered. Don't make me laugh, you bastard, it hurts.'

'Don't make daft jokes then.'

'If I'm stuck in this bloody coffin for six weeks, I'm gonna go stark raving bonkers.'

'You're already stark raving bonkers, that's how you got here. What did you think you were doing?'

'Dunno, can't remember.' He drew a deep breath and the rest of his intended riposte became a strangled yelp as pain shot down his side.

'Are you okay?' Danny asked with unusual concern.

'Bloody stupid question.' He clutched at the sheet, screwing it into a ball.

Danny pressed the bell and held the door open.

The nurse's shoes squeaked.

'Get rid of him, he's trying to make me laugh,' Johnny gasped with his eyes tight shut.

The nurse shooed Danny out. A nurse with a foreign accent. He'd never heard anything like it, her sentences turned up at the ends. She laid her palm on his forehead. He opened his eyes and stared in astonishment. She had skin the colour of chocolate and tendrils of hair like tiny black springs escaped from under her starched white cap.

'Me name is Nurse Arnold but if you are good you can call me Dorcas.'

She wet a cloth to sponge his forehead. 'Better?'

Johnny grimaced. 'Mm.'

'I'll get you something for the pain.'

'Can I have a fag?'

'You can smoke if you promise to be good.'

'What if I'm not good?' he said.

She laughed. 'Then I shall be cross.' She pronounced it "crass".

Nurse Arnold sat and waited patiently while he smoked. He watched the smoke drift upwards, took a long drag, dropped the butt in the ashtray and held out his arm.

'Ready when you are.' He watched the needle go in, astonished to see the palms of her hands were as pink as his own, so were her fingernails.

'Did your mama not tell you it's rude to stare?'

'Sorry.'

'Try to get some rest now.'

The young nurse carried a tray. 'How are you feeling today?'

'Dunno,' he mumbled. 'What day is it?'

'Tuesday.' She offered him a spoon.

He turned his head away.

'Please. Just a little, to keep your strength up.'

Johnny knocked it clean out of her hands.

The girl went out still clutching the bowl and almost collided with someone.

'What have you done?' Len said.

'Nothing.'

'Johnny, this simply won't do. That poor girl is in tears out there.' Len retrieved the spoon.

Sister Denley appeared. 'Leave that please, Lucien. Would you excuse us for a moment?'

Len went to wait in the corridor.

'Mr Hunter,' the sister's voice was stern, 'I will not have my staff intimidated.'

Johnny grunted.

'However ill you are, and however you choose to behave elsewhere, while you are here you will treat my staff with respect. Do you understand?'

'Yes.' Johnny spat the word at her.

Len came back in. 'Excuse me, Sister Denley?'

'Yes?' She didn't sound as if she was in the mood for a chat.

'I wondered if I might help?'

'In what way?'

'Perhaps I can persuade him to eat something,' said Len. 'It's got to be worth a try.'

'Stay with me,' Johnny grabbed his arm.

Len winced and tried to prise Johnny's fingers open. 'Let go. I'll be back in a minute.'

Johnny released him. 'You will come back?'

'Yes, of course.' Len retreated, pulling his shirt cuff down to cover the bandage on his wrist. 'I won't be a moment.' A few minutes later he returned with a plate.

Johnny glared at the ceiling. 'What do you want?'

'A favour.'

'Oh yeah?' He eyed the plate suspiciously. 'Well, I want a fag.'

'If you eat some of this I'll fix it with Sister Denley.'

'Maybe. What is it?'

'Humble pie perhaps?' Len said.

'Stop mucking about.'

'Buttered toast.'

He nibbled without enthusiasm at a triangle of toast. He dropped it on the soup-stained bedspread. 'I'm not hungry.'

Len held out the other half slice. 'The deal is you eat this if you want a cigarette.'

He took another bite. 'Will that do?'

'I suppose so,' Len said.

'I wondered where you'd got to yesterday.'

'I'm so sorry I didn't make it last night, I took Maria to the cinema. It was a double feature so too late to look in on you.'

'Thank God for that, I was worried something might have happened. That she might be suspicious.'

'Why would she be? One feels somewhat guilty for misleading her. Don't you ever feel guilty about Francesca?'

Johnny looked away. 'Not really.'

'Sister said you may have a cigarette. Actually, I brought you some more.' Len put two packs of Woodbines on the locker and gave him a little box. 'I'll be sorry to miss your birthday.'

He tried to prise the lid off with his thumb. 'When do you go?'

'First thing tomorrow.' Len flipped the lid open.

'Oh, Len.'

'Do you like it?'

'Of course I do. Thanks, mate.'

'I'm afraid the old one was rather mangled. This one has an expanding strap so it should slip on easily enough. Give me your hand.'

Len touched his arm and the hairs rose as if caressed by a live wire. 'I ain't half gonna miss you.'

'Are you all right, dear?'

'Of course I'm not!'

His mother flinched. 'Please don't get upset, Johnny.'

'I'm sorry, Mum. I didn't mean to lose my rag.'

He looked at his watch. If Francesca was coming she'd be here by now.

'That's very nice,' she said.

'A friend gave it me.'

'It's an awfully expensive present to get from a friend; it looks just like real gold. Your birthday isn't till Friday.'

'Mum, can you go and see if there's any sign of Fran yet?'

'Yes, of course, dear.'

It seemed an age before she came back alone.

'I couldn't see her. Don't look so worried, I expect she'll be in tonight.'

The tea trolley arrived. Francesca did not. The young nurse came to give him his tea and his mother left. His hopes were raised when the door opened again but it was Sister Denley with her numbing needle.

She turned up later, after he'd given up on her and dozed off.

'I was afraid you weren't coming any more.'

'I got kept in after school. I'd already had a ticking off for leaving school at dinner time last week and I didn't go in at all on Friday. I told them that Mama hadn't had time to write me a note but they knew I was telling fibs because one of the teachers saw me in town.'

'When you didn't turn up this afternoon I was afraid you weren't coming any more. I thought perhaps—'

'You thought I'd told on you?' She was angry. She let go of his hand and looked at his arm, the one in plaster, the one with Len's drawing on it. Then she looked at him, her mouth a tight line. 'I promised not to tell and I won't. I'll never tell a living soul. Can we forget about it now?' She stood up.

'But you haven't been in for days. I thought you didn't want to see me any more. Len's gone, I couldn't bear it if you left me too. Stay a bit longer. Please, Fran.'

'Don't be such a misery, you should think yourself jolly lucky I came at all after everything. I've had an awful day but I still made the effort so you should ruddy well be grateful.'

'I'm sorry.' He gestured at the locker. 'My fags are on there, I think.'

He lit the cigarette with the Zippo. They passed it back and forth, smoking in silence.

'Danny dropped in yesterday; I think it was yesterday. He said the stream burst its banks.'

'Yes, at the weekend. Tilly's field is in a right state and so is the stream.'

'There used to be wild daffodils by the stream,' he said.

'There still are. Mind you, their leaves are all pointing downstream now and squashed flat like they've been run over by a steamroller. In some places the bulbs got ripped right out the ground.'

'Fran, what is it?' He reached up to stroke her hair. 'You're crying.'

'No, I'm not. The smoke went in my eyes.' She ground out the butt and put the ashtray down.

'Don't go. Not yet. What's the matter?'

'That was Len's lighter, wasn't it?' she said.

Francesca sat in the park where Triton loomed dark and forbidding under the louring sky. She sat by the lake with her feet on the bench, hugging her knees. She didn't understand what she had seen the other day. Len was nice, and he was going out with Maria. He couldn't possibly be a queer, could he? A man being dragged past by a choking Alsatian jogged her memory. The Wolfenden Report, it was called. It had been in the paper on Danny's birthday, she was sure because she'd read it to him. They hadn't understood why, if being queer was criminal, the law ought to be changed.

THIRTEEN

A nurse gave him a drink, she had allowed him a smoke too. His good hand searched the locker. She had forgotten to put his cigarettes away. Footsteps approached and he dropped the butt in the ashtray, a tell-tale wisp of smoke spiralling upwards to disturb the still, tidy air. As the door opened the smoke eddied and he braced himself for a ticking off but it was his mother.

She prattled on. He wasn't listening; there were more important things on his mind. Francesca hadn't shown up, again.

Danny rolled up his sodden cap and stuffed it in his pocket. A few people were waiting outside the men's ward; some sat on the row of chairs clutching dripping umbrellas, others stood patiently by the closed doors. Curtains drawn across two square panes hid the ward beyond. Danny whipped out a comb and ran it through his hair, bobbing down to view his reflection in the glass. He was taken by surprise when a nurse flung the doors open. He stashed the comb in his jacket pocket.

'Hi, kid.'

Johnny grunted.

Danny pulled up a chair.

Johnny opened his eyes. 'You're soaking wet!'

'Yeah, it's tipping down again and I couldn't find my lid. It's okay for you, nice and warm and dry.'

'I don't know what you're complaining for, I'd swap warm and dry anytime if I could get out of here. And no one's been in, not even Fran.'

'I don't know why I bloody well bothered.' Danny went to hover over Sister Denley at her desk.

She glanced up. 'Yes, Daniel?'

'Is my sister about? I've got a message for her.'

'I believe she's in the kitchen.'

Danny went down the corridor. The ward kitchen was empty. He found Maria in the sluice. She flung a cigarette out of the open window and slammed the sash down.

Danny chuckled. 'Gotcha!'

'You nearly gave me a heart attack, I thought it was old Seddons.' She pushed the window up and flicked ash off the sill. 'It's such a long time between my afternoon break and going off duty.'

'Dad says if it's still raining when you knock off he'll come and get you. Have you seen my lid anywhere? I can't find it.'

'I haven't seen it for ages. Aren't you going to see Johnny?'

'I already have. He's in a mood.'

'Go and cheer him up then.'

'I tried to but it didn't do any good.'

'He's finding it very hard. His father seems to think he crashed on purpose to get out of doing National Service.'

'That's ridiculous, he couldn't wait to leave home,' Danny said.

'That's what I thought.'

Johnny spent the rest of the evening hoping for another visitor but she didn't come. The night staff came on duty. The light was turned off. The sleeping pills didn't work; he couldn't stop worrying about Francesca.

Footsteps approached his door and paused.

'Hello, Dorcas,' he called.

She flicked the switch to flood the room with light. 'How did you know it was me?'

'Your shoes squeak.'

'Would you like a hot drink?'

She returned with the despised invalid feeder.

'Is something worrying you, Johnny?'

'What do you think? Oh, I don't know… it doesn't matter. I could do with a fag.'

She sat with him while he smoked.

'Dorcas, where do you come from?'

'I am from Cornwall, in the far west, with sunshine and warm seas.'

'I don't believe you, my granddad comes from Cornwall. You're not even English.'

She smiled, a broad smile that showed off bright teeth. 'I am from Black River, in the county of Cornwall on the beautiful island of Jamaica.'

'Another Cornwall? In the West Indies?'

'Truly.'

'Well, I'll be damned!'

'Now are you going to be a good boy and go to sleep? Otherwise we will have Sister Branch complaining that I am keeping the patients awake.'

She pulled the door to and squeaked off.

Dawn finally came. Grey and dreary, it did nothing to lift his mood. Maria came on duty flourishing a birthday card. They'd all signed it. He knew their dad's name was Carlos; their mother, always known as Ma, was called Consuela.

In the afternoon his mother brought another card, her neat writing including his father.

'How's my brave boy?'

'I'm seventeen, Mum, not seven.'

She took a box of handkerchiefs and a parcel from her wicker basket. 'They're from both of us.'

He rolled his head to view the cardboard box with an orange bow.

'I thought some more fruit would be useful. Your dad would've come but he's still at work. It's a bit difficult just now what with me being off.'

'Thanks, it's very nice.'

Danny lugged in something the size of an attaché case.

'Happy birthday, mate. I didn't know what to get so I thought you might like a lend of this. The sister said it would be all right.' He elbowed the box of fruit aside to dump the portable radio on the locker and put something in the drawer. 'It's tuned to Radio Luxembourg and there's some spare batteries for it.'

'Smashing.' He didn't dare ask why Francesca hadn't been to see him.

'How're you doin', kid?'

'Don't ask.'

'United did all right in the week,' Danny said.

'Did they?' he said without enthusiasm.

'I'm surprised Murphy managed to scrape a team together.'

'Who's Murphy?'

'He's in charge now Busby's out of action. They beat Sheffield Wednesday three-nil.'

Francesca came with her arms full, juggling a coat and a paper bag and a bunch of bananas. She looked pretty in the green dress sprinkled with little white dots, a red cardigan and her ponytail tied with a red bow. Dangly silver earrings twinkled with her every move and thickly applied make-up almost hid her scar.

'Hello!' She dropped her coat on a chair and put the bag and the bananas next to the radio. 'Oh! You've already got some.'

Johnny smiled, relieved. 'I was afraid you weren't coming.'

Her glance flickered momentarily to his arm, then she looked him straight in the eye. 'Happy birthday. I'm so sorry I didn't come yesterday, I got detention.'

'She means she got caught bunking off again.' Danny leapt to his feet. 'Gotta go, Penny's waiting. I'll see you later, kid.'

'Your sister looks like a Christmas tree.' Danny's girlfriend had been waiting right outside. 'Pity she didn't leave her hair down.'

'Penny!' Danny pulled the door shut behind him but it was too late.

Francesca looked mortified.

'Frankie,' Johnny held his hand out. 'You look really nice.'

Francesca burst into tears and fled.

'Fran! Hang on a minute.' But she didn't come back.

His father turned up next, looking shifty and smelling of beer.

'Your mother went on about your birthday so I thought I'd better look in. Who gave you the wireless?'

'Danny lent it me.'

'Dreadful shame about Duncan Edwards.'

'What about him?'

'I thought you'd have heard.'

'Heard what?'

'He passed away this morning. It was on the news.'

They were, at last, saved by the bell that signalled the end of visiting hour. He lay in considerable but bearable discomfort listening to Radio Luxembourg. Someone had arranged his cards on the windowsill. He closed his eyes. The scrawny old staff nurse came in and switched Dickie Valentine off in mid-croon.

'I was listening to that!'

'I thought you were asleep.' She took his blood pressure, entered numbers on the chart then clipped it to the foot of the bed and dropped her pen. Stooping to pick it up she banged her elbow.

He swore at her.

Nurse Arnold came on duty. 'How is the birthday boy?'

He didn't answer.

'Johnny?'

He shut his eyes and turned his head away.

'I'll get you something for the pain. You must tell us when it is bad.'

'It's always bad and it's worse when that clumsy cow bashes into the bed.'

'Do you need anything else?'

Johnny shook his head and reached for his cigarettes. She gave him the ashtray and went away. He sensed her standing on the other side of the partition, watching until the cigarette was safely stubbed out. He'd dropped ash on the sheet, Nurse Arnold came back, folded it over twice and tucked him in firmly.

'You're making damn sure I don't escape.'

'I see you got a wireless set. Shall I turn it on for you?'

'Yes please.'

'You got a parcel here.' She gave him the brown paper bag.

Johnny tipped it up and a paperback fell out. 'James Bond!'

'Who bought you that?'

'My friend's sister.'

'You want your sleeping tablets now, Johnny?'

He swallowed them obediently. Dorcas left the radio on.

Next day Francesca arrived in jeans, with little gold sleepers in her ears and her hair in plaits.

'Infinitely lovely,' he said.

'Don't tease.'

'I'm not, Frankie. Honest, I'm not. I was afraid you weren't coming yesterday, then when you ran off...'

'I thought...' She slung her coat on the back of a chair, took a slightly squashed cigarette packet from the back pocket of her jeans and lit up.

'Penny had no business saying that,' he said.

'I can't stand her.' Francesca let out a sigh. 'But she is pretty.'

'No she ain't, she's all perm and paint. Give us a drag.'

She took a puff and passed him the cigarette. 'Do you remember taking me out?'

'Of course I do. On the back of my bike with your arms round my waist, hanging on like grim death. Going to the pictures to see Harry Belafonte…'

'That was last autumn. Johnny, the other day—'

'*Island in the Sun*,' he said triumphantly. 'See, I can remember stuff. Did you know there's a Jamaican nurse here?'

'No, Maria never said.'

'I shouldn't think Maria knows her, she works nights.' He took another drag, coughed and stubbed the cigarette out. 'I was afraid you weren't coming yesterday.'

'I'm sorry, Johnny. I got here in the end though.'

'Yeah, but you only stayed five minutes. Thanks for the book.' He hadn't the heart to tell her that reading needed too much effort, it made his good arm ache to hold the book up.

A trolley rattled down the corridor and stopped outside. 'That's good, you can save somebody a job,' Mabel said and put his cup on the locker.

Francesca picked it up cautiously, as if it was about to bite.

'Get on with it or it'll be stone bloody cold.'

'Sorry.' Francesca held the cup with both hands. 'Sure you don't want me to get a nurse to do it?'

'Give it here.' He spilled surprisingly little. 'They're taking my stitches out tomorrow,' he said when she put his cup on the locker.

'Piece o' cake. It just pulls a bit.'

'I know that, but they've got to take the plaster off to get at them.'

'Don't worry, it'll be fine. They cut it off, take the stitches out and put some more plaster on when they've finished.'

He was getting used to injections; they didn't hurt unless the needle was blunt. As it took effect his mind began to float. He was quite enjoying the sensation until the porters came in and started making a commotion.

'All aboard the *Skylark*!' They loaded him onto a trolley and wheeled him down the corridor with a nurse bringing up the rear. A man approached with a pair of cutters.

'Don't you bring them things near me,' he yelled and lashed out with his good hand, having nothing else to defend himself with.

'I thought he was supposed to be sedated.'

'He is,' the nurse replied.

A porter held his shoulders down while they hacked off the plaster. By the time they started on his arm it wasn't so scary until the man wrenched the cast apart. When he saw his hand he quickly looked the other way.

A man hiding behind a surgical mask was trying to cut off his arms and legs with tree loppers. Another man, similarly attired, was unpicking stitches. He knew that when the man got all the way round his leg would fall off. He screamed. Every time he screamed a searing pain went down his side. He knew that the pain came every time he screamed but he couldn't stop.

'It's all right, Johnny,' said his mother. 'It's only a dream.'

Sister Denley took the bell away from her, though it had not been necessary; half the building must have heard him.

A few minutes later Mr Barrington came in. 'Now then, Johnny, how are we today?'

Johnny glowered at him. 'Well, you look okay, I'm fuckin' awful. I fell off my bike, you know.'

'Johnny!' His mother looked embarrassed. 'I'm so sorry, Doctor.'

'Don't apologise for me, Mum.'

'Hm!' The surgeon went out, not bothering to close the door.

'How could you be so rude? Whatever will he think?'

'Oh Mum, for God's sake. Why does it always matter what people think?'

'If the boy's well enough to swear at me, he's well enough to be on the ward.' Mr Barrington had the sort of voice that carried. 'We'll move him tomorrow.'

Francesca came in when his mother left. She must have been waiting till the coast was clear. Johnny groaned.

'What's the matter?'

'My arm hurts a bit,' he said with considerable understatement.

'Shall I call a nurse?'

'No, they've given me some stuff. I'm waiting for it to work.'

'How was it?'

He looked at her.

'Having the stitches out?' she said.

'Okay. I'm bloody knackered though.'

'I've been helping Mama clean out the caravans, it'll be Easter soon. Mind you, the camping field is still a bit squishy after all that rain.'

'Mm,' he mumbled, doing his utmost to stay awake.

FOURTEEN

Next day after breakfast Maria brought in a pyjama jacket. She did up the buttons, took out a pair of scissors and snipped through the hem at the back. He gasped in astonishment as she held the cloth firmly with both hands and ripped it from hem to collar. She eased the sleeves onto his arms and hitched the collar round his neck.

'What's all this in aid of?'

'You're moving.'

Two porters arrived and prepared to shift his bed. One was the man who held him down when they took the plaster off.

'Now what?' Johnny eyed them suspiciously. 'What are they going to do to me this time?'

'Nothing to worry about, lad, you're going up in the world. You'll love it,' the man assured him. 'You'll have someone to talk to.'

They wheeled him halfway down the long row of beds and slotted him into a gap. The view was marginally more interesting than in the room he had left. The student nurse came along with his belongings.

'Where's the radio?'

'Sister says you can't have it in here, it might disturb the other patients.' She arranged things in his locker and poured water in the invalid cup. 'Do you want a drink?'

'No!' said Johnny. 'Not with everyone watching.'

'The other patients aren't going to go away every time you have a drink,' she said.

A rail suspended from the ceiling circled the bed, the curtains hung either side of him, pushed back against the walls. 'Can't you pull those?' He pointed at the curtains and the cup went flying.

'I'm not supposed to, not unless it's necessary.'

The ward maid was still wielding her mop when Maria came past. 'You want to be careful, you might break something.'

'Stop trying to make me laugh.'

'That's better.'

'Doesn't anything make you cross?'

'No, but you want to watch out, I think you're trying Staff Nurse Seddons' patience.'

Lunch proved more of an ordeal than usual for both Johnny and Student Nurse Hobbs. She insisted that eating was not a function which warranted closing the curtains and he had to endure the humiliation of being fed in front of the other men.

He was in a mad rush. He must find it before they took it away. He vaulted the gate, took the steps two at a time and ran for the door. In his haste he pushed at the door until he noticed the sign instructing him to pull. He tore down a corridor and reached another at right angles to it. In breathless panic he swung left then right, not certain which way to go. He could hear voices but couldn't make out which direction they were coming from.

'It's all right.' A firm hand gripped his shoulder. 'Calm down, sonny.' An old man in a dressing gown was leaning over him.

'I am bloody well calm,' Johnny shouted at him. 'Leave me alone.'

'You were having a nightmare.'

The ward stirred into activity. There was a sense of anticipation, or in some cases of feigned indifference. Staff

Nurse Seddons flung open the doors and a tide of visitors surged in carrying his mother with it. She made her way along the row of beds, peering short-sightedly at each.

'Oh, there you are, dear.' She stopped.

'Yes, Mum, here I am. Did you think I'd escaped?'

She produced a nervous smile. 'They told me you'd been brought in here. That's good, isn't it?'

'What the hell is good about it?'

'I brought you some more cigarettes.' She put her handbag on the table which spanned the foot of the bed, barely clearing the frame over his legs. 'You're getting through an awful lot.'

'There's not much else to do.'

'I suppose not. At least you've got some company in here, that must be nice.'

He couldn't be bothered to respond.

'You know, people to have a chat with or play cards.'

'How'm I supposed to do that stuck here flat on me back?' he snapped. He explored the locker top with his fingers.

She jumped up. 'What do you need?'

'My lighter, you silly old bag.' She looked as if he'd slapped her. 'Sorry Mum. I can reach, it's on here somewhere.' His hand groped further. There was a clang. 'Bollocks!'

'Johnny!' She leapt to her feet again.

'For God's sake stop jumping up and down like a jack-in-a-box.'

A passing nurse picked up the ashtray. 'Is this what you're after?'

'Thank you, Nurse,' his mother said.

He lit up, the ash lengthened.

His mother leaned forward. 'Johnny—'

'Do stop fussing, Mum.' The ash fell in the ashtray.

'I was afraid it was going to go on the sheet.' She jumped as the double doors crashed open.

The tea trolley finally reached his bed and Mabel decanted his tea into the invalid cup.

'I don't want any,' Johnny said.

The nurse was back. She stationed herself opposite his mother. 'Johnny, nobody's going to notice. They're all too busy talking to their visitors and drinking their own tea.' She lowered her voice. 'If you won't drink anything you'll be back on a drip and you don't want that, do you?'

Danny clomped down the brightly lit corridor in his heavy boots, paused outside the ward's open doors then loped down the row of beds. 'Hi kid. I see they've sent you to join the hoi polloi.'

'Yeah.'

'You don't look too happy about it. Aren't you pleased not to be stuck in there on your own?'

'Not really. They wouldn't let me bring the radio in.'

Danny picked up the chair next to the bed, twirled it round, straddled it and propped his chin on his knuckles.

'Wanna fag?' Johnny offered him the packet.

'Ta. Are we allowed to in here?' Danny helped himself to a cigarette.

'Oh, yeah. It's the only good thing about it, they let me smoke without an armed guard.'

'What's wrong with being in here?' said Danny. 'At least you've got someone to talk to now.'

'Oh, shut up.'

'Suit yourself.' Danny stubbed out his cigarette and left, passing Francesca on her way in.

She turned the chair the right way round and sat down. 'What's the matter, Johnny?'

'Dunno,' he shrugged. 'Why didn't you come in with Danny?'

'I came in earlier. I didn't half get a fright when you weren't in your room. Maria came and told me you were in here but your mum was here so I went for a walk. There's a moorhen's nest in the park. The chicks look like little clockwork toys.'

Johnny beckoned her nearer. 'Fran, it's awful in here,' he whispered.

'That's why you're looking so fed up.'

'There's no bloody privacy. They won't pull the curtains at dinner time. It's bad enough anyway but it's even worse when everyone's watching.'

She made a face at him. 'I know how boring it is being stuck in here. I was in the children's ward, remember?'

'I know.'

'You never came to see me once. Not once in all those weeks and I was so very bored.'

Their silence was covered by the buzz of other conversations. 'It was my fault you broke your leg,' he said at last.

'Of course it wasn't. How on earth do you make that out?'

'Because you wouldn't have fallen out the tree if I hadn't dared you to climb it.'

'Don't talk rot, it was nothing to do with the dare. I would've climbed it anyway because I wanted to,' she stated.

He looked doubtful.

'Danny's coming back for me soon, he's gone to get the jeep.'

'Why?'

'Because he can't carry his radio on the bike, can he?'

In the morning the nurses drew the curtains round his bed before the morning ordeal. Only too aware that the flowered fabric was no barrier to sounds or smells and the other patients must know what he was enduring, he let rip with a stream of invective.

Footsteps approached, the curtains rippled. 'Mind your language please, Johnny,' said Sister Denley. 'The entire ward can hear you.'

Later his neighbour came begging help with his crossword. He sat down with his pencil poised. 'It doesn't fit,' the old man said.

Johnny sighed. 'Let's have a look.'

Mr Fletcher held the folded newspaper above him.

'I'm paralysed not short-sighted,' Johnny snapped, snatching the paper. 'If you spell four down right then it'll fit. It should be CK, not KE.' Johnny handed the paper back and the man scrubbed at the offending letters with his rubber.

'Clear off,' said Johnny. 'I'm bored.'

Maria came over. 'Don't you be so rude to Mr Fletcher.'

Mr Fletcher looked up. 'That's nothing to his language earlier on. He got a right ticking off from Sister first thing, didn't you, lad?' He winked at Johnny.

'She ought to be called Sister Sternly,' Johnny said.

'If you want stern you should try Staff Nurse Seddons.' Maria held an airmail envelope. 'Shall I open it for you?'

'No! I'll read it later.'

'I only wondered where he was. I expect I've got one waiting at home.'

'Probably.' He finally got rid of her and Mr Fletcher and opened the letter. Len said he was posting it from Port Said along with one to Maria. That was a relief. If Len hadn't written to Maria as well it might have led to awkward questions. Len wrote regularly. One week there was no flimsy blue envelope and Johnny was angry and upset. The following week two letters arrived on the same day.

FIFTEEN

'Hobbs!' Nurse Seddons summoned the student nurse. 'Go and tidy Johnny Hunter. How can a boy who can hardly move make so much mess?'

'Yes, Staff.' The girl came over. She ran a comb through his hair and steadied herself on the bed head to pluck something from the bottom of her shoe. She picked two more from the bottom of his bedspread. 'How did you get grapes down here?'

'He was playing bowls with 'em,' Mr Fletcher said.

Johnny scowled. 'I was aiming for the table.'

Nurse Seddons looked at the watch pinned to her apron and glared at them over the rims of her spectacles.

'Wizened old hag.'

'Hush, Johnny, she'll hear you.'

Maria took pity on the girl and came to help. 'Buck up!' she hissed, folding the top of the sheet over and pulling it straight. 'You know how old Seddons goes on about visitors being entitled to their full hour. Mind you, she won't allow them one second extra if we're late letting them in.'

Visitors were, eventually, admitted to clutter up the tidy ward under Nurse Seddons' disapproving gaze.

His mother unbuttoned her coat and opened her handbag. 'Hello dear. What a nice day, so much better than the weekend.' She produced cigarettes and chocolate bars.

'Ta.' He took the offerings. 'What about the weekend?'

'There was a bitter cold wind and it was trying to snow. It laid up on the moors.'

'It does that.'

'Not at Easter it doesn't, not usually. Do you want something to read.'

He yawned. 'If you like.'

'Are you tired?'

'Yeah, there's some bastard opposite who snores all night.'

Mr Fletcher's wife arrived in a loud floral-print frock and his mother moved to let her past.

His mother sat down again. 'Or how about a jigsaw? To pass the time.'

'How the bloody hell can I do a jigsaw?' Johnny yelled at her. Mrs Fletcher turned round.

'What are you gawping at?' Johnny demanded.

The woman shook her head and turned back to her husband.

'You got to make allowances, Enid,' said Mr Fletcher. 'The poor lad can't help it. He can't even sit up.'

'Shut up!' snarled Johnny. 'Bleedin' well mind your own business.'

'Is everything all right, Mrs Hunter?'

'Yes thank you, Nurse,' his mother said. She glanced over her shoulder.

'Why do you keep looking at the door? You've been doing it ever since you got here.'

'I thought your father would be here by now. He's finishing early today.'

'What for? He don't usually bother to come and see me.'

'He said he'd try to get here this afternoon. Mr Barrington wants to talk to us.'

'What about?'

'About you of course, dear.'

Sid turned up, crimson acne clashing with his carrot-coloured hair. He had swapped his crutches for a walking stick.

'Hi, Johnny. I see they let you out of solitary.'

'Hi yourself. It's good to see you.'

Embarrassingly, his mother tried to relinquish her seat.

'I'm fine thanks, Mrs Hunter,' said Sid. 'Honest.'

'Are you sure?'

Sid scratched his leg. 'It don't half feel weird without the plaster on. I've just finished doing the physiotherapy and thought I'd come and see you.'

'I'm supposed to go soon,' said Johnny. 'I might see you there.'

'Yeah, you'll be getting rid of your plaster soon.'

'I'm still going to be stuck here for ages, then they're sending me somewhere else.' A thought occurred. He threw back the covers. 'Sid! You gotta sign it, everyone else has. There's room here somewhere.'

Sid searched his pockets for something to write with.

'Mr Hunter! Stop exposing yourself.'

'I'm not,' Johnny protested indignantly and twisted his head round.

Maria turned away to hide a smile.

'I'd better get cracking,' said Sid. 'See you soon, mate.'

Danny and Francesca arrived to deposit orange squash and paperbacks on the table spanning his bed.

'Hello, Mrs H,' said Danny.

His mother got up. 'I'd better go, he's only meant to have two visitors at a time.'

'I can wait outside,' Francesca offered. 'If we take it in turns you can stay till the end.'

'Come over here, lad, you can pretend to be one of mine,' Mr Fletcher said in a stage whisper. 'That'll shut the dragon up.'

Danny hovered in no man's land between the beds. 'That dragon's my sister,' he whispered back.

'Sorry, lad. I didn't mean no offence.'

Danny laughed. 'She's like it at home too.'

'How come you're here so early?' Johnny asked.

'We're going to the pictures tonight,' said Francesca. 'We're going to see *Doctor Blood's Coffin*; it's a horror film.'

'I'd never have guessed.'

'Don't be sarcastic,' said Francesca. 'Penny doesn't like horror films so I'm going.'

His mother looked scandalized. 'They'll never let you in, dear. You're nowhere near old enough.'

'Yes they will. Danny's going to buy our tickets and I'll put some lipstick on and borrow Maria's high heels.'

'Left to myself I'd sooner watch a western,' said Danny, 'but there y'go.'

He became aware of somebody looming over him.

Mr Barrington pulled up a chair. 'Johnny, I've spoken to your parents and explained that you will be transferred to Stoke Mandeville before long.'

'Is that the place in Buckinghamshire?'

'Yes. I know your mother is concerned about the distance but their physiotherapy facilities are second to none.'

'But I won't get any visitors,' said Johnny. 'Why can't I do that here?'

'You will to begin with. I also asked your parents to consider your long-term future and your father has agreed to approach the local authority with a view to locating a suitable ground-floor property.' Mr Barrington left him wondering what he wasn't being told.

The plaster-room staff were prepared for another bout of hysterics when Johnny arrived to have his casts removed. This time he knew what to expect.

'You're quiet today. What's wrong? Aren't you pleased to be getting this lot off?' The nurse looked more closely and blushed. 'I see your friends have been busy.'

When they finished hacking off plaster they took him to be X-rayed, covered him with a blanket and abandoned him on a trolley in the corridor.

'Nurse!' Johnny finally caught somebody's attention.

'They won't keep you long, you have to wait until the films are developed.'

'Do I have to wait where everyone can see me?'

'I'm sorry,' she said.

'Well, can you find me something to read?'

She brought back a dog-eared copy of *Woman's Own*. 'It's all I could find.'

After an eternity they took him back to the plaster room. Mr Barrington arrived to supervise while a new cast was applied to his wrist. They got their tantrum.

SIXTEEN

The bus drew up at the farm gate and Ma clambered down the steps encumbered by a basket, a cardboard box and two string bags.

Danny took the box from her. 'We were wondering where you'd got to, it's nearly teatime.'

'Is okay, is a stew in the stove. I find poor Mrs Hunter crying so I take her to the tea shop. Go in the house and I will tell you.'

Danny filled the big kettle and lifted the hob cover.

'I find her sitting in the bus shelter. She went to look at a house, is council exchange,' she said, stacking groceries in the larder.

'What was she crying for if they've found somewhere at last?' Danny asked.

'Is no good. She says it is lovely and it has a backyard as well but there are stairs at the front door. Everywhere near the river got stairs so it's not much better than what they got now.'

'What about the yard? Can't they get a wheelchair through there?'

'There are stairs at the back alley too and that is ever so narrow. The woman next door take her pram up the stairs at front. I tell her the council got other houses and she say she'd be happy with a ground-floor flat, but they tell her there's a housing shortage and it could be months before there is anything else.' She stood on tiptoe to hug him. 'We are so lucky.'

'I know we are, Mama.'

'If your Papa never heard about the job here we would still live in the attic at Southampton. Johnny's mother tell me he will go in the nursing home if they don't find the place to live so I tell her about Mr Durrant and how he lives in the nursing home since he had the stroke and is really very nice.' She opened the back door, picked up a brass bell and shook it vigorously. Moments later the tractor chugged up the track. Carlos came stamping his boots on the path to shake mud from them.

'I take Mrs Hunter for tea and cake to cheer her up,' Consuela announced.

'Good idea,' said Carlos. 'How's Johnny?'

'Same. The greengrocer has no garlic. He says to me why you don't grow this?'

'That's not such a bad idea,' said Danny. 'Enough for us and a little bit more. You might be able to sell some to the Italian restaurant. What d'you reckon, Ma?'

She stood with her hand on the back of a chair, staring into space.

'Mama?'

She came out of her trance. 'Johnny could stay with us, we got plenty room.'

A draught from the front door blew down the passage. Maria came in and slammed her handbag on the kitchen table.

Her mother put a mug of tea in front of her. 'Bad day?'

'That boy is in-*furiating*.'

'Johnny?'

'Who else?' Maria shook her head. 'He's been driving poor Nurse Hobbs demented with his tantrums. Now he won't talk to us. He's so stubborn. He'd rather lie there in agony than admit he's in pain. I don't know which is worse; when he shouts and swears and throws things, or when he sulks and won't eat.'

'He don't hit his mother again?'

'No, Mama. I'm sure that was an accident. He was waving his arm about and he caught her with the back of his hand. I can't wait till he gets a wheelchair; it's got to be easier once he's up and about. I hope.'

'Then he goes to the other hospital?'

'Yes, Mama. Let's hope his parents have found somewhere to live by the time he's discharged from there.'

'We've been discussing that.' Their mother lapsed into Spanish. 'We won't let them send Johnny to the nursing home.'

'What are you on about?' said Maria. 'There's nothing we can do.'

'I've had an idea. If his parents haven't found somewhere suitable by the time he leaves hospital we're going to ask if he can stay here.' She went into the passage and flung open the door to the next room. 'He can share with Danny. It's perfect, all on the level for a wheelchair and there's plenty of space for another bed. It's so obvious I don't know why we didn't think of it before. The nursing home is fine for Mr Durrant but he's nearly eighty.'

Maria, sitting at the kitchen table with her mug in mid-air, looked astounded.

'Over my dead body,' said Danny. 'I'm not sharing, not even with Johnny. He probably snores.'

'Well, that's the end of that daft idea,' Maria said.

'I could have the old caravan and he could have my room all to himself.' Danny also switched to Spanish. 'Do you think they really would let him stay here?'

'I've no idea,' Carlos said.

'You can't have the caravan,' said Consuela. 'People might want to rent it.'

A cat slunk past with its head down and disappeared into Danny's room.

'I know Johnny's dreading the nursing home but are you sure this is such a good idea?' Maria said.

'What is wrong with it?'

'Mama, have you thought this through? For one thing do you really want him and Dan under the same roof? Heaven knows what they'll get up to.'

'Hey!'

'Be quiet, Danny,' ordered his father. 'What can Johnny get up to now?'

'You'd be surprised. And have you any idea how much work it is looking after someone so badly crippled?'

'A bit like looking after baby?'

Maria nodded. 'Yes, Mama. A heavy seventeen-year-old baby who throws things and shouts and swears at you.'

'So how would his mother look after him even if they do find a house? She doesn't weigh as much as a sparrow.'

'At least it would get him away from his dad,' said Danny. 'He's a nasty piece of work.'

'He is really nasty,' said Ma. 'All boys need a smack sometimes but I think he used to take a belt to Johnny. The poor child's back used to be covered in bruises.'

'That settles it,' said Carlos. 'We'll ask someone.'

'Who do we ask?' Consuela looked at Maria. 'The hospital or his parents?'

'What are you arguing about?' Francesca stood in the doorway.

'We're not arguing,' Maria said in English.

'Yes, you are.' Francesca came into the kitchen and folded her arms. 'You only speak Spanish when you're having a row.'

After tea Danny went to the café. The place was buzzing. Skinner and Bert faced each other across the counter.

'Hi, kid.'

'Hi, Skinner.' Danny took a handful of coins from his pocket.

'You been up the hospital?' Bert asked.

'Yeah. Johnny's fed up.'

'I expect he's looking forward to going home,' Skinner said.

'He can't go home,' Danny said.

'They're on the council estate down by the river.' Bert couldn't resist putting in his twopenn'orth. 'They've got an upstairs flat.'

Danny strolled over to feed the jukebox. 'His mum has been trying to find somewhere else but she hasn't had much luck so far.'

'So, where will he go?' Skinner pushed his mug across the counter for a refill.

'They're sending him to another hospital. It's miles away. After that he'll have to go in a nursing home,' Danny said.

'That don't sound like much fun.' Bert, in competition with Tommy Steele from the juke box, raised his voice.

'No, it don't,' said Danny. 'It's full of old people.'

'Still, it's got to be better than being stuck in hospital,' said Skinner. 'How long will he stay at the other place?'

'A few weeks I think.'

'You never know, his folks might have found somewhere by then,' Skinner said.

'I guess. If not, my mum's had a brilliant idea.'

A screech of tyres heralded the arrival of Penny's Austin. She scraped through the gears until she found reverse. She stepped out of the car to reveal grey slacks and a figure-hugging scarlet sweater.

'Looks like you've got company,' Bert said.

'Darling!' Penny swept into the café on a cloud of perfume and curled herself round Danny. 'Two coffees,' she said without a glance at Bert, who put two glass saucers on the counter and busied himself with the coffee machine. He placed the frothing cups on their saucers.

Penny pushed her cup back across the counter. Her nail varnish matched the sweater exactly. 'It's dirty!'

Danny gaped.

Bert examined the offending cup and found a smudge of pink lipstick on the rim. He poured the contents into another cup. 'That do you?'

'It most certainly will not. I want a fresh cup.'

Danny's swarthy skin turned a shade darker.

Bert wrenched at the handle of the coffee machine. 'Fancy yourself as a conni-sewer, don't you, duchess?'

Penny ignored him. Danny took their drinks to a table by the window and went back for the sugar bowl.

'What's this brilliant idea of your mother's?' Bert asked him.

'She thinks Johnny could stay with us and she's getting in touch with the hospital but I don't know what they'll say.'

Bert nodded in Penny's direction. 'What does she think of the idea?'

'I haven't told her yet.'

When they left the café he held the door open for her, hoping to impress.

She tied a black chiffon scarf over her auburn curls. 'Don't go too fast, I don't want my hairdo ruined.'

He didn't bother to point out that the seafront wasn't far enough to get up a decent turn of speed. He parked near the pier and they strolled along the prom until they reached a brick shelter.

'It's getting a bit nippy,' said Danny. 'Let's go in here.'

A ship rounded the timber wharf, coming down-channel on the tide, her lights reflected in the water. She passed a stone jetty and headed out to sea; the steady pulse of her diesels faded. They sat on the wooden bench enveloped in a cloud of cigarette smoke and perfume. The moon peeped from behind a cloud, silvering the waves. 'Isn't this romantic?' He slid his arm round her shoulders.

'Don't smudge my make-up.'

He kissed her carefully, bearing her lipstick in mind, and reached a little further. Cautiously his hand found its way inside her coat until it rested on the tight jumper, crept further until it cupped a breast. Encouraged by his success so far he allowed his free hand to hover above the suspender and stocking-top area of her tailored slacks and select a landing site. The slap knocked him against the wall.

'Stop groping me.'

'Ow!' He rubbed the back of his head and tried to resume the kiss but she wasn't having any of it.

'You look a bit damp, lad,' Mr Fletcher said as Danny sauntered down the row of beds the following night.

'Yeah, I still can't find my lid and it looks set in for the night.'

'Yes, I don't think my missus will turn out in this weather.' Mr Fletcher shook out his newspaper and turned the page.

Danny pulled up a chair.

'I saw Sid again today,' Johnny said.

'How's he getting on? He seemed all right at the weekend. His mum don't hardly trust him out of her sight but he managed to get down the caff for a bit.'

'He kept on about how he's got his medical soon, to see if he's fit enough for the army.'

'Ma saw your mum the other day,' Danny said.

'She never said.'

'They went for tea and cream cakes. Ma says if your mum don't find somewhere by the time they let you loose you might be able to come and stay with us.'

'Oh.' Johnny unhelpfully seemed even less inclined to talk than usual.

'You don't have to sound so interested.'

'What's the point? They'd never bloody well let us.'

'All right, keep your hair on. I don't know what you're so grumpy about, you've got shot of that plaster coffin at last.'

'But they still won't let me sit up. And they put my arm back in plaster.'

'Well, it is a bit smaller this time.'

It was that time of day when the night nurses were ready to go home and the day staff had just arrived. They were all clustered round Sister's desk and nobody was watching him. Johnny jammed his elbows into the mattress, tensed his arms as hard as he could and with a tremendous effort prised himself up a few inches. He surveyed his surroundings from this novel vantage point until someone spotted him and came to fuss. The porters arrived soon after breakfast.

'Big day today,' announced the physiotherapist, 'your new waistcoat has finally arrived.'

Johnny watched him unpack the cardboard box. 'It's pink!'

'It's flesh-coloured,' the man said. He took metal strips from the box and slotted them into channels sewn the length of the linen garment. 'It will feel rather strange sitting up after all this time; you may feel a little unwell at first but you'll soon get used to it.'

Not only was the thing a ghastly pink, it was laced like a woman's corset. A nurse came and they rolled him on his side, arranged it beneath him then rolled him back again. The nurse fastened a row of hooks down the front and began to adjust the laces.

'Do I get left room to breathe?' Johnny asked as they stood on either side of him pulling it tight. Finally the nurse buckled a flap which covered the laces. They had a new pyjama jacket ready for him.

'I can do it,' he snapped and won a modicum of independence by buttoning it up himself.

SEVENTEEN

Danny clattered down the ward. 'Hey kid! They finally got you sitting up, you lazy devil.'

'I don't half feel funny.' His tongue stumbled over the words.

'What's the matter?' Danny rolled a cigarette. 'You look awful.'

'Leave me alone.'

'But Johnny—'

'Fuck off!' He turned his head away.

'I might just do that. Here comes your mum.'

'Where's my fags?' he demanded before his mother had a chance to take her coat off.

'Here you are, dear.'

Johnny ripped off the cellophane with his teeth and lit up.

'It's good to see you sitting up,' she said.

'For Christ's sake, Mum.'

Danny cleared off. When he came back to Men's Surgical there were only a few minutes of visiting time left.

'You feeling any better?'

'Yeah. I'm absolutely fine.'

Danny looked at his toes. 'There's no need to be sarcastic. I'll be in tomorrow, is there anything you want?'

'Yeah, there is.' Johnny raised his voice. 'Can you nip out and get me a new back and a new hand?'

'Don't have a go at me.'

Johnny scowled at him, willing him to look back.

'It ain't my fault, Johnny. I know how long it took you to build that bike but it's gone now.'

'Yeah, so's my jacket. They tore it to shreds getting it off what's left of me. I've got to wear this bloody stupid straitjacket and it ain't exactly black leather.' Johnny shut his eyes and turned his head away.

'United are up for the cup next weekend.'

'So what?' he muttered.

'Against Bolton. I'm amazed they got this far after Munich an' all.'

'I won't get to hear it, will I?'

'What if I bring in my radio?'

'You know I'm not allowed it in here.' The conversation was becoming hard work.

Mr Fletcher was earwigging and he leaned towards Danny. 'Now there's an idea, lad. Why don't you go and ask?'

'It's worth a try.' Danny went to the sister's desk and cleared his throat. 'Excuse me, Sister Denley.'

She glanced up from her paperwork. 'Yes?'

'I just wondered...'

'Yes, Daniel?'

'Well, Johnny's really fed up, and he's gonna miss the cup final.'

'Several patients have been grumbling about that,' the sister said.

'Please, I don't suppose...' Danny hesitated.

The sister raised questioning eyebrows.

'Get on with it, lad,' Mr Fletcher called.

'I wondered if I could bring in my radio.' Danny lurched from foot to foot. 'Just for the match on Saturday afternoon.'

The first Saturday in May arrived. At afternoon visiting time men were conspicuous by their absence. Danny lugged the radio in and dumped it on the table spanning his bed.

'I've tuned it in for you.'

'That's very kind of you,' his mother said. 'Isn't that kind of him, Johnny?'

'I'd better get cracking or I'll miss the start,' said Danny. 'I'll see you to the bus stop, Mrs Hunter.'

'Is it that time already? My word, this afternoon's gone quick.'

Danny escorted his mother out.

Patients began to fidget, furtively glancing at their watches or craning their necks for a view of the clock on the wall above the doors.

Nurse Seddons occupied Sister's desk. She checked her watch, looked at the bell – ready on top of the desk – then resumed her writing.

Mr Fletcher checked his watch. 'Blooming marvellous,' he said.

'What is, dear?' Mrs Fletcher asked.

'Usually she can't wait to ring that bell. She's doing it on purpose, I'll swear she is.'

'Anyone would think you're trying to get rid of me.'

'I am, Enid. The football starts at three. We're allowed to have the wireless on once you've all gone.'

'You're unbelievable, you are, Fred. Even in here, on a Saturday afternoon, all you can think about is a football match.'

'But it's the FA Cup, United are playing Bolton Wanderers.'

'Manchester United? The team that they call Busby's Babes?'

'Yes.'

'The team whose plane crashed in Germany and all those poor boys were killed?'

'That's them.'

'Oh, Fred. Why didn't you tell me?' Mrs Fletcher gave him a perfunctory kiss and gathered up her bag and coat. 'I'll see you tomorrow, dear.'

Halfway to the doors she stopped and turned back. 'How have they got enough players then?'

Mr Fletcher flapped his hands, shooing her out.

In ones and twos wives, mothers, sisters and girlfriends departed. Soon only one girl remained, seated beside a bed opposite. Some of the more daring patients donned dressing gowns and slippers until a glare from Nurse Seddons stopped them.

The hands of the clock crawled towards the hour. The ward held its breath.

Mr Fletcher leaned towards him. 'Turn it on, lad.'

'I can't reach the bloody thing.'

Nurse Seddons' hand moved towards the brass bell. Before the clapper touched its sides men had flung aside their bedcovers and hurried, hobbling and groaning, over to his bed and the radio. The last visitor had to fight her way out through the mob. 'Turn it up a bit,' her bedridden husband shouted.

They sat on the beds on either side of him, creasing the counterpanes and bringing the wrath of the staff nurse, but she was thwarted by those who had dragged chairs over and gathered in her way around his bed.

Nurse Hobbs tidied scattered chairs quickly at the far end of the ward, becoming slower and slower as she approached the huddle round the radio. She smoothed the covers on abandoned beds, lingering near the centre of the long room. An elderly man's bell dragged her away. She pulled the curtains round him.

The crowd roared and the commentator's voice reached fever pitch. The probationer could stand it no longer and joined the patients. She leant forward, her hands on the rail at the foot of Johnny's bed.

'Nurse!'

Nurse Hobbs leapt like a startled antelope. 'Coming, Staff.'

'How long has Mr Hughes been sitting on that bedpan?'

As Nurse Hobbs went out carrying the cloth-covered bedpan a collective groan rose from the listeners. She stopped in the doorway to look back.

United lost two-nil.

Weekdays they put him in a wheelchair and carted him off to the physiotherapy department. Once he had looked forward to it and sometimes he met Sid there, but Sid was better now and wanted to buy another bike, to join the army, to do all the things that he would never do. At least the physiotherapy sessions gave him a chance to escape from the ward for a bit.

'I'm fed up. This is hopeless.'

'You've got to persevere,' the man said. 'After so many weeks in bed it's going to take a while to get fit again.'

'I ain't never going to be fit though, am I? It's a bloody life sentence.'

'You're getting stronger every time I see you. Is your back still painful?'

Johnny responded with a snarl.

'As for this hand, you need to work on it.' The man tapped his useless fingers. 'You've got to give it time.'

A porter arrived. 'Time to go home,' he said cheerfully and propelled him down the corridor.

A nurse took his dressing gown. 'Hello, Johnny. How are you today?'

'Knackered,' Johnny gasped.

She helped the porter lift him on the bed and poured a glass of water. 'Here you are.'

Johnny swallowed the painkillers and collapsed against the pillows. He wasn't left in peace for long. Porters shoved the lunch trolley through the open doors, nurses ferried plates. The hospital menu rotated on a fortnightly basis and after a few weeks Johnny knew it off by heart. Liver and-bacon today, Nurse Hobbs arrived to cut it up for him, with rice pudding after. That came round weekly. He couldn't stand rice pudding but at least nobody needed to cut it up.

He endured the indignities heaped on him; the wheelchair enraged him, the cheerful kindness of the nurses aggravated him. He hated the bed baths. Usually the young probationer got that thankless task. One morning she had nearly finished and was washing his legs. 'Is the water still warm enough?' she asked.

'How the blazes would I know?' The words were no sooner out of his mouth than he regretted them. He sensed she found the whole business as embarrassing as he did.

A trolley rattled, stopping at intervals. 'Does he want some tea?' said a voice from outside the curtains.

'He sure does, Mabel,' he said.

The nurse gave him the cup, put the saucer on the table next to the bowl of water and started on his feet.

'Thanks,' he said.

Someone rushed past; the curtains eddied in the draught.

'Hobbs! I need you now.' The sister's summons sounded urgent.

The probationer ran. Nurses never run, Maria had told him.

The girl had left him exposed. In her haste she had left a gap in the curtains. The skinny sticks that used to be his legs lay useless before him, and he worried that the man in the next bed might be able to see. He put the cup on his locker and tugged at his pyjama jacket. It more or less covered his genitals but did nothing to hide the catheter.

'She's abandoned you, lad,' his neighbour said.

Johnny jumped.

'Gone and left you,' Mr Fletcher went on. 'Fickle, these girls.'

'Yeah,' agreed Johnny. 'What's going on?'

'They're all round the old boy in the corner.'

The sheet was neatly folded back out of reach. In the end Johnny made a grab for the towel. This manoeuvre sent the cup flying. The noise brought the staff nurse, who glared at him over the rims of her spectacles.

He clutched at the towel, afraid she planned to take it away. 'I'm sorry, it was an accident.'

'And I'm the Queen of Sheba,' she said.

'It was,' protested Johnny, 'this time.'

She muttered crossly and disappeared before he had a chance to ask her to cover him up properly.

The ward maid arrived with a mop. 'Oh, Mr Johnny, you 'ave made a mess and no mistake.'

'I'm sorry, Mabel. It really was an accident, honest.'

'You've got it all down the screens too.' She pulled at the cloth.

'Don't! For gawd's sake cover me up first.'

She did so. He whipped the towel out from beneath the sheet and she hung it on the rail at the back of his locker.

'Mabel, can I have another cup? I only got a mouthful of that one. Please.'

'Course you can. I'll be back in a jiffy.'

His mother fluttered in, perched nervously on the edge of a chair and twittered at him.

Danny ground to a halt at the end of the bed. 'Hello, Mrs H.'

'Hello, Danny.'

'How're you doing, mate?'

Johnny shrugged.

'They're really pleased with him.'

'I hate it when you do that, Mum.'

'There's no need to shout, Johnny. Do what?'

'Answer for me. I can speak for myself, Mum, I am here.'

'I only meant—'

Danny whipped out his tobacco tin. 'Want one?'

'I'm sorry, dear, I've got to go. I don't want to miss the bus.' His mother took flight.

Danny twirled her vacated chair round and sat astride it. 'Have you heard about my folks' brilliant idea?'

'Mum did say something. As a last resort, she said, but it might not come to that because it sounds okay.'

'What does?'

'The flat she's gone to look at, that's why she went dashing off.' He sighed. At least now he could do that without his ribs hurting. 'It's ages before Len gets back.'

'I expect Maria's looking forward to seeing him. A letter came for her this morning.'

'I got one too, from Hong Kong. I wonder where he is now.'

Nurse Seddons picked up the bell to ring the rabble out.

EIGHTEEN

Danny walked in the back door and stopped short. The coconut matting was missing and bare bricks gleamed damply at him. He went back outside to take his boots off. The well-scrubbed table held milk in a jug and a bowl full of sugar cubes. His mother took the best cups and saucers down from the dresser and polished them with the tea cloth.

'Did you tidy your room for the lady?'

'Of course I did, Ma.'

She had just made a fresh pot of tea when they heard the taxi outside. Danny went to the front door. The hospital almoner stood at the gate having a good nose round. Bullet shot across the yard, his tail wagging an enthusiastic greeting and the woman took a step backwards straight into a cowpat.

'Mrs Morley?' Danny made a grab for the dog's collar and dragged the gate open.

'Good afternoon.' The woman picked her way across the farmyard with great care, evidently expecting other hazards to be lying in wait.

Danny led Mrs Morley along the flag-stoned passage – past the two steps which led up to the sitting room – and showed her into the kitchen. His mother took her coat, poured her a cup of tea and washed her shoe in the sink. She opened the back door and gave the bell a vigorous shake.

His father appeared in moments. A hen fussed in at his heels. He shooed it out, closed the bottom half of the door and prised his boots off. Mrs Morley's gaze strayed to the beamed ceiling. Things Danny had never noticed before leapt into view; dangling flypapers, the wooden rack where his mother hung washing when it rained. His father ran his hands under the tap and wiped them on corduroy trousers balding at the knees.

'Please to meet my husband,' his mother said.

'Good afternoon, Mrs Morley.' They shook hands.

His brothers chased Bullet through the room leaving the back door swinging open behind them. 'Is Miguel and Alvaro, my littlest boys.' Ma introduced them after their departure.

The flypapers swirled in the breeze. Mrs Morley cupped her hand over her tea.

'Is a good idea for Johnny to stay, please to come look at the room.' Ma led the way into the passage and threw open the door.

Massive wooden lintels protruded from the thick wall, crowning the high window and the glass-panelled doors leading to the yard. A new blue candlewick bedspread covered his bed and the flagstones fairly shone in the sun. He wondered if, when his mother had hung the carpet on the fence to beat the living daylights out of it, she'd scrubbed the flagstones too. The upright piano stood halfway along the wall where it would have to stay. There was no way they could get it into the sitting room. He had tidied up as promised, piling stray belongings on the sofa. He realised too late that it would have looked better if he had put the cushions on top. Now they were buried beneath his guitar and his leather jacket, topped by an apparently unconscious black and white cat.

The hospital almoner ran a disapproving finger along the top of the piano.

'He can share with Danny, plenty of room for another bed,' his mother said.

'Not on your life,' said Danny from the doorway. 'You know I want the van. Anyway, this would be perfect for Johnny, it's all on the level so he'd be able to get in the kitchen or outside.'

Ma flung open the doors to the sunny courtyard. 'You can't have the caravan. What if we get a booking?'

'Is not a problem,' said Carlos. 'You have the van, Johnny have your room.'

The house had grown round a brick courtyard. A low stone wall divided the yard in two with the kitchen on one side and a later brick addition on the other. Outside a solidly-built horse cropped grass in a paddock; on the far side of which apple trees swayed gently in the breeze, their blossom long gone.

'There's the toilet.' Danny pointed to a dark-green door at the end of the yard. 'So he wouldn't need to get upstairs to the bathroom.'

Ma led the way back inside and gestured dramatically at the hall shelf, 'And see, we have the telephone in case of emergency.'

The sitting room door was open when his mother showed the woman out. Mrs Morley paused by the steps and peered in. The television set had pride of place – a luxury Danny remembered their landlord buying many years ago – an upright wooden cabinet with a row of knobs beneath a small convex screen. Under Mrs Morley's disapproving scrutiny it became old-fashioned and the comfortable armchairs grew shabby and worn. Danny's dream of the caravan faded beneath her probing gaze.

Johnny was getting the hang of the wheelchair. Straight runs were okay but getting round corners was a nightmare. They'd taken the cast off at last and put a splint on his wrist but his fingers were still numb and he couldn't grip anything. He frequently escaped from the ward, anything for a change of scene, and was just as often brought back. He became marooned in strange places and had to wait for someone to turn him round. On one of his expeditions he discovered the lift. He'd genuinely forgotten about the time, and was whisked off to physiotherapy twenty minutes late and in disgrace. They seemed more resigned than annoyed and he seemed to be making no progress at all.

One day he finally completed the ward's only jigsaw to find the last two pieces were missing, Mr Fletcher was no match for him at draughts and nobody wanted to play cards. He got thoroughly bored playing patience and with nothing to do on the ward he went exploring. He found offices in a ground-floor corridor. Miss D. Turnbull, Matron, a brass plate announced; the door wasn't properly closed and voices came from inside.

'The farm is totally unsuitable,' said a woman. 'It's certainly not a practical house for a cripple. It's a rambling old place, altered a great deal over the years I shouldn't wonder. There are small flights of steps everywhere and the stone floors must make it terribly cold in the winter. And it's far from hygienic, there are animals all over the place and the smell of cattle is overpowering.'

Another woman spoke. 'It is a farm after all. Actually, I think Kingfishers has distinct possibilities.'

Johnny's ears pricked up.

'Did you mention something about French doors and a downstairs lavatory?' the voice went on.

The first woman sniffed. 'There are some old-fashioned metal glazed doors, probably put in before the war in an attempt at modernisation and there is an outside toilet.'

'They've known him for years, he was at school with the eldest son and don't forget the daughter is a nurse.'

'The only washing facility on the ground floor appears to be the kitchen sink, but it does have hot and cold running water.'

'I believe they have a television,' Mr Barrington's voice boomed.

Johnny edged nearer.

'I did see a TV set,' said the first woman. 'Mind you, it's out of the ark.'

'It may not be perfect but what are the alternatives? The nursing home or trapped in an upstairs flat.'

'Perhaps we should consult the patient's parents?' Mr Barrington suggested.

There was a crash as he rammed the door open. It swung inwards to reveal Mr Barrington and two women sitting round a table. He hadn't got the wheelchair lined up properly and it was wedged in the doorway. He pulled a cigarette packet from the pocket of his hospital dressing gown and lit up. 'Has anyone thought of consulting the patient?'

A woman came up behind him. 'I'm sorry, Mr Barrington. I'd no idea he was—'

'Coming to gatecrash our meeting?' Mr Barrington glanced at Johnny. 'Our patient appears to be stuck. Please could you extricate him.'

'I can do it,' Johnny said.

'In that case,' said the surgeon, 'your assistance will not be required.'

The woman went away. They shuffled papers while he tried to shove himself back into the corridor. He pulled and pushed at the wheel, trying to align himself with the doorway, and had another stab at entering the room. 'Fuck!'

The stout woman in blue stood up. 'Young man! Would you kindly allow someone to help you whilst there is still some paint left on my door?'

His book slid to the floor and he looked round to see who was near enough to pick it up for him. Nurse Seddons flung open the double doors and visitors flowed in. Len and Danny marched down the ward together.

Johnny's face lit up. He waved.

Mr Fletcher chuckled as Len approached. 'Hello, sailor. Do all the nice girls love you?'

Len put his cap on the locker and stooped to hide a rising crimson tide and retrieve the fallen book.

Johnny beamed. 'Aw, mate. How long are you back for?'

'Till Sunday. I was only due an overnight but I managed to wangle a couple of days. Oh, Johnny, it's so good to see you.'

'It's good to see you an' all. How come you're still in uniform?'

'I came straight from the station. You look so much better. I understand you're to stay at Danny's for the weekend,' said Len. 'That's why I tried for an extended leave.'

'Yeah. After that I'm going to be stuck in some other hospital bloody miles away.'

'It's an absolutely brilliant place, my father used to work there,' said Len. 'It must be easier to read now they've got you sitting up.'

'How're you doin', kid?' Danny asked from the end of the bed.

'He looks dreadful,' Len mouthed at Danny.

'He's been as miserable as sin since they took the plaster off and he gets dizzy turns when he sits up.'

'Shut your big gob,' snapped Johnny. 'I just felt a bit funny one day, that's all. Have you got any fags?'

Danny produced his tobacco. 'You can't have smoked all yours already.'

'Nip out and get me some more, Dan.' Johnny flipped open his wallet.

'Haven't you got any change? I don't need a ten-bob note just for a packet of fags.'

'I'll need a couple at least.'

'We do have a village shop, you know.' Danny departed on his errand.

Len pulled up a chair. 'What's wrong? You didn't send him away so we could sit around not speaking.'

'I needed some fags.'

'Don't give me that. What's the real reason?'

'I'm not sure if it's going to work, staying at Danny's.'

'It'll be fine. Maria has the weekend off to look after you and you'll have your invalid chair.'

'I'm not a bleedin' invalid.'

'I'll come round as often as I can. Oh, Johnny, you have no idea how much I've missed you.'

'Do you think we'll get a chance to be on our own?'

'That's going to be a touch difficult with Maria there, never mind the rest of them.'

Danny returned with a stock of Woodbines. 'All ready for tomorrow then?'

'Yeah, Mum brought my things in earlier.'

The morning ordeal was over and Johnny waited for the breakfast trolley in a fever of impatience. He ate a token meal and complained bitterly when they left him in bed. He sat there worrying that the stone path to the yard would be too narrow for the wheelchair, that he wouldn't be able to negotiate Danny's bedroom door, that Danny's kid brothers would laugh at him behind his back. Eventually the painkillers sent him into a doze in spite of himself.

Mr Barrington did his rounds.

'Last chance to poke and prod?'

Len's father produced a rare smile. 'I hope it works out for you, Johnny. You'll find Stoke Mandeville an invaluable experience.'

Nurse Hobbs helped him dress; screens were permitted. She pulled his trousers on. 'They're a little on the short side but they'll have to do.'

'Didn't Mum bring my jeans in? They'll be long enough.'

The girl took the jeans out of his suitcase and looked at them dubiously. 'I don't think they're going to fit.'

'Bloody hell! You ain't tried yet.'

The curtains parted. 'Is there a problem, Nurse?'

'I'm sorry, Sister. He's nearly ready.'

'I wanna wear my jeans.'

'Johnny, they are much too narrow to accommodate your urine bag, you will have to wear the trousers.'

He knew she was right, it was no use shouting, it wouldn't change a thing. This was how things would be for the rest of his life.

NINETEEN

The bed arrived first, in a brown van labelled Perkins & Sons Removals. Francesca, perched on the farmyard gate see-sawing between nervousness and excitement, jumped down when it came into view.

The man in the passenger seat wound down the window and leaned out. 'Kingfishers Farm?'

'You're to go round the back.' She swung open the gate and the van reversed down the track, coming to a halt opposite the cowshed.

The men carried the new bed through the courtyard into Danny's old room. It was accompanied by a bedside cabinet in hospital beige, a large cardboard box and two parcels. Maria was getting the room ready for its new occupant. Francesca followed the men in, eager to find out what was in the parcels. One contained pillows, the other a quantity of bed linen.

'What's in the box?' Francesca asked.

'Things he'll need.' Maria pushed it to one side. 'I'll put them away later on.'

Their mother came in, drying her hands on her apron. 'So much stuff for one weekend.'

'It'll be so much easier with a proper hospital bed, Mama. I don't want to do *my* back in. It's got wheels so it's dead easy to move,' Maria said, positioning the bedhead against the wall and flicking the brake on with the toe of her shoe. 'And we'll definitely need it if he does come back to stay when Stoke Mandeville has had enough of him. Mind you, you might not want him back after this weekend.'

'I think you exaggerate, he is not so bad. Where you want this?' Their mother ran her hand over the shiny surface of the modern wipe-clean cabinet.

'Better put it over there.' Maria pointed to the far side of the bed. 'It'll be easier for him to reach. He's always knocking things over because his locker's on the wrong side.' She knelt in front of the box to unpack, putting a glass bottle and a bedpan in the locker along with several packages whose contents were a mystery to Francesca.

Danny wrestled a square table through the sitting room door and down the steps to the passage. He leant on it with both hands to get his breath back.

Their father came in. 'You want some help with that?'

'I could've done with some help getting the blasted thing out. Come on then, Maria wants it in there for the bedside lamp.' The room didn't look so very different except the sofa lacked its usual clutter and his old bed leant against the wall between the wardrobe and the piano with a curtain draped over it. A wooden towel rail stood under the window. He had rescued it from the dairy and sanded and varnished the thing until it looked like new. A marble-topped washstand fitted in the corner with an enamel bowl on it and two large jugs underneath.

'Don't just stand there watching us,' said Maria, 'or you'll miss the bus and get detention again.'

'Look who I met on the bus home,' Francesca called.

Mrs Hunter lingered in the passage as if she needed permission to enter. Johnny sat in his new room with his hand tucked down beside him as if he was ashamed of it.

'Hello, Mrs Hunter,' said Maria. 'Come on in. Can I get you a cup of tea?'

'Thank you, that would be lovely.' Mrs Hunter crept in. 'Hello Johnny, what a lovely big room.'

Maria joined Francesca, leaving the door ajar. 'I forgot she's never been here before,' she whispered.

'It's very kind of them to have you,' said Johnny's mother. 'You will behave won't you, dear?'

'Of course I will, Mum. Hello, Fran.'

Francesca, hanging about in the passage in her gymslip, gave a self-conscious grin. 'Hello!' She loosened her school tie, dragged it over her head and threw it at the row of pegs on the wall where it lodged precariously on top of someone's cap.

Johnny grinned back.

Francesca ran upstairs to change. When she came down everyone seemed to be in Johnny's room. She left through the kitchen. She walked through the orchard, along the path parallel to its lower boundary that wandered along the contours of the hillside above the river. The path led out of the orchard to a tangle of long grass and cow parsley. Anyone straying from it could easily fall in the hidden stream if they didn't hear the water tinkling below the weeds which met over the narrow chasm. The ground to her left fell away steeply and water skipped over rocky ledges to the estuary. The tide was out and wading birds dabbling on the mudflats became little black dots from this distance. Once, walking down towards the river, she had come upon Father O'Brien, sitting in the middle of nowhere peering through a pair of binoculars at the birds below. For no good reason she had found the encounter unnerving and had run back home. She turned her back on the estuary and walked towards the bridge. On the opposite bank a stile crossed the barbed-wire fence which had robbed her of the chance to be pretty. She passed the bridge and continued up towards the high barn. Under the willows the stream widened into a pool and dappled sunlight glinted on the water. She sat with her back against a tree trunk hugging her knees. It was deeper on the opposite side where the current had undercut the bank. The tree over there was the one she had fallen out of when she was little, when she broke her leg and cut her face. It would be strange having Johnny to stay. He must have been so bored in hospital. She remembered only too well what it was like to be stuck in bed for weeks on end with her leg in plaster but she was lucky, her leg had mended. She almost missed the flash of turquoise; all that remained of the kingfisher was a quivering branch. She peered closely at the place where it had been; several chunks of dark red clay had fallen from the opposite bank. She took off her shoes and socks, rolled up her jeans and dipped her toes in. The clear, shallow water was cold, by halfway it was past her ankles and on the far side it nearly reached her knees and she had to take care to keep her balance in the invisible current sweeping round the bend. Within reach of the bank she steadied herself on an overhanging branch and plunged her hand in the water. The coloured pebbles were little stone cubes, just like the one Al had found when they unblocked the stream. When she reached home Johnny's mother had gone and Maria was with him.

'Sister Denley said you need some new trousers. We could go into town tomorrow and get you some.'

'Good idea,' said Johnny. 'If you measure these then you can find some a bit longer.'

'I meant that you could come and choose them.'

'Not bloody likely.'

Francesca tapped on the door. 'Can I come in?'

'Hello, Fran. I wondered where you'd got to.'

'Oh, just around. Where's Danny?'

'He's shifting some of his stuff. The jammy sod has bagged the old caravan,' Johnny said.

'Yes, I know.'

'I'm afraid you're stuck with the piano. There's no way we can get it in the sitting room,' Maria told him.

'Will it be all right if I practise sometimes?' Francesca said.
'Course it will,' said Johnny. 'Are you coming in?'

Francesca and her mother were at the kitchen table shelling peas when Maria answered the door. Len carried a shallow cardboard box. He planted a kiss in the air close to Maria's left ear. 'My father arranged for North's to send a few pairs of trousers on approval. Johnny can keep any that are suitable. My father suggested he put them on his account if that's all right.'

'He is a very nice man, your father. You want stay for tea, Len?'

'That's very kind of you, Mrs Gomez, but he's expecting me. He's going to a conference tomorrow and my leave ends on Sunday so this is my only chance to spend an evening with him.'

'Perhaps you stay for tea tomorrow?'

'Thank you, I'd love to.'

'This is really helpful,' said Maria. 'Johnny wasn't too keen on the idea of going shopping.'

'Do you think he needs anything else?' said Len. 'How about shirts?'

'I should think those fit him. If anything they're probably a bit big. I'm hoping he'll put some weight back on soon. Thank goodness you're here, he's been so tiresome this afternoon. He didn't want to have a rest after lunch, he swore at me and said he didn't need one and what did I think he'd been doing for months. He did want to sit and smoke all afternoon.' She pushed a door open.

Johnny's face lit up. 'I thought I heard voices.'

'I wanted to come round earlier but Dad said you'd need time to settle in. How are you doing?'

Johnny waited in the gloom of the passage watching Francesca lay the table for tea.

'Where's Johnny going to sit?'

'He go next to Maria,' said Ma. 'You sit by me tonight.'

'Shall I give him a knife, Mama?'

'If you want but he don't need one.'

Francesca went to the back door and gave the brass bell a vigorous shake. Her brothers tumbled in and raced to the sink to splash each other.

'Wash properly and get out the way,' their mother said. She drained a saucepan in the sink, creating a cloud of steam that instantly fogged the window. 'Can you get Johnny sat down before everybody comes,' she said, vigorously mashing potatoes.

'I'm already here,' Johnny called, 'and I'm already sat down, I just need to get through the bloody door.'

'I'll do it,' Francesca said.

Danny came in, took his boots off and padded across the brick floor in his stockinged feet.

Maria put a plate in front of Johnny.

'I don't like peas,' he said.

'Is not what you like, is what you got,' Carlos said.

Johnny scraped sauce off the fish with his fork and prodded at it.

'What's for pudding?' Miguel asked.

'No speak with your mouth full,' said Ma. 'Is rhubarb, our own, Johnny. I know you like, your mama tell me. And we got cream tonight.'

'Clotted cream?'

Ma nodded. 'Our own too.'

'Smashing,' said Johnny. 'I haven't had clotted cream for ages. In hospital they drowned everything in lumpy custard.'

After tea Miguel ran off. He came back with a cardboard box.

'Does anyone want a game of Ludo? Do you want to play, Johnny?'

'Go on,' urged Danny. 'You might as well, I'm going to.'

Miguel set up the board and gave the dice to Johnny. 'You can have first go if you want.'

'I'm bored!' Johnny said.

'You can't stop now, we're in the middle of the game.' Alvaro leaned across the table to give the dice to Miguel but Johnny snatched them from his hand and hurled them across the table. They bounced onto the floor.

Danny scraped his chair back to look under the table. 'Under your chair, Mig.'

'Play nicely, boys. Why can't you go on without him?' Ma said.

'Fran can take your turn,' Mig said, trying to be helpful.

'No I can't,' said Francesca, 'I haven't finished the drying up.'

While little Al was retrieving the dice Johnny gave the board a shove, sending the counters sliding from their squares. 'Silly kids' game.' He pushed at the table to move himself away from it.

Al scrambled to his feet and gave him a furious glare. 'What did you do that for? You've gone and lost my place.'

'He's lost everyone's places,' said Mig. 'It's not fair, why did he have to come and stay with us?'

'There was no need for that,' Danny said and took Johnny to his room.

Maria took his shoes off and put them neatly side by side under the bed. 'If you stand on his other side,' she said to Danny, 'we can lift him together.'

'It don't need both of us.' Danny bent down. 'If you put your arm round my neck, that's it. Ready?'

'Get on with it,' Johnny said through gritted teeth.

Danny put one arm round his shoulders, the other under his knees, scooped him up and deposited him on the bed. 'Blimey! You don't hardly weigh nothing.'

'Go away, Dan,' said Maria, 'I want to sort these out.'

Johnny watched her unpack half a dozen pairs of trousers. There were no jeans.

'Whatever doesn't fit can go back and you won't have to try all of them. I'll find the tape measure and we can work out which fit best.'

By the time he had tried on two pairs he'd had enough. 'I ain't here for you to play dressing up with.'

A knock on the front door finally made her leave him in peace.

'Is it convenient?'

'That you, Len?' shouted Johnny. 'Course it's bloody convenient, get in here.'

'Hello, darling, you don't have to knock you know. And you can park your bike round the back if you want,' Maria said.

'He's in a mood,' Francesca called from the kitchen.

'I'm not in a mood,' Johnny said, 'I'm just knackered. My back's aching and I don't want to play dressing up or silly kids' games.'

'Have you had your painkillers?' Len asked.

'Not since this afternoon.'

'And how is Maria supposed to know when you need them if you don't tell her?'

Maria brought tea and Johnny's pills. 'I thought you were spending the evening with your father.'

'He's packing for the weekend so I thought I'd pop round for a while.'

'Maybe things can start to get back to normal between us now.'

'What?' Len looked blank for a moment. 'Oh, yes of course. I only have until Sunday though.'

'We'd better make the most of it then. Mind you, I'm being paid to look after Johnny so we can't go out.'

'Why not?' said Len. 'We could all go. Technically you'll be working if Johnny comes too. Do you think your father would let us use his Land Rover?'

'That's not a bad idea, the fresh air will do him good. We can fit his wheelchair in the back.'

'We could go somewhere in the morning, into town perhaps?'

'Stop talking about me as if I'm not here,' Johnny said.

A hefty kick swung the door open. Danny had a large stoneware jug in one hand and a clutch of mugs in the other.

Maria looked surprised. 'Aren't you going to youth club?'

'No, I thought I'd give it a miss this Friday. I said I'd take Penny out tomorrow.'

'What've you got there?' she said. 'It had better not be cider, I've just given Johnny his tablets.'

'It's only lemonade, Sis.'

'That's all right, then. I've got some ironing to do, give me a shout if you need anything.' She folded the trousers away and left them to it.

'Anyone wanna drink?' Danny asked when the door closed behind Maria.

'Not half!' Johnny said.

Danny held the jar in both hands to pour a cloudy liquid into their mugs. He gave one to Johnny and rammed the stopper back in the jar. 'Bottoms up!'

Len took a sip and grimaced. 'What is it?'

'Scrumpy,' Danny said.

'I'm not sure this is such a good idea. He's just had —'

'Don't be such a spoilsport, Len,' said Johnny. 'It's only home-made.'

'I suppose one won't hurt.' Len perched on the edge of the bed and took a sip. 'It tastes better than it looks.'

'Don't let my mum hear you say that about her cider,' Danny said.

Danny opened the French doors and went out. A latch rattled, the toilet door slammed.

'I was beginning to think he was going to hang around all night,' Len said.

'I think he is, he's only gone to the bog.'

'Are you okay, Johnny? You do look a bit tired.'

'I'm absolutely bloody knackered.'

The toilet door crashed shut and Danny came back.
'Ain't you got cows to milk tomorrow?' Johnny said.
'Yeah, better make this the last one.'

TWENTY

Johnny's dream about a crowing cock was cut short by a slamming door. The bedspread beneath his hand had changed from harsh linen to candlewick. He opened his eyes. Daylight broke in a line above the curtain rails and fanned across the ceiling. The cock crowed again. The measured tread of nurses' shoes, the smell of disinfectant and the squeak of trolley wheels had been replaced by the clatter of footsteps running down stairs, the smell of bacon frying and the sound of a radio.

Ma had left the kitchen bell on his bedside table in case he needed anything during the night. He was about to ring it when the door swung open.

'Are you awake?' Maria wore a white dress adorned with blue roses – blue? She carried a white cup with a spout.

'I see that bloomin' thing's followed me here.'

She drew back the curtains. 'Actually it's a new one, so try not to break it.'

Low sunshine spilled into the room and Johnny winced. 'What time is it?'

'Just gone six.' She gave him his painkillers and held the cup for him. 'How's your hangover?'

'I haven't got a hangover,' he said, but he swallowed the tablets and all of the water.

He could hear Ma in the kitchen. 'I don't do him the breakfast in bed you know, he not in the hospital now—' The kitchen door slammed shut, cutting her off in mid sentence.

'Mama will do your breakfast later,' Maria said. 'But she'll want to get everyone else out of her hair before then. Do you want to get up or would you like a cup of tea first?'

'Tea would be smashing. My mouth tastes like the bottom of a parrot's cage.'

'That's your own fault for drinking cider. I should have known you and Dan couldn't be trusted together,' she said and went out, leaving the door ajar.

Johnny was trying to see where his cigarettes were when the French doors burst open and Danny barged in.

'Doesn't anybody ever knock in this place? It's as bad as being in hospital with people walking in and out all the time.'

'Sor-ry!' Danny sprawled on the settee.

'You're up early too.'

Danny seemed to find this funny. 'I slept through my alarm and Dad had to come and wake me up. Did you sleep all right?'

'Sure did.' Johnny sounded surprised. 'Where are my fags?'

Danny went in search of them, leaving doors wide open. 'Have you seen Johnny's cigarettes, Ma?'

'On the dresser. Don't leave him on his own if he smoking in bed.'

'I've been smoking in bed for months and I ain't set light to anything yet,' he shouted indignantly. Danny brought the cigarettes and he lit up. 'Ah, that's better.'

Maria came back with two mugs and she tipped the contents of one into Johnny's cup.

'Where's mine?' Danny said.

'Get it yourself, you lazy sod. Why aren't you working?'

'Dad's taking the cows back. He told me to come and see if you needed any help.'

'Well, you're not helping are you, you great lump? You're sitting around doing nothing. And you should have known better than to give Johnny cider.'

Danny threw a cushion at her and disappeared in the direction of the kitchen.

Johnny grinned.

'I don't see what's so funny,' said Maria. She shoved the cushion behind his head and gave him the cup. 'See if you can manage like that.'

'Why didn't you let me drink it myself in hospital?'

'We're not allowed to, in case patients choke or scald themselves. Anyway, it makes too much mess.' She took the bowl from the washstand and put it on the table by his bed. 'I won't be long, shout if you need anything, I'll only be next door.' She took away the bell.

She came back with an enamel jug, elbowed the door shut and half filled the bowl with warm water. Johnny's mind wandered while she washed him and strapped his wrist. She took the corset out of the locker and he rolled obediently and held his arms out of the way while she fastened the ghastly pink thing.

'Time you got up, even if you have got a hangover.'

'I'm fine and Danny can get me up, can't he?'

'I suppose he can, it's about time he did something useful.' She took the bowl away.

'Can I come in?' Francesca stood just outside the door.

Johnny grinned at her. 'Sure.'

'Did you sleep all right?'

'Like a log. I think it helped with it being properly dark. That and not having people walking to and fro all night.'

'Not to mention the fact that you were full of scrumpy. Maria's furious.'

'That might have had something to do with it, I have got a bit of a thick head.'

'Serves you right.'

Danny stuck his head round the door. 'Fran, Ma says your breakfast is going cold.'

'I'm coming. Have you had yours?'

'I thought I'd wait and keep Johnny company.'

Danny parked him at the kitchen table. Ma placed a plate in front of him and a dish of fried bread beside it. He studied his breakfast: scrambled egg, fried tomatoes and mushrooms. Nothing on the plate needed cutting up and he ate nearly all of it. In hospital he had barely picked at food that had gone cold by the time somebody came to cut it up for him.

'Do you want any more?' Danny pointed at the last two pieces of fried bread.

Johnny shook his head, his mouth full.

'I'd best get back to work, then.' Danny strode out of the kitchen with a slice in each hand.

Ma finished washing the dishes and sat down beside him. 'Is there anything you need?'

'I don't think so. That was smashing, I can't remember when I last had fried bread.'

'You want anything else you must say. I find you a jigsaw?'

Johnny was at a loss. For so long he had no choice of what to do; even when he wanted to do something he had been forced to accept that he could not. 'I don't know. Can I just sit here for a bit?'

'Of course, I go feed the chickens.' She left him alone.

Johnny studied the familiar room wondering what had changed. Several minutes elapsed before he realised the coconut matting that used to cover the brick floor had been taken up. The only mat left was in front of the sink.

'Maria! Can I have my book?' he shouted.

She came and stood in front of him with her hands on her hips.

'Please,' he added.

She pushed him into his room and opened the doors to the courtyard. 'It's a nice sunny morning, you can read it in the fresh air.'

'Wait a sec,' he said.

She stopped pushing. 'Now what?'

'I need my fags too. Where's Fran?'

'In the dairy, helping Mama start a new batch of cream.'

'What time did Len say he was coming?'

'He didn't say but I hope he won't be too long,' said Maria. 'We're supposed to be going out when he arrives. Dad said we could have the jeep when Danny gets back from the milk run. There's plenty of room in the back for your wheelchair.'

'Now hang on a minute, I never said I wanted to go anywhere.'

'Here he is,' she said.

'The front door was open,' said Len. 'Where's the Land Rover?'

'Danny's taking the milk,' said Maria. 'He'll be back soon. See if you can persuade Johnny to come out, he doesn't seem too keen on the idea.'

Maria straddled the gear lever, sandwiched between Danny and Johnny. Len brought up the rear on his bike.

Johnny wound down the window. 'I can smell the sea.'

Danny parked on the front near the fishermen's pier and Len pulled in behind them. The tide was out and several people had spread towels on the sand and were soaking up the sun. Children paddled at the water's edge. A woman with her skirt pulled through her legs and tucked into her waistband held a toddler's hands while it squealed at the cold water lapping its toes.

Danny unfolded the wheelchair and Len transferred him to it.

'Let's see how fast this chariot goes.' Danny broke into a trot along the promenade.

'Be careful,' Maria shouted at his retreating back.

'It's okay. I ain't going to crash it.'

Len sprinted to catch up. 'You'll be had up for speeding if you're not careful.'

'It ain't a bleedin' toy you know,' Johnny muttered. 'Let's get out of here. People are looking.'

'Let me,' Len said.

Danny relinquished his hold on the chair and Len pushed him across the road and down a side street. Danny and Maria straggled behind them.

Johnny folded his arms. 'It's cold.'

'That's because we're in the shade,' said Len. 'You'll be all right in a minute. Shall we go to the café? It's only round the corner.'

'No!' Johnny spotted a red and white striped pole. 'I could do with a haircut though, it's got awful long.'

'Good idea.' Maria caught them up. 'You haven't had it cut since Easter.'

'How come?' Len asked.

'They were always carting me off somewhere when the barber came round, so I kept missing him.'

'Here we are.' Len came to a halt outside the barber's shop.

Being Saturday morning it was busy and a row of customers sat waiting their turn. A young boy jumped up to hold the door open, eyeing Johnny with undisguised curiosity. The doorway was obviously too narrow for Johnny's chair and Len leaned across.

'No! No way,' protested Johnny. 'Don't you bloody dare, not with everyone gawping at me.'

On the way back Danny stopped behind a queue of traffic waiting to turn into the high street. Len paused behind them, his feet planted on the ground, gazing at the nearest shop window. The jumble of items in Leadbetter's Marine Store could hardly be described as a display – at the front, an open wooden box nestled between an elephant's foot holding umbrellas and a heap of tennis racquets with broken strings. The box contained an old typewriter. Len pulled alongside the Land Rover. 'I'll catch you up,' he yelled. A horn tooted, Len jumped, realised the traffic was moving and pulled into the kerb. "Two and sixpence" announced a pencilled label tied to the box. A bell above the door jangled as Len entered a shop crowded with junk that stretched back to a sash window so filthy it let in hardly any light. Len started as a rasping cough revealed an elderly man lurking in the shadows.

The proprietor clambered, complaining, into the window space. While Len waited for him to retrieve the box he explored the gloomy interior. A double bass languished in a dark corner behind an assortment of golf clubs and walking sticks, a large cobweb reached from the instrument's tuning pegs to the ceiling. The shopkeeper reappeared and a brief examination of the Corona's dusty keys proved they worked but it was in dire need of a new ribbon and the box's leather handle was broken. He tied it on the back of his bike with a tatty piece of string which the man charged him an extra sixpence for. Len went to the stationers to buy a typewriter ribbon and some paper. His next port of call was a shop in a side street near the station. The narrow shop smelled of oil and shoe polish and at the back a man held a shoe against a circular brush in a row of spinning belt-driven wheels.

A ginger-haired youth in a brown overall came to the counter. 'Len! You on leave then?'

'Hello, Sid. I didn't know you worked here.'

'It's me dad's shop.'

'How's the leg?'

'It's pretty much okay now, thanks. Mind you,' Sid leaned forward and lowered his voice, 'they won't let me get another motorbike.'

'I'm not surprised.'

'What can I do for you?'

'Any chance you can repair this?' Len showed him the handle.

Sid turned to the cobbler. 'Dad!'

'What's to do?' The man put the shoe down.

'Can you fix this?' Sid showed him the box.

'Well now,' the man scratched his ear with a blackened fingernail, 'I could, but it's worn right through, you'd be better off getting a new one made. There's a saddler a couple of miles up the Exeter road. You can't miss it, it's next to a pub called the Horse and Hounds.'

'Thanks, I will.' Len picked up the box. 'Be seeing you, Sidney.'

Len took the typewriter home, gave it a thorough clean and inserted the new ribbon. He found the saddler's shop next to the village pub. It would be hard to mistake it, filled with items of tack in varying stages of repair.

The bell tinkled as he opened the door and man in a leather apron turned round. 'Yes?'

Len put his empty wooden box on the counter. 'Could you make a new handle for this, please?'

'If you leave it with me, I'll have a look when I get a minute.'

'How long will it take?' Len asked.

'People usually ask how much it will cost first.'

'It doesn't matter how much it costs but I am in a bit of a hurry for it.'

'Are you sure? It's only an old box.'

'Quite sure,' Len said.

'How much of a hurry?'

'I was hoping to collect it this afternoon.'

'I'll see what I can do. Come back about five.'

When Len reached the farm Francesca called to him from the doorway of one of the outbuildings round the farmyard.

'What's going on? They got home a lot earlier than I thought they would and Johnny was in a foul mood. And where did you get to?'

'I'll tell you later.'

They found Johnny's room had been turned into an impromptu barber's shop. Johnny had a towel draped round his shoulders and Maria flourished comb and scissors. Danny lounged on the sofa, watching.

'Hello, mate!' Johnny looked round when Len pushed the door open. 'Where've you been?'

'I'd keep still if you value your ears,' Danny said.

'You're finally getting that haircut then,' Len said.

'Does it look okay?' Johnny asked.

Maria stood back to survey her handiwork. 'A touch more, I think.'

'I think it suits you a little bit long,' Francesca said.

Maria went in search of a dustpan and brush.

'Shall I get a mirror?' Francesca asked and dashed out before anyone had a chance to answer her.

'Get me on my feet, then I can see in that one,' Johnny said. With his arms round Len's and Danny's shoulders he studied his reflection in the oak-framed mirror hanging from a nail above the washstand.

'Lost three stone and grown three inches,' Danny remarked.

'I have not.'

'You bloomin' well have, you'll be catching up with me soon.'

Maria crouched on the floor sweeping up snippets of hair.

Francesca returned with a hand-mirror and she held it up so that Johnny could see the back of his head. 'Thank goodness you've cheered up.' Her smile vanished. 'Look out!'

Johnny dropped like a stone. Len was taken completely by surprise but Danny managed to hang onto him.

'Are you all right?' Len lowered him into his chair.

'Bit dizzy. Gimme a minute.'

'Dizzy!' said Danny. 'You passed out.'

'I'm okay now,' Johnny snapped.

'I'm real glad you stayed for dinner,' Johnny said. The others had gone back to work but he and Len were still eating. 'Are there any more sausages?'

'All gone, Johnny,' Ma said.

'You can have one of mine.' Len transferred a sausage to Johnny's plate.

'Don't,' said Johnny as Len leaned over to cut it up. He jabbed at the sausage with his fork and it shot across the table taking several baked beans with it.

Len laughed and reached for it.

Johnny slapped his hand, picked up the sausage with his fingers and bit off the end. 'Don't watch me.'

'I'm not.' Len avoided looking in his direction. When he licked his fingers and pushed his plate away Len fetched his tablets and a glass of water.

Johnny pushed the glass away. It toppled over and he watched, stony-faced, as water trickled over the tabletop, darkening the wood. He ignored the tablets and shoved himself away from the table but he couldn't get his chair to line up with the doorway.

'Why don't you take him to his room?' said Ma. 'I expect he's tired.'

'Good idea.' Len took hold of the wheelchair's handles.

'I wish I could work this bloody thing for myself,' snarled Johnny. 'Then nobody would have to take me anywhere.'

Len steered him into his room. 'Do you want all those pillows or would you prefer to lie down?'

'Lie down.'

Len put most of the pillows on the old sofa and lifted him on the bed. He fetched the painkillers and Johnny gave in.

'I wish we could be on our own again, like we used to,' Johnny said.

'So do I, but I don't see how on earth we can. Nothing is ever going to be like it used to be.'

'It's bloody baking in here, open the doors.'

Len carried a dining chair over to sit in the sun by the open door.

Pain relief kicked in and Johnny dozed. Len went to look for Maria. He found both sisters in the kitchen; Francesca washing the dishes, Maria drying them.

'He went out like a light,' Len said.

'I think he found this morning a bit tiring,' Maria said.

'It's a beautiful day, shall we sit outside while he's resting?'

'I'd feel a bit guilty doing that. It seems like I'm being paid for doing nothing.'

'You'll be within earshot if he needs anything. Come on.'

'All right.' Maria dried her hands and hung the towel on the rail in front of the range. 'There are some deckchairs in the harness room.'

'Where's that?'

'The door next to the stable.'

By the time Len had lugged the heavy wooden deckchairs round the corner into the paddock and wrestled them into position – twice catching his fingers attempting to put them up – he was sweating. 'Would you like a drink?'

'Yes, please,' Maria replied, perched uncomfortably on the edge of a chair.

As Len headed for the kitchen he glimpsed her out of the corner of his eye, adjusting the deckchairs to a more upright position. Francesca was at the sink, peeling potatoes.

'Is it all right if I make some tea?'

'There's some in the pot. Help yourself.'

Len went to the range. 'I think it may need more hot water.'

'It probably needs topping up. You have to lift up the lid to put the kettle on. Be careful, it's hot.'

Len raised a lid and found it stayed upright on its own. He slid the kettle onto the iron hotplate. 'It is quite warm in here.'

'That's the trouble with cooking on a range, but we wouldn't have any hot water if it went out.' She leaned across the sink to push the window open further. Hardly a breeze stirred although both doors were open. 'Here, let me. I expect that'll be stewed by now. What's Johnny doing?'

'He's having forty winks.'

She wiped her hands on her jeans, emptied the pot and stood on tiptoe to reach the tea caddy. 'I'm not surprised, he looked worn out. Whatever were you up to this morning?'

'Nothing much. A bit of a walk on the seafront; he didn't seem to want to do anything else.' A spoon nestled among the tea leaves. 'How many spoonfuls should I put in?' Len said.

'Four or five. What made him pass out like that?'

'His blood pressure must have dropped. He's not used to standing up.'

'Being held up, you mean,' she said.

When Johnny woke Len was on his own in the yard, stripped to the waist, immersed in the *News Chronicle*.

'Anything in the paper?'

'Not a lot. The Queen has opened a new airport at Gatwick. You certainly picked a good weekend. Do you want to come out in the sun?'

'You bet!'

'Let's get you up then.' Len hoisted him into his chair.

'You'll need to open the other door or this thing won't fit through.'

Johnny unbuttoned his shirt and dragged it over his head. Len smoothed Ambre Solaire on his pale arms. 'I've missed you so much.'

'Keep your voice down, the kitchen window's open.'

Johnny snatched the suntan lotion and rubbed it on Len's shoulders, finishing with a dab on his nose.

'Behave!'

Johnny chuckled, then quickly became serious. 'I wish I didn't have to go away. They gimme a taste of freedom then go and take it away again.'

'They've got a brilliant physiotherapy department there. Dad is hoping it will make quite a difference.'

'How's it going to make a difference? I ain't never going to walk, am I?'

'I wish I didn't have to go tomorrow, but I'll be back in August.'

'That's ages.'

'It's only a few more weeks, and you'll be back before I am.' Len squatted on his haunches and stroked Johnny's arm. 'It's hard for me too. I wish things were different but… Johnny, I'd give anything to put the clock back but I can't.'

'Don't start blubbing for gawd's sake.'

Len stood up and turned his back.

'Len, I'm sorry. I don't want a row. It's just, I miss you when you're away, I wanted to make every moment of this weekend count and it's nearly gone already.'

'It's hard for me too, being away for weeks on end.' Len shoved his hands in his pockets, still with his back to Johnny. 'Do you still want me to stay for dinner this evening?'

'Won't your dad mind?'

'He's at some do for the rest of the weekend.'

'Take me in, I'll ask Ma.'

'No need, she offered yesterday. I've got to collect something but it won't take long.'

Len crossed the farmyard to his T-Bird.

'I thought you were staying for tea,' Francesca called from the shade of the dairy.

'I am. Sorry, I didn't see you in there.'

'Where are you off to then?'

He squinted into the cool, whitewashed interior. 'I have to collect something before the shops close.'

Francesca skimmed cream from a churn into a shallow basin and placed it in a large china sink. 'Is it a present for Maria?'

'It's something for Johnny, actually. You really must excuse me, I'll be back soon.'

'Thank you, Mrs Gomez. That was excellent,' Len said.

Danny finished a second helping of shepherd's pie and pushed his chair back. 'Six-Five Special's on soon so can we take our pudding in the sitting room?'

'Yes, of course,' said Ma. 'Do you want to see it, Johnny?'

'I suppose so.'

Len pushed him along the passage and carried him up the steps.

Francesca dashed past them to rearrange cushions. Maria took them away from her and stood back to let Len get to the settee.

'Is that okay?'

'Yeah.' Johnny took out his cigarettes, shook one onto his lap and groped in his pocket for his lighter.

Maria dragged a low table across the room. One leg caught on the edge of the carpet and an ashtray slid from the centre of the table. 'Drat!'

Len positioned the table in front of the settee.

'Do get a move on,' said Johnny. 'By the time the set's warmed up it'll be finished.'

Danny dumped a tray of china mugs on the table and took his own mug to the armchair by the fireplace, his long legs stretched out in front of him. The girls claimed spaces on the settee either side of Johnny.

'Sit down, Len,' said Danny. 'You're making the place look untidy.'

Len picked up his tea and hovered. 'Where are your parents going to sit?'

'They don't watch this,' Maria said.

Len took possession of a mug and the remaining armchair. Mig and Al claimed the hearthrug, Bullet squeezed between them, facing the set with his chin on his paws.

When the programme finished Maria collected up dirty mugs. 'Do you want to go to your room now, Johnny?' she asked.

Johnny shrugged.

Danny bent to pick him up.

'Wait!' Johnny said.

'What's up?'

'Wait till the others have gone,' he whispered.

'Keep your hair on, it's no big deal.'

Mig and Al chased the dog out. Maria took the tray and Francesca was hauled off to the kitchen to help her.

Danny took him down the steps; Len followed at a discreet distance.

'I'd best get cracking,' said Danny. 'I promised to take Penny to the pictures.'

'Fine, I need to fetch something but I'll be back in a jiffy.'

Len brought in a square wooden box, put it on the table next to the bed and lifted the lid.

Johnny stared at it.

'Do you like it?'

'What is it?'

'It's a typewriter. You'll be able to write to me.'

'How does it work?'

'It's hinged in the middle.' Len took the machine out of its box and set it on the tabletop. 'It unfolds like so.' He demonstrated and wound in a sheet of paper.

'But I can't type.'

'Nor can I. How hard can it be?' Len sat on the bed and picked out letters with his index fingers. His hands hovered over the keyboard and he tapped another key.

Johnny pushed himself forward. 'Let's have a look.'

love you forever

'Christ Almighty! You can't write that.'
'There's nothing to show that I did. You could have written it to Francesca.' Len wound the page up but Johnny was there before he had a chance to slide the carriage back.
'Let me have a go.' Johnny got as near as he could. It was awkward because the table was lower than the one in the kitchen and his knees didn't fit underneath. He pulled the typewriter to the edge of the table and jabbed keys at random with his index finger until two keys shot up at once and jammed together.
'Take it easy,' Len said, unhooking them. He wound the paper up again.

love you forever
ytrewqazgh

'How do you make the spaces?'
Len showed him. Then he showed him how to change to capitals but this proved more difficult, requiring the use of two fingers at the same time; some letters were too far apart and his fingers wouldn't stretch to the required key while he was still holding down the shift button.
'This is maddening, it's like when you can't reach on the piano.'
'I didn't know you played the piano.'
'Well, I can't any more, can I?' Johnny held up his bandaged hand. 'Danny's dad showed me how when I was a kid.'
'Do you think anyone would mind if I had a go?' Len crossed to the instrument, lifted the lid and gently depressed a few notes. 'Which is middle C? I never can remember.' Johnny pushed himself within reach to prod middle C. Len picked out a tentative tune. 'I had lessons but I'm a bit rusty I'm afraid. I wish I could play jazz but it wasn't exactly on my music teacher's curriculum.'

Giggles came from the doorway. The girls were watching.

'I can do boogie-woogie,' Francesca said and came to demonstrate.

'I thought you wanted to watch something on the telly,' Johnny said.

Maria smiled at Len. 'I was coming to see if you'd like to join us.'

'Why don't you go and watch your programme? We're going to sit in the garden for a while.'

Johnny gave a sigh of relief. 'Well done, mate. I was afraid they'd hang about all night once they got started.'

Francesca's bedroom window was wide open. She leaned on the sill with her chin on her hands. The sun had set but the heat was oppressive and the thick, cloying scent of privet hung in the air. The boys were sitting on the bricks in the courtyard with their backs against the low wall. The wheelchair stood apart, abandoned. Dusk faded. The kitchen light went out. Len lit a cigarette for Johnny, another for himself, slid his arm along the wall behind Johnny. Their cigarette ends glowed in the darkness.

'Whatever are you doing lurking in the dark?' Maria said from the landing.

Francesca started violently and swished the curtains shut. 'Nothing. Are you going to bed?'

'Not yet, I thought I'd watch the telly till Johnny wants to go to bed. Len said he'll help me as Danny's out. Isn't that kind of him?'

'Yes.'

'And he's coming round first thing tomorrow. I was worried about leaving Dad to keep an eye on Johnny, so I was going to skip mass and go in the evening. Now I can go with everyone else.'

'Won't Len want to go to church?' Francesca said in surprise.

'He said he doesn't bother when he's on leave.' She kissed Francesca's hair. 'Goodnight then, my lovely. Sleep tight.'

When she went downstairs Francesca went back to the window and parted the curtains. The low, nearly full moon picked out a shimmering path across the sea. She could just make out Tilly, standing silently in the corner of the paddock. The yard was in total darkness and it was unusually quiet. Len's lighter flared. A shared cigarette, a murmured conversation she couldn't quite hear. A sudden movement made her step back from the window. The light went on in Johnny's room, shining on the bricks, the wheelchair, Johnny. Len went back into the yard and stooped to lift Johnny into his chair. Johnny's arm lingered round his shoulders for longer than necessary and Len made no attempt to pull away. An approaching motorbike broke the spell. By the time the Vincent's engine cut out they were indoors.

Francesca ran downstairs to intercept her brother. 'What have you got there?'

'I picked up the local paper in town,' Danny said with his hand already on the doorknob, and before she could stop him he walked into Johnny's room brandishing the *Advertiser*. 'There's a picture of Skinner in here.'

Johnny reached out. 'Give it here then.'

Danny folded the paper and handed it over.

Johnny scanned the article and began to cackle. 'No wonder he calls himself Skinner.'

'What's it say?'

'He's come a cropper, broke his collarbone.'

'That ain't funny.'

'He's called Cedric; that is. *Local man injured at the Isle of Man TT*,' Johnny read the caption out loud, '*Cedric Tripp, forty-three—*'

'Blimey!' said Danny. 'He's nearly as old as Dad.'

'Do you want me to read it or not? *Mr Tripp…*' Johnny choked and spluttered. 'That's enough on it's own without the Cedric. *Mr Tripp suffered concussion and a broken collarbone whilst competing in the island's annual Tourist Trophy motorcycle race when he lost control of his machine at Cronk-y-Voddy…*' He dissolved into helpless giggles and the rest of the article stayed unread.

'Poor Skinner. I think you're horrid.' Francesca flounced out.

TWENTY-ONE

The top half of the back door was latched back and a lethargic black and white cat stretched lengthwise along the strip of sunlight on the brick floor. The collie was asleep under the table. The frying pan sizzled.

Ma buttered and cut several slices of bread. 'Johnny, how you want your eggs?'

'With the middle still runny. Can I have some bacon too?'

Danny advanced with a knife and fork, obviously intending to cut up his breakfast. Johnny gave him a hefty shove. Caught off guard and off balance Danny staggered backwards and trod on Bullet's tail. The dog yelped and cleared the lower part of the back door in a single bound. The cat briefly raised one ear.

Danny turned on him. 'What did you do that for?'

'Leave me alone,' Johnny said.

'Okay then, get on with it.' Danny threw the cutlery on the table and went out slamming the door behind him.

Johnny rolled up a rasher with his fingers, dipped it in the egg yolk and bit into it. He had polished off the bacon and was making a mess with the remains of the eggs when Maria appeared.

'What was all the door slamming about?'

'Danny's gone off in a huff,' he said, mopping his plate with a slice of bread.

'I hope not,' said Maria. 'He's meant to be driving us to church. Where's Mama?'

'Dunno,' Johnny said with his mouth full.

Francesca ran downstairs clutching a small blue handbag and began a frantic search through the dresser drawers.

'Now what have you lost?' Maria said.

'I can't find my gloves.'

She turned the handbag upside down. A tangled heap fell out on the tabletop. She shook her mantilla and a lipstick rolled free. She pulled out a box of matches and some empty sweet wrappers. 'They're not in here. I told you.' She dashed back upstairs.

'Well, they must be somewhere.' Maria threw the sweet wrappers in the coal scuttle.

A bike rumbled along the track and stopped outside the back door. Johnny looked up expectantly as Len walked in. 'They ain't ready yet, Fran's still trying to find her gloves,' he said.

Len began a desultory search in the hall. The boys came down in clean shirts and school blazers and Ma shooed them out of the front door and into the Land Rover before they had a chance to get dirty. Danny waited by the driver's door. He reached in and tooted the horn. Maria tracked down the missing gloves underneath the telephone directory. Danny switched on the ignition. Carlos closed the front door, poured himself a mug of tea and shook his head. 'Is the same every week, always a mad rush. Good job they sit down when they get there.' He took out his tobacco pouch and filled his pipe, pressing tobacco into the bowl with his thumb.

Johnny caught Len's eye. 'Can we take our tea in my room?' he said, pushing his mug towards Len.

'I'm supposed to be looking after you,' Carlos said.

'You don't need to,' said Len. 'I'm sure you've a great deal to do and I can give you a shout if we need anything.'

Carlos picked up the *News of the World*. 'Are you sure?'

'Absolutely,' Len said.

Len took Johnny in his room and went back to collect their mugs, drank his tea and stood with his hands in his pockets looking out of the open French doors.

'Alone at last,' said Johnny. 'Come here.'

'We're not alone though, are we? I feel damned awkward with Carlos liable to walk in any minute.'

There were a couple of loud and solemn dongs, a moment of silence, then several bells clamoured simultaneously. Len looked startled. 'What the blazes is that?'

Johnny giggled. 'You never heard church bells before? The village ain't far away as the crow flies. Come here, we're quite safe, Carlos will be making the most of an hour's peace.'

'If that's what you call it.' Len closed the doors.

'Don't shut them, it's already too hot.' Johnny rolled up his right shirtsleeve and repeatedly rubbed his other elbow down his side in a futile attempt to push the other sleeve up.

'Here, let me.' Len knelt beside him to fold it back, he laid his head on his knee. 'I'm going to miss you so very much.'

He stroked Len's yellow hair. 'I'll miss you an' all.'

There was a commotion outside and Len scrambled to his feet.

'It's only a couple of ducks having a row,' said Johnny. 'Do you think we'll ever get a chance to be by ourselves? Properly I mean, like we used to?'

'I'm sure we can manage something when I come home again. It's really a question of transport but I'm not sure my father will allow me to borrow the car.' All too soon doors slammed, footsteps trooped along the passage, voices approached.

'We're home!' Maria put her head round the door. 'Your mum's come back with us, Johnny. She wanted to say goodbye.'

'I'll have to go now.' Len thrust his hands in his pockets. 'Best of luck, Johnny,' he said with stilted formality.

Johnny listened to the growl of the departing Triumph. His mother stayed long enough to irritate the hell out of him. When

Ma Gomez asked if she would like to stay and eat with them, Johnny raised his eyes to heaven. Thankfully she explained that she must go home and get dinner ready for his father. She accepted Danny's offer of a lift home with excruciating gratitude and he let out a sigh of relief.

In the afternoon Maria started on his packing. She had Danny take the battered brown suitcase down from on top of the wardrobe and began to fold his shirts. 'Which books do you want to take with you?'

He sorted through the pile of paperbacks, stacking those he had read on the table and leaving the rest on the bed.

Francesca stuck her head round the door. 'Tea's nearly ready.'

'I thought my lid would turn up when I cleared my stuff out,' said Danny, peering on the top of the wardrobe.

'And did it?' Johnny said.

'No,' said Danny. 'I ain't seen it in ages.'

'You can't have needed it much if you haven't missed it for months,' Francesca said.

'How do you know it's been missing for months?'

'I didn't, I mean I don't,' she said.

'Why all the mystery over a missing skid lid?' Johnny asked when Danny left them.

'You borrowed it that night,' Francesca whispered.

'What night?'

Francesca seemed to have lost the ability to speak.

'You mean when I smashed up the Triton?'

She nodded.

'Danny's lid?' He moved closer to her. 'Len's dad said my lid saved me. Mum wanted me to buy one and I couldn't remember so I thought I must have.'

'I lent you Danny's because it started raining.'

'I can't remember a thing. What's wrong, Fran?'

'You're going in the morning. You've been here two whole days and I've hardly seen you.'

The bell clanged a summons to tea. Mig and Al chased each other down the stairs, jumping the last two to crash-land in the passage.

Johnny declined an evening in front of the television with the others. He wanted to be on his own. Danny hadn't shut his door properly so he shouted for him to come back but nobody heard because of the blaring television he hadn't wanted to watch. A tortoiseshell cat sidled through the gap, glared at him balefully for a few seconds then sprang. It landed on his lap and nuzzled against his hand until he stroked it.

'Good puss.' He dropped his hand.

Puss wasn't so easily put off. He soon gave in to a campaign of insistent nudging and stopped racking his brains, trying to remember what he had done that fateful evening. Puss purred like an over-revved engine. When Danny stuck his head round the door it jumped down and stalked out through the French doors.

'Maria wants to know if you want a cuppa.'

'I'd love a coffee,' Johnny said.

'Don't give him coffee, it'll keep him awake,' Maria called from the kitchen.

Johnny made a face.

'I'll fix it,' Danny mouthed at him. He came back with two mugs, gave the larger one to Johnny and sat on the edge of the bed.

Johnny sniffed his drink.

Danny winked. 'I made it in my cup,' he said.

Johnny grinned back. 'Who was she? The cat.'

'What makes you think it was a she?'

'Because no girl can resist me.'

Danny laughed. 'Big'ead. It was Pudding.'

'Pudding?'

'Yeah, don't you remember? The kittens that were born last spring, just before you, um…'

'Bloody hell!' Johnny took a sip of coffee. 'It's grown.'

'Kittens do that.'

'Have you still got the others?'

'We kept Pudding and the black an' white one, Pie. Ginger went to the lady at the shop and the pub took the black one. They've called him Satan.'

It was Johnny's turn to laugh, spilling his coffee.

'I should drink that while there's still some left,' Danny said.

Maria wore black lace-up shoes and her nurse's uniform with its black belt and silver buckle but no apron or cap. Her mother helped her strip Johnny's bed. 'He was very quiet this morning,' she said. She tied the laundry in one of the sheets and pinned a list to it.

'You think he get on okay?' said her mother.

'Yes, I'm sure he will. The laundry van will call for these later on.'

'It is so kind of Mr Barrington to arrange. Len does take after his father. Fancy him getting the typewriter for Johnny. He is a very thoughtful boy.'

'Don't you start getting any ideas, Mama. I'd better get a move on. It was only a long weekend but it feels like I haven't been to work for ages.'

'You think we manage okay when Johnny comes back?'

'Yes Mama, if you're quite sure you want to. It's an awful lot of extra work to take on and I won't be here during the day. Hopefully he'll be able to do more for himself by the time he gets back.'

PART TWO

KINGFISHERS FARM

TWENTY-TWO

Johnny wheeled himself to the courtyard outside his room, yawned and stretched. Danny took the suitcase inside and came back to perch on the edge of the low stone wall that divided the yard in two, leaning forward with his elbows on his knees to avoid the willow hurdles jammed in the cracks between the wide stone blocks.

'That fence wasn't there before,' Johnny said.

'We put it up to give a bit of privacy for the holiday flat. We've got some old people with a dog staying this week and I guess they didn't fancy a caravan. It'll give you a bit of space an' all.'

'A dog? Isn't that a bloody nuisance?'

'It's as old as its owners. I don't think it's capable of chasing anything. The ducks quacked at it and it ran away; the poor thing didn't even bark back. The flat's let right through the school holidays and we've got loads of campers in the field. The other caravan's let out too.'

'There you are.' Francesca came out to join them. 'Your room's all ready. Are you all right?'

'I'm knackered. It's a helluva long way.'

'Tell me about it,' Danny said.

'That time he went to see you he didn't get back home till gone midnight,' Francesca said.

'I'm going in.' Johnny crossed the yard. He managed okay on the bricks but when he reached the French doors he got stuck at the threshold so Danny gave his chair a shove that shot him into his room, which seemed bigger somehow. The towel rail had been moved and the washstand was missing. What else?

'You've shifted your old bed.'

'Yeah, we put it in the holiday flat and look, Dad's plumbed in a washbasin with hot and cold running water.' Danny turned on the taps and water gushed briefly but the flow became a dribble. 'Except when some clot turns the kitchen tap on.'

'Do you like the ceiling?' Francesca said.

Johnny looked up. The space between the beams had been painted dark blue, the background to a constellation of stars and a crescent moon. 'Bloody hell!'

'I did it,' Danny said.

'It was my idea,' said Francesca. 'No more boring ceilings. Now you can see the sky even when it's cloudy.'

Ma came in wiping her hands on her apron. 'Johnny! Is good to see you.' She gave him a hug.

'It's good to be back.'

'Tea ready soon. Are you hungry?'

'Not very, we stopped at a caff on the way.'

Danny opened the wardrobe door. 'The cupboard's all yours now. I've put the rest of my stuff in the van. D'you want any help unpacking?'

'I might leave it till later.'

Maria put in an appearance. 'Did you have a good journey?' She stood behind his wheelchair and gripped the handles. 'I can do it myself,' he snapped and propelled himself into the passage. He turned to go in the kitchen. Mig, at the sink washing his hands, stared.

Johnny glared at him.

'Sorry.' Mig looked at the floor. 'I thought your other hand didn't work.'

'It don't, they gave me a new brace for my wrist. What's for dinner?'

'Shepherd's pie.' Ma dished up. 'Your mother says is your favourite.'

Carlos took an earthenware jar from the dresser, drew the stopper and poured cloudy liquid into tumblers.

'Scrumpy!' Johnny accepted a glass.

'I broke open a new jar to celebrate,' Carlos said.

'To the holidays.' Mig picked up a glass. 'Only another week.'

'Hey! That's mine,' Danny said and took it away from him.

'Can't I have some?'

'It is a special occasion,' Ma said.

'What about me?' said Al. 'It's my holidays too.'

Francesca laughed. 'We're not drinking to the school holidays.'

Carlos raised his glass. 'We will drink to Johnny coming home.'

Johnny was more tired than hungry. Ma scraped his leftovers into the dog's bowl and set to work on the washing-up.

'Do you want to watch telly?' Mig said.

Johnny shook his head. 'I'm going to have a fag.' He went through his room to the yard.

'Got a spare one?' said Danny, following him. 'I meant to get some baccy before the shop shut. I'm nearly out.'

'Sure.' Johnny tossed the packet over.

'I'll take you in if you're tired,' Danny said when they finished smoking.

'I don't need taking in.'

'There's no need to be so touchy.'

Johnny wheeled himself across the yard and rammed the doors open. Danny got him on the bed and he leant back against the pillows. 'I could do with another drink.'

Danny went in search of scrumpy.

Francesca joined him. 'It's lovely and cool in here with the doors open.'

Johnny lit another cigarette. 'Do you want one?'

Francesca leaned forward for a light. Her tan made the scar more noticeable, paired white dots on either side showing where her stitches had been. She touched her face in an unconscious gesture.

He reached for her hand. 'Is everything okay?'

'I had to own up about giving you Danny's lid. He wasn't half cross.'

'I can't think why, he only wore it when it rained.'

She very gently kissed his cheek.

'I won't break you know,' he said.

Danny came back with the cider jar and three mugs. 'No, you've already done that all by yourself. Do ya want some or not?'

'Yeah,' said Johnny. 'I ain't half tired.'

Danny stopped pouring.

'It's only half full!'

'Maybe that's enough if you're tired,' Danny said.

Johnny sighed. 'Perhaps you're right.' He folded back his shirt sleeve. The new splint reached from his knuckles well beyond his wrist. He unbuckled the straps and took it off, exposing his own scars.

Francesca examined the leather brace. It was beige and lined with soft material. 'It's very stiff. Isn't it uncomfortable?'

Danny picked it up. 'So that's your secret for getting round corners.'

'Yeah, now I can use this hand to push with.'

'What are you lot up to?'

Danny spun round. 'Maria! I didn't hear you coming.'

'Evidently. Does Dad know you're helping yourselves to the cider? And another time take his shoes off before you put him on the bed.'

'They're hardly likely to be dirty, are they?' retorted Johnny. 'It's not like I'll have trodden in anything.'

TWENTY-THREE

The cockerel woke Johnny. He heard Carlos come downstairs and hesitate outside his door before going in the kitchen. There was a clang as he set the kettle on the hob, and more clanging as he riddled the stove and loaded it with coal.

He was about to call out for his cigarettes when the back door slammed shut. His door creaked open slowly and a cat slunk in and disappeared under the bed. A little later Ma puffed down the stairs and pushed his door open. She held an overflowing basket of dirty clothes.

'Are you awake?'

'Yeah. Do you know what Maria did with my fags?'

She clattered about with the stove then brought his cigarettes, he lit one and she took the packet away again. She returned with tea and tablets, sitting on the settee waiting for him to finish smoking.

The girls' footsteps sounded on the stairs.

'Good morning, Johnny.' Maria came in dressed for work; blue dress, white apron, black stockings and black lace-up shoes. Francesca waited in the passage in her school summer dress.

He was in the yard swinging a pair of small dumb bells back and forth when a taxi delivered his mother to the farm. She struggled with a big, battered suitcase containing the rest of his belongings until Ma relieved her of it and put it in his room.

'Johnny is outside exercising,' Ma said.

His mother found no reply to this incomprehensible remark. She stood by the doors and watched in amazement as he swung the weights. 'His hand's better,' she said.

Johnny unhooked the strap from his right wrist and put the weights on his lap. His mother's smile faded.

'Hello, Mum.' He grinned, out of breath, released his brakes and wheeled himself to the doors. His mother clutched her bag with both hands, realised she was in the way and stepped aside. Ma gave him a push over the threshold.

'Don't stare at me, Mum, I ain't a bleedin' freak show.'

His mother flinched.

'I can do it from here,' he said.

Ma let go and led the way to the kitchen. Johnny waited for his mother to follow and brought up the rear to park himself at the kitchen table while Ma took cups and saucers from the dresser. She gave him a mug.

He grinned. 'She don't trust me with the best china.'

His mother didn't say a word.

'Mum.'

'Yes, Johnny?' His mother looked as if she was about to burst into tears.

'I didn't mean to be cross.'

'We know you didn't,' Ma said, knowing this was the nearest to an apology his mother was likely to get. 'You think nobody understand.'

'How can you bloody well understand?' He banged his fist on the kitchen table with such force that the best teacups rattled in their saucers.

After tea he took himself off to the yard where he found Francesca leaning on the wall at the far end with her hands in her pockets.

'I wish I had some jeans, my old ones are no good.'

'Why don't you ask Danny? He might have a pair he's grown out of.'

'They'd be too big for me.'

'Even if they are they're hardly going to fall down, are they?'

'You don't need to rub it in.'

'Just stating a fact.'

'D'you know what I like about you?'

'No. What?'

'You don't pussyfoot round me. Mum drives me nuts, she don't dare open her mouth in case she says the wrong thing.'

Ma called Francesca away, leaving Johnny alone in the quiet of early evening. Though still hot and sultry, clouds were building behind the apple trees. He lit a cigarette and watched the smoke spiral up in the still air. Maria brought him a cup of tea. Before long she came out again to fuss and pester. He didn't want another cup and he didn't want to go in yet. The first breath of wind came suddenly, so secretly he hardly felt it. It began to get dark and he checked his watch, the one Len had given him; it wasn't as late as he thought. Time, which had gone so quickly when Len was here, now dragged but Len's stint in the navy would soon be over. The breeze got up and the first drops of rain sent him heading for shelter, but before he reached the doors the heavens opened. Once he could have covered those few yards in seconds, now it took an age. He gave a hefty push to bump himself over the threshold and grabbed the towel by the washbasin. Rain blew in, spattering the flagstones with dark droplets.

'Fran!'

She ran down the passage and burst into his room. 'What's the matter? Oh heck, you're wet through.'

'I had noticed. Gimme a hand to bolt the doors.'

Maria came to take charge. She towelled his hair dry, took his wet clothes away and put him to bed like a naughty child. She sent Francesca for an old newspaper to fold under the damp edge of the carpet.

'I hate being stuck in bed.'

Francesca flung her arms round him. 'Please don't get upset.'

'Well, I do, and I hate having to keep asking for things. I hate not being able to do things, and I hate it that the things I can do take ten times as long as they used to. Sometimes I wish they'd just left me to die.' Her crestfallen expression stopped him short. 'Oh, Frankie. I'm sorry.'

She kissed his cheek. 'I love you, Johnny Hunter. I always have and I always will.'

He stroked her hair. 'Don't leave me on my own.'

'Never, I promise.'

They sprang apart as the door handle rattled.

'You two can stop smooching,' Danny said.

'What the hell's got into you?' Johnny said.

'Penny chucked him,' Francesca said.

'Who'd she catch you with this time?'

'She hasn't. I mean, I never…'

'Pull the other one,' said Francesca. 'You couldn't keep a secret if your life depended on it.'

'Don't you ever knock?' Johnny grumbled.

'Why should I knock? It's my house,' Danny said.

'But it's my room.'

Ma came in with a tray of rattling mugs. 'He's right, you know, is his room now.' She put the tray on the coffee table and sank wearily onto the settee.

Johnny groaned.

'What's the matter?' Danny and Ma asked in unison.

'Everyone treats this like a sitting room. It's not fair, I never get no privacy.'

Danny looked astonished. 'What do you want privacy for?'

'Because I'm bloody fed up. If you lot want to end a conversation you can just get up and leave, I can't do anything about it. It doesn't matter how much people try to help, they have no idea how it feels.' He closed his eyes and turned his head away. An embarrassed silence lengthened. He opened his eyes and pointed at the tray. 'Any chance of getting a cup before it goes stone cold?'

Next morning Maria helped him wash and put his socks and trousers on. She took a clean shirt from the wardrobe and left it on the bed. 'I'll go and see if your back support is aired. Mama hung it in front of the stove to dry off overnight.'

He lit up and blew a smoke ring. Smoke swirled and eddied through a shaft of sunlight slanting in through the open doors. A bulky form cut off the sunny strip.

'It's all right for some. You gonna laze around in bed all day?' Danny asked.

'I'm waiting for Maria.'

'It's a smashing day; you wanna wait outside?'

'Okay.'

'Let's try it. This thing's got wheels.' Danny nudged the brakes off with the toe of his boot, flung open the French doors and rattled the bed into the yard.

'The suspension ain't much cop,' Johnny said through clenched teeth.

'Will you be okay if I leave you on your own for a sec?'

'Course I will. I ain't going nowhere, am I?' He closed his eyes, enjoying the smell of damp grass, the sun on his bare skin. The boys went off to school, crockery rattled in the kitchen.

'Quack!'

For a moment Johnny thought he was dreaming. It was a great improvement on his usual dreams. He opened his eyes to a cloudless blue sky.

'Quack!'

He craned his neck. The duck circumnavigated his bed, stopped and fixed him with a beady stare.

'Shouldn't you be in the pond?' he asked it.

'Quack!' it informed him and vanished under the bed just as Danny came back.

'I think I'm going nuts, I've been talking to a duck.'

'You are nuts. Your breakfast's ready.' Danny looked round the yard. 'Where's this duck then?'

'Fuck the duck.'

Danny gave the bed a shove and almost ran over the bird which shot out from beneath the bed with a protesting squawk.

'Told you,' Johnny started giggling.

Francesca appeared. 'Mama says… What's so funny?'

'Duck,' Danny spluttered, pointing at the yard.

'What?' She frowned at him.

'He was…' Danny plonked himself on the edge of the bed and doubled up with laughter.

'I was out there.' Johnny, giggling, dabbed at his eyes with his shirt.

'Talking to this duck,' Danny said.

'Shut up! I was not.'

'There was this duck under the bed, and he said…' Danny stopped laughing.

'Well, go on then. What did he say that was so funny?' demanded Francesca.

'It wasn't especially funny really, you had to be there for it to be funny.'

'Huh!' Francesca turned on her heel and collided with her mother. 'Oops, sorry.'

'You put that shirt on or just screw it up?' Ma enquired.

His intended retort was forestalled by Maria bringing the hated pink garment.

'He can't finish getting dressed till he's got this on.'

'Sorry, I forget. Bring him soon, his breakfast ready.'

'I thought I might as well eat while you were sunbathing,' said Maria. 'Roll onto your side, please.'

Johnny held his arms out of the way while she fastened the thing round him. The moment his eyes closed his mind began to wander.

The alarm clock shrilled. He kept it on a tin tray covered in pennies so that it made more noise. He turned it off and waited till his father shouted 'Are you awake yet?' and slammed the front door on his way out. He stumbled out of bed, threw his clothes on and helped himself to a cup of stewed tea from the pot on the kitchen table. His mother came home from work in time to make him toast, then he too slammed the front door and ran down the concrete steps to leap astride his bike still licking marmalade from his fingers. He rode like the wind and reached the garage with a minute to spare.

He let out a deep sigh.

'Is that too tight?' Maria asked.

He shook his head.

'Give me your arm.' Maria held his shirt.

'I can do it.' He slipped his arms in the sleeves, gathered up the back and hitched it over his head.

'Now that really will screw it up,' she said.

Johnny sat in the yard and watched the tractor chugging up the track. It stopped and a few moments later Danny appeared at the open sash, leaning over the kitchen sink splashing water on his face and neck. 'If he wants to sit in the sun he ought to have a hat on.' He spoke to someone out of sight.

'I give him your old one,' Ma said.

'It's on the ground now,' said Danny.

Johnny put his book on his lap to light a cigarette.

'Take him some lemonade.'

'Ma, you're a genius. I thought I'd nip up to the village tonight. I could take him with me.'

'Good idea, he not go out the house since he come back.'

Danny brought him a mug of lemonade and pushed him

into the shade on the other side of the yard. A collection of dog-ends on the bricks marked the spot he had vacated.

'I don't want to bloody move.'

'You'll fry if you stay put.' Danny picked up the hat and shook it. 'Why is it covered in fag ash?'

Francesca answered the door. The old man seemed a bit long in the tooth for a camper. 'Milk and eggs round the back,' she said.

'I bain't after groceries, miss. I've come to see Johnny Hunter.'

'Oh!' she said, stupidly surprised.

'I'm Jim Trevelyan.'

'Who is here?' Consuela shouted.

'A man to see Johnny.'

At the mention of his name Johnny himself put in an appearance. 'Granddad!'

'I should have realised he wasn't dressed like a holidaymaker.' Francesca still stood at the open door. A bus stopped by the gate and disgorged a pair of schoolboys.

Consuela closed Johnny's door. 'Do I ask him to stay for tea?'

'How should I know?'

'Who's staying for tea?' Mig said.

'Is Johnny's grandfather.'

Having been forcibly prevented from interrupting the visitor Mig and Al went to change and came downstairs to linger in the passage in vain. They were promptly sent to fetch their father from the fields but Mr Trevelyan declined the invitation to dine with them.

'Where are we going?' Johnny demanded as Danny pushed him along the road to the village. It was still warm, the hedges abuzz with insects.

'Wait and see.'

'Why not use the motor?'

'Because Dad's using it for the greengrocer's order, and besides, we're not going far. What did your grandfather want?'

'He wanted to see me, and to know how Mum is.'

'Why don't he ask her himself?'

'It's a bit awkward. Dad isn't Catholic so they got married at the register office and Mum's parents never forgave her.'

'That's such a shame.'

'Yeah. He's still not speaking to her, even though he's been on his own for all these years.'

The road narrowed as it neared the stone bridge over the stream. The sound of engines made Danny push him close into the hedge, two motorbikes swerved past. The riders waved.

'I've changed my mind. I want to go back.' Without any warning Johnny braked and his chair slewed sideways.

'Too late, we're nearly there.' Danny let the brake off and pushed him over the bridge. 'It took long enough persuading you to come out and I'm not taking you straight back home again.'

'Did you see who it was?'

'Don't know.' Danny stopped pushing. 'I never realised this bit was uphill. It's quite steep really.'

'I didn't recognise the green thing.'

'Nor me, I don't know anyone who's got a Bantam.'

Near the village shop the grass verge gave way to pavement and Danny dragged the wheelchair backwards off the road. Soon they ground to a halt at the bottom of a concrete path leading to a single-storey building set back from the road. The village hall did service as a scout hut, cricket pavilion or, on Friday nights, youth club. Rock 'n' roll blasted through the open door. Pushbikes leant haphazardly against the wooden walls, another lay discarded on the grass next to a row of neatly parked motorcycles.

'Oh no, Dan. I really ain't in the mood.'

'Well, we're here now. We might get a chance to nip in the pub after.'

The owner of the BSA dismounted and took off his helmet to reveal a mop of ginger hair.

Johnny grinned. 'Hi, Sid.'

'I see your mum made you buy a lid,' Danny said.

'It was the only way she'd let me have another bike. Won't it be smashing if this weather lasts till the bank holiday?' Sid said.

'Let's stay out here, Dan. It'll be like an oven inside.'

'Shut up whinging. I didn't push you all this way to go straight back home again.'

'Wait a sec.' He twisted round.

'Careful!' Danny said.

Penny's father put in an appearance, standing in the doorway with his arms folded. 'He's barred!' he said, looking over Johnny's head.

'But that was ages ago,' Danny said.

The other rider came up behind Johnny. 'Yeah, you can't bar him now, Mr Robinson. That's not fair.'

'He's still barred.'

'Yeah, but that was before he, um…' Sid's ears turned scarlet.

'He means I can't get up to any mischief now, don't you, Sid?' Johnny said.

A girl in a yellow blouse and full skirt appeared in the doorway. 'What's going on?'

Penny joined her, sleek and predatory in a black cotton blouse and a houndstooth-check pencil skirt reaching just below her knees. More teenagers gathered at the top of the steps, leaving Tommy Steele singing the blues to an empty room.

'I think it would be best if you took him home,' said Mr Robinson. 'Before you attract any more attention.'

'I am here you know,' Johnny said.

'Don't try to be clever with me, Hunter. You're still barred.' The man pointed at Danny. 'And you're too old!'

'I'm not eighteen yet. Anyway, he can't get in without me.'

Danny lowered his voice. 'And if I'm not allowed in then Penny is way too old.'

Mrs Robinson stuck her head out of the open window. 'George!' she said in a stage whisper. 'You can't bar the boy now. You're making yourself look ridiculous.'

Johnny fidgeted, aware that all eyes were on him.

'What are you doing?' Danny asked.

'Turning out my pockets.' Johnny produced cigarettes, lighter, small change. 'To show I'm behaving, Mr Robinson. Don't you wanna frisk me?'

'That won't be necessary.' Mr Robinson took a step back. 'All right, you can come in. But one hint of trouble from either of you and you're out.' He turned his back on them and vanished inside.

Danny dragged the chair backwards up the path. Johnny leaned over and felt behind him.

'You're gonna fall out if you keep doing that,' Danny said.

'I can't reach my knife,' he whispered.

'Are you nuts?' Danny whispered back. 'What the hell did you bring that for after last time? Only you could be that daft.'

'You never said where we were going, did you?'

Inside, Mrs Robinson was hiding behind a tea urn, being deafened by the record player. Danny shoved him into the games room.

A small boy faced them across a ping-pong table. 'It's Johnny Hunter!'

'What?' his opponent half-turned, whisked his attention back to the ball and flailed his bat wildly but too late.

Johnny caught the ball.

'Do you want the table?' the boy asked in a squeaky voice.

'Nope.'

'Is it all right if we carry on then?'

'Yep.'

'Oh, I don't know. Why don't we show 'em how it's done?' Danny asked.

'I said I don't want to.' Johnny tossed the ball back. 'What are you staring at?'

'They thought you was dead, mister. But I told 'em, dead men don't bleed, I said.'

'You found me?'

'Yeah, up there.' He gestured at the window. 'You was right underneath the bike. It took me dad, a copper and two ambulance men to get it off of you.'

Penny came in and stood behind Danny. 'What did you bring him for?' she said, making no attempt to hide her annoyance. Danny grabbed her elbow and steered her back into the other room.

'What's eating you? I don't understand why you don't like him.'

The urchins were still gaping at Johnny who looked round in time to see Penny pull her arm away and walk off. Danny shrugged and came back. 'Scarper!'

The kids scarpered, leaving their bats on the table. Danny picked one up and bounced the ball, swiped it hard and hit it again as it bounced off the wall.

Johnny watched him. After a few minutes he picked up the other bat, and as the ball flew off the wall he reached to intercept it, knocking it straight into the net. Danny reached over and flipped it with the edge of his bat. Johnny stopped the rolling ball and tried to scoop it up with the bat. It rolled smartly onto the floor. 'Bugger!'

'Shh! We don't want old man Robinson chucking us out when we've only just got in.'

'Well, I'm not fussed about staying, I never wanted to come in the first place. I'd rather be in the pub.'

'We could go after, but we need to go in with someone else,' Danny said.

'I always got away with it an' you're taller than me.'

'That's because you're a lanky bastard but you ain't standing up no more. Besides, I'll probably need a hand to get you down the steps when we've had a few.'

'I forgot about the bloody steps. Is there any scrumpy indoors?'

'Sid's old enough,' Danny said hopefully.

They went straight home.

TWENTY-FOUR

The weather broke on the first day of August with an almighty thunderstorm. It rained relentlessly for the rest of the weekend. When Johnny woke up on bank holiday Monday it was barely light. He tried to go back to sleep. A gust of wind rattled the doors and he resigned himself to a day cooped up inside. He waited for the cock to crow but heard nothing except rain lashing against the windows. He couldn't quite reach to turn the light on so he tried to turn over, fidgeting and wriggling till he touched the flex of the reading lamp. He pulled it until the switch was within reach, peered at his watch and was surprised to see it was gone six. He hadn't heard anyone come downstairs. He hadn't even heard the cock crow. Somewhere a door slammed repeatedly. How could they all have overslept? Lightning flashed and the bedside light flickered; the peal of thunder was so loud he almost dropped his watch. He swung the bell Ma left by his bed at night.

Something bounced noisily across the yard. Another fusillade clattered against the windows, accompanied by distant shouts and urgent footsteps. The door to the passage opened.

'Be with you in a sec, mate.' Danny didn't come in.

There were more running footsteps and a door slammed. Johnny lay and waited impatiently. His door opened slowly and the dog trotted in.

'Stay!' Johnny commanded.

Bullet stopped dead for a second then shook himself vigorously, sprinkling the room.

'Dan! Come and get your bloody soaking wet dog out of here and bring my fags in.'

Mig and Alvaro burst in from the yard and Mig held the doors open. Danny came in carrying a block of wood under each arm. Johnny gaped as the younger boys lifted the settee and Danny slid the wood under it.

'What the hell's going on?' Johnny demanded.

'The stream's gone,' said Danny. 'Burst its bloomin' banks again.' He hauled the bed over by the doors and started to roll up the carpet.

'What about this?' Alvaro had his hand on the wheelchair.

'Stick it in the sitting room for now,' Danny said, balancing the rolled-up carpet across the arms of the settee. A gust of wind blew the doors open.

'I'm getting wet,' Johnny protested.

'I ain't got time to fetch you a brolly.' Danny dragged the bed back a bit, went out and shut the doors behind him. He returned with a wheelbarrow full of small, bulging sacks. Mig went out to help him.

'No, get inside,' Danny yelled. 'Bolt the doors.'

Mig secured the doors and Danny piled sandbags against them.

'Hey! Where the bloody hell are you going with that?' Johnny demanded as Mig proceeded to fold up his wheelchair and make off with it.

'Danny said to put it in the sitting room.'

'Come back! Oi! I'm talking to you.'

Mig kicked the passage door open and took his chair away.

'Mig! Bring it back this minute.'

'What are you shouting about?' Maria wore gumboots and dungarees with a hairnet over her curlers. 'Didn't anyone ever tell you it's rude to stare?'

'Mig's stolen my wheelchair.'

'Don't talk daft, he's just putting it in a safe place.'

'He might break it.'

'That's rich coming from you; stop making such a fuss. Anything you need?'

'I need my fags and I need to get out of here.'

'I'll get Fran to bring you a cup of tea.'

'And my fags,' he shouted as the door swung to behind her.

Francesca brought coffee and cigarettes. She too wore gumboots. She wedged several pillows behind him. 'I can't stop. Mama's helping Dad take the cows to higher pasture.'

'What about my bike?' Johnny wondered out loud, but she, like the others, had abandoned him. He lit a cigarette and watched the depressing downpour. A thin trickle of red mud started to snake across the yard. He stubbed his cigarette out, drained the last of his coffee and glanced towards the French doors. Dirty twig-laden water swirled round the corner and across the yard to dribble down the drain under the kitchen window. 'Gawd! Frankie, the water's coming. Frankie!'

Francesca appeared with a mug in her hand. 'It'll be fine, there are plenty of sandbags.' She sounded unconcerned. 'Typical, it always goes and rains on bank holidays.'

'Is that for me?'

'You might as well have it, I'll get another one.' She gave him the mug.

Bullet bounded in and stopped by the bed. He waved his tail slowly, shedding drops of water on the stone floor. He put his head on one side.

'Don't you dare,' said Johnny.

Francesca dragged the dog out by his collar. Johnny watched the volume of water increase rapidly, carrying mud and rubbish into the yard. It rained so hard that dirt splashed up the bottom panes of the French doors. Twigs blocked the drain and the water level began to rise, imperceptibly at first. A sudden gush brought a sizeable branch hurtling straight across the yard. It hit the door, breaking the bottom pane of glass.

'Frankie! It's coming in.'

Suddenly everyone was running.

'We need to get Johnny moved,' Maria shouted.

Danny ran in and whipped a blanket off his bed. 'I've got him,' he said and scooped him up.

'But I ain't dressed yet,' Johnny complained as Danny stomped up the sitting room steps to dump him on the settee wrapped in the blanket.

Danny almost collided with Maria in the doorway. 'I'm going to be late for work.' She pulled a mac over her uniform and picked up her shoes.

'Is okay, you go.' Ma, in stockinged feet with a coat over her apron, took off her sodden headscarf and draped it over the handle of the coal scuttle. 'I get him dressed this morning, Francesca will help.'

Eventually the gale blew itself out. Next day the sky was clear, the air crisp and cool. Mud and twigs covered the yard. Francesca came; in jeans, gumboots and an old check shirt that Mig had grown out of she swept up the debris, piled it into a wheelbarrow and disappeared round the corner of the house.

'Poetry in motion,' Johnny said to himself. A few minutes later she elbowed his door open, put two mugs of tea on the table and perched on the edge of the bed.

'Look what I've got.' She took half a dozen little stone cubes from her pocket and tipped them on the table. 'I'd forgotten all about them, I found them in the stream after the last flood.'

Johnny turned them over. 'I wonder what they are. I hope my bike's all right, I think it's in the barn over there.'

'It'll be fine. It's built on a bit of a hill, which is why it's called the high barn. We mostly use it to store machinery.' The door opened and she hastily got to her feet.

'Is he ready to get up?'

'Yes, Mama.'

'We manage okay yesterday, is good for Maria not have so much to do.'

Maria found the pebbles when she got in from work. 'What are these dirty old stones doing on here?'

Francesca cupped her hand under the edge of the table, scooped them into it and rinsed them under a running tap.

'Now you've got his washbasin all muddy. Go and throw them away.'

Francesca took them outside and arranged them on the window ledge to dry. One was as red as the banks of the stream, two were the colour of clotted cream, another two the grey-blue of an undecided dawn and the last was a bold, proper blue.

It was getting late and Francesca was sitting on his bed smoking one of his cigarettes when there was a crash from the kitchen; she hastily dropped it in the ashtray.

'What the hell was that?' Johnny made for the door but Francesca beat him to it. He followed her into the passage. Danny was leaning on the kitchen sink, shaking and cradling his left hand. The back door was open, swinging in the wind.

Francesca closed it. 'Whatever's happened? Are you all right?'

'Do I look all right?' gasped Danny. 'Bloody, sodding thing.'

'Maria?' Francesca came flying out and shoved past him. 'Get out the way, Johnny.'

Maria ran down the stairs. 'What's wrong?'

'He's hurt his hand,' Francesca said.

Maria looked at Johnny.

'Not him, Danny.'

Maria marched into the kitchen and pulled out a chair. 'Sit down.'

Danny ignored the chair, hitched his bum on the table and leaned over, still clutching his hand.

'Come on, Dan, I can't help if you won't let me have a look at it.'

Ma appeared at the top of the sitting room steps. 'What is all the fuss?'

'Danny's hurt his hand.' Maria turned to her brother. 'How did you do it?'

'Came off the bloody bike, didn't I?' Danny said through gritted teeth.

'Someone get me the first aid box,' Maria ordered.

Francesca took a tin box from a dresser drawer.

Maria attacked Danny's glove with a pair of scissors.

'Don't do that!'

'Keep still. It's ripped to bits anyway.' She cut through the shredded leather and eased it away from his grazed skin.

Francesca looked the other way.

'Get a bowl of water,' said Maria. 'Not too hot.'

Ma set a half-filled bowl on the table. Maria dipped the inside of her wrist in the bowl then plunged Danny's hand in.

'Ah!'

'I've got to clean it. It looks worse than it is, you won't need stitches.'

Johnny watched blood swirl until the water resembled a glass marble.

'Is good you had the gloves on or it would be worse,' Ma said.

'It certainly would,' Maria said.

Danny let out a yell when she poured iodine on his grazed skin.

'Tea please, nice and sweet.' Maria made short work of bandaging his hand. 'Fetch the aspirins, Fran.'

Francesca ran upstairs. Ma poured tea.

Danny began to shake again. 'Could someone go and see if my bike's okay?'

Francesca picked up the motorcycle gauntlets. 'What shall I do with these?'

'You might as well chuck 'em out,' Danny said. 'They're no use now.'

'Don't do that,' said Johnny. 'Can I have the other one?'

'What for?'

Johnny pulled his shirt sleeve up to show his brace. 'Why do you think?'

'I would have thought,' said Maria, 'that a black glove would make it even more obvious.'

'Is anyone going to see if my bike's okay?' Danny stood up, wobbled and sat down again. 'It's in the lane. I skidded on the mud turning in.'

TWENTY-FIVE

The sun shone and insects buzzed in the hedges as Danny strolled along behind the herd, his hand wrapped in a grubby bandage. He wondered what was for tea and if the shooting brake in the distance was an Austin. It was. It came to a halt when it met the leading cow. The driver leaned out. 'Are we on the right road for Kingfishers Farm?'

'Aye, that you be.' Danny offered them an exaggerated local accent and nudged the red rump in front of him with a stick. The animal continued to nibble grass from the roadside.

The woman passenger wound down her window. The leading cow, an orange-red Devon, stepped daintily up to the Austin's running board, scrutinised the woman with her big brown eyes then, still gazing at the fascinating stranger, defecated with a pungent plop.

'Ugh!' The woman withdrew her head and wound the window up.

Danny squeezed past the cows. A teenager and a small boy occupied the back seat. 'Are you the Latimers?'

'That's right.'

'Sorry, won't be a tick. I'm Danny Gomez; I just need to get this lot through that gate there.' He pointed to a field entrance a short way up the road. 'You'll have to back up a bit. Sorry. We weren't expecting you till later on.'

'We made pretty good time actually,' said Mr Latimer. 'We stopped in Dorchester for lunch.'

'I don't like the country,' complained a small voice from the back seat. 'It smells.'

The car reversed and the cows ambled to their field. Danny shut them in safely and returned to the car.

'It's right there, just before the farmyard. He sprinted down the road to pull open the five-barred gate and waited while they parked in front of the porch.

Ma came from the farmyard. 'Is Mr Latimer?'

'Mrs Gomez.' The man briefly doffed his trilby and turned to hold the passenger door open for his wife.

'Good evening.' Mrs Latimer held out her hand.

"Ello. Please to go in, the key it is in the door.'

They entered directly into a sitting room with a settee in front of the fireplace and a dining table under the window opposite.

'The men they have made the dining room for a bedroom.' Ma showed Mrs Latimer. 'Is okay?'

'Perfectly,' said Mrs Latimer. 'Thank you for going to so much trouble.'

'Is no trouble.' Ma threw open the door of a small kitchen. 'I leave milk and butter on the table for you. Please, always remember to shut gates behind yourself.'

Outside, Mr Latimer had the car boot open.

'Need any help?' Danny asked.

'Can you take this, please?'

Danny carried the suitcase to the porch and left it on the stone step. He turned his attention to the older of the two boys. 'Hello, you must be Nigel. Do you need a hand at all?'

'I can manage fine thanks, or I will when you get out of my way.' The teenager gave his brother a shove with his elbow.

'I don't want to,' the small boy complained, tumbling out of the car holding his nose. Nigel Latimer unearthed a pair of wooden crutches that his kid brother seemed to have been using as a footrest, propped them carefully against the open door and hauled himself to his feet.

'I thought you used a wheelchair,' Danny said.

'I can't wait for them to unearth it from the luggage, I'm as stiff as a board after all this time.' The boy tucked the crutches under his arms and made his way to the door, swinging himself across the gravel with an easy grace that took Danny by surprise.

'What have you done to your hand?' the little boy asked.

'Bashed it falling off my bike,' Danny said.

'I've got a bike at home.'

'Inside with you,' Mr Latimer said as he unearthed a wheelchair from the back of the car, filled it with bags and pushed it to the porch.

Danny left them to it, ran round to the yard and ducked under a fully laden washing line. Johnny sat by the kitchen window with a book on his knees.

'They've arrived!' Danny announced.

Johnny looked up, frowning at the interruption. 'Who's arrived?'

'The Latimers.'

'Who the hell are they?'

Francesca came round the corner carrying a wicker basket and began to unpeg laundry. 'The family that's renting the holiday flat. Don't you ever listen? Mama told us at breakfast time they were coming today. The flat suited them better than a hotel because their son uses a wheelchair and they wanted somewhere with a bedroom downstairs. He's still at school so he must be a bit younger than you.'

'I forgot. My head don't work no more, it's like…' he shook his head, 'like when you push the button on the jukebox and nothing happens.'

'Johnny, love.' She dropped the pegs in the basket and squatted beside him.

Next day Johnny sat in the farmyard, shirtsleeves rolled above his elbows. 'Dan, how much longer are you going to be?'

'Give me a chance, I ain't finished bottling yet.' Two little girls from the camping field trotted past with buckets and spades. Their parents followed laden with bags and a picnic basket, bound for a bus to the seaside. 'The place is full of bloomin' kids, they keep trying to get in the yard.'

Johnny backed into the patch of shade by the haystack and peered through the open door, watching milk trickling from the cooler.

A woman approached and leaned on the gate. 'Hello, I'm after buying some milk.'

Johnny pointed. 'The kitchen door's round the back, you don't need to come through the yard.'

Danny emerged from the cool shade of the dairy and pointed to the rear of the house. 'Milk, eggs, Mum will sort you out.'

The woman left.

'Grockles!' Danny said. 'Mustn't complain I suppose, the more there are the more rent we get, but they do make a bloody mess and as for that idiot who left the gate open last week—'

Johnny shushed him. The woman was talking to Ma. 'Your sons tell me you sell eggs too.'

'Yes, and tomatoes.'

'Ma didn't say I'm not hers,' Johnny said.

'It's the middle of the holidays, she ain't got time to explain who you are to every Tom, Dick and Harry.'

'Oh, I don't mind.'

Another woman came down the track with a small boy in tow. A boy in a wheelchair brought up the rear, wearing jeans and a singlet, with his wheels straddling the strip of grass between the ruts. The small boy started to climb the gate and his mother told him to get down. He made a reluctant retreat and looked at Johnny. 'Were you born like that?'

Johnny, enraged, looked round for something to throw at him.

'My brother was.'

'Paul! Come here this minute,' his mother said.

The occupant of the wheelchair drew level with the gate. 'Sorry, my little brother's a pest.'

'Am not!'

'I'm Nigel Latimer,' said the boy. 'You must be Johnny.'

'Yeah, and that's Danny.' Johnny pointed at the dark doorway.

'I know, we met last night.' Nigel's bare arms were almost as white as his vest but as well muscled as Danny's. 'We've come for some more milk.'

Danny brought the milk, screwing up his eyes against the sun. 'Morning, Mrs Latimer. Here you are, straight off the cooler, you won't get it fresher anywhere.'

Paul was staring at the paddock. 'I've never seen a horse like yours, he's got hairy hooves.'

'He is a she,' said Danny. 'She's called Tilly.'

Tilly raised her head at the mention of her name and walked over to the fence in the hope of a sugar lump.

'Why has she got hairy hooves?'

'To keep her feet warm, of course,' Johnny said.

'I'm nearly finished here, Nigel. Do you want to wait for us?' Danny said.

Minutes later Carlos appeared to load the Land Rover and Danny emerged from his lair to hold the gate open for Johnny. Danny pushed him down the track between the house and the cowshed, leaving Nigel to bring up the rear. The field beyond the milking shed was cluttered with tents and both caravans were occupied. A woman sat cross legged on a picnic blanket outside one of them, watching a child in a white sun bonnet tottering unsteadily across the grass. The child stopped and stared, her thumb in her mouth. The woman glanced at them then quickly turned back to the toddler.

Ash and cinders spread on the ground near the house made the track easy to negotiate but further on it had been deeply rutted by tractor wheels. 'Do you need a hand on this bit?' Danny called over his shoulder. 'It's pretty bumpy.'

'I think I can manage, thanks,' Nigel said, valiantly forcing his wheels round.

Opposite the camping field the paddock was edged by a post and rail fence topped with barbed wire. At the orchard boundary the fence gave way to a hedge where a straw bale had been propped upright against the bushes.

They found Nigel's kid brother cavorting in the paddock with his arms outstretched, making a screeching noise. 'Look at me! I'm a Spitfire.'

Tilly grazed nearby; a child with nothing edible held no interest for her. Flies settled on her nose and she tossed her head and snorted. The little boy gave a shriek and ran off to find his mother.

'That's got rid of him,' said Nigel. 'Is the bale of straw for your horse?'

Johnny went a few yards along the path by the house. 'Ignoramus. It's not for eating, it's for the stable floor.'

'Tilly eats grass or hay,' said Danny, 'I use the bale for a target.'

Nigel gaped. 'For a gun?'

'For my bow. Do you want a go?'

'Oh, yes please. We do archery at school,' said Nigel. 'This might not be quite so bad after all.'

'What might not?'

'A holiday in the country isn't my idea of fun. There's nothing to do in the country. My parents thought it was a good idea because they'd found somewhere with a downstairs bedroom and another cripple lived here so I'd have someone to talk to.'

Danny burst out laughing at his expression of disgust.

'Seriously, why do they assume that handicapped people must automatically have interests in common?'

Danny fetched his bow and a handful of arrows from the tack room and walked over by the pond. He fitted an arrow, pulled until his biceps bulged and loosed the arrow, which lodged firmly in the centre of the bale. Nigel struggled on the uneven grass but reached a spot near Danny, who handed him the bow.

Nigel examined it. 'I've never seen one like this before.'

'He made it himself,' Johnny said.

Nigel positioned himself sideways on to the target and squinted down the shaft. His arrow hit the straw close to Danny's, bounced off and fell to the ground. He edged closer to the pond.

'Better not get too near,' said Danny, 'you don't want to fall in.'

'It's a funny place for a pond.'

'It was a bomb crater.'

'Honestly?'

'Oh yeah. In the war this was all dug up to grow spuds and one night a Heinkel dropped a socking great bomb in the middle of it.'

'That must have been some bang,' Nigel said.

'It was more of a ginormous thud really. It made a whacking great hole and shattered every window in the place. They say I can't remember cos I was only a baby but I can; it rained down earth and spuds all over the place. They tried to fill the hole in but it filled up with water every time it rained so in the end they gave it up as a bad job and got some ducks.'

'Aren't you having a turn?' Nigel called.

Johnny, still on the path, shook his head. He turned his back on them and headed for the courtyard.

Nigel looked surprised. 'What's up with him?'

'When he came off his bike it clouted him, broke his back and nearly took his hand off, so he can't pull the bow any more,' said Danny in a low voice. 'He's a moody bastard sometimes, 'specially when his back's playing up.'

'Is that why he wears that glove?'

Danny took quick, careful aim. 'Yeah.'

Later Nigel found Johnny in the yard surrounded by cigarette ends, his head in a book. 'Danny's gone to help his father. Oh my!' He spotted the coloured stones on the windowsill. 'Where did you get these?'

'I'd forgotten about them. They're Francesca's.'

'Dad thinks this house is really interesting. He says the new part we're staying in is Georgian.'

'That's not new.'

'Well, it's newer than the rest. He reckons the oldest parts date from before the Civil War and your garden wall is made of dressed stone,' Nigel said, pointing to the blocks under the fence.

'What's dressed stone when it's at home?'

'It's when a stonemason has chiselled the sides or carved them to make frames for doors and windows. My father was wondering where they came from.'

'Why?'

'He wants to ask the local museum about them.'

'What are those little stones then?'

'Roman tesserae; they used them to make mosaic floors in their villas.'

'Bloody hell! I thought they were rubbish like the rest of the stuff Fran collects.'

TWENTY-SIX

Next morning was cloudy. Johnny sat by the half-open kitchen door gazing vacantly across the paddock. 'I'm bored.'

Nigel appeared, bowling along the path scattering hens.

'Not you again,' Johnny said.

'Don't be so rude, Johnny.' Ma pulled the bottom of the door back to let Nigel in. 'Your mother ask about the bus to Exeter, she gone shopping.'

'I know,' said Nigel. 'She's taken Paul with her and Dad's scouring the countryside looking for Roman remains so I'm at a loose end.'

'I'm not busy this afternoon. We could go to the pictures.' Francesca perched on the table in jeans and one of Mig's old shirts and her hair in a ponytail. 'There's a horror film on.'

Nigel gawped, evidently not used to seeing girls wearing boys' clothes.

'Yeah!' Mig was enthusiastic.

'They won't let you in, you're not old enough.' She jumped down and held out her hand. 'How do you do. I'm Francesca.'

'Nigel, hello.'

'S'not fair. You're not eighteen Fran, how come they let you in?' Mig went off in a huff.

'What are you going to do this morning?' Francesca asked.

'I don't know.' Nigel yawned.

'Are we keeping you up?' Johnny said.

'Sorry, I was awake half the night. I thought it was supposed to be quiet in the countryside.'

'Isn't it?'

'It was noisy all night, what with the sheep and the cows; it was bad enough getting used to the smell. Then there were the motorbikes and when I finally got to sleep a chicken started crowing.'

'That chicken's a cock'rel and he's meant to be loud. You should have kept the window shut.' Johnny was unsympathetic. 'And the bikes would've been on their way home from the pub.'

Danny came to help himself from the teapot on the range. 'The sun's trying to come out.'

Maria came in search of her handbag. 'Why don't you ask Dad if you can have the morning off? Maybe you could take Nigel for a picnic?'

'Gosh!' said Nigel. 'How many of you are there? Are you coming?' he asked Maria.

'I can't, I'm going to the hairdressers.'

Francesca returned transformed in red gingham skirt and black high heels. 'We can go as soon as you're ready, Johnny.'

'Not in those you can't,' said Maria. 'I do wish you wouldn't borrow my things without asking, it's absolutely infuriating.'

'Sor-ry!'

'Could you please behave when we've got guests? Won't it be a bit of a squash, with Johnny and Nigel?'

'I can go in the back,' Francesca said.

Maria raised her eyebrows. 'With two wheelchairs?'

'They'll be okay folded up and hitched on the side.' Francesca took herself off and returned two minutes later and two inches shorter in black sandals.

They piled into the jeep with Nigel straddling the gear stick, wedged between Johnny and Danny. Francesca perched on a wooden crate in the back nursing a basket of sandwiches. Mig stayed behind to sulk.

Danny parked near the piers. A ferry was steaming across the estuary towards them and Nigel wanted to watch it dock. It slowed almost to a halt as it approached the stone pier; passengers lined the rails, ropes were caught and tied to bollards and the throng streamed down the gangplank, in their shirtsleeves and summer hats, carrying buckets and spades, fishing rods and picnic baskets. Francesca strolled along the promenade beside Nigel.

Danny realised Johnny wasn't keeping up. 'Aren't you coming?'

'I've seen it come in hundreds of times,' Johnny said, staring at the sea between the fishermen's jetty and the ferry pier. The sun shone on water so clear he could see the sandy bottom and the rocks the piers were built on. The pale green water rose and fell with the rhythmic breath of a sleeping dragon.

'Francesca tells me you like fishing,' Nigel said.

Johnny gave a violent start. 'I didn't hear you coming.' He swung round to face the pier where several fishing boats were moored; it was covered with a jumble of wooden boxes, creels and tackle. 'I used to fish from the end there. You can catch conger eels when the tide's coming in.'

'How about some ice cream?' Nigel said.

'Good idea.' Danny grasped the handles of Johnny's chair.

'Don't you dare, I can do it myself.'

Nigel headed for a kiosk nearby. He got up quite a turn of speed on the smooth, flat promenade until a small child with a fully laden ice-cream cone darted in front of him. He almost collided with her and the ice cream fell on the ground. The little girl clutched the empty cone, staring in consternation at the small mound of vanilla melting between them. Then she began to howl.

Her mother ran up, shouting at Nigel. 'Look what you've done. Why don't you look where you're going?'

The child stopped crying, stuck its thumb in its mouth and resumed staring, at Nigel this time. The ice cream had become no more than a puddle.

'I'm really very sorry,' said Nigel. 'Let my buy her another one.'

'You've no right to be whizzing about like that, barging into people,' the woman said.

Danny hurried up but before he could utter a word the woman turned on him.

'Are you supposed to be looking after them? They shouldn't be allowed to go round upsetting normal people.' Her hand came down smartly on the back of the little girl's legs. 'How many times have I told you not to run off like that?'

The child started screaming again.

Nigel backed off.

'Seems to me its mother was doing more damage than you,' Danny said.

While everyone's attention was diverted Johnny took the opportunity to slope off. Francesca shouted after him but he pretended not to hear. He reached the fishermen's pier and wove in and out among nets and boxes, perilously close to the edge. How he missed the tang of diesel and stale fish.

'Oi! Watch yourself.' An old man leaned on the boat's rail. 'Get away from the edge.' The fisherman shifted his gaze from the wheelchair to its occupant. He squinted at Johnny. 'Aren't you Jim Trevelyan's grandson? You shouldn't be mucking about on here, it bain't safe.'

Johnny grinned insolently. 'Scared I'll fall in?'

'That's not funny. We've had enough trouble from you lot riding yer bikes on here, without you coming in one of them there wheelchair contraptions.' The man heaved a box of plaice aside. 'What have you been doing to yourself?'

'Fell off me bike, didn't I.'

'Well, you don't want to be falling off here an' all.'

'Afraid I'll drown?'

Danny sprinted onto the pier. 'What the bloody hell do you think you're doing?'

'I was only having a look,' Johnny said as Danny seized the handles to turn his chair round.

'Keep him away from here, it's dangerous,' the fisherman advised. 'I hope you get better soon, lad.'

Johnny scowled. 'I am better. This is as good as it gets.'

'Bloody idiot,' said Danny. 'What if you'd fallen off the edge?'

Danny and Francesca sat on the low wall around a flowerbed to eat their ice creams and watch the holidaymakers; children constructed elaborate sandcastles or paddled at the edge of the water, further out heads bobbed in the gentle swell, several wearing swimming caps.

'I've never been swimming in the sea,' Nigel said.

'Can you swim?' Danny said.

'Of course I can swim. Dad and I often go to the baths in the holidays. We generally go early in the morning when it's almost empty.'

'We could go to the end of the prom and have our picnic. It's quieter along there,' Francesca said.

'Good idea,' said Danny. 'We'll drive down, it'll be quicker.'

The far end of the seafront was deserted except for a man with a shrimping net wading through the shallows. On their left dark red cliffs towered above them, below these a ledge of rock jutted into the sea. At this end of the promenade the drop from the concrete was only a few inches deep.

'I won't be able to operate this on the sand,' said Nigel. 'You'll have to pull me backwards.'

'No problem.' Danny tilted Nigel's chair and dragged him back until the wheels ground themselves into the sand. He went to fetch Johnny from the prom.

'I'm not—'

'Oh, yes you are.' Danny seized the handles and tipped his chair back.

The shrimp man reached the rocky ledge and upended his net, which was as wide as he was tall. He took a bag off his back, shook the contents of the net into it and waded back the way he had come.

'The sea looks awfully inviting,' Nigel said.

'You should've brought your crutches,' Danny told him.

'You're strong enough to give me a piggyback into the water but I'm afraid I haven't brought my swimming trunks.'

'Swim in your underpants,' said Danny. 'They'll dry in the sun.'

Nigel glanced at Francesca.

'It won't be the first time I've seen boys in their underpants,' she said.

'Shall we?'

So Nigel let Danny carry him into the sea. He ducked down to wet his shoulders. 'Brrr!'

'It feels warm once you get used to it.'

Nigel floated on his back.

'You had enough yet?' Danny yelled at him.

'No, just having a breather. I'm going to try for those rocks.'

'Race you!' He made the mistake of giving Nigel a head start and was forced to put in some effort to catch up with him. He touched the ledge only seconds before Nigel, clambered out and turned and knelt to help him. 'Take care,' he warned. 'The barnacles are really sharp.'

Johnny lit a cigarette and watched Danny and Nigel sitting side by side on the rocks, their feet dangling in the sea, chatting like they'd known each other for years. 'I wonder what they're talking about.'

Francesca sat by his feet. 'Don't know. Can I have one?' She lit the cigarette from his. 'Isn't it lovely?'

'I suppose.'

'It's better than being stuck indoors because it's raining.'

'Those two seem to be getting on famously.'

She jumped up. 'I've left the sandwiches in the jeep, they'll get all hot and squidgy.'

'Len will be back soon,' said Johnny when she came back with the basket. 'I hope Nigel doesn't keep on hanging around then.'

Danny emerged from the water with Nigel, allowed him to slither to the ground then sprawled on his back, his arms flung above his head.

'That was marvellous.' Nigel rubbed at his hair with his shirt, causing it to stand on end, wet and spiky. He spread his damp shirt out on the hot sand. 'Anyone got a comb?'

Francesca peeled back layers of greaseproof paper and shared out ham sandwiches. 'We ought to have bought some crisps.'

'We can get some at the pictures,' Danny said.

The man with the shrimp net returned, emptied his net and ploughed away again. Danny finished his sandwich and turned on his stomach. 'I'm nearly dry, how about you?'

'Here we are,' Danny said as they passed an imposing art deco building, marble steps spanned the entrance. He pulled up round the corner. 'You never said it was a western.'

Francesca looked crestfallen. 'I could have sworn it was a horror film this week.'

'I'm not coming,' said Johnny.

'What d'you mean, you're not coming?' she demanded as Danny went to unload the wheelchairs. 'We're here now.'

'I am not being lugged up those steps in full view of everyone.'

'For heaven's sake, Johnny, we're here now.'

'You can go if you like. I'm staying right here.'

'You'll have to get out or Nigel can't.'

'What if we went to Exeter?' said Danny. 'The Odeon hasn't got steps.'

'Do you know what's on there?' said Nigel. 'We could go by train. It would be an expedition. I hardly ever go anywhere by train.'

This idea lasted only as long as it took Johnny to discover what the proposed travel arrangements involved. 'I ain't goin' in no guard's van,' he stated flatly.

'Why don't we go to the café instead?' Francesca said.

'But—'

Francesca put her hand on his arm. 'It's okay, Dan, we can go to the pictures after tea.'

'No I can't, Dad only let me have the day off because I promised to help him pack beans tonight.' Danny put Johnny's chair back in and hitched the rope round it.

'I don't want to go to the café,' Johnny said.

'Oh, for pity's sake.' Francesca scrambled in the back.

Danny got in, slammed the door, crunched the gears and found reverse.

Johnny was still hot after Carlos got him to bed and took the corset off. He lay on his side to read, with the sheet pushed down to his waist. Nigel, Francesca and Danny had gone to the pictures; at the last minute Maria decided to go too.

'Was it any good?' he shouted when they came home.

'Not bad,' said Maria. 'I get quite enough blood and gore at work, so a western was something of a relief except Dan kept up a running commentary on the film's mistakes. Who put you to bed?'

'Your dad.'

'I had to squat on the box in the back again,' said Francesca. 'But because Nigel was with us they let us in at the fire exit round the side and we sat right at the front because that's where wheelchairs go.'

'What was it about?'

'Cowboys and Indians,' said Maria, 'and something about a stagecoach. Then I nodded off.'

Johnny burst out laughing.

'Well, that's put you in a better mood,' Maria said and left him alone with Francesca.

'Where's Danny disappeared to?'

'Gone to help Dad pack beans,' Francesca said.

'Go on then.'

Francesca looked bewildered.

'The film,' he prompted.

'The baddies pretended to be goodies and fight off the Indians but really they were planning to rob the stagecoach. Then the sheriff's posse caught them. I don't know how she can possibly doze off through all those gunfights.'

'I wish I could have gone.'

'Well, you could have if you weren't so blooming obstinate.'

'Don't be cross, Fran.'

'Don't sulk then.'

'I'm not bloody sulking,' he mumbled with his face in the pillow.

TWENTY-SEVEN

On Sunday the Latimers attended St Michael's in the village and Danny drove the family to Mass at the Catholic church in town leaving Johnny and Carlos to fend for themselves. As usual Ma called Carlos a heathen Communist. As usual he ignored her.

In the afternoon Johnny sat on the path alongside the paddock, watching Danny and Nigel take aim at the straw bale. Tilly stood over by the apple trees in the shade, swishing her tail at flies. Len would be home soon; he couldn't wait. He made his way slowly towards the courtyard.

'Don't go in yet,' Danny said.

'I'm too hot. Where's Nigel?'

'Gone in for tea.'

'I need to get this thing off before I melt.'

Danny helped him on the bed and fetched two chunky glasses. 'Do you want some cider, Fran?'

She shook her head. 'Johnny, did Mama leave some of the bendy straws in your drawer?'

Maria came home from work and poked her head round the door. 'He'll have to have his tea in bed if you've taken his support off.'

'I'm not hungry, I hate eating in bed,' Johnny shouted but Maria had gone upstairs to change and didn't hear.

The phone rang. 'Somebody get that?' Ma called.

Danny answered it. 'Hello? Yeah, we're all okay, hang on.' He stood in the doorway holding the handset at the full extent of its flex and held out the receiver to Johnny. 'Surprise!'

Johnny listened, beamed. 'Hello? When did you get back? No, it's not too late, of course you can come round now, can't he, Dan?'

'Course he can.' Danny, marooned in the doorway, held the handset aloft with the flex looped from it to the socket on one side and to the receiver on the other.

'Danny says to come on round. I thought you weren't back till tomorrow. Okay then.'

Len arrived in a matter of minutes. Danny let him in. 'Do you want a drink? Seeing as Johnny's already got one.'

'I thought we could go to the Horse and Hounds for a drink,' Maria said.

'Well, I—'

'You go and say hello to Johnny while I run and get a cardigan.' She spirited Len away before they had a chance to say more than two words to each other and left Johnny fuming.

Danny went to hose out the cowshed. He had nearly finished when Nigel came round the corner with his father in tow. It was still very warm but Mr Latimer wore a jacket though he had ditched his tie. He took a pipe out of his pocket.

'These pebbles you found…' old man Latimer struck a match and applied it to the pipe. It flickered and went out. 'They were from the stream over there, weren't they?' he said, using his pipe stem as a pointer.

'That's right,' Danny said.

'I think I've discovered,' Mr Latimer struck another match, sucked at the pipe several times and blew out a cloud of smoke, 'their possible origin. There's a field just beyond the trees,' he puffed on his pipe again, 'which seems in its topmost part to have a great many hummocks.'

Danny waited a moment, not quite sure whether Mr Latimer had finished his sentence. 'Yes, it's full of old stones. My dad and the farmer next door use them for walls and such like.'

'Ah!' said Nigel's father. 'I see.' He wandered off, abandoning his son.

Danny took Nigel in the kitchen where the large earthenware jar waited invitingly.

'Scrumpy's out, d'you want some?'

'Scrumpy? Isn't that home-made cider? I can't, my mum would go mental.'

'She need never know,' Danny winked and rolled a packet of mints across the table.

'Where are your parents? Won't they mind?'

'Why would they mind? Anyway, they're in the sitting room watching telly. Shall we take these through to Johnny's room? This heat was making him ratty but he's okay now.'

Nigel, with a three-quarter-full glass wedged between his thighs, followed carefully, trying not to spill its contents. He ground to a halt in the doorway and goggled in amazement.

The doors to the yard stood open and Johnny lay naked on the bed with only a sheet covering his lower half. Francesca perched beside him.

Johnny grinned. 'Like the tattoos? It's Triton, the sea god.' He rolled over and held up his other arm. 'And a mermaid to keep him company. I had them done ages ago, place in Dartmouth. Don't just sit there, either come in or clear off.'

'It's getting a bit dingy,' said Francesca. 'Shall I turn the light on?'

Nigel regained the power of speech. 'I thought you were tired.'

'No, just too hot, I needed to strip off,' Johnny said.

'So do I.' Danny pulled off his T-shirt and stooped to peer out of the window. 'I reckon there's a storm coming, the sky's gone a funny colour.'

'Gawd, it's hot.' Johnny pushed the sheet down as far as decency allowed. A drinking straw bobbed in his mug.

Danny went to the washbasin and splashed water on his face, turned and flicked water in the direction of the bed.

'Missed!' Johnny finished his drink, beckoned Francesca and whispered in her ear. She filled his mug with water and gave it back. He sucked up water and pointed the straw at Danny.

'Oh no you don't.' Danny skipped into the passage and the water cascaded harmlessly on the carpet. He returned in a couple of minutes brandishing a water pistol.

Johnny squealed as the jet of water hit him. Nigel backed away until he crashed into the wardrobe.

The front door slammed; Len and Maria walked in.

'For heaven's sake, how childish can you get? Hello Nigel, what are you doing in this madhouse?' she said.

'Trying to keep out of the way mostly.'

'Len, this is Nigel.' Maria performed the perfunctory introduction.

'I'm on holiday,' Nigel expanded.

'Oh, right. Hello.'

Maria went out leaving the door open. Water gurgled from the kitchen tap.

'I need a piss,' Johnny announced.

'Out, you lot,' Francesca ordered. She opened the door to Johnny's bedside locker and the others trooped out.

'Here you are.' She gave Johnny his bottle. 'You're soaked.'

'That's Danny's fault.'

'Not entirely.'

'Oh bloody hell. I thought I was in time.'

'It's okay. Don't worry, no one knows,' she said.

'You know.'

'Turn over.'

Johnny rolled obediently. By the time Len returned she was towelling him dry.

'It's become extremely overcast,' Len said.

'Time Nigel left or he'll get wet. Wetter, I mean,' Johnny said as Francesca tucked in the sheet.

Len found Danny in the kitchen feeding Nigel peppermints. 'Your parents won't smell a thing, I promise.'

'You'd better get cracking, it's going to pour any minute,' Len said.

Danny went with Nigel; lightning flashed as they crossed the yard. The rain began with big, slow drops. Lightning flashed again followed by a peal of thunder and the heavens opened.

Len leaned on the windowsill. 'It's quite heavy now, I hope he made it in time.'

Johnny laughed. 'He wasn't meant to stay dry. It'll cool him down.'

Danny ran in from the yard, shaking water from his hair. He grabbed the rail at the end of the bed. 'You still need to cool off?'

'Don't you dare! I've only just changed his sheets,' said Francesca, 'and shut the doors properly, the rain's coming in.'

Danny picked up his T-shirt. 'At least this is dry.' He bolted the doors and took hold of the curtains.

'Leave them open,' said Johnny. 'I want to watch the storm. Get my tablets, Len.'

'Maria says you're only allowed one if you've had a drink,' Francesca said.

'It was worth a try.'

'You wanna be careful. One of these days you ain't gonna wake up cos you've stuck too much booze and pills down your gullet,' Danny said.

'That's exactly what I'd like.'

'I was only joking.'

'I wasn't.'

Francesca squatted next to the bed. 'Johnny darling, please don't.'

'Don't you Johnny darling me.' He pushed her and she made a grab for the table to stop herself falling.

'Oi! That's enough.' Danny strode towards the bed.

Johnny laughed.

Len knew better than to argue with Johnny in this mood. He put his hands in his pockets and kept out of it.

'You're a pig, Johnny Hunter. Come on, Dan,' said Francesca. 'I'll get his tablets while he's saying goodbye to Len, then I'm going to watch the lightning with him till he goes to sleep.'

'I thought you were cross with him.'

'What's the point? We all know he can't help it.'

Len turned up next day so soon after Maria left for work that Johnny suspected he'd been watching the house, waiting for her to leave. Francesca was helping her mother in the dairy, the boys were in the fields harvesting beans and they were left to their own devices. It was too good to last. Inevitably Nigel turned up.

'Haven't you got a family of your own to pester?' Johnny said.

'They've gone to a museum but I thought I'd come round here instead. Dad thinks the mosaics must be somewhere nearby if the dressed stone came from the farm next door.'

'What the hell are you babbling about?' Johnny said.

'The stones in your yard,' said Nigel. 'The ones the fence poles are stuck into.'

'I'm sometimes tempted to stick a pole in someone.'

Nigel cleared off, baffled by Johnny's change of mood.

'There was no need to be quite so rude,' Len said.

'Why not? I wish he'd clear off but he won't take a hint, he's always there and he won't shut up.'

'He seems a nice enough chap. Apparently he stays at a hospital in Middlesex during term time. The place sounds rather like boarding school; they have a tutor come in daily. He's hoping to take his O levels next year.'

'That's what Fran wants to do. She's staying on for an extra year.'

'Really? I thought she was already sixteen. Nigel suggested we might borrow Danny's bow later on.'

'Do what you want, like you usually do.'

'Johnny, that's not fair.'

Len disappeared and Johnny sat in the yard, thankful to be left on his own. Ma came out to give him the sun hat but he chucked it away the moment her back was turned. He tilted his head back to let the sun fall on his face, closed his eyes and concentrated on the swirling shapes on the inside of his eyelids. The pain was still there, but masked by the painkillers so he was less aware of it. The shapes were crimson, the colour of frustration, rage and hate. They met at a central point and vanished. More whirled in from the sides to take their place. Ash fell from his cigarette onto the hat he had dropped.

'Johnny!' Len's voice came from an infinite distance.

'Johnny.' Len shook his shoulder gently.

The red haze disappeared. 'What?'

Len stood behind him and pulled his shoulders back. 'When you let your arms dangle like that it makes your shoulders all hunched.'

'What's it matter?'

Len picked up the hat and brushed ash off, leaving a grey smear on the brim. 'Danny won't be too pleased if you burn a hole in his hat.'

'He don't wear it no more, he's got himself a cowboy hat.'

'It's hot out here. Do you want to go in now? Maybe lie down for a bit if you're tired?' Len said.

'I'm not tired. I don't want to go back to bed. I hate being stuck in bed. I'm sick of it. I hate it. I hate it. I hate you,' Johnny exploded. 'And I hate this fucking wheelchair.' He slammed his fist on the arm of his chair. 'And I hate that fucking hat.' He snatched it from Len and threw it on the bricks.

'Temper, temper.'

'Why don't you go away and leave me in peace?'

'You need a hat in this sun, you'll burn.' Len pushed him across the paddock.

'I'm not a kid.'

'Then don't behave like one.'

Johnny snapped his brake on. 'I'm not.'

'Stop it, Johnny.' Len picked him up and carried him. He left him on the grass in the shade of the apple trees. 'I'll leave you to have your tantrum in peace then, shall I?'

Johnny shouted and swore but Len ignored him and walked away.

The tractor came into view. Danny was driving, naked to the waist and wearing a straw cowboy hat, he towed a trailer laden with wooden boxes full of runner beans.

Len had nearly reached the house when the tractor stopped. Danny ran round the corner and cannoned into him.

'Look where you're going, you nearly knocked me flying.'

'Sorry. What's up? I could hear Johnny yelling over the row the Fergy makes.' Danny spotted the empty wheelchair. 'Where is he?'

'I dumped him in the orchard. He's having a ranting tantrum.' Danny laughed. 'A what?'

'I mean, he's having a tantrum and ranting and raving at me so I left him to it. At least he won't get sunstroke down there.'

'Might as well go and get a drink I s'pose, now I'm here.'

They headed for the back door.

'He practically bit Nigel's head off this morning,' Len said.

Ma dispensed lemonade and advice. 'Give him some time to calm down.'

'He's really fed up. We could take him to the pub later on, it might cheer him up a bit. What do you reckon?'

'We'd have to carry him up the steps,' said Len. 'You know what a song and dance he'll make about that.'

'I guess I could ask Dad if we can use the jeep later.'

'I'll be back shortly.' Len left abruptly.

Ma poured another tumbler of lemonade. 'Take a drink out to Johnny.'

Danny found Johnny lying on his back, staring through the branches at the sky, calmly smoking a cigarette.

'You alright, mate?'

'Never better.'

'No need to be sarky. I brought you some lemonade.'

Johnny tossed his dog-end into the long grass and rolled over. A wisp of smoke spiralled upward.

'You shouldn't do that with the grass so dry. Last night's cloudburst was no use at all.'

'You don't half fuss.' Johnny propped himself on his elbow and reached for the lemonade. 'Where's Len gone?'

Danny shrugged.

He passed Len on his way across the paddock. 'He's in one of his moods.'

'When isn't he?'

'Where've you been?' Johnny demanded.

'I went to find Danny's father to ask if I could borrow his Land Rover tomorrow,' Len said.

'What for?' Johnny gazed skywards through half-closed eyes.

'I thought we could go to the seaside. It's perfect, bags of room for your chair in the back.'

'My chair won't work on the beach. You should know that, you twerp.'

'I can carry you.'

Johnny was instantly wide awake. 'No way. Absolutely no way.'

'Why not? I do here.'

'People will stare.'

'We could go to Shining Sands Cove. No one goes right over there, even during the summer holidays.'

Johnny asked if Len could stay overnight so that they could get an early start. He planned to get out of the house before Nigel tried to tag along.

TWENTY-EIGHT

Johnny opened his eyes. The calm, clear light of early morning seeped through the gap above the curtains. He shifted sideways on the bed and dragged a pillow from the bedside table to shove behind his head. The window was open and the curtains flattened against the glass, then slackened to drop back over the sill, the sequence repeated hypnotically.

Len had pulled the couch across the door to the passage. He slept curled up with his mouth slightly open, his straw-coloured hair stuck out in all directions, untidy as a seagull's nest. He stirred and murmured in his sleep. It must be hard for him too, coming to terms with the consequences of the crash. Footsteps sounded on the stairs. Johnny let out a heavy sigh.

Len stirred, rubbed his eyes and stretched. 'What's up?'

'I've been waiting for you to wake up. I need a fag.'

Len groped on the floor. 'What did I do with them?'

'They're under the settee.'

Len put his hand on the floor to peer underneath. 'So they are.' He retrieved a square red packet and scrambled to his feet.

'What time is it?'

Johnny looked at his watch. 'Nearly quarter past.'

'Quarter past what?' Len yawned hugely.

'Six.'

'Good God!'

'I can't believe you didn't hear Carlos come down.'
'Dead to the world.'
'Gimme a fag, Len. I'm desperate.'

Len lit a cigarette and gave it to him. When he finished he ground the stub out in the ashtray and pulled aside the covers. 'Fancy a cuddle?'

They lay on their sides on the narrow bed like two spoons in a cutlery drawer. Len kissed the back of Johnny's neck, squirmed and grunted.

'Mind, you'll fall out.'

'I'm coming,' Len breathed in his ear. 'I'm…' and he fell out of bed, crashing into the table. He crouched on the floor, rocking back and forth and rubbing his elbow. 'Shit!'

Johnny rolled over and spluttered.

'It's not funny.'

'It is from here.'

A knock on the door shocked them into silence. 'Are you all right in there?' Francesca said.

'Fine thanks.' Len picked himself up. 'I, er, I tripped on the carpet.'

Johnny exploded in a paroxysm of laughter.

The door opened an inch and collided sharply with the back of the settee. 'The door's stuck.'

'No, it's not. I put the couch in front,' Len whispered.

'Whatever for?'

'To stop anyone barging in,' Len said, hopping on one leg to pull on his jeans.

'Why are you whispering?'

'It's very early, I don't want to disturb anyone,' Len said.

The morning was cloudy but dry; Johnny decided they should go anyway. 'Bring a towel just in case.' He had Len bandage the old plastic splint to his wrist; he didn't want to get the new one wet.

By the time Carlos finished the milk run they were in the farmyard waiting. Len sat him on the passenger seat, folded his chair and opened the rear door of the Land Rover. Bullet bounded across the yard and leapt in, his tongue lolling from the side of his mouth and his tail thumping expectantly.

'Come on out, you rascal.' Len propped the wheelchair in the back and grasped the dog's collar.

'Woof!' Bullet's tail thumped harder.

Johnny adjusted the rear-view mirror to get a better view. 'Hurry up and shift him, we want to get there today.'

Len tugged. 'Come on, boy!' The dog splayed its legs and his claws scraped on the metal floor as Len dragged him out, making a noise that could curl teeth.

Johnny began to laugh.

Len finally ejected the dog, backed sedately into the haystack, stalled and swore. He found the starting handle and cranked the engine. He was not in the best of moods when he finally settled behind the wheel. 'Who the devil left that mirror at such a ridiculous angle?'

Johnny giggled helplessly.

'I'm glad you find it so hilarious.' Len drove out of the yard, put the handbrake on and jumped out to close the gate. Bullet gazed at him reproachfully with his ears at half mast and tried a hopeful wag.

Len drove straight through town to turn onto an unmade road. After half a mile negotiating the bumpy track he parked on the grass close to the cliff path.

Once, they had raced together down through the undercliff, elbowing each other out of the way. Negotiating the narrow path carrying Johnny proved more difficult than Len had anticipated; he couldn't see where to put his feet. In the end he hoisted Johnny on his back with his arms hitched under his knees. Near its end the path steepened and Len swore as he missed his footing. He was sweating by the time they reached the cove. Red cliffs enclosed the crescent of sand. A dead calm sea merged with the grey mist. They sat side by side leaning against a rock, raucous cries from gulls on the ledges above only serving to intensify their sense of isolation.

'Are you warm enough?'

'Yeah. Perfect, our own private little world at last.' Johnny sighed and slid his arm round Len's shoulders. 'Nobody can see us, we're safe down here.' He began to unbutton Len's shirt.

'Oh, Johnny, Johnny.' Len undid the few remaining buttons.

The tide went out, gradually, exposing smooth, wet sand. Offshore rocks emerged, stretching from the headland. A cormorant hunched, inert as the rock it stood upon. The mist dispersed and the horizon became visible, a pewter slit dividing sea from sky. The sun peeked out from behind a cloud.

'I might have a dip,' Len said.

Johnny hurled a stone at a rock pool but missed, hitting a rock so violently that it ricocheted.

'Careful!'

'I know, I'm lucky to be alive. So they say. I just wish I could go in the water.'

'Can you still swim though?'

'Yeah, there was a pool at Stoke Mandeville, but they had all the gear to get you in and out.'

'I can carry you in. Do you want to give it a go?'

In no time his clothes lay in a heap on the sand. When Len began to unfasten the detested surgical corset he reached over, tugging at the waistband of Len's Y-fronts, dragging them down to uncover Len's tight, white buttocks and expose a solitary tattoo.

'Remember when we got these done?' Johnny stroked the triskelion.

Len gathered Johnny in his arms and waded waist-deep before lowering him into the sea. The flash of envy and anger at Len's strong legs and working muscles vanished when he hit cold water. He forced himself to relax in spite of the sudden chill, letting his head fall back, resisting the temptation to see if his legs were floating. The slight swell made him feel dizzy and water seeped into his ears. 'Let go.' He tried a backstroke, his flailing arms narrowly missing Len's head. Len ducked instinctively. Johnny kept going, arms swinging, water splashing, using his injured hand as a paddle. Seawater splashed in his mouth. Len grabbed him as he spluttered and spat.

'You okay?'

'Hey! I'm free.' He slipped like an eel from Len's outstretched hands. Len hovered, ready to catch him.

Len staggered out of the water and laid him on the wet sand. He dried him, unravelled the soggy bandage from his wrist, bound the splint on with a dry one, helped him dress. Only then did Len shake the sand out of his own clothes.

'Yes!' Johnny shook his clenched fist in the air. The yell sent gulls wheeling, screeching skywards.

'What was that for?'

He shrugged. 'I just felt like it.' He reached out, grabbed Len's hair and dragged him down on the sand for a rough, urgent kiss.

Len sat up. 'Don't look now but there's some chap with field glasses watching us.'

Johnny giggled. 'Let's give the peeping Tom something to look at shall we?'

'Shut up, you idiot. Why the blazes did you have to shout like that and attract his attention?'

Johnny twisted his head round. 'Blimey! It's old Bri.'

'Who?'

'Father O'Brien.'

Len sat back on his heels. 'Are you sure?'

'Course I'm bloody sure.'

Len stiffened, rooted to the spot. 'Oh, shit! He knows my father, he's bound to say something. Oh Johnny, what are we going to do?'

'Perhaps he didn't see us,' Johnny said.

After dinner Johnny sent Len to the village shop. He lay on the grass by the pond with his back to the afternoon sun, propped on his elbow prodding at the water with a stick when Father O'Brien put in an appearance.

He rolled onto his back and smirked. 'You'll excuse me if I don't get up, Father.'

The perspiring priest shifted from one foot to the other like a black crow. He focused on a spot near Johnny's feet, cleared his throat and began at last. 'It's good to see you looking so much better. In fact I wondered if you might feel able to attend Mass soon. I'd need to hear your confession first, of course,' he added.

'Whatever can I have to confess, Father? I don't go nowhere or do nothing.'

'Good afternoon,' Len said and tossed Johnny a packet of Woodbines.

Father O'Brien jumped.

'Ta, you took your time.' Johnny ripped off the cellophane with his teeth. The abandoned twig floated into a patch of duckweed. He held out the packet. 'Father?'

'No, thank you. I don't indulge.'

Johnny sniggered.

Father O'Brien retreated.

'What did he say? He must've recognised us,' said Len. 'What if he says something to my father? What if he tells the police? Oh dear God, what are we going to do?'

'Stop panicking, he was a long way away.'

'But he had field glasses don't forget. Why else would he turn up now? We could end up in court, in prison even.'

'They wouldn't put me in prison.'

'Have you never heard of prison hospitals. What are we going to do?'

'Will you stop marching up and down,' mumbled Johnny, cigarette dangling from his lips. 'I suppose I could go to confession, just in case.'

Len stopped pacing. 'What good will that do? You'll only confirm what he already suspects.'

'Apart from saving my immortal soul you mean?'

'It's not a bloody joke. We could be facing a prison sentence and you're planning to tell him he's right?'

'Exactly, then we'd be safe,' Johnny declared.

Len frowned. 'I don't understand.'

'Because if I do confess then he's not allowed to tell anyone, no one at all. Not ever.'

Francesca left the house straight after tea before she got roped into helping wash the dishes. She headed for the orchard, angry because Len had borrowed the jeep and taken Johnny out. She wouldn't admit to jealousy; that would make it real. She ran through the trees and followed the path upstream. The willows grew closer than the apple trees but a few shafts of sunlight found their way through the branches to sparkle on the water. She sat on the bank by the pool, rolled up her jeans, took off her shoes and socks and dangled her feet in the cold water. She wondered why Father O'Brien had come to see Johnny and remembered the day she had come across the priest scanning the estuary through his binoculars. Had he been spying again, and not just on the birds?

A sheep peeked through the barbed-wire fence guarding the opposite bank. A commotion of black and tan collie came bounding down the field, followed by the farmer. The sheep fled. The man whistled and the dog crouched, creeping forward stealthily as the flock became a ragged column straggling across the field.

'Come by,' the man said without raising his voice and the collie darted to the left. He scampered obediently to the farmer's commands until the sheep approached an open gate on the far side of the field where he made short work of sending them through.

The sun set by the time Francesca made her way back to the farm. The boys were in the paddock. Len sat on the grass at Johnny's feet, smoking, and she lingered under the trees in the twilight, reluctant to show herself.

Johnny pointed. 'There! See? I told you there were bats.'

'I can't see any.'

'Over the pond.'

'So there are.' Len scrambled to his feet and stood behind Johnny's chair, a hand on his shoulder.

Johnny covered Len's hand with his own, twisting his head to look at him. It was very quiet. An owl hooted, another replied.

'Oh, Johnny, Johnny,' Len murmured.

A torch flickered in the lane.

Johnny tensed. 'Someone's coming.'

Len took a step back.

A couple crossed the camping field, unfastened a tent flap and crawled inside. Francesca ran across the grass.

'Where've you been?' Johnny said.

'I went for a walk. Do you know why next door have moved the sheep?'

'Have they?' said Len. 'My father mentioned something about archaeologists digging up a field in the village but I'm afraid I wasn't really listening.'

Headlights swept across the paddock as the Latimers' car pulled up on the far side of the farmhouse. Nigel made his laborious way over the bumpy grass. Francesca waved to him.

'Oh, no! Not him again.' Johnny made no attempt to lower his voice.

Nigel drew level with them.

'You bloody spastic. Why don't you fuck off?'

'At least I didn't have to go to all the trouble of falling off a motorbike,' Nigel retorted.

Nobody moved, nobody spoke. Johnny glared, Nigel returned his gaze. A stunned silence hung in the air, the shadows deepened.

Nigel gave in first. 'I should be getting back,' he muttered, lowering his eyes.

TWENTY-NINE

'Mr Latimer was talking to the men digging up the field on the other side of the stream,' Francesca said at dinner time next day.

'Already?' said Johnny. 'Whereabouts are they?'

'Up the top near the gate, nearly opposite the high barn.'

'This I gotta see,' he said.

Danny took him round in the jeep and parked in the lane beside Yelland's Farmhouse to unload him and open the field gate. Nigel's father was nowhere to be seen but a tall, stooping man with a panama hat and a bow tie was staring intently at an oblong of bare earth. Danny stopped pushing a few yards away from him.

Francesca emerged from the willow trees and dashed up the slope, plaits swinging wildly. 'I told you to wait for me,' she panted.

She stopped at the shallow excavation. 'It's a very neat hole.' Outlined by string tied at ground level to red and white striped poles, the hole was only a couple of inches deep, a bit deeper on the same side as the gate because its base was level but the field was not. A woman with short hair and glasses hanging round her neck like a necklace stood near the man in the hat. A young man in a lumberjack shirt leaning on a spade completed the workforce.

'We're from next door,' Francesca said.

'Isn't that where the tesserae were found?' The man held out his hand to her. 'Professor Boulton-Brown.'

'I'm Francesca Gomez. Can I help? It's the school holidays so I've got time.'

'Thank you for your interest, young lady, but I already have an assistant, my student, Malcolm.' He flapped his hand in the direction of the young man and eyed Danny's muscular build. 'But perhaps you might be able to assist with the heavy work?'

'No offence,' said Danny, 'but I've got plenty of my own work to do.'

'Quite. I would like to see your parents when it's convenient, to discover exactly where the artefacts were found.'

'The what?'

'The tesserae,' said the man in the panama hat. 'They're small stone cubes.'

Francesca folded her arms at him. 'I know what tesserae are, thank you.'

'That won't do you much good.' Danny walked over to join her. 'It's us that found them.'

'And me that found out what they were.' Johnny, unable to escape and exasperated at being ignored, tried unsuccessfully to operate his wheels on the rough grass. 'Come on, let's go home.'

Danny began to pull him backwards.

'Please! Wait a minute. Before you leave would you mind showing me where they were discovered?'

'What's the point if you won't let us help?' Johnny said.

Francesca dragged the gate open and Danny made short work of hauling the wheelchair back towards the lane.

The professor watched them go. 'Perhaps...'

Danny stopped.

'As you are so interested, perhaps you would care to observe the excavation.'

'I guess it's better than nothing,' Johnny muttered.

Francesca took the professor to the stream to show him where the little stones had come from. After a while the professor came back. She did not.

'You just missed Nigel,' said Francesca when they got home. 'He came to say goodbye, they're leaving first thing tomorrow.'

'Oh! I missed him,' said Johnny. 'What a shame.'

'Just as well you weren't here. You can be unbelievably spiteful sometimes.'

'Me?' Johnny looked the picture of innocence.

'You were really horrid to Nigel.'

'He was always hanging around when he wasn't wanted.'

Next morning Danny wedged Johnny's wheelchair in with the milk churns and delivered him to the field next door before delivering the milk. The jeep drove off leaving him to watch the archaeologists at work, like an overseer in charge of a chain gang. The turves stacked at the far end of the hole were balanced by a growing mound of earth at his end. The student broke up the soil with a mattock and the professor knelt in the hole scratching away with a pointing trowel. Johnny figured it would take him a long time to get much deeper with that and he wondered why he didn't use a shovel. The woman, who turned out to be Mrs Boulton-Brown, sat at a trestle table cleaning bits of broken pot in a chipped enamel bowl.

The young man approached him with a bucket full of soil which he prepared to tip on the rapidly growing heap.

'Don't!' Johnny shouted.

'What?' Soil trickled from the rim of the bucket.

'Don't chuck it on there. There's something sticking out of the pile.'

'I can't see anything.'

'Look, by that brick.'

The young man put the bucket down and pulled out a chunk of terracotta. 'I don't know how we missed that.' He brushed mud off and turned it over. 'Roof tile, I think.'

'Not that. Look!' Johnny almost screamed in frustration. 'The thing next to it, there's something green there.'

The twerp unhooked a small trowel from his belt and prodded at the loose earth.

'Give it here!' Johnny, now seething with frustration, snatched the trowel. 'You'll lose it if you're not careful.'

A miniature avalanche sent a small object tumbling down the side of the spoil heap. Johnny made a grab for it.

'I say, may I have my trowel back please?'

'In a minute.' Johnny poked at the lump of verdigris with the point of the trowel and earth crumbled away. He picked at the object with his fingernail. He spat on it and rubbed it on his trousers, exposing a pair of ears. 'Hey! It's a rabbit.'

'Please can I—?'

'Here!' Johnny tossed the trowel like a knife thrower. It stuck in the spoil heap with its handle pointing skyward.

Its owner retrieved it. 'Please may I have the artefact? I'd better show the professor.'

'No bloody fear. I found it.' Johnny slipped the dirty scrap of metal in his pocket.

'But Johnny—'

'Hard luck, you threw it out,' said Johnny.

The Land Rover arrived and the young man turned to see who it was. Danny parked at the end of the lane and vaulted the gate.

'Here's my lift.'

Al came running as soon as they pulled into the farmyard.

'Have they found any buried treasure yet?'

Johnny wound the window down. 'No. But they got all excited about some broken crocks and a bit of tile.'

'Ask if I can come. I can bring my own spade.'

'They're not digging properly. The student broke up the ground with a mattock while the professor scratched about with a little pointing trowel. I did find this.' Johnny fumbled in his pocket.

'Let's have a look,' Al said.

Johnny showed him the bit of metal. 'It's a rabbit.'

'Cor!' Al picked it up between his finger and thumb.

Danny unfolded his chair and slammed the rear door. 'Where'd you get that?'

'It was on their rubbish heap.'

'You can't keep it,' Danny said, lifting him down from the cab.

'Why not?'

'Because it don't belong to you.'

'It does now.'

'But that's stealing.'

'No, it ain't. I found it.' Johnny looked round for Danny's kid brother but he'd vanished. 'Where's Al gone?'

Danny laughed.

'It ain't funny, Dan. He's pinched my bleedin' rabbit.'

'Malcolm tells me you found something yesterday.' The man in the panama hat glowered at Johnny over the rims of his spectacles. 'Stealing artefacts from an archaeological site is a serious matter.'

'I didn't steal it, I found it. Someone had chucked it on the rubbish tip.'

'Nevertheless,—'

'You can have it back if you let me help.'

'Young man, are you trying to blackmail me?'

'I just want to do something. If you're so keen to have it back…'

The professor looked around. 'I really can't see that there is anything you would be able to do.'

'What about some pot washing?' Mrs Boulton-Brown rose from the trestle table. 'I could show him what to do and I'm sure he'd be most careful.'

'I suppose so.' The professor didn't sound at all certain. 'Would you be able to manage that?'

'Forget it.'

'I'm sure my husband didn't mean to be insensitive. You can help clean some of the artefacts for me, but do stop when you've had enough. I'm well aware that it's not the most exciting part of the proceedings but it's very necessary. Please Johnny, I'd appreciate your help.'

'Here you are then.' Johnny fumbled in his pocket. 'It's a rabbit.'

'Thank you.' Professor Boulton-Brown gave the object a cursory examination. 'It is a Roman brooch in the shape of a hare and I hope you haven't damaged it,' he declared and put it in a clear plastic bag. 'Rabbits are not indigenous to this country, the Normans brought them in over the eleventh century.'

Johnny stationed himself at the table and Mrs Boulton-Brown gave him a shallow slatted box lined with old newspaper.

'You can arrange the items on the paper to dry,' she said and left him in charge of a bowl of muddy water and an old toothbrush.

He spent most of the morning cleaning bits of broken pot. He held the brush in his good hand, dipped each item in the cold water, anchored it on the table with his other hand and scrubbed at it with the brush.

'Keep it in the bowl,' advised Malcolm. 'You're spattering mud all over yourself.'

'The water's dirty, I can't see what I'm doing if I keep it in the bowl.'

Malcolm changed the water for him, refilling the bowl from a large tin can.

Johnny took his glove off, wiped it on his trousers and stuffed it in his pocket. It was less messy putting things in the bowl and holding them steady with his right hand while he cleaned them.

Malcolm passed on one of his regular trips to the spoil heap.

'This red bit's got a pattern on it,' called Johnny. 'It's a lady but her head's missing.'

Malcolm put his bucket down to take a closer look. 'Ye gods! It's Samian ware.'

'Is that important?'

'I'll say. Do be careful. Give it a very gentle brush, just enough to get the mud off without damaging the patina.'

Johnny frowned. 'What's a patina?'

'Sir!' bellowed Malcolm. 'Sir, come and look at this.'

Mrs Boulton-Brown put it in a plastic bag and wrote on it.

'What's that say?' Johnny asked.

'It's the context number,' she explained. 'YF58 stands for Yelland's Farm 1958; this is YF58/6. Each part of the excavation has a separate number, depending on where the finds are from.'

'But they're all from the same hole.'

'Yes, but objects can be from different strata; different layers. Things from high up have been deposited later than things found lower down. Which means that items lower down are likely to be older, generally speaking.'

'As long as it's a sealed context.' Malcolm loomed with another bucket of soil.

'Don't confuse the issue, Malcolm, I'm trying to keep this simple.'

'Why? D'you think I'm thick because I can't walk?'

'No, of course not. I'm sorry, I didn't mean—' She looked so embarrassed he almost felt sorry for her.

'So, what's a sealed context when it's at home?'

'Suppose we were to dig down and find a layer of debris, perhaps where a wall had collapsed. Everything beneath it would be sealed in, therefore we could be certain that what lay under the debris was older than that which was above,' the professor's wife explained.

'Like a jigsaw puzzle, only in 3D.'

The professor clambered out of the hole. 'You comprehend the idea exactly, young man.'

'Except when someone comes along centuries later and unhelpfully digs a drain straight through the middle,' said Malcolm. 'Then it's no longer sealed.'

'Quite so,' the professor agreed, pouring water on his hands from the can. His wife produced a ragged towel.

'Would you care to join us for luncheon, Johnny?'

'Thanks, Mrs B, but Danny's picking me up.'

'You had better wash your hands.' She offered the towel to Johnny. 'Just look at the state of you, I don't know what your mother will say.'

'She's not…' Johnny began. He wiped his right hand on the towel and dabbled the other in the dirty water. He was getting fed up with correcting people; he couldn't be bothered. 'She won't mind, I'll get cleaned up properly when I get home.'

'You've been a great help this morning, Johnny. Are you coming back later?'

'Maybe. What's a patina?'

'I'll tell you this afternoon,' she said as the jeep jolted along the lane towards them. 'Here's your brother.'

When they got home Ma looked stupefied. 'What you been doing? You all wet and muddy.'

'It don't matter, I can't feel it.'

'That's not the point. Now I must wash your hand thing and it take so long to dry.'

He went to his room, unbuckled his brace, dropped it in the sink and turned on the tap to rinse off the mud.

Francesca stuck her head round the door. 'You are in a mess.'

'That's because they've given me something to do at last. I've been washing the rubbish they found in the hole, I don't know what they want to clean it all for. Malcolm even told me to be careful with a piece of pot that was broken centuries ago.'

'Have they found the mosaic floor yet?' She knelt down and rummaged in his locker.

'No. What do you think you're doing with my stuff?'

'Found it!' She held up his old splint triumphantly.

Len turned up after dinner. 'What on earth have you been doing?'

'He's been helping the archaeologists wash their broken crockery.' Francesca held out a pair of jeans. 'Mama found these for you. They're an old pair of Danny's, she'd put them away until Mig grew into them but you might as well try them on.'

They were a bit baggy but at least they were long enough. Len wanted to see the dig so Francesca showed him the shortcut over the bridge.

'Danny's mother has offered to put me up tonight so that I can come with you tomorrow, but Maria wants to go to a dance this evening,' Len said when they came back.

'Okay by me, we need to keep her sweet.'

So Len went home and came back after tea in a suit and tie, reeking of Old Spice with his fair hair Brylcreemed into submission, carrying a bag of old clothes for the morning. Maria made a pretty entrance in black high heels and an orange dress with no sleeves.

They returned to find the black and white cat fast asleep on Johnny's bed, the tortoiseshell purring on his lap and Danny draped along the settee with his feet dangling over the arm. The cider jar stood on the table.

'How was the hop?' Johnny asked.

'Actually, it was all right,' said Len. 'Maria introduced me to a chap who recently started working at St Anne's. I gather he's hoping to become a GP eventually. We had a most interesting chat about university.'

'How frightfully nice for you.' Danny's voice was laden with sarcasm. 'We decided on a boozy night in. The others have gone to bed.'

'Do you two need anything?'

'No,' said Johnny, 'go and get yourself a glass.'

Len found Maria in a billow of orange with her elbows on the kitchen table and her head in her hands.

'Are you okay?'

'I'm just tired, that's all.'

'You should have said, we could have come back sooner. Why don't you call it a night?'

'I've got to see to Johnny.'

'That's all right, Danny and I can do it,' Len offered.

'Okay. But don't forget he's only allowed one sleeping tablet if he's been drinking and don't keep him up half the night.'

'Don't worry, I won't.'

Danny poured more cider; Len refused a refill, Johnny did not. Eventually Danny left them.

'At last, I thought he'd never go.'

'We could hardly ask him to,' said Len. 'He does live here.'

Johnny dropped his shirt on the floor. 'About time we got a bit of privacy. Shut the curtains, will you?'

Len bolted the French doors, drew the curtains and dragged the settee across the door to the passage. He took Johnny's shoes off and lifted him on the bed. He undid Johnny's belt buckle and flies. The door to the outside toilet banged shut and Len nearly jumped out of his skin.

'Turn the radio on,' said Johnny. 'Then nobody can hear us.'

Len turned on Radio Luxembourg.

Johnny lay back and watched Len massaging his legs, his hips. He reached out, his fingers pushing down, creating havoc in Len's carefully combed hair.

'Can you feel anything?' Len asked.

He rolled his head from side to side. 'Not yet.'

'Oh, Johnny.'

'Don't start snivelling.'

Len's hands roamed over him and he watched in wonder as his cock stood to attention. He moaned.

Len raised his head. 'Can you feel that?'

'Don't stop now for gawd's sake.'

'I don't want to hurt you.'

'I'm not a bleeding china doll, an' I'm fed up with people treating me like one.' He pushed Len's head down. With no sense of touch the experience had a detached, clinical quality. The climax was so unexpected that he gasped.

'You can feel it.'

'No, not a bloody thing.'

THIRTY

Danny mounted the steps to his caravan. The key was, as usual, in the lock so it wasn't until he went to light the Calor gas lamp that he realised his matches were missing. 'Damn!' He checked his other pockets but they weren't there, and neither was his tobacco.

To begin with, crossing the yard, it didn't strike him as odd that the curtains were closed. The radio was playing and the light was still on but when he tried the handle he realised the door was bolted. A chink between the curtains gave a limited glimpse of the room and he was about to knock when he stopped dead.

Len, naked and on his knees, leant over the bed; Johnny was stroking his hair.

For a second Danny stood rooted to the spot staring in horror, quite unable to believe his eyes. His hand dropped to his side, he spun away from the doors and flattened himself against the outside wall to hide as though he had committed the crime. When he was sure he had not been heard he tiptoed away to let himself in at the kitchen door. He found a box of matches, helped himself to Johnny's cigarettes and headed back to his caravan for a sleepless night.

In the morning Danny put the cigarette packet back on the dresser and poured himself a mug of tea. Bullet came to sit at his feet, his tail gave an expectant swish. Getting no response he tried licking Danny's hand but his master pushed him away. Bullet put his head flat on the floor between his paws and gazed at him mournfully until Ma came into the room. He sprang up with his tail wagging.

'There you are,' she said to Danny, opening the stove to take out a tray of bacon. 'He is full of the beans. After breakfast you give him a good long walk, yes?'

Danny grunted and took a sip from his mug of stewed tea.

Francesca tossed knives and forks on the table as if she was dealing playing cards. 'What's up with you, Dan? Cat got your tongue?'

'Francesca, you help me in the dairy this morning,' Ma said.

'Oh, but I wanted to go to the dig with Len and Johnny.'

'You go after. He's been sleeping better lately, don't you think?' Ma said.

Danny chucked his empty mug in the sink and left without a word, slamming the door behind him.

Francesca straightened cutlery. 'What's got into him?'

Len drew the curtains back. 'Danny forgot his tobacco tin last night.'

'He'll be back for it. Hurry up, the sooner we have breakfast the sooner we can get cracking.'

'Impatient, aren't you?' Len bundled him into his wheelchair, parked him at the washbasin and went in search of sustenance.

'Good morning, Mrs Gomez. May I have some coffee?'

'You help yourself, your breakfast in the middle oven.'

'Is she all right?' Len asked Francesca.

'Not really, she's a bit harassed and Danny never came back for breakfast. It's unheard of for him to miss a meal.'

Johnny wheeled himself into the kitchen. 'Are you coming today, Fran?'

'I can't, I've got to help Mama. We can hardly keep up, what with everyone wanting clotted cream.'

After breakfast Johnny grabbed his cigarettes. 'Bloody hell! There's only two left.'

'That's all right,' said Len. 'I've got plenty.'

'You don't understand, it was nearly full.'

'You must have smoked them.'

'Len, it was a new packet, don't you remember? I couldn't get it open and I lost my rag when you tried to help. I couldn't possibly have smoked nearly all of them.'

It was Len's turn to look horrified. 'What if he came back for his tobacco tin and saw us?'

'Stop panicking. We don't know he came back.'

'Oh, please no. What if he says something?'

'Even if he did come back for his baccy he can't have seen us. You shut the curtains.'

A horn tooted. Len started violently.

'That'll be him,' said Johnny. 'Get me in the bloody motor and stop fussing. Fran probably pinched them.'

But it wasn't Danny, it was Carlos. He dropped them at the end of next door's lane and drove off.

When the Boulton-Browns stopped for a tea break Len made the mistake of asking why little labels had been fixed in the hole with nails and got one of the professor's lectures.

'They show the context numbers,' the professor said. 'General Augustus Pitt-Rivers introduced the stratigraphical method. He worked in the late nineteenth century…'

Pitt-Rivers? The name sounded familiar. *Wasn't he had up for gross indecency a few years back?* It had been in the papers; three men, one of them a lord. It was a long time ago, before he left school. His mother had left old newspapers spread on the newly washed kitchen floor and he'd knelt on the wet lino to read about the trial. It couldn't possibly be the same Pitt-Rivers. If he'd been digging holes in Victorian times he'd be over a hundred by now.

'… when I was directing an excavation in southern France last year. Of course that was Roman too,' the professor concluded.

245

It didn't seem like a good idea to ask if the general was related to the jailbird. Mrs Boulton-Brown joined them.

'Why is the ground a different colour over in that corner?' Johnny asked, mostly to get them talking about something else.

She laughed. 'You're very observant, young man.'

'Why is it though? It's all the same earth.'

'In this case,' she said, forestalling her husband, 'it's a sign of burning, where there has been a fire, but post holes, pits and shafts may be filled with soil of a different colour as well, so you see it's not all the same earth.' She tipped dregs of tea on the grass and packed the plastic cups and Thermos flask in the picnic basket.

The men stepped back in the hole. Johnny turned back to the trestle table and resumed his pot washing. He dropped pottery fragments in the bowl, anchored them with his bandaged hand and set to work on them with the tatty toothbrush then laid them in the box to dry in the sun.

Len squatted at the edge of the hole watching the archaeologists unearth pieces of broken pot. 'Do you suppose they will find a mosaic floor?'

'I dunno,' Johnny said.

Len stood up and strolled over to the table. 'Why don't you stop for a while? You've been doing that all morning.'

'Okay, I've nearly finished this lot.' He put the brush down and struggled to undo the safety pin that fastened the bandage on his wrist.

'Here, let me.' Len knelt in front of him to unwind the wet bandage and he dried his hands with Mrs Boulton-Brown's towel. 'How very odd! Why on earth should your good hand be as wrinkled as a prune and the other not?'

'I ain't got a clue. Here's Dan, it must be dinner time already.'

The Land Rover stopped at the gate. It wasn't Dan but Carlos again.

'Consuela is busy. She left you something in the kitchen,' said Carlos. 'We're all busy this time of year and it doesn't help with Danny being in a silly mood.'

They found a plate of sandwiches on the table covered with a damp tea cloth. The boys had eaten and gone. There was no sign of Francesca.

'I thought Fran was coming to the dig with us after dinner,' Johnny said.

'Maybe she's still in the dairy.'

'She'll turn up. Let's take ours in my room.' He put a tray on his lap to carry the sandwiches and a jar of pickle. Len picked up their mugs.

Danny chose that moment to come in; he paused in the doorway while his eyes adjusted to the comparative gloom of the kitchen. When he saw them he clenched his fists. 'Get away from him.'

Johnny and Len exchanged glances.

'Keep your filthy hands off him. Don't you go anywhere near him.'

Johnny gave Len a shove towards his room. The pickle jar wobbled. 'I think he must have—'

'Shut up! How could you let him do that? It's disgusting.'

'Ah, so it *was* you that took my fags. Who've you blabbed to?' Johnny demanded.

'No one.' Danny had the look of a small boy who'd been caught scrumping apples.

'That'll be a first,' Johnny muttered.

'I haven't said a word. Who on earth could I tell?' Danny advanced into the room. 'Are you still here, you bleedin' pervert?'

'I'm sorry,' Len said.

Danny knocked a mug clean out of his hands and tea splashed their jeans, the bedspread and the carpet. The mug rolled under the bed.

'Get out! Get out and don't come back.'

Len put the other mug down and began to gather up his things.

Johnny picked it up. It was now only half full. 'What about my tea?'

'Fuck your tea!' Danny stormed out.

'Len…'

'I'll have to go, we daren't risk him telling anyone.' Len gave his shoulder a brief squeeze.

'Don't worry,' said Johnny. 'I'll have a word with him when he's calmed down. He'll come round.'

'Somehow I don't think so.' Len dabbed at the bedspread with his handkerchief. He picked up the mug. 'It's not broken. It landed on the carpet.'

The front door banged and footsteps ran down the passage. 'Hello!' Francesca bounced into the room and stopped dead. 'What's going on?'

'Nothing!' said Johnny.

'I'm going home,' said Len.

'Do you want me to give Maria a message?' she said.

'No,' said Len. 'No message.'

Danny trudged across the fields, neither knowing nor caring where he was going. He found himself at the high barn and felt along the top of the door for the key to the padlock. He lifted the sacks off the wrecked Triton and stood looking at it for a long time. He took a tin of chrome cleaner from a shelf, found an old rag and set to work on the bike. Working slowly and methodically, he polished the forks, the cam-covers, the exhaust. When he should have been collecting cows for afternoon milking he was hard at work on the wheels, carefully polishing each individual spoke. When the light faded he abandoned his self-imposed task and carefully covered the bike up again. He locked the doors, crossed the plank bridge and climbed the stile to Yelland's Farm and the main road. He walked to the village and went to the Horse and Hounds to drink cider on an empty stomach.

Ma was at the stove vigorously stirring a saucepan when Carlos came in with Mig in tow. Carlos took his boots off and went to the sink.

'Danny's gone missing,' he said, washing his hands under the tap.

'He never turned up for milking this afternoon.' Mig leaned on the wall to pull his boots off. 'So I got lumbered.'

'Perhaps he's gone into town,' Ma said.

'His bike's still in the yard,' said Carlos, 'and he was acting very suspiciously this morning.'

'Perhaps it wouldn't start,' Mig said.

Maria got home, dumped her bag on the table and collapsed on a chair. She kicked her shoes off and looked at her parents. 'Is something wrong?'

'Danny's disappeared,' Mig said.

'How do you mean, disappeared?'

Francesca came in. 'Is tea ready yet?'

'Have you seen Danny?' Ma picked up a thick cloth. She slid a large casserole dish onto the table. 'Stay back, is hot.'

'I haven't seen him since…' Francesca frowned. 'I don't think I've seen him since this morning.'

'He'll turn up,' said Maria. 'He's big enough and ugly enough to take care of himself and he's never been known to miss a meal. I for one am going to have my tea and get changed.' Maria massaged her ankles. 'I wish I hadn't gone dancing last night, my feet are killing me.'

Johnny rammed the door open. 'At least you can feel your bloody feet.'

'Johnny!' Maria never got the chance to tell him off for swearing because Al burst in and stood on the doormat, muddy and breathless.

'Am I late for tea?'

'Have you seen Danny?'

'He was in the high barn earlier on,' Al said.

'I'll go and get him.' Carlos picked up his boots.

'He's not there any more.'

Francesca turned on him. 'Well, where is he then?'

'He was on the other side of the stream last time I saw him,' said Al. 'Going towards the road.'

Francesca pulled her chair out. 'That's all we need, Len's gone too.'

'Gone? What do you mean, gone?' Maria said.

'He just said he was going and when I asked if he wanted me to give you a message he said no,' Francesca said.

When the sisters were on their own Maria tackled her.

'Len seemed all right last night when I explained I'd started seeing someone else now. We were never going steady and it just sort of fizzled out when he went back to sea.'

'He just said that he was leaving. You could've cut the atmosphere with a knife. He looked ever so upset and Johnny had a face like thunder.'

'I wonder what they were rowing about,' Maria said.

'I haven't got the foggiest.'

Next day Carlos hauled a reluctant Danny out of his bed. Francesca was in the middle of breakfast when they finished milking. 'Yours is in the oven. Are you all right, Danny?'

Danny took one look at the egg, bacon and sausage and fled. Ensuing noises from the outside toilet confirmed that he was throwing up.

'Absolutely, completely useless,' grumbled Carlos. 'He didn't come home till the middle of the night.'

Francesca was busy at the sink when Danny came back. 'Dad's ever so cross. How's your head?'

'Okay.'

'Dad's absolutely furious with you for bunking off yesterday.' She leaned forward and plunged her hands in the hot, soapy water. 'And if Len doesn't come back they'll wonder what's going on.'

'So?'

'If Johnny had to leave here for any reason…'

'Why would he do that?' He looked up in surprise.

'Something happened yesterday. I think…' She took a deep breath. 'Heavens above, Dan, you're making this bloody difficult.'

'Don't you let Mama hear you swearing.'

'Stop being so holier than thou, you swear enough. Since you're here you might as well dry the dishes.'

Danny picked up a tea cloth and took a plate from the rack. 'Not indoors I don't. Anyway, there's worse things than swearing. Much worse. Things you wouldn't know anything about.'

She threw the dish mop in the bowl with enough force to splash them both. 'If *worse things* come out, then they'll send Johnny to the nursing home after all and what sort of a life would he have there?'

'It's not Johnny I've got a problem with.'

'Len will be off to university in a few weeks.'

'I wanted that pervert outta here, not Johnny.'

'So you did see them.'

Danny looked incredulous. 'He told you?'

'If you tell they'll send him away, they really will. Come on, Dan, you've been friends for ever, you can't fall out because of a little thing like this.'

'Little!' Danny slammed the plate down on the table and shook the cloth at her. 'It's hardly little, it's a criminal offence for a start. It was horrible, disgusting.' There was a thud as Johnny rammed the door open. Together they turned towards him.

'What are you two rowing about?'

'Nothing,' Danny said.

'We're talking about you,' said Francesca. 'He's found out.'

'I know, he told Len to clear off.'

'How could you let him do that?' Danny demanded.

'I didn't let him, I told him to.' Johnny spoke quietly. 'And if you two don't stop shouting the whole damn house is going to hear.'

'Stop it, both of you.' Francesca turned on Danny. 'Why can't you leave him alone? He can't help it.'

'Oi!' Johnny protested.

'Shut up!' she hissed. 'Just damn well shut up.'

Johnny, dumbfounded, shut up.

Francesca held her breath and waited for Johnny to explode. He picked up the plate Danny had banged on the table. The other half dropped in his lap, cracked clean across.

'Sort it out before he blabs to everyone,' Francesca told Johnny. She snatched the cloth from Danny to dry her hands. 'And you need to be a bit less self-righteous, I know all about you and Penny.' She marched out of the room, slamming the door behind her.

Danny leaned against the sink, folded his arms and stared at the floor. 'I can sort of see how with all those weeks at sea; I mean, no chicks, y'know? But how could he? And to you of all people. I mean he went out with Maria. I wish you'd never laid eyes on him. I always said he wasn't one of us.'

'Put a sock in it, Dan. I told you, it was my fault.'

'You don't think I believe that? Why d'you keep sticking up for him?' Danny stayed glued to the sink.

'It is safe to come over here. It's not catching.'

'Eh?'

'Being queer. It's not catching, you know.'

It was still dark when Johnny woke. A fox screamed. He switched on the bedside light. When his eyes became accustomed to the brightness he looked at his watch. Ten past three. He reached for his book. After a while his arm began to ache. He put the book down and stared at the painted ceiling, his brain whirling.

There was a soft tap on the door and Francesca stuck her head round. 'Are you still awake?' It opened wider to reveal a vision in yellow pyjamas. 'What's the matter?'

'Len's cleared off, Danny knows all about us and I'm stuck like this for ever and you need to ask me what the matter is?'

'Don't get upset. Things are never as bad as they seem in the middle of the night.'

'Well, they couldn't be much worse, could they?'

'They're liable to get a whole lot worse now. How could you be so stupid as to let Danny find out?'

'I didn't exactly plan for him to see us.'

'Danny, of all people; you might as well've shouted it from the rooftops.'

'It don't make no difference now, there's not a thing I can do about it. With a bit of luck he'll unload his conscience on old Bri then keep his trap shut. If he says anything to your parents I'm sunk. God knows where I'll wind up. To be honest I'm past caring.'

'Stop it! You're mighty lucky you're still alive.'

'Still alive to do what?'

'Shh! Try and keep out of trouble for a start. You're missing him already, aren't you?'

'Don't shush me,' he yelled.

'Please be quiet,' whispered Francesca. 'You'll wake someone up.'

'Anyway, what are you doing creeping about in the middle of the night?'

'I got up for a drink and saw your light was on. D'you want some tea?'

'I need a fag.'

She fetched his cigarettes and a mug of tea. 'Sure you don't want anything to drink?'

He shook his head and lit a cigarette.

'Does it hurt?'

'A bit.'

'Shall I wake Maria?'

'No, let her sleep, I'll survive till the morning. Unfortunately.'

'Will it make it worse if I sit on the bed?' she asked, not taking the bait.

'Don't worry, I'll bloody soon tell you if it does.'

She sipped her tea. 'Why don't you like the curtains shut?'

'So's I can see the sky. Aren't you cold?'

'My feet are.' She wriggled under the covers, snuggling against him. 'Turn the light off.'

A streak of light crossed the sky. 'A shooting star,' Francesca said.

'They're called meteors. Len used to see them when he was on watch at night.' There were a few more faint shooting stars but none as good as the first. He reached across her to switch the light back on and get his book.

Maria found them in the morning, both fast asleep with the light still on. Francesca was curled into Johnny's back, her slippers thrown casually under the bed, the book on the floor.

'Dear God Almighty!'

Francesca leaped out of bed. 'I only shut my eyes for a minute.'

'Dad will skin you alive.'

'Don't tell him. We weren't doing anything wrong,' Francesca pleaded.

'That's not the point.' Maria picked up the book.

'It's my fault.' Johnny rolled onto his back. 'I was still awake and Frankie came in to talk to me. She got in because she was cold. Nothing happened, honest.'

'I might believe you but perhaps we'd better not mention it. I'll speak to Len's father and see if he'll prescribe something stronger for you. For goodness sake, Fran, don't just stand there shivering, go and get dressed.'

Carlos took him to the dig. He scrubbed at the things the archaeologists gave him with little enthusiasm until he heard the engine. The T-Bird stopped by the gate. 'Better not let Dan catch you here or he'll blow a gasket,' he called out.

Len picked his way round the edge of the hole. 'It's safe for the moment, I saw him in the distance driving the tractor. What's he said?'

'Nothing. His dad thinks it's got something to do with Penny. His dad found out they've started going steady again. Well, Carlos read the riot act, he said Dan had to choose between his work and his love life or he won't get paid, so things are back to normal. Sort of normal.'

'Thank heavens for that. I was terrified he'd say something.' Len squatted on the grass next to him.

'Don't sit there, you'll get splashed.'

Len moved to one side. 'I'll have to write to Maria. I've no idea what to say.'

'You'll think up some excuse or other. She thinks me and Dan aren't speaking because I said something nasty about Penny.'

'That doesn't explain why I left without saying goodbye.'

'You can say you suddenly felt sick.'

'That's true enough.'

THIRTY-ONE

The disappointed archaeologists found no coins to date the villa and no mosaic floors. Centuries of disturbance had destroyed all trace of them although they did find more scattered tesserae. Dislodged by ploughing and washed downslope by the rain, many had finished up in or near the stream. Stone from the building had found its way into walls all over the village, in barns and farmhouses, even the church. They concluded that the villa had burnt down, and they filled in their hole and packed up their buckets and spades; taking with them the rubbish they had collected from the hole and Johnny's chance to meet up with Len.

September arrived in a flurry of showers and blackberry-stained fingers. Sid was in the army now. Danny had been disappointed when he wasn't called up. Carlos was not disappointed, neither was Ma. Danny picked up discarded cigarette butts from the newly deserted camping field, chased old newspapers over the windswept grass and was keenly supported by Al and Mig scouring the field and surrounding hedges for empty glass pop bottles to return to the village shop for a bit of extra pocket money. Once the field was cleared of its seasonal accumulation of litter the grass could begin to regrow. The tractor chugged up and down the track, its trailer laden with boxes of apples. Miguel had grown out of his school trousers, Alvaro had grown out of everything so one fine morning Ma caught the bus to town. Everyone else had gone to pick apples, including Francesca, whose school uniform still fitted her.

Bored left indoors on his own Johnny had a brainwave. He telephoned Len then ordered a taxi. With the driver's help he got in the car without too much trouble. The driver folded his wheelchair, put it in the boot and drove him to a tree-lined avenue where imposing houses stood back from the road. They turned down the gravel driveway and came to a halt in front of the mock-Tudor mansion.

Len waited in front of the elaborate brickwork of the porch. 'I'm so glad to see you.'

'Not half as glad as I am to get here.' The driver unloaded his chair, Len gave him a generous tip and helped Johnny out of the car, which was much harder than quitting the jeep. He was grateful it wasn't raining or he'd have been soaked through in the time it took. Inside the house he was confronted by an expanse of parquet, a strong smell of lavender polish and a grandfather clock whose hypnotic brass pendulum swung solemnly in the corner; the polished mahogany table mirrored a bowl of late roses and a strip of Axminster climbed the wide oak staircase opposite the front door.

'Blimey! You could fit Mum's flat in your hallway.'

Len laughed and threw open a door. 'Shall we go in here?'

The room had wall-to-wall carpet and a modern television set and a radiogram. Chintz curtains matched the armchairs. Johnny went to the window. The grass was more bowling green than paddock and led to a paved area. A gaping hole in the paving caught his eye.

'Christ Almighty! You've got a bloody swimming pool.'

'Yes, but it's not in use at the moment, it leaks. Shall I ask Mrs Stannard to rustle us up some tea?'

'Mrs Stannard?'

'Our housekeeper.'

'Oh!' Johnny said, somewhat overwhelmed.

'I'll go and find her, won't be a sec.'

While he was gone Johnny inspected the contents of the bookshelf. There were a few proper books but most of them were medical textbooks. The pictures on the walls were proper paintings, not photographs. Len came back with a record case.

'Why don't you keep them with the radiogram?'

'I keep them upstairs with my record player.' Len lifted the lid. 'Dad uses this for his classical stuff.'

Mrs Stannard brought a tray with a brown china teapot and a silver tea-strainer. The sugar bowl had a muslin cover with blue beads round the edge. Len offered him a plate.

'Ta.' Johnny munched a chocolate biscuit and gave the pictures another inspection. 'Who's the stern old gent?'

'That's my grandfather. The old fellow isn't nearly as fierce as he looks. The mountain is Snowdon. I painted it for my mother when we were on holiday.'

'You painted it? You mean for real?'

Len laughed at his astonishment. 'Yes, for real. I wanted to phone you but I wasn't sure, in case Danny answered or Maria for that matter. I didn't know what to do.'

'Don't phone the farm, I'll phone you when there's nobody about.'

'I know Danny's still here, I saw him outside the café with Penny Robinson so I didn't stop. He'll hear about his National Service soon, won't he?'

'He isn't going. They ain't taking no more soldiers.'

'Blast! I leave for university soon. We need to make the most of what time we have left but how can we with him around?'

'Why can't we meet here? I managed the taxi okay this morning.'

'Perhaps you could manage Wednesday, it's Mrs Stannard's day off.'

They sorted through Len's records, played blues by musicians he had never heard of. The time flew by and when Mrs Stannard came to collect the tray she asked if they wanted lunch.

Johnny looked at his watch. 'I've gotta get back.'

'Where did you say you were going?'

'I didn't, there was nobody about.'

'Crikey! They'll be wondering where the hell you are. I'll call a taxi.'

October was damp and dreary but above all lonely, with Danny ignoring him and Len at university. Len, back with his own kind. His lover, his best mate, gone; leaving only an intoxicating memory. Ma put an eiderdown on his bed, a darker blue than the bedspread with a paisley pattern in an even darker blue. She plugged in an electric fire. First thing every morning Carlos would turn it on, giving the room time to warm up before Ma came to help him get dressed.

As autumn progressed he stayed indoors, spending the mornings huddled by the kitchen stove. In the afternoons Ma lit the fire in the sitting room and Carlos carried him up the steps to sit on the sofa in front of the television. Ma found an old travel rug, a legacy of old Mr Durrant, the tartan a confused array of red, yellow and blue stripes and squares, and tucked it round his legs while he sat watching everything from The Lone Ranger to Rag, Tag and Bobtail. As soon as he heard anyone coming he flung the rug aside.

One morning a despondent cry from the kitchen brought Maria running down the stairs. She shut his door as she ran along the passage, abruptly cutting off the early morning news. Raised voices came from the kitchen. Johnny rolled on his side with his back to the door, pulled the blankets over his head and closed his eyes.

'I'll help you this morning,' Carlos said.

Johnny rolled on his back and stared in surprise. 'Where's Ma?'

'She's very upset. The Pope, he is dead.'

'I thought you didn't believe in all that.'

'Consuela does.'

'Who's milking the cows?'

'Danny can manage on his own.'

By the time he was ready for breakfast Ma had calmed down but as soon as Carlos appeared she started jabbering in Spanish. Johnny couldn't understand a word. Carlos picked up the coal scuttle and went out.

He pushed his plate away and parked next to the stove. 'What were you arguing about?'

'We not argue,' said Ma. 'I only say Danny shouldn't go out singing tomorrow. On a time like this it is disrespectful.'

'Eh?'

'Don't you talk to each other? He goes on Friday nights with his guitar.'

'To the pub?'

'*Si.*' She tucked the rug round his legs. 'You're shivering, Johnny. Can't have you get cold.'

'Don't!' He pushed her away.

'Is okay, nobody going to see.'

'You can see.'

One October evening, trying to calm down after an almighty row with Maria born of rage and frustration, Johnny sat in the courtyard in the cold, under wispy clouds whipping across a haloed moon, and shivered. He lit a cigarette, surprised to discover he felt calm now that he had come to a decision. His plan was complete and it was time to put it into action.

Francesca intruded on his reverie. 'What on earth are you doing sitting out here in the dark?'

'Just thinking.' He chucked the dog-end across the yard.

'Aren't you cold?'

'I'm always bloody cold.'

He had hidden enough sleeping pills but he couldn't do it at the farm; nobody left him in peace for long enough. He lit another cigarette. He would have liked to be near the sea but this was impossible because even in October there were bound to be people about, digging for bait or walking their dogs. He had a fleeting thought of Shining Sands but he hadn't a hope in hell of getting near the undercliff – never mind the cove itself – without implicating anyone else. Eventually he began to type. It was difficult enough one-handed but he had to stop every time someone came in. When they asked what he was writing he told them to mind their own business. It took several days. He explained how he'd pretended to take both sleeping pills but hidden one as soon as Maria's back was turned. He told her he was sorry. He told Francesca that he loved her and she must not be upset. There were more messages in the same vein. The one to his mother was the most difficult. He added a postscript telling Father O'Brien that he was sorry. This last message was ambiguous; was he sorry for committing a mortal sin or for some other reason?

He would need a solicitor to make a will but this was obviously impossible to do in secret. He had no idea he needed to be over twenty-one to make a will. He hoped that whoever was in charge afterwards, his father presumably, would respect his wishes. After considerable thought he typed a list of instructions disposing of his possessions; the rosary he left to his mother, his watch to Len and his records to Francesca. At the bottom of the page he typed *The Mark Of Johnny Hunter* and drew a cross underneath.

The final letter was laboriously handwritten in block capitals.

DEAREST LEN,

I CAN'T DO THIS ANYMORE. BY THE TIME YOU READ THIS I'LL BE GONE I'M SORRY

> PLEASE DONT BE UPSET, REMEMBER
> WHAT REAL GOOD TIMES WE HAD
> I LOVE YOU MORE THAN I CAN SAY
> JOHNNY

He typed the envelopes and hid the letters in the breast pocket of his jacket. He asked Francesca to buy some stamps from the post office.

'Mama can get some when she collects your National Assistance.'

'Why can't you get them after school?'

After nearly three weeks of deliberation the cardinals elected John XXIII.

He'd got hold of a bottle of red wine on one of his outings to Len's house. After Carlos helped him to bed he'd opened it for him. Francesca came in to say goodnight.

'Keep me company for a while.' He had her fetch the gramophone from the sitting room and they listened to Elvis singing *Love Me Tender* over and over. She sat by his side and shared his glass. 'Cuddle me,' he said.

She curled up behind him, her arm round his waist. She kissed the back of his neck. 'What's the matter?'

'Nothing, not any more. Do you remember riding on my bike? You'd put your arms round my waist and cling on for dear life.'

'I remember.'

'What happened to it?'

'It's safe, Danny helped Dad collect it.'

'I wonder if it's as broken as me.'

'Oh Johnny, stop being morbid.'

'I wanted to know where it was, that's all.'

'They put it in the high barn, near the willow trees. We told you.'

'I love you, Frankie. Always remember I love you.'

'He's putting on a brave face but he's got that shut-down look. Like when he was stuck in hospital and used to close his eyes to shut us out,' Francesca said.

'What d'you expect me to do about it? Shouldn't you be getting ready for church?' Danny snapped.

She wiped her face on a tea cloth.

'Don't cry, Sis.'

'Can't you make it up with him now Len's gone?'

'I don't know how. Do you reckon he's been acting weird lately?'

'I know what you mean, he hasn't lost his temper for days and there's been no shouting or swearing or throwing things. I think he's up to something,' said Francesca. 'He was acting really strange last night, he kept going on about his bike.'

Once the family cleared off to church Johnny announced that he was going out. When Carlos cross-questioned him he said Sid was on leave and he was going to meet him at Bert's café. He picked up his lighter and two cigarette packets. He patted his jacket pocket, the letters were safe. He asked the taxi driver to take him to the Star; when the man asked if he was sure he said again that he was meeting a friend. He had the driver drop Len's letter in the pillar box by the village shop. When they reached the remote inn the driver got him out of the car with some difficulty. It would be so good never to have to go through this rigmarole again. He was early. The inn sign with its single star guarded a closed door. He planned to go round the back in any case, where he juddered laboriously over the cobbles.

The yard was cluttered with barrels and crates of empty bottles. A pair of geese came honking round the corner but they lost interest when he didn't chase them or run away. Smoke rose from a chimney and he lit a cigarette. A sudden breeze snatched at the smoke and the weak sun went in. When the landlord appeared he asked for a pint jug of rough cider, the man brought it out and set the thick glass on top of an empty barrel. From the other cigarette packet Johnny shook several capsules onto his makeshift table. A bloke he'd known from Bert's café scooted round the corner on a pushbike and asked if he was all right. He replied with a grunt and a curt nod. The geese returned to honk at the newcomer, who wheeled his bike across the yard keeping it between himself and the birds and propped it against the wall by the back door. Car doors slammed. A two-stroke screamed to a halt out front, revved briefly then cut out.

What would Len be doing now? A fine drizzle began to fall, barely a wet mist. He washed the first yellow capsule down with cider, swallowed another. He dropped the next and it rolled into a crack between the cobblestones. He had another smoke. One by one he consumed the rest of his hoard, jammed the pint jug between his thighs and lit up. He reached out to put his glass on the barrel and lost his grip. The glass slipped through his fingers, bounced off his knees and smashed on the cobbles. His fingers wouldn't grasp the fag and smoke went up his nose. This was it then. The sound of breaking glass brought the geese honking. Not right, should be music. The last thing he heard was the geese.

THIRTY-TWO

As soon as they got home Francesca ran to Johnny's room.

'He's not there,' said her father, 'he went to meet Sidney Randell.'

'He can't have, Sid's been posted to Yorkshire,' Danny said.

The telephone rang.

Danny drove like the wind. He found Johnny slumped in his chair, his damp, greasy hair hanging over his face. The landlord had thrown a blanket over him to protect him from the drizzle.

'He's still breathing, I checked,' said the landlord. 'I've called an ambulance.'

'How long ago?'

'As soon as I found him, then I recalled he were a friend o' yourn.'

'No time.' Danny loaded Johnny's limp body into the Land Rover. 'Phone the hospital, tell them I'm bringing him in.'

Directory enquiries produced the university telephone number and Danny stood shivering in the passage waiting for the operator to connect the trunk call. At last he was put through to a porter's lodge and left an urgent, garbled message.

Len rang back breathless and panic-stricken. 'I'm so sorry,' Len said, wracked with remorse, not thinking what he was saying or to whom. 'Are you sure he's going to be all right?'

'Absolutely,' said Danny. 'They think he'd only just passed out when the bloke found him. He's had his stomach pumped and he's feeling pretty sorry for himself but he's going to be okay.'

'Thank God for that, I'll come right away, I'll get the first train.' The pips went. 'Please tell him…'

Danny and the girls were still up when Len arrived. Maria let him in. She hadn't seen him for months, not since his unexplained row with Johnny. She wasn't sure if he knew she was going steady with Peter.

'I came straight from the station, I hope your parents won't mind.'

Francesca threw her arms round him. 'Len, I'm so glad you came.'

Len returned the hug. 'How is he?'

'He's going to be all right. Do you want something to eat?'

'No thanks, I had something on the train.'

'Where's your case?'

'I didn't bring one.'

Francesca fetched mugs from the dresser.

'Not for me,' said Maria, 'I'm on duty at seven.'

Len almost fell onto a chair, put his elbows on the table and his chin on his hands. 'I should never have left,' he said when Maria had gone. 'I should have stood up to you, Dan, but I didn't dare. I thought you might—'

'Snitch? What do you take me for? And what if you hadn't gone?' Danny said. 'He must have been planning it for ages. He didn't want to live any more, if you can call it living, like he is now.' Danny looked him straight in the eye. 'I don't suppose it helped with me being so angry.'

'That's not true, I know it's not,' said Francesca. 'He was all right till the weather changed. You know he was.'

'It's all my fault,' Len insisted. He looked at Danny. 'I shouldn't be here, I didn't think.' He stood up.

'Sit down, it's okay,' said Danny. 'I don't have a problem with you being here.'

'But I thought—'

'Siddown! Look, I'm sorry about before, I shouldn't have gone off the deep end. And if anyone upset Johnny it was me but I'd got no idea he was so unhappy he'd try and do away with himself.'

'Will you both stop blaming yourselves? Len, does your father know you're here?'

It was clear from his look of surprise that he hadn't given it a thought. He glanced at his watch. 'I really should go. It's rather late and he has quite enough disturbed nights.'

'There you are then, don't worry him till the morning. You can stay here, can't he, Danny?'

Danny hesitated.

'Can't he?'

'I suppose so,' Danny said.

'Thanks, I appreciate it.' Len held out his hand.

'I guess we're stuck with you then.' After a moment's hesitation Danny shook hands. 'After all, life's too short.'

'No, Francesca. I can't possibly sleep here.'

'Of course you can. Where else? And it's not as if you haven't slept in here before. Don't worry, our parents don't know anything about what happened in the summer.'

Len sat down on the bed. He couldn't look her in the eye.

She sat beside him and took his hand. 'Danny will never tell because if anyone got wind of the truth he couldn't bear the shame, he thinks it would reflect badly on him. In the summer he wasn't angry with you, not really. He behaved like he did because it was such a shock to discover his best friend was, well, different.'

'Stop it, Fran, you of all people shouldn't have to explain. I am so, so sorry.'

She put her arm round his shoulders. 'It really wasn't your fault. None of it was. When the weather got cold he was in pain most of the time and he wasn't thinking straight, he thought he couldn't carry on any more.'

'He was always the tough one.'

'He still is. It isn't the coward's way out like they say, that's not true at all. It takes a lot of guts to commit a mortal sin.'

'I always meant to ask, whose idea was it to hang the crucifix on the wall above the bed?'

'Mine,' she said. 'Johnny needed all the help he could get, whether he believed in it or not.' She'd held back the tears for so long and now, to her great embarrassment, months of anguish flooded out.

Len looked on helplessly. 'Don't, Fran, please don't.'

'What happened, what he did, it wasn't your fault, it wasn't anyone's fault. Johnny once told me you'd make a better doctor than your father because you understand people. He said you're kind and sensitive.'

'Oh Fran, my father was never deliberately unkind. He was just never there after mother died. Maybe before, I don't know. He never hit me. Did you know Johnny's father used to take a belt to him?' Len didn't seem to realise that his cheeks were wet too.

'You're tired, why don't you try and get some sleep? I'll find you a sleeping tablet.'

When she came back Len was sound asleep, curled up on the eiderdown still fully dressed. She draped a spare blanket over him and quietly closed the door. She went to the bathroom to put the pill bottle back, then remembered how he'd cut his wrist that dreadful night when Johnny had been so close to death. She took the bottle to her room and hid it under her pillow.

Next day Len telephoned his father to explain that he was staying at the farm. He got a thorough dressing down for leaving university so abruptly. At St Anne's he soon discovered he couldn't walk in whenever he liked as he had after the accident. Then Johnny had been on Men's Surgical where his father was in charge. The medical ward was quite a different matter and he was forced to wait for visiting time.

Danny wasn't happy. 'Whatever possessed you to ask that toffee-nosed pansy to stay? What do you think Ma is going to say? As for Dad, he'd kill him if he knew what he'd done.'

'But they don't know, do they? And nobody's going to tell them. Len's gone home now but they were fine with him staying over last night.'

Johnny was completely apathetic; there was no screaming, no shouting, no throwing things.

'I'm so glad you're all right. I don't know what I'd do if anything happened to you,' Francesca said.

Johnny didn't respond.

'Why are you being such a misery? You're okay now. You should be thankful someone found you in time.'

'I'm not okay and I didn't want to be found. It would've worked if they'd only left me alone.'

When the staff pointed out to Johnny that he risked being prosecuted for attempted suicide if he didn't accept treatment he didn't even try to argue. He was sent to a psychiatric unit in Exeter. His parents were persuaded that the move was in his best interests.

Matron was in Gerald's office when he telephoned the consultant to make sure Johnny's nursing requirements were fully understood. He explained about the head injury and subsequent memory problems and stressed that no treatment should be given which would exacerbate his condition. The psychiatrist assured him that his concerns were noted.

THIRTY-THREE

Visitors streamed down the corridor, Len and Consuela followed them to a day room. Men of varying ages sat, stood or, in one case, huddled on the floor in a corner, but there was no sign of Johnny. They found a nurse, who directed them to a ward. A man with unkempt grey hair, clad in a dressing gown, paced up and down between the rows of beds muttering at the lino. The nurse ignored the old man and pointed to a bed at the far end.

'He's over there.'

Johnny lay on his side with his back to them. In striped hospital pyjamas two sizes too big he looked much younger than his seventeen years. He clung to Len and sobbed and they could get no sense out of him. The old man stopped, raised his head and shouted, wagging his finger at an invisible adversary.

'Why aren't you up? Where's your surgical corset?'

Johnny jerked his thumb over his shoulder.

Len looked in the locker, avoiding the old man, who was perambulating again. 'Have you been up at all?' Len stood up.

'I don't know,' Johnny said.

'Haven't they given you a wheelchair?' Len looked round.

'There's one over there in the corner,' Consuela said. There was; it had four small wheels.

Len knelt by the bed and took his hand. 'Oh, Johnny. What are we to do?'

Consuela spotted a small stack of chairs and fetched one, executing a bizarre waltz around the old man. She pulled Len out of the way, sat down and seized Johnny's good hand. 'You got to get better, Johnny. You get better and come home soon,' she instructed.

Johnny buried his face in the pillow.

'Is no good.' She turned to Len. 'Go to phone your father, find out what to do.'

Len found a call box in the entrance hall. 'Dad, I don't know what they've done to him but he's in a terrible state, physically as well as mentally. He's totally incoherent, he's not wearing his spinal support and his wrist isn't even bandaged.'

Len went back to the ward. Consuela had given Johnny a handkerchief. He blew his nose. 'I want to go home.'

'At last, a comprehensible response. Listen, Johnny, Dad says you can discharge yourself because you came here of your own accord. They didn't force you to come. Do you understand what I'm saying?'

'Can't I come home with you? Please. They're not going to want me back at the farm.'

'We do want you,' Ma insisted.

'Why didn't the others come then?'

'They wanted to,' said Len, 'but visiting is restricted to weekends and they only allow two visitors.'

'Doesn't anybody wash you? Is not right.' Ma found a comb and did his hair.

'Francesca's really upset,' said Len. 'Danny's worried too, he thinks it's his fault.'

A smartly dressed woman marched in, not bothering to close the doors which crashed shut behind her. 'There you are, Daddy. Don't you know it's visiting day? Why aren't you in the day room?' The woman, apparently not expecting a reply, seized the old man's arm and propelled him into the corridor.

Len went in search of nursing staff and found a man in a white coat with his feet up on a desk, reading the *Racing Times*.

'I need to speak to the person in charge, please.'

'I'm the charge nurse for this ward.'

'I need a discharge form for Johnny Hunter, he wants to leave this afternoon.'

'Not possible, he needs to be seen by a doctor before he can leave.'

'He's a voluntary patient, he can leave whenever he likes if he signs the necessary form.'

'But he can't sign the form, can he?'

'He can make a cross and I can witness it.'

'Are you over twenty-one?'

Len struggled to keep his temper and asked if he could telephone his father. He offered to pay for the call. Eventually the man gave in.

'I'm having a bit of difficulty getting hold of a discharge form,' Len said and handed the receiver to the male nurse.

'I'm Lucien Barrington's father,' Gerald's booming voice announced. 'What exactly is the problem regarding Jonathon Hunter's discharge?'

'We can't allow him to discharge himself unless there's a responsible adult present. Your son tells me he's only nineteen and the woman with him isn't even English.'

Gerald was furious. 'How dare you. Do you know who you are speaking to?' The nurse did not. 'Put me through to his consultant.'

'I'm sorry, sir, there are no consultants on duty at weekends. It will have to wait till Monday, at the earliest.'

'Bloody part-time doctors,' said Gerald without lowering his voice. 'Then put me through to whoever *is* in charge.' He was put through to a junior doctor, apparently the only person on duty at weekends. The requisite form was finally produced.

Johnny drew a cross on the dotted line and Len signed below it.

'Where's his watch?' Len demanded.

It transpired that Johnny's watch was locked in the safe with his money. The charge nurse did not know the whereabouts of the key and they would have to wait until Monday.

Len was becoming increasingly worked up. Consuela almost had to drag him out of the office. 'Come back to Johnny before our time is up. Why don't we take him home now and come back for these things on Monday?' she said.

The doctor came in while they were getting Johnny dressed. 'Are you Lucien Barrington? Your father spoke to me earlier.'

'We've decided to take him home with us now,' Len said.

'Yes, of course. You've filled in a discharge form?'

'It's in the office, I witnessed it for him. I'll be back on Monday morning to collect his possessions.'

'I see no reason why he shouldn't take them now.'

'Apparently they are in the safe.'

'Naturally. Excuse me a moment, I'll get the charge nurse to open it now. I'm terribly sorry about all this.'

Len drew himself up to his full height. 'Not half as sorry as that male nurse is going to be.'

'I beg your pardon?' the doctor said.

'He told us he didn't know who held the key at weekends.'

Consuela took charge of Johnny's money, his watch and his knife. Len picked him up and carried him.

'Where's my chair?'

'Is at home, Carlos collect it the day after, after...' Consuela ground to a halt.

'After I tried to top myself? I couldn't even get that right.'

On the way home they stopped at a transport café and Consuela went to buy sandwiches.

'I can't go back,' said Johnny when she was out of earshot. 'You'll have to take me home with you.'

'Don't be silly, you've got to face the music sometime, you might as well get it over with.'

'Maria's going to be livid.'

'She's absolutely bloody furious,' said Len. 'You nearly cost her her job, you chump.'

'I can't go back, she'll hate me now. Nobody will want me after all the trouble I've caused.'

'She doesn't hate you. Actually, she's worried sick about you, so's Danny and Fran's beside herself, poor girl. As for the rest of them, do you really think Mrs Gomez would have come with me if they didn't want you there any more? Francesca was quite cross when she discovered that they'd only let two people in. They were arguing about who should visit you but Mrs Gomez put her foot down. She is understandably annoyed with you but really worried too. It was incredibly kind of them to take you in to start with and they're not ready to give up on you yet.'

Len stood in his father's office at St Anne's staring out at the drizzle.

'Gross negligence,' said Gerald. 'How has he got bedsores? How!'

'I was so angry, Dad. The chap was so obstructive, he practically smirked when I asked for a discharge form. As for the way he spoke to Mrs Gomez, he was so prejudiced.'

'How a person like that is allowed to work in a hospital is beyond me. I'll have the fellow sacked. I will not have some whippersnapper telling me what I can or cannot do. The staff had a duty of care but they appeared to assume that because he's a cripple it didn't matter. I have to admire the way Mr and Mrs Gomez have taken the boy on. They have a totally different attitude. They treat him as one would any other person of his age.' Gerald produced a rare smile. 'Carlos and Consuela; caring and considerate.'

When Gerald discovered Johnny had been given ECT treatment he was incandescent with rage. He telephoned the psychiatric department immediately.

'Against my specific instructions, totally unsuitable in a case like this. The family will sue for damages,' Gerald bellowed and slammed the receiver down. 'Their treatment of him was inexcusable. However much they offer won't make up for the harm they've done but it could go some way towards making life a little easier for him.'

Johnny didn't seem to care about suing anyone but the surgeon insisted. He felt so strongly he offered to pay the legal costs himself.

Maria tore him off a strip, she called him a nincompoop and said that if he even thought of doing such a stupid thing again she would throttle him herself with her bare hands. The animosity between himself and Danny had melted away, Francesca couldn't do enough for him and when she was at school Ma never left him alone for a minute. He felt smothered.

One day Gerald Barrington turned up at the farm. 'I don't think the boy appreciates how lucky he is to be alive,' he boomed.

Ma's reply was inaudible.

'What he needs is something to take his mind off things. He was interested in that archaeological excavation, wasn't he?'

'I don't think anyone's going to dig up a field for me in this weather,' Johnny called out. He was surprised when Len walked in too and even more surprised when Gerald Barrington gave him some books and left without Len. His heart skipped a beat when Len went to use the loo and Danny came into the yard but they seemed to be on speaking terms. They walked through the French doors together.

Len reluctantly returned to his studies. The books Gerald Barrington had brought were about kings and queens and wars from the olden days. Johnny found one that mentioned the West Country. He followed the Duke of Monmouth to Lyme then abandoned him. Francesca lent him her copy of *Lorna Doone*. She seemed shy these days, as if she didn't know how to talk to him any more.

'Why did you do it?' she asked one evening when they were on their own.

'I was fed up. Sometimes, when I wake up, just for a second I've forgotten. Then I try and turn over and it hits me like someone's punched me in the guts. I was so sure it would work.'

For a moment he thought she was going to cry but instead she knelt by his chair and hugged his knees. 'Oh, Johnny.'

On Sunday he and Carlos were left alone at the kitchen table when the others went to church. 'I don't need babysitting,' Johnny said. 'I'm not a kid.'

'And what if you need something?'

Johnny shrugged.

'Want to play chess?'

'No, you're too good at it.'

'You practise, you can beat me.' The chessboard was ready on the dresser; Carlos had planned this.

'Don't you ever get bored?' Johnny said.

'Bored how?' Carlos arranged chessmen.

'You're stuck here looking after the farm, don't you ever want a day off? To go on holiday? To see the world?'

'I travelled to come here. Here is everything I want; my home, my family, my animals. I'm a very lucky man.' Carlos spread his hands and smiled. 'Do you want to travel?'

'Yeah.' A dreamy look came to Johnny's eyes. 'I want to get on my bike and ride for miles. Go anywhere I want with nobody to stop me.'

'Is that what you were doing when you crashed?'

'I can't remember. I s'pose so.' Johnny gave a sigh. 'Don't you ever want to go home? Not even for a holiday?'

'We can't go back all the time that devil Franco is in power. Consuela misses her family but it is best not think about it. Life is very good here.' Carlos moved a pawn. 'You want to go home?'

'No.' Johnny shook his head. 'Why would I want to go home? My dad doesn't want a cripple for a son and mum treats me like a baby.'

'So, this is your home now. Are you happy with that?'

'I guess.' Johnny picked up a pawn and put it down again. 'How come you're so good at this?'

'You must look ahead to see what your opponent might be planning, then you plan your move. You must practise and you must concentrate.'

He'd never known Carlos talk so much. He took two pawns, lost several pieces. His hand hovered over a threatened knight, trying to work out whether he would place the piece in even greater danger if he moved it, when Carlos spoke again.

'What made you do something so stupid?'

'I suppose I'd just had enough.' Johnny made the move and banged his fist on the arm of his chair. 'Of this, of everything.'

Carlos picked up a bishop to pounce on Johnny's knight. 'Good thing someone found you in time.'

'I thought they would work quick enough, I couldn't believe it when I woke up.'

Carlos froze, his bishop poised in mid-air. The others walked in with Johnny's mother in tow.

'Is your mum all right?' said Francesca later. 'She looked awful when we got back from church. She started shaking when we came in. I thought for a minute she was going to faint.'

'I think she's still upset. I know I've made a bloody awful mess of everything, you don't have to rub it in.'

'At least it stopped Dad from beating you at chess.'

'You're right though, she was acting real peculiar. Anyone would think she was trying to avoid your dad. Have you noticed she usually comes when he's working?'

'He's always working, stop imagining things.'

When the officials at County Hospital learned that Matron had been present during Mr Barrington's telephone call to the psychiatrist regarding Johnny's injuries and the care he required, they immediately offered a substantial out of court settlement. Gerald wanted to pursue the case but was eventually persuaded that Johnny couldn't cope with any more hassle.

At the beginning of December Danny brought him a letter. 'It looks official, shall I open it? What's it say?'

Johnny ripped it open. 'They've sent an interim payment of fifty quid, I'll get the rest in a few weeks.'

'Cor! What you gonna do with all that dosh?'

'I ain't got a clue.' Johnny wasn't interested. 'It's a cheque. I suppose I ought to ask your dad to sort it out for me.'

'I'd get some decent wheels.'

'Mobile knocking shop you mean. What's wrong with Penny's car?'

'Nothing, I mean…' Danny squirmed. 'I wouldn't have to stuff my guitar in a rucksack when I want to take it out.'

'What do you want to take it out for?'

'I play in the pub sometimes,' Danny said.

'I bet Penny loves that.'

'I ain't seeing Penny no more.'

'Since when?'

'Since that stuck-up twerp from the car showroom started sniffing round her. I fancy the new barmaid at the pub but I haven't had much luck as yet.'

Mr Barrington called to see how he was and was taken aback when Johnny asked if he would cash the cheque for him.

'Don't your parents have a bank account? How is your National Assistance paid?'

'Danny's mum collects it from the post office in town.'

Mr Barrington said he would arrange for a bank account to be opened, advised him on investments and left him baffled.

Shortly before Christmas the cheque cleared and a card arrived from the Latimers.

'I ought to have sent one to Nigel,' Francesca said.

'Don't you worry,' said Ma, shovelling sausages onto Johnny's plate. 'I send a Christmas card to them.'

That evening Maria went to a dance with her new boyfriend so Francesca helped Johnny get ready for bed.

'What about new clothes, and some Christmas presents?' she suggested.

'I dunno what anyone wants.'

'A peace offering for Maria wouldn't hurt either.'

'I really didn't mean for her to get into trouble.'

'Well, you managed it anyway. Do you need anything?'

'Any cider going?'

She set two mugs of tea on his bedside table. 'We could get Dad to drop us off in town tomorrow, if it's not raining.'

'Not on a Saturday, too bloomin' busy. We could go in the week.'

'I can't, I'm at school,' Francesca said.

'I forgot.'

They went into town on Saturday. Francesca looked at winter clothes. Johnny showed a total lack of interest, he shrugged and let her choose for him and flatly refused to try anything on. The expedition nearly ended at the second shop. Francesca was looking at shirts and he sat gazing into space.

'Do you need any help, duck?' the shop assistant asked him.

'No,' he snapped. 'And I ain't your fucking duck.'

Francesca came over. 'Don't be so rude,' she whispered.

'I'm not rude, other people are,' he said, seething with anger and making no attempt to lower his voice. 'Bloody nosy lot. The worst ones are those who won't ask outright. You know they're dying to ask how I got like this but they won't say straight out. Oh, I'd say, I thought I'd try to break every bone in my body, it seemed like a good idea at the time.'

'Stop it, Johnny.' She seized the handles of his chair and pushed him out of the shop.

'I just hate being talked to like a six-year-old,' he muttered. The record shop sparked some response. He listened to music through the headphones and made several purchases.

'I need to go in the bookshop,' she said.

The shop had very little space between the shelves. Francesca browsed, he squeezed himself into the non-fiction section. 'D'you think Len would like this?' he asked her, holding up a book on astronomy.

'He's almost like his old self,' she told Danny when she called to say they were ready for a lift home. 'We'll wait by the phone box in the high street.'

Johnny began to shiver. 'It's getting dark.'

'Well, it is December.' Francesca tucked the hideous rug round him. 'I don't suppose he'll be long.'

Too tired to protest he let her wrap him up. A row of Christmas trees on the pavement opposite almost hid the greengrocer's shop. A man carried them inside one by one, preparing to close.

'Frankie, I haven't got anything for Ma. Nip over there and get her a bunch of flowers.' He gave her a ten shilling note.

'You look after these, then.' She put the shopping bags on his lap. 'Shall I get some for Maria too?'

'I forgot her too.' He thumped the arm of his chair with his fist. 'Oh, why don't my bleedin' brain work?'

By the time she came back with two huge bouquets Danny had arrived and Johnny was already on board. The shopping and his chair were stowed in the back. Danny held the driver's door open. 'Johnny was cold so I got him in, you'll have to get in my side.'

Francesca knelt on the driver's seat to drop the flowers in the back then squeezed past the steering wheel. 'I made Johnny buy some warm clothes,' she said. 'Didn't I?'

'Mm.'

She settled herself between them. 'And we went in the bookshop and the record shop.'

Danny pulled out the choke and waited for a bus to go past. A woman holding a well-branched fir tree was standing at a stop up the road, the bus pulled in and she fought her way on, tree and all.

'We should've got a Christmas tree,' Johnny said.

'We don't usually have one,' Francesca said.

Ma gave him a hug when Johnny presented her with the flowers. To his surprise Maria hugged him too. 'You're a darned nuisance but we all love you.'

Francesca took the books and records to his room. She helped him sort them out and wrap them. Later, as they laid the table for tea, he heard Maria vent her annoyance on her sister.

'You've only bought one pair of trousers. You know he's enuretic, what were you thinking?'

Francesca rounded on her. 'He couldn't try them on, could he? If they fit then we can get some more the same, can't we?'

THIRTY-FOUR

Christmas at Danny's house was like nothing Johnny had ever experienced. Not only was there no tree, they didn't even put any decorations up. Then, the day before Christmas Eve, things began to happen. Consuela rushed him into his clothes and after breakfast Danny dumped him in the sitting room with a book. Francesca was on her knees in front of the fireplace arranging rolled up newspaper and kindling.

'It's freezing in here,' Johnny complained.

'Well, you can't go in the kitchen, Mama's busy.' She wiped her hands on her jeans and fetched his eiderdown and the electric fire, switched on both bars and took everything off the mantelpiece. 'You'll soon warm up.'

Carlos staggered up the steps with a basket full of logs, stacked them on either side of the stone fireplace and lit the fire.

'How am I supposed to read when everyone keeps coming in and out?' he enquired of Carlos' retreating form. He was to spend Christmas Day with his parents and he was dreading it but at least there would be a Christmas tree.

On Christmas Eve he ate a hurried breakfast amongst a litter of Kilner jars and baking tins. Al brought in a big cardboard box and Ma shooed him out, then she took Johnny back to his room. He didn't stay there, the kids were in the sitting room and he parked himself at the bottom of the steps to see what they were up to. Miguel was balanced on top of a stepladder holding one end of a paper chain.

'So you do decorate,' Johnny said.

Mig turned round, wobbled dangerously, dropped the paper chain and hung on to the steps with both hands.

'Where's the tree?' Johnny asked.

'We don't have a tree, we have a Nativity set,' Francesca said. She stood on a stool by the fireplace arranging the statues on the mantelpiece. She placed a pair of brass candlesticks on either side. 'Don't you have a Nativity set at home?'

Ma had been shut in the kitchen all day. Maria came home from work, quickly changed out of her uniform and went to help her mother. Danny and Carlos left the kitchen door open and went upstairs chatting in Spanish. Mouth-watering smells wafted along the passage. He hadn't eaten since Al bought him a sandwich at midday. Danny and Carlos came down scrubbed clean and in their Sunday best, they put him in his chair and threw the kitchen door open.

Johnny expected tea to be ready but tea wasn't the word, tea didn't do it justice. A feast lay before him; ham and shellfish, lamb with vegetables, and wine. Strong, red, Spanish wine; Carlos filled their glasses, diluting Al's with water. There were no crackers and the pudding wasn't a Christmas pudding but by the time they finished he was fit to burst. They adjourned to the sitting room to pile more logs on the fire and exchange presents. Danny was delighted with his new skid lid.

Francesca gave him a squishy parcel. 'It's from all of us but it was Mama's idea.'

Johnny unfolded a travel rug, smooth and black with muted blue and green squares.

'It's Black Watch tartan,' Francesca said.

'Thanks, it's nice,' he said, and it was certainly a great improvement on the horrible fluffy thing that had belonged to Mr Durrant but he resented the need for it; having a rug draped over his knees made an old man of him. Francesca fetched her fiddle, Carlos and Danny picked up their guitars and they sang in Spanish what he guessed must be Christmas carols. Late in the evening everyone apart from himself and Carlos piled into the Land Rover and set off for Midnight Mass.

'Are you sure you don't want to go too?' Carlos said.

'No, that was smashing but I'm absolutely knackered. Is there any more of that wine?'

Carlos held his finger to his lips and winked. 'We'll get you to bed then I bring some more. What Consuela don't see she can't complain about.'

Johnny got his Christmas dinner next day. The roast was chicken and his father complained when he picked up the leg to eat it with his fingers. The table was scattered with plastic novelties and discarded paper hats and his mother was about to dish up the pudding when the letter box rattled. His father went to the door, grumbling at the interruption, to let Len in.

'I hope I'm not intruding.'

His mother rose to the occasion. 'You've finished your dinner early, we weren't expecting you. Can you manage some Christmas pudding?'

'I'd love some, Mrs Hunter, I'm so sorry to interrupt your meal. My father was called out to an emergency so I hoped you wouldn't mind if I popped in for a few minutes. I didn't realise you'd still be eating.'

'Of course, we don't mind, do we, Norman? I'll find another plate.' She scurried away.

'Thank goodness you're here,' Johnny said. Dinner had been a trial he could have done without. Carlos was going to collect him after tea but he had been dreading the interminable afternoon that stretched before them.

'Dad had barely started to carve the turkey when he was called out and Mrs Stannard had gone home by then so I was at a loose end,' Len said in a low voice, not wanting Mr Hunter to overhear. 'I ate a few roast spuds then came round here.'

'So nobody's pulled your cracker yet?' Johnny remarked with a wicked grin.

Len looked alarmed and shook his head warningly.

His mother came back and dished out the pudding.

'Watch your teeth, Mum booby-traps it with threepenny bits,' Johnny advised.

'Do you want some more, Johnny?' his mother asked.

'No thanks, I'm full. I could do with putting my feet up for a bit.'

'That's all right, dear, I've got your room all ready. I put the fire on in there to warm it up a bit.'

'Shocking waste,' his father muttered.

She had made up his bed. 'Mum,' he protested, 'I'm not going to bed, I just need a break for a couple of minutes.'

He pushed the eiderdown to one side and with Len's help slid onto the bed, rumpling the counterpane his mother had so neatly arranged.

'You've put on a bit of weight since the summer,' Len said.

'Is that enough pillows for you, dear?'

'Plenty, don't fuss, Mum, this'll do fine.' Johnny took out his cigarettes.

His mother went in search of an ashtray.

'Are you sure your parents don't mind me coming round?'

'I'm glad you did. Mum doesn't dish up dinner till the pub shuts and Dad comes home, that's why we were still eating. I think they're as pleased to see you as I am. Dad can't think of anything to say, mind you he never could, but now he can't even bring himself to look at me.'

'It was kind of your mother to offer me pudding.'

'Danny's folks had their dinner on Christmas Eve, real fancy fish and the foreign veg Carlos grows in the greenhouse.'

Johnny dozed off. Len went to find Mrs Hunter, who refused his offer of help to wash the dishes. Mr Hunter was reading the *Radio Times*. He grunted a non-committal greeting, turned the wireless on to warm up, and shouted. 'Buck up, Win, you'll miss the Queen. Where's Johnny?' he demanded when she appeared.

'He's worn out, Norman, he's fallen asleep.'

Len tiptoed to Johnny's door and crept in. He was fast asleep. His hair, so very dark against his pale skin, had fallen forward; Len gently brushed it back, and the long, dark eyelashes fluttered.

'Comfy?' Len asked.

'I ain't a kid,' Johnny said and without warning slapped his face.

Len left the room without a word. He went to the bathroom and peered in the mirror propped on the windowsill.

'Len!' Johnny called. 'Len, please.'

'What?' Len stood in the doorway, a livid mark on his cheek.

'I'm really sorry, I didn't mean it. And don't you dare say that I can't help it or I'll hit you again.'

Len smiled in spite of himself. 'Is it safe to come within range?'

'I really am sorry.'

'I know. Do you want to get up? I must warn you, your father is snoring away in his armchair and your mother is preparing tea.'

'Gawd! I can't face another whopping great meal yet.'

Thankfully Carlos arrived early, surprising in a suit.

His mother insisted they take slices of Christmas cake with them, wrapped in red paper serviettes. 'I'll shine the torch for you, those steps are dreadful in the dark,' she said, opening the front door. Len went first carrying the folded wheelchair. No sooner had the torch beam faintly illuminated the concrete steps than a door opposite opened and light flooded the street.

'Quick! Come back in.' His mother beckoned Carlos inside, flattening herself against the wall to let him back in. Carlos blocked the narrow hallway, with Len behind him carrying the chair.

'What's wrong?' Carlos demanded.

'The neighbours will see you,' she said.

'What if they do?' Carlos said and took Johnny back to the living room.

'Shut that bloody door, you're lettin' all the heat out, woman.'

'I'm sorry, Norman.'

Not until the people across the street finally waved their guests out of sight and round the corner and their door closed leaving the street in darkness, were they permitted to go on their way.

'I don't understand,' Carlos said.

Len opened the passenger door. 'I don't think they wanted the neighbours to see you carrying him down the stairs,' he whispered.

'Is a secret?'

'No, but,' Len loaded the wheelchair in the back and mounted his bike, 'it's hard to explain.'

'I'm an embarrassment,' said Johnny. 'I don't much like anyone seeing me either.'

Carlos muttered something in Spanish and climbed in the driver's side.

Johnny was surprised to see Francesca sitting on the farmyard gate. 'Why are you lurking out here in the dark?'

'Mama's being annoying,' she said and pushed him across the yard. 'Are you coming in, Len?'

Len was fiddling with something on the back of his bike. 'Yes, I won't be a minute.'

'Your mum's lovely,' said Johnny. 'She don't mind if I eat with my fingers. My mum insists on cutting everything up even if it don't need it. Your Ma has never tried to hide me like she was ashamed.'

'You hide yourself away, though.'

'No I don't, I went into town with you before Christmas.'

'You know what I mean. When's the last time you went anywhere you might meet someone you know? You never go near Bert's café any more, do you?'

Francesca pushed him into the passage, into light and warmth. He unbuttoned his jacket, revealing a Fair Isle pullover.

'What in the world are you wearing?'

'Mum made it. I had to put it on, didn't I?'

Len caught them up and gave Johnny a parcel wrapped with fancy paper which he wrestled with until Francesca, sitting on the bed swinging her legs in impatience, fetched a pair of scissors to let him extract a small radio set.

'It's a transistor,' said Len. 'They're all the rage.'

Johnny balanced it on his lap and twiddled knobs. He was rewarded with a selection of whistles and a snatch of foreign speech.

'Try it over here.' Francesca put it on the table by the bed and tuned it to the *Light Programme*. She found his slice of Christmas cake. 'Sure you won't want it later?' she mumbled with her mouth full.

'I'm still full from dinner time, you might as well finish it off. Is Danny about?'

'Asleep in front of the telly.' She licked the tip of her finger and used it to mop up slivers of icing.

Ma had invited his grandfather to dinner on Boxing Day. Carlos collected him from the Anchor on the seafront and installed him in the cosy farmhouse kitchen to spin yarns to the youngsters. Consuela produced her version of an English meal but the astonishment of roast beef with garlic caught his grandfather unawares and he grinned at the expression on the old man's face. After the meal playing cards took over from plates until Al fetched a small cardboard box and Johnny tried in vain to beat his grandfather at dominoes; they were too engrossed in their game to notice when Danny left to start up the jeep and Carlos went to attend to his livestock.

'Please, not to be cross,' Consuela said when the jeep doors slammed.

The old man placed his last domino. 'What are you up to, Mrs Gomez?'

'Is season of goodwill, forgiveness,' Consuela said.

The old man's seat faced the open door to the passage. His daughter stood at the front door, squinting into the dark interior.

'Is my fault,' said Ma. 'I decide is silly no speak.'

Johnny stared aghast as his mother burst into tears. Consuela pushed him towards the door and he held out his hand. 'Mum, I'm sorry. I didn't know anything about this. Honest.'

'Come on, mate, best leave the grown-ups to it,' said Danny and shoved him into his room.

'Whatever possessed her?'

'You know what Ma's like when she gets an idea in her head. She thought it was daft for them to keep avoiding each other.'

'You don't understand, your mum's stirred up one hell of a tin of worms. He blamed Mum when Grandma died.'

'It wasn't your mum's fault though,' Danny said.

'I didn't suppose she deliberately arranged a visit from the Luftwaffe.'

'Listen.' Danny sat on the edge of the bed. 'Your mum told mine all about it. It all started when she, your mum, fell in love with a soldier. He wasn't Catholic and they ran off to Exeter and got married in the register office. Her parents were furious, said they were living in sin and wouldn't have her darken their door but when you came along your grandma used to visit her in secret. In other words, if the old goat hadn't been so stubborn it might have been you and your mum visiting them. And wandering the streets when the bombers came over.'

Danny tiptoed into the passage and stood by the kitchen door.

'What?' Johnny mouthed.

Danny shrugged his shoulders and shook his head. He closed the door quietly behind him. 'Can't hear a thing. I'm not even sure they're still in there.'

Johnny never did find out what Ma said to them but whatever it was they spent New Year together for the first time that he could remember.

THIRTY-FIVE

January dragged and the weather stayed stubbornly cold, damp and misty. Early one morning Consuela and Winifred wrapped themselves in their winter coats and hats and set off to catch the ferry for the train to Rossiter's department store and its January sales. They came back laden with new saucepans for their kitchens, candy striped bed linen for him and school shirts and jumpers a size too big for Danny's kid brothers to grow into. Ma tucked in the crisp new blue and white sheets and Johnny spent whole mornings in bed, reading in the warm, returning to the unlucky Duke of Monmouth whose rebellion did not end happily.

'The postman brought something for you.' Francesca tossed a letter on the bed and knelt in front of the electric fire rubbing her hands together.

'It's bloody perishing, ain't it?'

'It's really pretty outside, the bushes are covered in sparkly fairy dust and there's even ice on the pond. What is it?'

'Eh?'

'Your letter, it looks important.' She drew back the thick curtains to let weak sun shine through the French doors. The bottom of each pane was covered in icy fronds. 'Aren't you going to open it?'

He picked it up, gave it a cursory glance and dropped it on the table. 'It's only something official.'

'Even so, you ought to open it.'

'Later.' He tugged the blankets up under his chin. 'My feet are freezing.'

'I'm not surprised,' she said, rubbing at the window with her fist. 'There's ice on the inside. It's beautiful, it looks like ferns.' She swung round to face him. 'What did you say?'

'I said I'm bloody cold.'

'You said your feet were cold.'

'Did I?'

'Well, are they?'

'I think so.'

'That's no answer.' She dragged aside the blankets and took hold of his feet. 'Can you feel that?'

'I'm not sure.'

She went back to the window and held her palms flat against the hoar frost.

'Christ Almighty!' he yelled when she put her cold hands on him.

They both started talking at once until Maria came running.

'He can feel his feet,' Francesca yelled, jumping up and down in excitement. Her euphoria was short-lived. He could feel his left foot when she touched it with really cold hands but the feeling in the right one had only been in his imagination and there was no movement whatever from either.

Francesca held out the letter. He ripped open the envelope and glanced at the contents without enthusiasm.

'It's from the bank, the rest of the money is in my account.'

'That's good, isn't it?'

'Oh, yeah, it means I can buy anything I want. Anything except what I really want.'

In February snow and aeroplanes again proved a lethal combination, in the United States this year. Danny, fed up with Johnny hogging the gramophone playing Buddy Holly records all day long, pointed out that he didn't need to be carried up the sitting room steps every time he wanted to use the thing if he could afford to buy one of his own. He prised Johnny out of the house by insisting he must choose it himself and they brought home a super-modern record player that took a stack of half a dozen singles, automatically dropping each record onto the turntable one after another.

A few days before his birthday Johnny woke with a roar of pain. He stifled it instantly but footsteps were already running down the stairs. The light came on and Francesca stood gaping at him, resplendent in winceyette pyjamas.

'What's wrong?'

'Foot hurts.'

'Are you sure?'

'Of course I'm bloody sure. Oh, geeze!' He clutched the rail at the head of the bed, his face contorted with pain.

'I'll get Maria.'

'Bugger Maria! Do something now.'

She whipped the blankets aside. His left foot was twisted and the tendons in his ankles stood out like overwound fiddle strings. 'I don't know what to do.'

'Please, Fran.'

'I think you've got cramp.' She pressed his foot against her hip, forcing it up, massaging his knotted muscles.

'Oh, that's better. Christ, that hurt.' It may have hurt like hell but he couldn't move it, however hard he tried.

He was dressed but still lolling on the bed, listlessly flicking through an old copy of the *Beano*, when Ma ushered Mr Barrington into his room. The surgeon deposited a stack of books on the bedside table.

'What's all this I hear?'

'How should I know?'

'Johnny, don't be rude,' Ma said and shut the door on them.

'Mrs Gomez tells me you had some feeling in your foot yesterday.'

'I got bloody awful cramp in the night,' Johnny said.

'May I?' Without waiting for an answer the surgeon took his socks off and started prodding. 'Feel anything?'

'I think I can feel something, sort of, I'm not sure. It's like when your foot's gone to sleep cos you've sat on it.'

'I thought you might need some more reading matter.'

'Ta.' He gave the top book a cursory glance; *A Concise History of the English Civil War* didn't look very exciting. An unpleasant feeling in his foot, something between a tickle and a pain, made him yell.

'Can you sit on the edge of the bed?'

Johnny hauled himself round to let his legs dangle over the side.

'You've no movement at all?' the surgeon asked.

'None.'

'Hmm. Should you experience any sensation such as pins and needles I want to hear about it immediately. I think it could be worth trying some more physiotherapy.'

Ma reappeared bearing a tray with teacups and a plate of custard creams. Danny followed the biscuits like a bloodhound follows scent.

'What you really need is something to do,' said Len's father. 'You didn't take A levels, did you?'

'No, they only did them at the grammar school.'

'What about O levels?'

'Not really, I left school when I was fifteen, didn't I?' Johnny couldn't figure out why Len's father wanted to pester him with such peculiar questions.

Danny butted in. 'He could've gone to grammar school, he passed the eleven-plus.'

'In that case, why didn't you?'

'Dad said the uniform was too expensive. I didn't want to anyway, Danny wasn't going.'

'And you have got an O level,' Danny said.

'How did that come about?' Mr Barrington said.

'He took it a year early.'

Mr Barrington glared Danny into silence. 'In which subject?'

'I got two as it happens; English and history. I had to take the exams at the grammar school.'

'Two! Never does anything by halves, look what a good job he made of falling off his bike,' Danny taunted.

Johnny threw his empty mug at him.

Danny snatched at it. 'Not a bad shot for a cripple.'

'Not a bad catch for an arsehole.' He launched himself at Danny and caught him off balance, his momentum took Danny down too and Mr Barrington winced as they crashed to the floor where they wrestled, rolling and cursing. Johnny slammed his fist in Danny's face.

Danny grunted and somersaulted out of the way. Johnny leaned on his elbow, panting.

'Are you all right, mate?' Danny said.

'I hate you, you bastard.' Johnny made a grab for his ankle but Danny sidestepped. 'I hate all of you,' Johnny said and looked round for something to throw.

Danny nudged the mug out of range with his foot while Mr Barrington took hold of Johnny under the arms to heave him back on the bed. 'I'm pleased to see your fighting spirit returning, Johnny, but do try to take a little more care.'

At home that evening Gerald Barrington poured himself a large Scotch and soda and telephoned his friend Sir Henry Fordham, who, in addition to being head of orthopaedics at a London teaching hospital, was Lucien's godfather.

'Henry, I need a favour. I'm hoping you can pull some strings for me.' He proceeded to explain Johnny's situation. 'The boy needs something to occupy his mind. I've heard some talk of scholarships for handicapped students and I thought perhaps you could ask around and find out what, if anything, is available. He has shown something of an interest in history.'

'What are his academic results like?' Henry spoke as he worked, quickly and precisely.

'He has no A levels. His sole qualifications are at O level, in English and history, both of which he sat a year early.'

'How come?'

'He left school at fifteen.'

'You've got to be kidding, there's not a chance. You want to sponsor this maimed youth, no, even better, this suicidally depressed youth with no qualifications, to attempt an academic course?'

'He's surprisingly bright for a working-class boy.'

'He'd need to be.'

'There's something else,' said Gerald, afraid he was about to finish off all hope for the idea that had seemed quite reasonable half an hour ago. 'Johnny not only uses a wheelchair, he injured his hand in the accident and has some difficulty writing. If there were any chance of him getting a place, he would need an amanuensis.'

'I'll call you back.'

Henry returned his call within the hour. 'This young protégé of yours, I might have found a solution. How does the boy feel about university? He does realise it's nothing like school, all down to organising one's own work schedule and so forth.'

'I haven't mentioned the idea to him yet. I didn't want to get his hopes up until I had some definite information.'

'You don't even know if he'd be interested?' Henry's voice rose to a squeak.

'Why, what were you going to say?' Gerald was on tenterhooks.

'Only that very few places have suitable facilities for handicapped students but I have heard of a possibility. Remind me, where is Lucien?' He barely gave Gerald time to answer.

'I thought so, I've been chatting to the chap in charge of their history faculty, very forward-looking college; ground-floor adapted living quarters are available in hall and they're offering a diploma in ancient history. Mind you, the campus is not ideal for anyone with a physical handicap. To date the only occupant was a deaf student. It's a two-year course and they've not had many applicants yet so the boy could be in with a chance.'

'I can't thank you enough. Johnny's an intelligent young man and it seems such a waste to survive his injuries only to spend the rest of his life reading trashy novels.'

'I have to admire your optimism,' Henry said.

On Saturday Johnny watched Ma fitting cake candles into little plastic holders. She had gone and invited his mother to tea.

'Don't tell her.'

Ma looked up. 'Don't tell who what?'

'Don't tell Mum about my foot. You know she'll only get her hopes up and then be really disappointed when nothing happens.'

'*If* nothing happens, only the Holy Mother knows. Father O'Brien tell us about the priest who took a coach of people to Lourdes last summer.'

'Please don't start Mum wittering on about Lourdes again, she went on about blessed Saint Bernadette for weeks.'

Len telephoned to wish him happy birthday; when Len's change ran out he escaped to his room. It would be Easter before he saw Len and that was weeks away. Francesca was upstairs playing the fiddle. For something to do he tried out the mouth organ.

She bounced into his room. 'You're playing the harmonica I got you for Christmas.'

'I heard you playing.'

She lifted the piano lid and struck a chord. 'Come on then, give us a tune.'

'I only know the theme tune from the *Dam Busters*.'

'Give it a go.'

But before he had the chance to try Danny interrupted them. 'We ought to celebrate now you're officially old enough to drink. You're coming out with me tonight.'

'I don't feel like it.'

'Oh, go on, Johnny, please.' Francesca was on Danny's side. 'You can't stay in on your birthday. I'll come too.'

'You can't,' Danny said.

'I can, I'm old enough as long as I only drink lemonade. Please come, Johnny, just this once.'

'Okay, I'll come out if it'll shut you up.'

'Right, then,' Danny rubbed his hands together, 'the Star it is.'

'No!' Johnny looked alarmed. 'I don't wanna go up there. I thought you meant the pub in the village.'

'They're expecting me at the Star.'

'Expecting you? How come?'

'Because I play there at weekends, you know that,' Danny said.

'I thought you went to the Horse and Hounds.'

'That's full of old fuddy-duddies, they don't want someone playing rock 'n' roll in there. You'll enjoy it, on a good night I can make a few bob passing the hat.' Danny left before he could think up an excuse.

'You used to like going there,' Francesca said.

'I really don't want to go to the Star. Everyone goes there, it's got steps outside and—'

'And you never want to go anywhere you might meet someone you know,' she said.

His birthday tea was eaten in strained politeness. Carlos missed the meal entirely because of a sick cow. After tea his mother caught the last bus home and he was left to himself until Danny turned up in his Sunday best. He tried one last time to get out of the proposed night out. 'What about the steps?'

'You know perfectly well we can get in round the back through the short-cut to the bog. You'll enjoy it once we get there. Besides, I need an excuse to speak to the new barmaid; if you and Fran are there it'll be easier to get her chatting.'

Danny parked in the yard behind the pub so getting out of the jeep without anyone looking was easily accomplished; going into a pub full of people was another matter. The door from the backyard was a narrow squeeze, so Johnny kept his arms tucked in and let Danny push him down the passage until they got to the bar. He figured regulars would gather near the fire so he parked by a table in the far corner. He need not have worried, the place was almost empty. He studied the tobacco-coloured ceiling, dingy brown paintwork and yellowing wallpaper. No wonder the landlord let Danny play here at weekends. No doubt everyone had deserted this old dump for a pub with a jukebox. Danny went to get the drinks in.

'Oh, no! Not another redhead.'

'That doesn't mean she's anything like Penny,' Francesca said.

She hung her duffel coat on one of the pegs by the door and came to sit next to him. Her unplaited hair flowed over her shoulders in glossy black waves and she looked really pretty in the green dress and silver earrings. Last time they came here she had her hair loose but she wore jeans and a jumper... Johnny nearly knocked his glass over. 'I took you out!'

'What?'

'That night, we came here, I remember now,' he said and downed half a glass of cider in one gulp.

'You came to the kitchen door,' she said.

Bikes rumbled to a halt outside, people swarmed in chattering and laughing, breaking his train of thought. The row of hooks was buried several coats deep. Danny got him another drink and he knocked it back. A guy he knew but whose name he couldn't remember made straight for him. He tried to move back but someone was standing behind him. He was trapped.

'Good to see you, mate, many happy returns, d'you wanna drink?'

'How the hell did you know it's me birthday?'

'Danny said so in the caff at dinner time.'

'Did he now?'

Johnny was still racking his brains for the bloke's name when he returned with a small glass. 'Get that down you, you deserve a proper drink now you're legal.'

More people plied him with alcohol and he began to feel less exposed. Danny rocked 'n' rolled until the copper-haired barmaid requested a folk song. He slackened the strings and plucked them with his head on one side, adjusting the tuning. He mouthed something at them.

'What's he want?' Johnny asked.

'He only knows the chorus,' said Francesca. 'Not to worry, I think I know most of it.' She pushed her way through the throng to join Danny by the fire and launched herself into the first verse. Johnny poured the remainder of his cider in her lemonade glass and started on the row of shorts.

Danny caught his eye but he shook his head. Danny navigated a middle eight and Francesca began to sing again. Customers joined in the chorus and Johnny could not help himself.

The landlord presented Danny with a brimming pint glass and an empty pewter tankard, the place was packed and when the tankard had done the rounds the landlord put it on a shelf behind the bar.

'Give us another song!' a man shouted.

'Couple o' minutes, I'm having a break,' Danny shouted back.

'Oh, go on.' A girl this time.

Johnny beckoned, trying in vain to attract Danny's attention.

'Let him have a breather,' Francesca said.

'It's kinda urgent,' said Johnny, 'I need a piss.'

'I'll take you.' She steered him into the passage. 'There's not much room, keep your hands in or you'll skin your knuckles.'

She pushed him into the yard and yanked open the toilet door. The naked bulb lit flaking paint and cobwebs. She pushed and shoved but getting him in there was no easy matter.

'It's too tight, go and stand in the passage doorway, make sure no one comes out.' An evergreen bush grew by the wall, he stationed himself beside it and undid his flies. The sky was clear, the moon was a couple of days past full and it shone brightly as she stood blocking the door to the bar, pretending to look the other way while he gave the bush a good soaking. Back inside they found Danny talking to the girl behind the bar. Francesca picked up the guitar and struck a chord, picked out a tune and began to hum Don't Be Cruel.

Johnny, well-oiled by now, couldn't resist; he was greeted by enthusiastic whistles and shouts of encouragement. He grinned and carried on singing. He followed it with a rendition of Love Me Tender which brought the house down.

Danny came up behind him. 'Always a good bet, Elvis,' he said.

It was raining by the time they left. Danny switched the headlights to full beam. 'Black as your hat.' He stated the obvious. The windscreen wipers clunked rhythmically to and fro. Francesca sat in front squashed between the two boys.

Johnny, drunk on a heady mixture of cider and applause, was nodding off on her shoulder. She tried to shove him away.

'You're very quiet, Sis. Are you okay?' Danny said.

'I'm fine, just a bit tired, that's all.'

Johnny roused himself. 'I haven't enjoyed myself so much in bloomin' ages.'

'That's because you're drunk as a lord,' said Danny. 'I wouldn't want your head in the morning.'

Rounding a corner the headlights caught a pair of glowing eyes in the middle of the road, Danny floored the brake pedal. 'Brace yourself!'

Francesca threw herself between Johnny and the dashboard. When they jolted to a halt the creature had vanished.

'Jesus wept!' Danny crossed himself.

'A deer!' Johnny was wide awake now.

'Whatever it was it gave me a helluva fright,' Danny said. He drove sedately though the village and home.

The cowshed light was still on but everyone had gone to bed. Danny tootled off to his caravan leaving Francesca to help Johnny.

'Your ear's bleeding,' he said and gave her a hankie.

She crossed the room and bent to look in his mirror, dampened the handkerchief and dabbed at her earlobe. 'I banged my head on the dash when we stopped.' She eased the gold sleeper out and examined the damage. 'Do you think it'll break if I try and bend it back?'

'It should be okay if you're careful. Try warming it under the hot tap first.' While she retuned it to its rightful shape he began to hum Don't Be Cruel.

She whirled round to face him. 'Yes, but it isn't me you're thinking of, is it?' She closed the door quietly but firmly behind her.

'Fran! Don't go yet.'

She opened the door a crack. 'What?'

He tried his most winning smile. 'Cup o' tea?'

She gave an exaggerated grin and stomped off, returning moments later with stewed tea from the pot on the stove.

'Ta.' Johnny patted the eiderdown. 'Sit down for a sec.'

She perched on the edge of the bed, facing him, heavy against his side. He ran his good hand up her leg under the full green skirt.

'No, Johnny!'

'Shh!' He stroked the inside of her thigh carefully, his hand crept higher.

'You mustn't.' She took his hand away.

'You know how much I fancy you.'

'You're incorrigible. I just don't understand how you can pretend to fancy me when we both know you're in love with someone else.'

'Why not? Danny can fall in love with half a dozen girls at once.'

'That's exactly it, girls. You knocked Penny back, that's how he got lumbered with her. How can you possibly be in love with a boy one minute then switch to liking girls? I can sort of see how some men might be…' She couldn't say the dreaded word. 'Some people might have different tastes but you can't have it both ways. I know you're not interested in me.'

'But you're not just any girl.' He put his arm round her shoulders to pull her closer. 'I fancy you too.' His hand crept back to her thigh. 'You're all right.' His hand reached her knickers. He stroked the thin cotton.

'Don't…'

His fingers strayed inside her knickers. 'Please, Fran,' he murmured.

Her breath came fast. 'Oh Johnny, Johnny.'

He carried on stroking, gently, rhythmically. 'I do fancy you, you know that.'

She gave an involuntary moan. When she shuddered he took his hand away.

THIRTY-SIX

Live music drew in customers. Danny was popular and most weekends he was at the Star, often with Johnny in tow. Since his birthday he was less self-conscious; with a few pints down him and Danny's encouragement he would often deign to join in. Their cover versions of Everly Brothers songs became a popular attraction on Saturday nights. Sometimes Francesca took her fiddle. One evening Johnny felt for his cigarettes and discovered the harmonica in his jacket pocket. He was persuaded to try a couple of tunes. When Danny pointed out that at least half Bert's customers patronised the Star Johnny at last agreed to visit the café.

Word got round and the Horse and Hounds asked them to play at a birthday party. With the additional attraction of a piano in the saloon bar Danny reckoned it would be rude not to use it and they clustered round, the boys singing, Francesca joining in with her fiddle. The Bell in town also had a piano. When they were asked to play there Johnny said he wasn't too keen on being gawped at by strangers so Danny and Francesca went on their own.

The postman brought an Easter card from the Latimers and a letter. Johnny rolled out of the back door and along the path to sit at the edge of the paddock. Out of sight in the fields beyond the orchard the tractor chugged. It was cool and crisp but the sun was out and the bush by the cowshed was covered in pale pink flowers. The field beyond was cluttered with tents and both caravans were let but there was no one about. The letter was about the history course, an exciting but daunting prospect. The interview wasn't at the university but in Exeter, and his recent memories of the place were pretty awful. Tilly trotted up to nuzzle his hair. He put his hand on the side of her head and pressed his face into her neck, felt her hot breath on his cheek. Francesca came looking for him and he held out the letter. 'I don't know whether it's even worth the bother. What do you reckon?'

The Easter holidays brought Len home.

'I've got an appointment about that history course. What the hell am I getting myself into?' Johnny said.

'It's only a viva, they won't expect you to write anything.'

'Eh?'

'It's only a chat, a few questions.'

'What about?'

'History I imagine, why you're interested in the subject, that sort of thing,' said Len. 'We've got the builders in, my father's having the pool repaired. He's hoping to get it back in working order.'

'You lucky blighter!'

'I was thinking, if it's ready before I go back, would you like to—'

'Try and stop me.'

Danny wandered in with his guitar; he lifted the piano lid. 'Give me a beat, kid.'

Johnny stationed himself at the end of the piano to thump out a one-handed boogie-woogie. Len sat down to watch.

'The Bell wants something a bit more substantial the weekend before Easter. I don't suppose you know anyone who's got a drum?' Danny looked hopefully at Len.

'Can't help you there, sorry.'

'That's a pity.'

'I say,' said Len. 'There used to be a double bass in Leadbetter's junk shop, he might still have it.'

'What are you still sat there for? Take the jeep and go and find out.'

Maria caught him in the farmyard unloading the instrument. 'Whatever do you want with that old thing? It's absolutely filthy.'

'It was Danny's idea. With a bit of cleaning up and some new strings...'

'But what on earth does he want it for?'

'He's trying to get a band together, he asked me—'

'A band? You're kidding, right?' Maria said.

'No I'm not. He wants me to play this.'

She looked flabbergasted. 'Can you play it?'

'Well, no, but I think I could learn.'

'Don't be ridiculous, I hope you said no.'

'It's a bit late now, I sort of agreed. He's trying to decide what we should call ourselves.'

'How about the holy terrors?' Maria suggested.

'There's no need to be sarcastic.'

'When Dan and Johnny were choirboys Dad used to call them the holy terrors. They were too.'

'I can't picture Danny as a choirboy.'

'He wasn't always so big,' said Maria. 'Actually he looked quite sweet in a surplice when he was little, they both did. You'd never have believed they could cause such havoc.'

Danny regarded Len's purchase with distaste. 'Best get yourself down the music shop sharpish, these strings are as much use as old ladies' knicker elastic.'

So a makeshift band assembled at the Bell Inn. Len, new strings installed, provided Danny with his beat and Johnny condescended to sing at the unfamiliar venue. When they stopped for a break Danny brought him a pint. 'I think we went down pretty well.'

'Not bad,' agreed Johnny. 'Reckon I could have done better on the bass.'

'Come on, he's only had a couple of days' practice.'

'I thought you couldn't stand him.'

'No! We're okay now, have been for a long time. I just, oh I don't know, I guess I just wanted him to go away and leave you alone. I didn't understand,' said Danny. 'Anyway, that's all done with now.'

'What made you change your mind?'

'You trying to do away with yourself, you bloody silly idiot. He turned up in a hell of a state and we called a truce.'

Easter, like Christmas, was divided between church and food, giving Ma an excuse to wear her best hat and provide lavish meals. His own mother always cooked a special dinner at Easter but Ma was in another league altogether.

Sid Randall came home on leave Easter weekend and Danny discovered he not only possessed a drum but had now been transferred to Wiltshire so could come home at weekends. With Len on bass and Sid's drum Danny had the makings of a rhythm section. At Danny's suggestion they called themselves the Kingfisher Boys.

One night Len turned up with a smug grin on his face. 'The builders have finished. Fancy a swim?'

'Do I ever. Is your pool fixed now?'

'Yes, we can use it tomorrow.'

Ma pulled out the laundry basket. 'I find you a clean towel.'

'Don't worry, Mrs Gomez, we've got plenty,' Len said.

He went to rifle through his wardrobe. 'Len! Give us a hand.'

Len came running. 'What a mess. What on earth are you doing?'

'Trying to find my swimming trunks.'

'I'll ask Mrs Gomez.' Len started putting things back in the cupboard. He held Johnny's bottle aloft. 'Better take this. You know what you're like near water, we don't want any mishaps.'

'You mean you don't want me pissing in your swimming pool.'

'Exactly. Have you anything to put it in?'

'I'll ask Fran if I can borrow her duffel bag.'

Len arrived at the farm bright and early. It was sunny and unusually warm for April. They sat at the kitchen table drinking coffee, waiting for Carlos to come back from the milk run.

'You'll need somewhere to change,' Len said.

Johnny laughed. 'I've already got my swimming trunks on.'

'What else?' Len wondered aloud.

'Take a spare bandage,' said Francesca. 'That one will get wet.'

'I told you, I've already got everything.' Johnny held up a comb to prove it. 'That sounded like the jeep. Come on, let's get cracking.'

Mr Barrington was in the kitchen hiding behind *The Times*.

'Morning, sir.'

The surgeon lowered his paper. 'Good morning, Johnny. Looking forward to your dip?'

Johnny beamed. 'I'll say.'

Len's father folded his paper and picked up a coffee pot. 'Do you two want coffee?'

'No thanks, Dad, we had some at the farm.'

Several cane chairs were arranged around the pool. Two had been set apart from the others, one of them piled with spotless white towels.

'It'll give you a bit of privacy,' Len said.

'I think your dad has seen me starkers often enough for it not to matter.'

Len's father placed his cup on a low table by the pool, pulled up a chair and shook open his newspaper.

Len folded his clothes tidily on a chair and gave him a pair of goggles. 'You might need these, there's rather a lot of chlorine in the water.'

'I thought it smelt a bit funny.'

Gerald Barrington lowered his paper. 'A few minutes only to start with, we don't want you getting too cold.'

'Dad, can you hang on to Johnny a minute while I get in?'

Len knelt on the edge of the pool, holding Johnny's shoulders.

'I was wondering how you were going to manage that.' Gerald supported Johnny while Len slid into the water and turned to lift him down.

Johnny let his head fall back and watched a solitary cloud sail across the sky, resisting the temptation to look at his feet. 'Let go, Len.'

'No, don't.' Len's father crouched by the side of the pool. 'I knew I should have changed into bathing trunks.'

Johnny splashed and Mr Barrington retreated. He kept going, using his arms as paddles in a ragged backstroke. Len waded after him. When they reached the other side he clutched the side for a few moments to get his breath back before pushing off again. He swam the length of the pool and felt for the rail. Len, doing a slow crawl, caught up with him.

'How deep is it?'

Len's shoulders broke the surface. 'I'm standing on the bottom.'

'My legs won't go down.' He finally achieved his goal. 'Look at me!' he shouted, clinging to the rail with his good hand. 'I'm standing up.'

Gerald Barrington rose in alarm, dropping *The Times* on the wet tiles.

Len hovered. His father watched. A shaft of sunlight reflected from an open window on the water.

Johnny overbalanced and plunged beneath the surface. Through his goggles the quivering sunbeam shone on the tiles below, a light as bright as the Triton's headlight… disjointed fragments of memory whirled. He thrust himself up and Len grabbed him as he broke the surface spluttering, spitting and gasping for air.

'It was a deer!' Johnny yelled. Water splashed in his mouth and he spat again.

'Time to get out,' Gerald Barrington said.

'Not yet,' Johnny protested, panting hard. 'Another five minutes. Please.'

'No, that's enough to begin with, you don't want to overdo it.'

Len took him under the arms and hoisted him out, leaving him on the edge clinging to the rail alongside the steps. Gerald Barrington draped a towel round him. Len climbed the steps.

'Good grief, boy, you're sitting without any support.' Mr Barrington fired questions at him. 'How's your back?'

'I'm fine,' panted Johnny, still trying to catch his breath.

'What was that about a deer?'

'Danny nearly ran one over a few weeks ago,' Len said. He carried Johnny to a chair and unravelled the soggy bandage on his wrist.

Gerald Barrington picked up his wet newspaper and cold coffee. 'Now I really must go and change, I don't want to be late,' he said as he walked off.

'Is your dad going to leave us in peace at last?' Johnny whispered.

'He has an appointment with a bunker and several Scotches,' said Len, towelling him vigorously.

'Eh?'

'He's gone to play golf.'

'Which takes hours?'

'Several.' Len lifted him into his chair.

Johnny grinned. 'We'll have the place to ourselves.'

'Mrs Stannard is here.'

He shot Len a look of disappointment.

'I'll get her to rustle us up some lunch. We'll have to get a move on though, she leaves at one on a Saturday.'

'Yes!' Johnny shook his clenched fist in the air with such enthusiasm that his wheelchair seemed to bounce.

'What did you mean about the deer? I thought you said Danny missed it.'

'I know why I crashed. I swerved to avoid a fucking deer.'

They squeezed in a couple more sessions at the pool but all too soon the holidays were over. Len went away again. His double bass stayed at the farm, where it lurked in the corner by the wardrobe, draped in an old curtain.

THIRTY-SEVEN

Francesca came in with her violin case. 'Are you busy? I can come back another time.'

Johnny folded down the corner of the page and put his book down. 'When am I ever busy?'

'I just wanted to try something out on the piano.'

'Go ahead. Pity Danny ain't going out tonight, I fancy a bit of a sing-song.'

She put the violin under the window and took his book off the piano lid. 'There was a time we couldn't get you out of the house, now you're raring to go.'

'It's something to do, ain't it? I don't mind if it's somewhere I know.'

'You enjoy being the centre of attention really.' She plonked out a Russ Conway tune. 'I heard this on the radio the other day but I can't quite get the middle bit.'

'It'd be okay if it weren't nosy parkers wondering why I'm stuck in this. Why isn't he going tonight?'

'I think he's had a bust-up with Jane.'

'Who?'

'That new barmaid,' said Francesca, 'she's the landlord's niece.'

'He wants to sort it out before Penny slinks back in there.'

'Don't even joke about Penny, she's a nightmare.'

'You're telling me,' he said.

She looked over her shoulder, fingers poised above the keys. 'What have you got against her?'

'Promise you won't tell anyone?'

'Oh Johnny, you shouldn't even have to ask.' She shut the piano with a bang and swivelled on the stool.

'She thinks she's God's gift but I turned her down flat. That's why she don't like me; she's used to getting her own way and she expects everyone to fall at her feet. I reckon she only started going out with Danny to try and make me jealous. It wasn't till her parents got wound up when they realised she was seeing a farmer's son that she got serious about him.'

'When was this?'

'When I got the new bike, I was busy fixing it up and she started hanging round the garage on Saturday mornings. She nearly blew a fuse when she saw you on the back one day. Turn the radio on, it's nearly time for the football results.'

Francesca took herself off. The news came on after the football scores and he switched it off. That was when he realised she'd moved his book. It was on top of the piano, tantalisingly just out of reach. By positioning his chair sideways on he could touch it and he tried to pull it nearer but this was a mistake because he only succeeded in pushing it further away. He shouted for help but canned laughter boomed from the television in the sitting room and nobody heard him. Francesca's open violin case was by the window; perhaps he could use the bow to knock his book down. He backed up to the wall and stretched sideways as far as he could, certain her bow was within his reach. The moment the chair tilted he knew the move had been a mistake. His chair swayed sideways, passed the point of no return and tipped him on the hard stone floor with a crash. They heard that.

Francesca sprinted along the passage, stopped dead in the doorway and let out a yell. She knelt beside him and tugged ineffectually at his shirt. 'Oh, Johnny! Are you all right?'

'Get me up.'

Seconds later Ma and Carlos appeared in the doorway. Carlos lifted him on the bed, Ma righted his chair and fetched him a mug of tea.

'You silly idiot,' said Francesca. 'What on earth did you think you were doing?'

Maria, who had been getting ready to go to a dance when Francesca shrieked, ran downstairs to see what the commotion was about. In the middle of all their fussing Peter arrived to take her out. When Johnny assured her for the umpteenth time that he was all right she finally stopped pestering.

'Just clear out and leave me alone.'

'If you're absolutely sure.' Maria turned her back on Francesca and looked behind her. 'Are my seams straight?'

'They're fine, now go and enjoy yourself.'

Johnny lay back exhausted. 'Don't you go yet, Frankie.'

'I don't intend to. You're not safe to be left on your own.' She sat down beside him.

He put his arm round her. Once he had envied Danny his big, boisterous family, now he was part of it. 'Be careful what you wish for,' he said.

'Johnny, what's the matter?'

'I ain't half bashed me elbow.'

'You stupid, stupid boy! You're darn lucky you didn't bash my violin, you could've broken it.' She stowed her bow in the violin case lid and snapped it shut.

'You care more about that fiddle than you do me.'

'Huh!'

'I could do with a drink. Go and see if there's any cider in the kitchen.'

'Please?'

'Please, and get my painkillers.'

'Don't you dare move,' she ordered and went to the kitchen.

He heaved himself over to reach his cigarettes.

Francesca came back with thick glass tumblers. 'You moved,' she said accusingly.

Danny followed brandishing a bottle. 'You sure you're okay?'

Johnny took the cigarette out of his mouth. 'Positive,' he snapped. His hand shook and ash fell on the bedspread.

'So what exactly did you think you were doing?' Danny poured out cider.

'I was trying to reach my book.'

'Oh, no.' Francesca put her hands to her mouth. 'I moved it when I opened the piano, I must've forgot to put it back after. Why didn't you call me?'

'Don't worry about it,' Johnny muttered.

'Do you want to get undressed yet?'

'I think I've had enough excitement for one night, thanks.'

Danny topped up their glasses.

Francesca stood up. Johnny ran his hand over her buttocks and down her skintight jeans.

'That's my sister you're mauling, man,' Danny slurred ever so slightly.

'And you're pissed, man.' He was in a lot of pain and didn't want anyone touching him.

Next morning Maria pulled aside the bedspread to discover Johnny was still fully dressed. He almost snatched the painkillers from her, gulped his tea and closed his eyes against the bright sunshine pouring in.

Carlos looked down at him with his hands on his hips. 'Self-inflicted; Danny is no use either.'

'Are you sure you're all right after your monkey tricks last night?' Maria asked as soon as her father left the room.

'Yeah. Go away.'

'Serves you right,' Maria said. She left a bowl of water on his bedside table, gave him a towel and a clean shirt and went off to work.

Soon afterwards Danny wandered in looking somewhat worse for wear. 'Have you had breakfast yet?' He picked up the bowl. 'Blimey! You ain't even washed.'

'Can you get me another cuppa?'

Danny had left the door ajar and he heard Ma's raised voice in the kitchen.

'He not feeling himself today.'

Johnny gave a snort of laughter, then grimaced. 'Aw, shit!'

Danny returned. 'What's wrong with you?'

'I feel bloody awful.'

Danny stood in the passage holding the phone, waiting to be put through. He put his hand over the receiver to speak to Ma. 'Are you sure?'

She glanced at Johnny. 'Maria give the painkillers to him this morning first thing same as always.'

'Hello? Mr Barrington? It's Danny Gomez, I don't know what to do.' Johnny could hear the panic in his voice. 'His painkillers aren't working.' Another whispered consultation with his mother. 'Over an hour ago. Lunchtime?'

Ma snatched the receiver. 'I don't think it will wait that long, Mr Barrington. We tried to get his own doctor but he gone out on call.'

'There's something seriously wrong here,' said Len's father. 'It really isn't a good idea to drink alcohol whilst taking painkillers, but that doesn't explain the state you're in today. Has anything happened that I should know about?'

'He fell over last night,' Ma said.

'How? Why didn't you call someone then?'

'He fell out his chair. When I go to bed he is okay, Danny and Francesca with him, nobody say that he hurt himself,' she said.

Mr Barrington turned to Johnny. 'Where does it hurt?'

'My elbow,' Johnny said through clenched teeth.

Gerald examined him and discovered a large bruise on his

left hip too. 'What the dickens have you been doing?'

Johnny remained stubbornly mute.

Gerald Barrington tried Danny. 'How did he fall?'

'I've no idea how he managed it; I wasn't here.'

'Well, who was here?'

'Francesca, I think,' Danny said.

'Your mother knows nothing, you weren't in the room when Johnny actually fell and Francesca is nowhere to be seen. You seem more concerned about getting into trouble over your drinking session than anything else.' Mr Barrington didn't try to hide his annoyance. 'Exactly what time did he take the last dose of pain relief?' he asked.

'Half past six,' Ma said.

Mr Barrington gave him morphine, packed the syringe back in his bag and took out his cigarette case.

'Can I have one?' Johnny said.

Gerald Barrington gave him a cigarette. 'Keep an eye on him,' he told Ma and strolled through the open doors to the yard. There, sitting on the bricks hugging her legs with her chin on her knees, was Francesca.

'I can't help if I don't know what happened. I gather you were with him, young lady.'

'I'm sorry, Mr Barrington.'

'And what have you to be sorry about?'

'It's my fault he hurt himself,' she said, looking at her feet. 'I'm ever so sorry.'

'How so?'

'I moved his book and forgot to put it back and he was trying to reach it when he fell on the floor.'

'Mrs Gomez, may I use your telephone?'

'Of course.' She turned on Danny. 'Why didn't you tell me yesterday night?'

'He said he was okay. Then he said he needed a drink and, well, we sort of forgot.' Danny faltered to a halt.

'You forgot?' Gerald roared.

'Well, he seemed to be okay,' Danny said.

The Bentley followed the ambulance to St Anne's. The men abandoned Johnny on a trolley in the casualty department.

'I need X-rays to find if he's done any damage. I intend to keep him in overnight for observation in any case,' Mr Barrington told the sister on duty.

Johnny let out a sigh; what a waste of a nice sunny day.

After breakfast the all too familiar hum of the hospital ward sent him into a doze. He woke to find Len's father standing over him.

'You can go home today, but I don't want any more horseplay.'

'Sorry. I only fell over, it's no big deal.'

'Stop smirking, boy, it isn't funny.' It was obvious Len's father was trying not to lose his temper. 'I mean it, Johnny, no more stunts like this. You don't seem to realise how serious this could have been. You've already done so much damage to your back, and I can't put your pelvis back together like a jigsaw a second time. Why on earth didn't you tell someone instead of lying there in agony?'

'I thought I'd just bashed my elbow.'

'And you felt no pain from at all from your hip?'

'None.'

'And why the dickens wouldn't you tell me what had happened?'

He shrugged. Thank goodness they hadn't given his mother false hope.

'That isn't bravery, Johnny, it's stubborn stupidity. You have to learn to admit when you need help.'

The family was still at church when the ambulance delivered him back to the farm on a stretcher. Carlos directed them to his room.

'Boy's to stay in bed,' one of the men said. 'I'm supposed to give this to Maria Gomez?' He proffered an envelope.

'My daughter. I'll give it to her when she comes home from church,' Carlos promised.

'It's good to be back,' Johnny grinned.

'Yes,' said Carlos. 'And next time you need something, call someone, don't you forget.'

They brought his mother home with them, in her best hat and matching gloves, clinging to her handbag like a lifebelt.

'Hello, Mum.'

She leaned over to kiss him. 'Oh, Johnny, you really must be more careful.'

'I'm fine, Mum,' he reassured her. 'The doc said to take it easy for a couple a days.'

'Mr Barrington has prescribed bed rest till the end of the week,' Maria translated. 'Though I'm not sure how he thinks that can be achieved.' She sounded cross. He certainly hadn't meant to get in her bad books again.

His mother perched uncomfortably on the battered couch between a stack of pillows and the black and white cat. 'You are looking a bit better, dear.' The door swung open and she looked round but nobody came in.

He glanced at the open door, laughed and patted the bed. 'Come here, boy.'

The collie bounded in. His mother watched in horror as it stood on its hind legs and put its muddy paws on the bedspread, wagging its tail and licking Johnny's face with enthusiasm.

'Get off, you great slobbering lump.' Johnny tried to fend him off. 'Sit!'

Bullet sat, ears erect, tail twitching, ready to spring into action at his slightest bidding. Ma brought in a tray.

'I am sorry, Mrs Gomez. The dog was on the bed before I could stop it.' Mrs Hunter dabbed ineffectually at the paw prints with her hanky.

'Connie, please.' Ma was unconcerned. 'Is no problem, it

brush off when is dry.' She slid the tray onto the bedside table, swept the cat off the settee and brushed off hairs with her hand.

Maria brought the biscuit tin, offering them to his mother first. Johnny helped himself. Munching them gave him an excuse not to join in the conversation, most of which concerned how to keep him out of trouble in the future.

'Mr Barrington says this new drug should knock out a horse, so it might just work for Johnny,' Maria was saying. He missed his mother's reply. He felt so tired. He closed his eyes for a moment and went out like a light.

In the evening Len phoned. 'How are you?'

'Okay, your dad didn't half tear me off a strip.'

'I'm not surprised, he went to a lot of trouble to find out about this scholarship. If you've mucked up your chance he'll be absolutely furious,' said Len. 'When is it?'

'Thursday, I think.'

'That's a damn shame. With luck they might be able to rearrange it.'

'It wouldn't have come to anything.'

'You never know, it's got to be worth a try. You do realise where the course is?'

'Yeah, we'd be in the same city but I'd never get to see you.'

'It's the same campus, you chump. They have more than one faculty.'

'Come again?'

'Different departments. You'd stay at a different hall of residence but we'd still be near each other.'

'What?' screeched Johnny. 'Why the bloody hell didn't you say so before?'

'I thought you knew. Why on earth didn't you tell Maria you'd hurt yourself?'

'I thought I'd only hurt my elbow. I never realised it was my hip making me feel so rotten.'

'You silly clot, it proves you must have some sensation coming back. If they do manage to rearrange your interview, for heaven's sake behave yourself. And absolutely no bad language.'

'As if.'

'Father has taken your mishap as a personal affront, he put you back together once and he doesn't want you ruining all his hard work. His exact words were "that damned boy's got a death wish".'

Johnny was holding the receiver so tight his knuckles had turned white. Now the hairs on the back of his neck prickled

THIRTY-EIGHT

'I'm gonna melt,' Johnny announced.

'I'm not surprised, it's bloomin' stifling.' Danny pushed him indoors.

'Get this bleedin' thing off me.' Johnny undid his shirt. 'It's too hot in this weather.'

Danny got him on the bed and undid the buckles.

Francesca came in and offered him a face cloth soaked in cold water. He sponged his face and neck.

'Chuck us a towel,' Danny said.

'Don't dry me.'

'It's to put on the pillow, you dope,' Francesca said. 'You don't want it soaking wet, do you?'

'There's a thought, it would keep me cool.'

Francesca folded his corset and trousers and put them on the shelf in the wardrobe, flung his shirt in the laundry basket and vanished with his sheet.

'Buck up, Fran,' Johnny yelled. How could she forget to put the sheet back on?

'What you shouting about?' Ma stuck her head round the door. 'Oops,' she laughed and turned away, still holding the edge of the door.

Johnny quickly covered himself with his hand.

'Francesca, what you doing? 'E is no clothes.'

'He has no clothes on, Mama,' Francesca corrected. She carried a sheet and a glass of lemonade with a bent straw.

'*Si,*' her mother agreed.

Johnny folded the crisp cotton across his middle. 'Ooh, cold. Lovely!'

'That's better,' said Ma. 'Can't have boys with no clothes lying about.'

Johnny took a sip of lemonade and kept his mouth shut.

The back door was wide open, the window too. Her mother balanced the iron on end, folded a shirt, added it to the growing pile on the kitchen table and brushed back a limp strand of hair.

'You make the milk go off if you leave it on the table.'

'Sorry Mama, I was trying to make room for Johnny's sheet.' She sat on the edge of the table. 'It's so hot.'

'If I let the fire out I can't cook,' her mother said.

'I know, thank goodness the exams are over, I can't concentrate. I wish we didn't have to wait so long for our results.'

'You are very lucky to stay an extra year and take exams.'

'I know, Mama. Why don't you send those to the laundry?'

'Because laundry is for Johnny's things.'

'Maria said we could use it for all the linen; his shirts count as linen, so why shouldn't ours?'

Her mother delved in the big wicker basket and held up a shirt without a collar. 'I don't send this where someone look at it.'

'It's seen better days,' Francesca agreed.

'Is no more use, put it in the rag-bag.' She tossed the shirt to Francesca.

'Aren't you going to turn the cuffs?'

'Been done once, too old now.'

Francesca sat on the table swinging her legs. She rolled the shirt into a ball. 'Can I have it? If I cut the sleeves off Johnny can use it for sunbathing. Not that he deserves it.'

'Why don't he wear a T-shirt like the others?'

'Because it would show what he's got underneath.'

'Does it matter?'

'Oh, Mama, you know how self-conscious he gets. He thinks people are staring at him and half the time he's right. He says it's either that or he's the invisible man cos people pretend not to see him at all. Even his mum feels sorry for him, you can tell from her face. He hates it.'

The front door slammed. 'Here comes Maria. Be a good girl and put the kettle on.'

'This heat is remorseless.' Maria kicked her shoes off. 'I can't be doing with that blasted hill in this weather.'

'Johnny gone to bed already.'

Maria looked surprised. 'It's a bit early, isn't it?'

'He was too hot, Francesca put his sheet in the fridge to cool it down.'

'Bed linen in the fridge! Whatever next?'

'I thought it was a good idea.' Francesca folded her arms.

'Well, it's not hygienic if you ask me,' Maria said.

'Nobody's asking you, are they?' Francesca jumped off the table, took the old shirt to the sitting room, found her mother's sewing scissors and hacked off the sleeves. She spent several evenings sitting by the open window in the overwhelming heat carefully hemming the raw edges. She proudly presented the now sleeveless shirt to Johnny and it rained solidly for two days.

'Typical, I might have known the weather would break as soon as Len's due back and I could use the pool,' Johnny grumbled. But he was wrong. After the brief interruption the long, hot summer resumed.

'That rain made hardly any difference,' said Danny. 'Everything's still dry as a bone and the beans are still wilting. Even the ducks are wilting.'

Summer blazed on. Len came home. The camping field was chock-a-block with tents, caravans, bicycles and noisy children.

They baked through July and sweltered through August; the bank holiday broke sunshine records all over the country.

Johnny sat on the toilet clutching the handrail Carlos had fitted, his forehead resting on his knuckles.

Danny kicked his heels in the yard; naked to the waist, berry brown, the straw cowboy hat on his head and a red bandana round his neck. 'Buck up. You've been in there *ages*.'

'Clear off then and let me concentrate,' Johnny yelled back.

'Can't do that.'

'Why not?'

'You might fall off.'

'Don't be daft. Whoever heard of anyone falling off a bog?'

'You've fallen off just about everything else. Aren't you ready yet?'

'Clear off.'

Danny came back a few minutes later and opened the door. 'You look dreadful.'

'Shut the bloody door.'

Danny shut the door.

A motorbike throbbed down the lane. The toilet door opened again. 'You can't spend all day in there,' Len said.

He dumped Johnny on the bed, went to the kitchen and came back with a bowl of prunes.

'No!' said Johnny. 'I'm not hungry.'

'Maria says you're going to eat them whether you like it or not.'

'I can't bloody stand them.' Johnny closed his eyes and turned his head away.

'Oh, no you don't. What she actually said was if you don't eat them she is going to come in here and shove them down your throat.' Len tugged him into a sitting position and piled pillows behind him. 'And if she doesn't then I will.'

Johnny registered his protest by spitting the stones as far as he possibly could. Len tried to hide a smile.

'What's so bloody funny?' Johnny hurled the empty bowl at him; it spun straight through the open doors and smashed to smithereens on the bricks in the yard.

Ma came running. 'What he break now?'

'He dropped a dish, Mrs Gomez. Where do you keep the dustpan?'

'Oh for heaven's sake!' Maria slammed the kitchen door behind her. Len caught up with her in the sitting room unlacing her shoes. 'Ah, that's better. You know I almost went in to give Johnny a piece of my mind.'

'Don't let him upset you,' Len said.

'I don't. Well, not usually. He's just so…' She clenched her fists and pressed her knuckles together. 'So infuriating sometimes.'

'I do wish you wouldn't wind her up. It makes things difficult,' Len said.

'I didn't upset her on purpose.'

'I know. Don't worry about it, she'll calm down.'

'Tell Ma I'm sorry about the plate.'

Len turned away. 'Tell her yourself.'

'You bastard!' Francesca came in and plonked herself on the sofa. 'You've really upset Maria.'

'I'm sorry. I wasn't trying to annoy her.'

'But you damn well succeeded, yet again.'

'Hey, it's okay.'

'It's not though, is it? It never will be okay, I'm sick of everyone knowing how many prunes I've eaten or whether I've had a shit today.'

They left him alone. Every door in the house had been propped open in the vain hope of a cooling draught. He smoked a cigarette, listening to them talking in the kitchen.

'I know you mean well but you're not doing him any favours if you keep on making allowances for him,' said Maria. 'All of you do. Can't you see it's not helping?'

'You are right, because he was hurt so bad we treat him differently. But it's difficult not to when there is so much he isn't able to do,' Carlos said.

Johnny strained his ears.

'I know he finds it difficult and frustrating, but he's better now and he's got to learn,' Maria said.

'It's not fair,' said Al, 'how come he always gets away with it?'

'He ought to be treated the same as everyone else,' said Mig. 'If one of us had broken a plate on purpose you'd have punished us. Wouldn't you, Dad?'

'She's right you know, he should be held responsible for his actions,' Len said.

Johnny couldn't contain himself any longer. 'Traitor!' he yelled.

Danny took Jane out, leaving them to their own devices.

Len stood by the French doors with his hands in his pockets. 'Switch your light off for a minute.'

'What for?'

'I thought I saw something. I believe there's a meteor shower due around now.'

'Can I see from here?'

'You'd get a better view outside.' Len dragged his bed to the far end of the yard and fetched a creaky deckchair to gaze at the cloudless sky. A sliver of moon rose, not bright enough to obscure the stars.

'I can see the summer triangle,' said Johnny. 'The Milky Way goes right through the middle.'

Lights went on upstairs. Johnny fidgeted.

'Are you warm enough?' Len asked.

'I can't get comfortable.'

'I don't know what you're complaining for, I've got a hell of a crick in my neck.'

'I'm a bit cold.' With Len's jacket draped round his shoulders they watched patiently. The Vincent throbbed to a halt in the lane.

'Danny's home.' A faint light shining from the caravan window confirmed Johnny's opinion. Bedroom lights went out and darkness settled over the yard. 'Was that one?'

'I thought I saw a glimmer out of the corner of my eye but I might have imagined it,' Len said.

'Well, we can't both have imagined it.' In the distance an animal screamed. 'Fox has got another one.'

'Have you taken your painkillers? You haven't, have you?'

Johnny shook his head.

'No wonder you're so fidgety.'

'I wanted to make sure I stayed awake but there ain't any fireworks in the sky after all.'

'It's often better after midnight,' Len said.

'Well, it must be damn near one o'clock and we've seen bugger all.'

There was a prolonged silence.

'Len?'

'Yes?'

'I need a piss.'

'Oh, for crying out loud.' Len fetched Johnny's bottle. He was halfway across the yard on his way to empty it when Johnny shouted and he tripped, spilling some of the contents over his socks. 'Damn and blast!'

'You missed it.'

'Shh! You'll wake the girls up.'

A light went on upstairs. Maria pulled the curtains apart and light streamed from the open window to frame Len, bottle in one hand, the other on the latch of the outside privy.

'What the devil are you up to?' Maria demanded.

'Turn the bloody light off,' said Johnny. 'We're watching shooting stars.'

'Just make sure he doesn't get cold,' Maria said.

Francesca stuck her head out of the next window. 'What is it?' She achieved a loud whisper.

'They're watching shooting stars.' Maria closed her curtains. Her light went off.

Len, standing on the bricks with wet feet, shivered. 'Can I borrow a pair of socks?'

'Help yourself.' Johnny was still chuckling when a star seemed to fall through the sky leaving a ghostly hint of its passing. 'Wow!'

Len was about to go indoors and turned back just in time to see the fleeting trail of light.

'Cor,' said Johnny. 'That's more like it.'

'Fantastic,' Francesca said.

Johnny twisted his head to look at the window above his own. 'Are you still there?' Another meteor zinged across the sky. Len came back with mugs of tea. 'You missed a good one a minute ago,' Johnny said, rolling on his side to gulp the contents. He watched entranced as the shooting stars came, one after another for several minutes.

Some shooting stars blinked as if someone had flashed a torch, others left brief trails of light behind them.

'Wow! How good is that?'

'Fantastic,' Len said.

After the burst of activity the meteors became less frequent but they watched until the early hours. Johnny gave a huge yawn.

'Do you want to go in?' Len asked.

'Might as well.'

Len attempted to drag the bed indoors without making a noise.

The next day after breakfast Johnny was preparing to take a rush at the threshold when he heard his name mentioned. He abandoned his attempt to get out to the yard and made for the kitchen instead. 'Should my ears be burning?'

'We're talking about you, not to you,' Mig said.

'You're to dry the dishes for a week,' said Francesca. 'As a punishment for breaking one.'

'No!' said Maria. 'We'll have no crockery left.'

'He didn't break anything when he washed up on the dig,' Francesca said.

'How do you know?' said Mig. 'All their stuff was already broken.'

Carlos interrupted them. 'This afternoon he can help me creosote the fence.'

This proved to be more trouble than it was worth. Johnny daubed the smelly stuff on the middle rails and Carlos did the parts that were out of his reach but he found it awkward manipulating a paintbrush with his left hand and Carlos spent more time hanging about waiting for him to move on to the next section than actually doing any work himself. In the end Carlos finished off the job because Johnny got more of the stuff on the grass, himself and his chair than on the fence.

Ma threw up her hands when she saw the state of him. 'I never see a boy in such messiness.'

Francesca found him sitting on the shady side of the yard with his eyes shut and his shirt undone. She perched on the wall, took a letter from her pocket and scrutinized the envelope.

'You won't find out unless you open it.'

'I thought you were asleep.'

He lit a cigarette. 'Well, I'm not. What's it say then?'

She ripped it open. 'Oh!' She looked at him then back at the sheet of paper.

'For gawd's sake! Have you passed or not?'

'Yes! All of them, every single one. Do you think you might get another chance at that interview?'

He turned away. 'A university course was only ever a pipe dream.'

'I'm so, so sorry,' she said.

'Why should you be sorry?'

'Because it was my fault you missed the chance.'

'Don't be daft.'

During that boiling hot summer Johnny wore the sleeveless shirt Francesca had hemmed with such care in penance for ruining his pipe dream, giving Triton and his mermaid frequent airings until his tan rivalled Danny's. He wore the shirt until Maria insisted it needed a wash and he was forced to hand it over. The glorious weather showed no sign of coming to an end. He made frequent use of the swimming pool at Len's house, skinny-dipping in the secluded garden on Mrs Stannard's afternoons off. On one occasion Len's father returned unexpectedly and almost caught them. Len was sitting on the edge of the pool when they heard the Bentley crunching on the gravel. He barely had time to lunge for a towel to cover himself before his father walked round the side of the house. Johnny was still safely in the water clinging to the rail giggling like a loon so it was not immediately obvious that he was naked.

'So this is what students do during the summer vacation.'

'You're home early, Dad.'

'I must say I'm glad to see I'm getting my money's worth from the repairs,' said Gerald.

'Everything all right?'

'Yes, I came home to change into something cooler.'

'That was close,' Len whispered when his father went indoors.

Johnny giggled. 'Your face! You needn't have worried, I could have told him you got it done so you could join Skinner's lot.'

'I'm not entirely sure my father would consider being tattooed for a motorcycle gang's initiation rite that much more favourably than the truth.'

THIRTY-NINE

Father O'Brien spotted the Bentley outside the Bell. He propped his bicycle at the kerb and entered via the saloon bar; the clamour from a crowd of youngsters in the public bar sent him scurrying past into the snug where he found Gerald Barrington sheltering from the noise.

'It's lively in here tonight. What will you have?' the priest shouted above the din.

'Eh?'

The music ended, immediately followed by enthusiastic applause. 'I said,' Father O'Brien bellowed into an unexpected silence, 'I said,' he repeated quietly, 'what will you have?'

'Scotch and soda, please,' said Gerald. 'Sorry about the frightful racket, which they claim is music.'

'Nevertheless, they haven't driven you out yet.'

'This shindig is Johnny's farewell do, so I couldn't really get out of it,' said Gerald. 'It's very encouraging to see him getting out at last and even I have to admit he does have a good singing voice. Shame one can't understand a word of it.'

Brendan O'Brien peered through the gap into the public bar. Gerald joined him. The landlord stood with his back to them, elbows on the bar, watching the band. Gerald cleared his throat loudly.

The man turned on his heel. 'Yes, gents?'

'I didn't know Lucien played the double bass,' Brendan said.

'Neither did I. He had piano lessons of course but he never seemed particularly keen. Oh good, it looks as though we've been spared for a while.'

They had a clear view through to the public bar. Danny balanced his guitar against a chair and waited to be served, chatting to a girl with dark hair neatly coiled into a bun. The barmaid pushed a tray of brimming glasses at Danny.

Len propped his instrument on the wall and joined them. The girl turned, smiled a greeting and kissed him on the cheek.

'Good gracious!'

'I know,' said Gerald. 'A nurse, and a foreign one at that. No wonder Lucien kept his private life quiet. I was beginning to think he didn't have one.'

'I, I…' Father O'Brien spotted a ginger-haired youth trapped in the corner behind a large drum. 'Oh, look, isn't that Sidney Randall?'

'Yes, he's on leave.'

With great care Danny reached across the drum with a brimming glass and the drummer took a long swallow before setting it down by his feet. Johnny manoeuvred himself within reach of the bar, grinned broadly and drummed his fingers on the arm of his chair.

'Apparently it's been going on for months,' Gerald said.

'It has?' Father O'Brien, watching Johnny, looked alarmed.

'Can I get you another?'

'Just a half, please. It was nice of Johnny to invite you; after all, it's quite unusual for him to get a place at university given the circumstances. He has a lot to thank you for.'

'More than you realise. The blithering idiot had a fall and almost missed his chance of a place. It was the devil of a business rearranging his viva voce. He's not doing a degree course, only a diploma. A couple of years of ancient history will be quite a challenge and that's exactly what he needs. Take the boy out of himself, stop him dwelling on things.'

Lucien took hold of the double bass and Johnny inched backwards into the space between him and Danny.

Gerald groaned. 'I do believe they're ready to start again. Good to see Johnny enjoying himself I suppose, one can't help but like him. He may be a bit headstrong but he would never have come through otherwise.'

Father O'Brien watched Johnny; the handsome face, the cocky grin. *Bless me, Father, for I have sinned.* Just as well he and Lucien would be separated, the further apart the better. 'How will he travel? He'll need someone with him no doubt.'

'Naturally. Daniel Gomez is to be his helper, he needs someone to live in and all the other applicants were women. The train is direct from Exeter so they should manage the journey without difficulty. I reserved a first-class compartment for them all.'

A breeze wafted through the open windows but Brendan O'Brien began to feel extremely hot. He took out his handkerchief and raised his eyebrows. 'All?'

'Did I not mention he'll be at the same campus as Lucien? Different halls of residence obviously but they won't be too far apart.' Gerald, in competition with the band, raised his voice. 'It really is most convenient. Lucien can show him the ropes and so forth.'

The priest gazed at his friend in horror. Gagged by the secrecy of the confessional there was nothing he could say. He took a sip of stout and mopped his brow with the square of Irish linen.

'Careful! You're spilling your drink.'

Brendan had a narrow view of Johnny singing his heart out in the adjoining bar. Suddenly the boy caught his eye and grinned. *Bless me, Father…* His own heart raced in time with the relentless tempo from the band. His dog collar had become abnormally tight. He ran his forefinger around his neck, tugging at the stiff, choking fabric in a vain effort to loosen it.

'My dear fellow,' said Gerald, 'are you unwell?'